APPLAUSE FOR AMANDA SCOTT

DANGEROUS ILLUSIONS

"Amanda Scott captures the Regency with a sharp pen and her dry wit, portraying the glamorous appeal and the sorrow of the era to a T. Readers will be enchanted . . . A true treat."

—*Romantic Times*

DANGEROUS GAMES

"Clever plotting and sweet sensuality turn *Dangerous Games* into a great read."

—*Romantic Times*

DANGEROUS ANGELS

". . . an exciting Regency romance filled with two great lead characters, a tremendous cast, and a brilliant storyline. If you haven't read the prequel, *Dangerous Games* . . . it is strongly recommended that you do so. Hopefully, this series will continue with the romance of an adult Letty, one of the most interesting children to appear in a long time."

—*Affaire de Coeur*

HIGHLAND SECRETS

"A tempestuous love story . . . Ms. Scott delivers a highly charged story with passionate characters and lush historical detail."

—*Rendezvous*

HIGHLAND TREASURE

"A marvelous, emotion-packed love story that holds the reader spellbound from beginning to end . . . A real treasure and a 'keeper.' "

—*Romantic Times*

DANGEROUS LADY

AMANDA SCOTT

Zebra Books
Kensington Publishing Corp.
http://www.zebrabooks.com

ONE

Lady Letitia Deverill's first order of business that cloudy spring morning was to visit her father's London solicitor and learn all she could about her interesting, unexpected inheritance. Thus, with a flourish and snap of the coachman's whip, her carriage and four turned from Villiers Street into the Strand, rather than up Pall Mall toward Mayfair, where one might have expected such a splendid rig to go.

Lady Letitia's coachman, the guard sitting stiffly beside him, and the tall, young footman standing up behind with his chin held high in haughty awareness of his worth, all sported elegant green-and-silver livery. However, if pedestrians turned to stare, it was not because of the grandeur but out of simple curiosity. To see such a noble equipage in that part of town was unusual. The nobility rarely ventured into the area, which had long been dominated by businessmen and men of law.

The lozenge on the coach door announced to all who understood such details that Lady Letitia enjoyed a close connection to his lordship, the Marquess of Jervaulx. She was, in fact, his only daughter, and she had come to London from Paris to assume her duties as a maid of honor in waiting to the young Queen Victoria. However, with Letty, first things always came first.

Her three most loyal companions accompanied her. The first

of these, Miss Elvira Dibble, a chaperone of stout figure and forbidding aspect, occupied the seat beside her. Facing them on the forward seat was Jenifry Breton, Letty's dresser. The third, Jeremiah, lay curled up beneath Letty's hand inside a large green velvet muff that matched her voluminous swansdown-trimmed carriage mantle. Lulled by the gentle rocking of the coach over the cobblestones, the little monkey slept.

Moments later, the coach drew up before the imposing bow-fronted building that housed Mr. Clifford's law offices, and the footman jumped down from his perch, flung open the nearside door, and flipped down the step. When Letty moved to descend, Jeremiah stirred. With a laugh, she drew him from the muff and handed him to fair-haired Jenifry, saying, "He had better stay here with you. I daresay Mr. Clifford will have enough to manage this morning without monkeyshines."

"Yes, my lady," Jenifry Breton said, smiling as she took the little monkey and tried to cradle him. Jeremiah sat bolt upright in her lap, however, chattering simian disapproval of his mistress's clear intention to exit the coach without him.

"Hush," Letty said, grinning. "You'll draw every eye in the street to me."

With quiet disapproval, Miss Dibble said, "They will look anyway, my dear. I doubt that folks hereabouts have seen such a turnout in a month of Sundays."

"Fiddlesticks," Letty said, giving the footman one gloved hand and using the other to hold her skirts out of her way as she stepped down to the flagway. "If you think this is ceremony, my dear ma'am, you never saw the extensive entourage that my grandfather considered his due."

"Perhaps I did not, but doubtless your grandfather ordered Mr. Clifford to visit him at Jervaulx House, which, as I reminded you earlier, is also what your father always does."

"Perfectly true," Letty said, looking back with a smile. "Had we not got into London so late last night, ma'am, I might have sent someone round to summon him. However, by the time I had sent a footman to the Strand and he had brought Mr. Clifford back to Jervaulx House, quite half the morning would have disappeared. I much prefer to do things at once, myself."

"Yes, I know," Miss Dibble said. It was a measure of the respect with which the marquess's household viewed her that when she emerged from the coach, the footman assisted her with the same deference that he had accorded his mistress.

"Don't keep them standing, Jonathan," Letty said to her coachman.

"No one won't try to move me," he replied, "and I doubt you'll be overlong in that place, Miss Letty."

"Now, Jonathan, don't be difficult. You know that you will become concerned for the horses if I take a minute above a quarter hour with Mr. Clifford, and I have no intention of leaving until I have made matters plain to him. You need not worry that I shall have to stand waiting for you at the curb, however."

The coachman grimaced. "I know that, miss. Clifford wouldn't never be such a gowk as to let you walk out the door without your coach standing ready to receive you. In point of fact, it is my belief that he'll want to put you right back inside it when he sees you in his office. It ain't no place for a lady of your quality, Miss Letty, if I may speak my mind on the subject."

"You will, anyway," Letty said, grinning. "But, Jonathan, even if Mr. Clifford is so forgetful of his manners as to express his disapproval of my presence in his office, do you think he will succeed in ejecting me?"

"No, miss," the coachman said with a sigh. His lips twitched, but years of practice kept him from breaking into a smile. He had known his mistress almost from the day of her birth, and had served her throughout her childhood. It was for this reason, she knew, that her father and mother had insisted that Jonathan accompany her to England.

Her footman waited patiently on the wide stone stoop, one hand poised to ring for admittance. Noting this, Letty said briskly, "Come, Elvira."

"You should listen to Jonathan Coachman," Miss Dibble said

in an undertone that would not carry either to the footman's ears or to those of the coachman. "He has only your interest at heart, my dear."

"Elvira, if you are going to preach, we shall soon fall out," Letty said. "My father likes Jonathan to accompany me because he knows I can trust him, not because he expects him to regulate my behavior. Thank you, Lucas; you may wait with the coach, if you please," she said to her footman when the door opened to reveal a visibly astonished porter ready to receive her.

The footman stepped aside to let her enter the office; but just then a tall, dark-haired man in a Prussian-blue redingote, its full skirt made long to the ankles, swept out past the porter. Startled, Letty stepped back, bumping into Miss Dibble and bringing the heel of her half-boot down hard upon the poor lady's instep.

Miss Dibble attempted unsuccessfully to stifle a cry of pain.

"Sorry," the man said curtly. Then, visibly collecting himself, he swept his tall beaver hat from his head and said to Letty, "I thought the porter had opened the door for me, ma'am. I never even saw you, but I trust you will forgive me."

"Certainly, sir," Letty said graciously. Despite his harsh expression, he was extremely handsome. She smiled, expecting him to stand back and let her pass. Instead, he brushed past her and continued on his way up the street.

"Well, good gracious me," Miss Dibble said, staring after him.

"He did apologize," Letty said, chuckling. "I expect he thought that was enough. Come, Elvira. It will do no good to glare at his back. He cannot see you."

The porter, still looking both surprised and bewildered, stepped quickly out of her path, and Letty entered a high-ceilinged chamber filled with expensive-looking furniture. Dark wood predominated, but many pieces bore polished brass fittings and rich red velvet upholstery.

Recovering his poise, the porter said politely, "Good morning, miss. How may I have the honor to serve you?"

"I have come to speak with Mr. Clifford," Letty said.

"I see. I expect you want the younger Mr. Clifford, but I am afraid—"

"I want Mr. Horatio Clifford," Letty said. "I am Letitia Deverill."

"I'll just see if he is available, shall I?" The porter turned toward the nearer of two tall, ornately framed doors at the rear of the chamber. He had taken but two steps, however, before he turned back abruptly. "Deverill, did you say?"

"Yes, Deverill."

"Would you perhaps bear kinship to—" He cleared his throat, then went on rapidly, "That is to say, would you perhaps be the *Lady* Letitia Deverill?"

"I am," Letty said calmly. "I ought perhaps to have explained at the outset that Mr. Horatio Clifford is my father's solicitor."

"To be sure, he has that honor, my lady," he said, adding more heartily, "Just you come with me now. Mr. Clifford would want to know where my wits had gone begging if I were to leave you standing whilst I apprise him of your arrival. Indeed, I hope you will not find occasion to complain of neglect. It is just that ladies of your quality seldom honor us with a visit, unexpected or otherwise."

"Just so," Letty said, smiling at him. "I would have sent a message, but I am in something of a hurry." She chuckled. "I nearly always am, I'm afraid."

"Then I shall not keep you waiting any longer," he assured her, hastening to open the door and putting his head in as he did so to say, "Mr. Clifford, such a delightful surprise this morning, sir. Lady Letitia Deverill—his lordship's daughter, you know—has condescended to pay you a call. Step right in, my lady."

Mr. Clifford proved to be a solid-looking gentleman with some fifty years to his credit. He arose with unhasty dignity from his chair behind an impressive cherrywood desk and stepped around to greet Letty. "Good morning, your ladyship," he said with easy formality. "I have been expecting to hear from you, for I had a letter from your papa not a sennight ago."

"Good morning, sir."

"I must say you have exceeded his lordship's expectations in having come all this way to see me," Clifford said. "There was no need, my lady, no need at all. I should have been quite pleased to wait upon you at Jervaulx House. Bring some tea for the ladies, Fox, straightaway, and don't send one of the lads in with it. Won't you sit down, my lady, and you, too, ma'am, of course?"

"Thank you," Letty said, taking the chair he indicated, while Miss Dibble sat stiffly upright on its twin. "I came to see you, sir," Letty added, "because I want to know more about the house I recently inherited. I know only that it lies in Upper Brook Street, in Mayfair, and that it was left to me by Mr. Augustus Benthall for reasons that no one seems to understand."

Mr. Clifford returned to his chair, peering at her over wire-rimmed spectacles as he sat down. To her surprise, his eyes were twinkling. "You are the second person to bring up that lack of understanding this morning," he said. "That would be a startling coincidence, except that I expect you both have arrived in town just now for similar reasons. Raventhorpe is to be a lord-in-waiting to the queen, and you have, I believe, been appointed to serve Her Majesty, as well, have you not?"

"Indeed, yes," Letty said. "I am to serve as a maid of honor in waiting, which sent my brothers into whoops when they learned of it. Not only do they believe me incapable of waiting for anything or upon anyone, but my family, sir, as you are doubtless aware, does not align itself philosophically or politically with the present government. I have every respect for Prime Minister Melbourne, and for Queen Victoria, of course, as does every member of my family, but Her Majesty does have a reputation for surrounding herself with loyal Whigs, does she not?"

"She does, indeed," he agreed. "That point has caused much controversy these two years past, however, because the monarch of our great country does not generally support one side over the other. Still, Her Majesty has a deep fondness for Lord Melbourne, and who can blame her, for she quite depends upon him to tell her how to go on in her august position. A young woman's needing a strong man to guide and support her can surprise no one, certainly."

Letty swallowed the contradicting words that leapt to her tongue, saying instead, "My brother Gideon says my appointment is just a sop. He says someone managed to convince Her Majesty that she must invite at least one Tory representative to court, and I do not doubt that he is right. That ought to cast me into dejection, I expect, but I am not so easily cast down, I promise you, and I daresay I shall find it all very interesting. However, at the moment," she added with a smile, "I must confess that I am more interested in learning about my house."

Mr. Clifford made a tent with his fingertips and stared at them thoughtfully before he met her steady gaze again and said, "I must say, my lady, I had expected to discuss this matter with your father. It is most unusual for an unmarried young woman— or a married one, for that matter—to demand explanations from her father's solicitor regarding matters of property. Now, if you were a widow—"

"Well, I am not, sir. Nor do I believe it would benefit me to become one."

"Legally it would give you powers that a single lady lacks, however."

"I do know that," she said, striving to keep the annoyance she felt out of her tone. "Though you may not realize it, sir, my family does not treat its women like children. We have opinions, and we do not hesitate to express them. Moreover, I have had the benefit of an excellent education, and my mother and father explained a good many other matters generally not taught to young ladies at even the best schools. You and I will get on much better, I believe, if you can manage to speak to me as you would speak to a gentleman."

"My imagination boggles at such a notion, my lady," the

lawyer replied, "but I will certainly strive to avoid offending you. Your father did warn me to treat you as I would treat any other heir, and I hope you do not think I meant any disrespect. Still, you are not yet one and twenty, and even gentlemen rarely take control of inherited property before achieving that age."

"I believe that Mr. Benthall attached no such condition to his will, however."

"That is quite true," Mr. Clifford admitted. "I daresay it never occurred to him that one might prove necessary."

"Then there can be no objection to my taking control of the house."

Apologetically he said, "There are tenants, I'm afraid."

"Yes, yes, I know. The letter we received last year from Mr. Benthall's man and my copy of the will both mention a Mrs. Linford and her sister, Miss Frome. I have no intention of turning them out or of interfering with them in any way."

"You could not do so if you wanted to," he said, settling back comfortably in his chair. "Benthall's will specifically ordains that they shall enjoy lifetime tenancy at no more than their present quarterly rent unless someone else begins paying that rent or you provide them with a house of equal elegance at an equivalent rent."

"Would the latter course be impossible?" Letty asked. "I do not ask because I have any desire to put them out, you understand, but only because I am curious."

"The Upper Brook Street house is one of the most elegant in Mayfair," he said, "which is to say, one of the most elegant in all London. Also, unlike most houses in Mayfair, it occupies a freehold property. You may not realize that nearly all the land in Mayfair is still owned by the Duke of Grosvenor, but so it is. Thus the small bits that are freehold have become particularly valuable. According to Benthall's man of affairs, there have already been two offers to buy the house."

"Indeed? Who wants to buy it? That gentleman who was here earlier?"

"No, my lady. Viscount Raventhorpe inherited the bulk of

Benthall's considerable estate. Not unnaturally, as one might say, he expected to inherit the house, as well. His mother was Benthall's cousin, you see. Over the past months, Raventhorpe has corresponded at length with Benthall's man of affairs about all this, but it occurred to him only recently that I might know why Benthall had chosen to leave the house away from his family. I'm afraid I was unable to help him."

"I see. Then who does want to buy the house?"

"The first offer came from Sir John Conroy. I don't know if that name means anything to you, but he is quite a well-known figure about London."

"He had the honor to be the queen's primary, unrelated advisor before she took the throne, I believe," Letty said.

"Indeed, he was," Clifford said, giving her a quizzical look that told her he wondered if she knew more than that about Conroy. She did, but she could see no good reason to mention her awareness of Sir John's fall from the queen's grace the instant Victoria took the throne, or that Jervaulx had warned her that Conroy saw the Tory party as just one more obstacle in the way of regaining the queen's favor.

After that brief look, Clifford went on to say, "According to Benthall's man, the only other offer came from a well-known admiral, but he withdrew his when he learned that Benthall had arranged for the two ladies to maintain lifetime tenancy."

"Let me see if I understand you correctly, sir. You are telling me that I can sell the house if I can find a buyer willing to accept my tenants on Mr. Benthall's terms, but that I cannot take full possession of the house myself until they die because it is unlikely that I could find an equivalent home for them."

"That is correct," Clifford said, nodding. "Not only would it be difficult to find a similar house, but it is unlikely that it would be worth your trouble or expense to do so, since you would have to accept their present rent, which is only forty pounds a year. Therefore, your only hope of taking full possession of the house before both ladies die lies in the second exception, which is if they allow someone else to take over payment of their rent. That condition is rather an odd one, because the ladies are said to be quite wealthy, but I expect Benthall feared that someone might try to take advantage of them in some way to gain control of the house for some purpose or other." With a ponderous effort at humor, he added, "Of course, legally, you could move in with them if you wish to do so."

"I see," Letty said, smiling dutifully. "I doubt that I will ever impose on them to that degree, sir, but I do hope that Mrs. Linford will not object to my calling upon her. My desire to see this excellent property is growing by leaps and bounds."

"She will welcome you with open arms," he said. His gaze shifted toward the door, and he added in a heartier tone, "Ah, Fox, just set that tea tray down in front of Lady Letitia's woman. Then you may take yourself off again. At least," he said to Letty with a smile, "I presume that you do not desire to pour out, my lady."

Grinning this time, Letty said, "We shall get on much better, Mr. Clifford, if you will cease to worry about what might offend me. I do not offend easily, I promise you. I like plain speaking and am prone to speaking quite plainly myself."

"You are a most unusual young woman, if I may make so bold as to say so."

"So I am told. Am I to understand, then, sir, that you have met Mrs. Linford?"

"Oh, yes, indeed. I took tea with her and her delightful sister, Miss Abigail Frome, shortly after Augustus Benthall's man of affairs communicated the details of his patron's will to me—such details, that is, as pertained to your father."

"To me, in fact," Letty reminded him.

"Yes, as it happens, my lady, but please understand that it never occurred to me that I would be dealing with anyone but his lordship. It simply is unheard of for young ladies to take an interest in such matters. I am an honest man, of course—"

"I do not doubt that, sir," Letty said, taking care not to smile. "Neither Grandfather nor Papa would tolerate a solicitor whom they could not trust entirely."

"I greatly admired your grandfather," Mr. Clifford said, "and I am grateful to know that I continue to enjoy the present marquess's confidence. But that does not make it less amazing that your father apparently trusts me to look after you, as well as his business affairs. He would not be wise to trust most men so far, you know, and I do not know that he is wise to entrust even me with something so precious."

"Do you mean the house, sir?"

"Certainly not. I mean his trusting me with your innocence, my lady. That is an astonishing burden for any father to put in the hands of his solicitor."

Letty's lips twitched, but she had little trouble hiding her amusement. "You will learn as you get to know me better, sir, that my father is not shifting any burden to your shoulders. I am quite capable of managing my own affairs."

"I have no doubt that you think you are, my lady, but—"

"I told him so, and I tell you so," Letty said firmly. "He believed me, and you will come to believe me, too, I promise."

"I am quite sure that I shall," Clifford said with a smile.

"Excellent. What I need from you now is to know exactly how far my responsibility extends. I shall, as I said, want to visit Mrs. Linford and Miss Frome, and see my property. But Mr. Benthall's will lacks detail, no doubt because he assumed that a landlord's specific duties are clear in law and that my solicitor would just talk things over with his. But I want the plain facts, sir. What exactly am I responsible for, if you please?"

"Why, nothing at all, my lady. I thought I had made that clear."

"You did no such thing. I must be responsible for something! One does not expect tenants to maintain the house they lease. Even I know that much."

"No, no, of course one does not, but it is your father, not you, who is responsible for such details. You are not—and here I hope I may take advantage of your permission to speak plainly . . ."

"Yes, please do so."

"Under law, you simply are not a legal entity, my lady. The plain fact is that our English courts regard an unmarried lady exactly the same way they regard a child, as a dependent person. That has nothing to do with individual justices or magistrates, I hasten to point out—only with the law. Under that law, your father bears all responsibility for matters pertaining to any property legally in your name. Nor will you bear responsibility when you marry, as I expect you will do very soon. A married lady is regarded as being one entity with her husband, and that entity—"

"—*is* the husband," Letty said flatly. Taking the cup of tea that Miss Dibble offered her, she added, "I know all that, sir. English law is chock-full of such foolishness, and despite that, rather astonishingly, it generally does work. Nonetheless, I also know that such matters can be rearranged in a Chancery Court."

"Indeed, they can," he agreed. "Still, I know of no case, even in Chancery, where a young woman has assumed full control of her property before the age of twenty-five."

"You say that you received a letter from my father, Mr. Clifford. Did he lead you to suppose that I should have to wait until I had attained such an age?"

Clifford grimaced but met her look directly. "No, my lady, he did not."

"I thought not. Did he lead you to suppose that I might be a burden to you?"

"No, he told me to advise you as I thought best, but I must remind you, my lady, that Mr. Benthall left you no money to go with the house."

"That, too, is true," Letty said, setting down her teacup and reaching into the cunningly-contrived slot in her muff that made it unnecessary for her to carry a reticule. Withdrawing a letter, she arose and handed it to the solicitor. "I anticipated your reluctance, you see, so that letter remains unsealed for the present. As you will note, it is addressed to the director of Child's Bank. Will you read it, please?"

He did so at once, and when he looked up, his eyes were wide with astonishment. "I've never heard of such a thing," he exclaimed. "Your father must be—" He broke off, flushing deeply.

"As you clearly were about to say, sir," Letty said smoothly, "my father must be fully confident of my ability. I promise you—as it was not necessary for me to promise him—that although he grants me full access to his London accounts, I shall not beggar him."

"No, no, I am quite certain . . . That is to say, this is all very unusual, and I hope you will not hesitate to send for me if you have questions about anything, my lady. Your father clearly believes you possess an understanding superior to that of most young women, but he cannot realize how easily some unscrupulous person might take advantage of so inexperienced a . . . a young person of either gender."

"That is precisely why I want you to describe my exact responsibilities, Mr. Clifford," Letty said with a patience she did not feel. "I readily admit that I do not know all the laws, or even which ones specifically pertain to my house. I am not inexperienced in other matters, however, and I can assure you that I shall attend competently to anyone for whose welfare I am responsible."

Angry chattering erupted in the outer office, and at almost the same moment, the door between the two chambers burst open and Mr. Fox said urgently, "I beg your pardon, sir! That is, I regret to say . . . Please, sir, there is a wild beast let loose and a young person chasing it. I can deal with most things, as you know, but monkeys in law offices is something I don't, and won't, hold with, sir."

Mr. Clifford leapt to his feet. "Monkeys!"

Also rising, albeit with less haste, Letty said calmly, "Only one, sir. I am afraid he belongs to me." Raising her voice, she said, "Come, Jeremiah. I am here."

As the little monkey darted into the room and leapt to Letty's arms, Jenifry Breton appeared in the doorway behind him and said ruefully, "I'm sorry, my lady. I attached his chain to his collar, but he unhooked himself, the little scamp. Then he got away, and when that man opened the front door, he just dashed inside."

"Never mind now, Jen," Letty said with a chuckle. "At least he did not get his hands on my pistol." Noting Mr. Clifford's scandalized expression, she said, "I was only teasing, sir."

"It relieves my mind to hear that you don't carry a pistol, my lady."

"Oh, but I do carry one," Letty said. "That is to say, I generally keep it in my coach when we travel. My mother gave it to me," she added demurely. "Jeremiah would never take it, though. I daresay the traffic frightened him, that's all."

"Indeed," Mr. Clifford said dryly. "Well, I trust that the others for whom you are so quick to take responsibility will prove more manageable than he is."

TWO

Viscount Raventhorpe strode swiftly up the Strand toward St. James's. He had dismissed his carriage before entering the solicitor's office, for he had not wanted to advertise his presence there either by leaving it standing at the curb or by having it go round and round the block. The Strand at Villiers Street was not a back slum by any means, but a nobleman's carriage would nonetheless soon draw notice.

He was a tall man, over six feet. Thus his long stride would cover the distance between Clifford's office and Brooks's Club in good time. Despite his carefully expressionless demeanor, his thoughts were in such turmoil that at Charing Cross he nearly stepped into the path of a team pulling a heavy dray wagon.

An urchin's cry of, "Hold up there, mister," brought his head up just in time to avoid disaster. Tossing a sixpence to the delighted lad, Raventhorpe paused just long enough for the dray to pass before striding on again into Cockspur Lane and Pall Mall, his long coat flapping around his ankles as he went.

He wondered if Clifford would speak to anyone else about their meeting. Solicitors were by nature generally a closed-mouth set, but one could never be certain. Over the past months, he had learned that many rules fell by the wayside when the richest man in London drew notice. Grimacing, he decided that, had anyone told him a year earlier that wealth could be as much of a curse as a blessing, he would have laughed himself to fits.

Until recently, he rarely had spared a thought for the opinions of others. Even now he told himself that no one's opinion mattered but his own. His life was orderly; and, aside from his duty to the young queen—agreed to before he had come into his vast inheritance—what he did or did not do concerned no one but himself. The difficulty was that he was finding it necessary to remind himself of that fact rather frequently of late.

Still, it irked him that Clifford now might think him so greedy that he could not bear even one of Augustus Benthall's many possessions to go to someone else. He had carefully explained to the man that he was simply curious about the odd disposal of the Upper Brook Street house, and concerned about the welfare of his great-aunts, its two elderly tenants. However, his interest had apparently surprised Clifford. Indeed, the solicitor had seemed downright disbelieving. His bushy eyebrows had shot upward as he said, "I believe your man of affairs must have made the details plain to you long since, when he read you the will, my lord."

"Not all the details," Raventhorpe had retorted, feeling his temper stir. "I'll grant you that the will made it clear enough that Augustus *believed* his aunts could remain in the house, but—"

"There can be no doubt of that, sir."

"That ought to relieve my mind, I'm sure, but I do not know how you can be so certain when Augustus left the house away from the family."

"The property was Mr. Benthall's to bequeath as he pleased, however."

"Yes, yes, I know it was, but surely you must understand my concern. We do not even know this person, this . . . this . . ."

"Lady Letitia Deverill has spent most of her life in France," Clifford said, his tone icy enough to inform Raventhorpe that he had stepped over the mark. "Her father, the seventh Mar-

quess of Jervaulx, has served our great country for many years
in a diplomatic post there."

Drawing breath, and smiling ruefully, Raventhorpe said instantly, "I beg pardon, sir, if I have given offense, but as I said,
I am gravely concerned about the welfare of my elderly rela-
tions."

"You might easily have left that concern to your solicitor's
attention, my lord," Clifford said softly. His eyes had narrowed
and grown steely, making him suddenly look far more formidable than he had only moments before. He said grimly, "The
most likely motivation for this call of yours is simple, not to
say vulgar, curiosity. I must presume," he added before Raventhorpe had gathered his wits to retort, "that you already have
taken up this matter with Benthall's man."

"I have, and he's as mum as mincemeat," Raventhorpe said.
"I own, sir, that I did hope you could cast light on this business.
Say what you will about my motives, for a man to leave an
excellent property away from his own kith and kin, to a family
whose politics not only conflict roundly with ours—"

"It certainly is a fine property," Clifford interjected, silencing
him.

The solicitor had said no more than that, but although the
steely look had softened, Raventhorpe was certain that Clifford
still disbelieved the purity of his motives. In truth, he was not
so sure of their purity himself, which stirred his temper now as
much as his failure to glean any useful information from Clifford did.

Having by that point accurately taken the solicitor's measure,
he had left without asking anything more about Lady Letitia
or her family. That she was the sole daughter of the Marquess
of Jervaulx he knew from Augustus Benthall's will, but he did
not think he had ever met her. In all likelihood, she and her
noble parents had attended the young queen's coronation the
previous May, and it was likely that he and she had attended
many of the same festivities at the time. It was even possible
that he had stood up with her for a dance at one coronation

ball or another. To be sure, such an instance would have required a proper introduction, but he met so many chits during any given Season that he had long ceased to take much notice of them unless they were diamonds of the first water or noteworthy heiresses.

The last thought brought a slight smile to his lips. He no longer needed to look for an heiress to undo the damage done over the years to his family estates. He could marry now where he chose, but he could see no reason to change his mind about Miss Susan Devon-Poole. Tall, blond, with a generally stately manner, and charmingly compliant, she would—as he had suspected nearly a year ago, shortly before the coronation—make him an excellent wife. Her respectable fortune, once a significant enhancement, now paled in comparison to his; but its existence would make her feel worthy of him. She would have to stop saying "my goodness me" every time she opened her mouth, but he would soon cure her of that.

That Miss Devon-Poole might reject him did not occur to him, for the notion was so absurd that it had not occurred to him even before he had inherited Augustus Benthall's vast fortune. Even then he had known his worth. The heir to the earldom of Sellafield, despite its wasted estates, had been quite eligible enough to attract her. She certainly would not reject him now that he was the wealthiest man in London.

He wondered if she suspected his interest. Though he had taken care not to exhibit it, not wanting to raise false hopes before he had quite decided, he suspected that she did. He knew that she had sent young Fothering to the rightabout, but that showed only that the chit had sense as well as beauty. Fothering would not suit her at all. With his fluttering attention to her, the scrawny fop always gave one the impression of a hummingbird attempting to drink nectar from an alabaster statue.

The walk from Villiers Street took him no more than twenty minutes. When he passed into St. James's Street, away from the traffic of Pall Mall, quiet closed around him until, as he passed Pickering's Court, a rattle of horseshoes and wheels on the cobblestones behind him broke the momentary stillness. A heavy town carriage soon drew abreast of him and a familiar voice shouted his name.

Turning, he saw that the carriage's lone passenger, a fashionable young man with wavy dark hair tumbling in wings over his forehead, had let down the window to lean out. Waving his beaver hat, he shouted at the man on the box, "Pull up, damn you! I want to get out."

The coachman complied, and Sir Halifax Quigley—known to his familiars as Puck—descended gracefully to the pavement.

Raventhorpe watched with amusement as his friend, who had been behaving like a rowdy schoolboy moments before, transformed himself into a young man about town the moment both highly polished shoes touched the cobbles.

Quigley wore a well-cut bottle-green coat, cream-colored smallclothes, a fashionably ruffled white shirt, and a well-starched cravat. As he moved toward the flagway, he restored his hat to his head and tucked a walking stick under his arm in order to straighten his coatsleeves and smooth his pale yellow gloves. He was shorter than Raventhorpe by a head, and built on slender, more graceful lines. "I hope you're going to Brooks's," he said as they met on the flagway.

"Where else?"

"Now, if that ain't just like you, Justin. Where else indeed? I haven't seen you in weeks, but here you are, walking along the street like a commoner, and you ask, 'where else?' Where's your carriage, my dear fellow?"

"At home by now, I expect. How are you, Puck?"

"Sound as a whistle, but don't think you can divert me that easily. Not when I've dismissed my carriage and condescended to walk with you."

"You needn't have done so."

"What was I to have done, then? Stand waiting on Brooks's stoop till you arrived? If you say that you'd have got into the carriage if I'd invited you to ride less than a block, I'll tell you to your head that I don't believe it."

"Then I won't say any such thing. I like that coat."

"Yes, so do I. You ain't just coming from Sellafield House at this hour."

"No."

"I knew it! Wrong direction."

"Your powers of observation amaze me."

"No, they don't. Never did." Puck remained silent until they had crossed to the other side of the street, then said, "If it ain't Sellafield House, then where *do* you come from, Justin?"

"I hesitate to snub you, Puck, but—I beg your pardon. Did you speak?"

"You know I didn't," his friend retorted. "I snorted, because you never hesitate to snub me, my lad—or anyone else, come to that."

Justin sighed. "Others tend more easily to heed my gentle hints, however."

"They're afraid of you, that's all."

"Dear me."

Puck chuckled. "You know they are. For that matter, when you lose that damned temper of yours, you can scare the liver and lights right out of me, too, even though I know you'd never do me any great harm."

"I trust that I may live up to your confidence."

"If that's by way of being a warning, it missed its mark," Puck said as they crossed Park Place. "You'd never strike anyone so short of matching your weight."

"Perhaps not," Justin said, turning to mount the wide steps of Brooks's. As they approached the front door, it opened, and when they entered the stately hall, the porter bade them a good morning, taking their hats and gloves, Puck's walking stick, and Justin's long coat.

"It's good to see you back in London, sir," the porter said to Justin. "Lord Sellafield is in the front morning room, by the bye. He asked that you wait upon him there if you should chance to come in."

"Thank you, Marston." Justin glanced at Puck. "I expect I

shall be detained some few minutes. Do you want to accompany me, or—"

"No, no," Puck said hastily. "I haven't had my breakfast yet."

"But my dear chap, it's nearly eleven o'clock!"

Puck raised his eyebrows. "I believe some deep meaning lies concealed in that observation, but I don't immediately perceive what it may be." Appealing to the porter, he said, "One can still get a passable breakfast here, can one not, Marston?"

"One can, indeed, sir."

"There, you see, Justin. Will you join me when you have attended to his lordship's wishes?"

"I will, but not to have breakfast. I ate mine several hours ago."

"Gad, is that why you noted the time? But surely you know that I do not rise with the sun, or ride in the park when there is no one to admire my seat or the cut of my coat! Nor do I have affairs of business to occupy my time. I ask you, what other purpose would serve to roust me out of bed before nine o'clock?"

"I can think of none," Justin admitted. "Go eat your breakfast, then, and I will join you when I can."

He found the Earl of Sellafield alone, sitting in a comfortable chair in one of the morning room's two window embrasures. The morning papers surrounded his lordship, most of them on the floor near his chair where he had dropped them.

"So there you are," he said gruffly, scowling at Justin as he lowered the paper he had been reading to his lap.

"Good morning, Father," Justin said. "How may I serve you?"

"Where the devil have you been?" the earl demanded. "I was out by the time you arrived yesterday. You were asleep when I got in last night, and although I thought I'd got up early enough to have a word with you this morning, they said you'd gone out. Moreover, you neglected to tell Latimer whither you were bound."

"I did not know you wanted me," Justin said, stifling irritation and glad that, for the moment at least, they had the room to themselves.

Sellafield snapped, "Good God, sir, it is no more than common courtesy to make your whereabouts known to the rest of your family."

"As you do, sir?"

"You keep a civil tongue in your head," retorted the earl, who rarely bothered to tell anyone where he was going or when to expect his return. "I'm still your father, by God, and I'll have none of your damned insolence. Sit down, damn you! I cannot talk to you whilst you loom over me like the Colossus of Rhodes."

Drawing a chair nearer, Justin obeyed, saying evenly, "How much?"

"Just a trifling amount," the earl said without pretending to misunderstand him. Casting his newspaper to the floor to join its fellows, he added matter-of-factly, "Yesterday was settling day at Tatt's, you know."

"I cannot see how that concerns me, however, or you, since you assured me that you would back no more horses until you could better afford to do so."

"Don't take that tone with me," the earl snapped. "I am not a child, and if I choose to attend the races, I must put money on my friends' entries, even when I've none of my own nags running."

"But since you have no money to waste—"

"Waste, is it? Now, see here—"

"Waste," Justin said firmly. "You should be putting your energy into restoring our estates, sir. Since they are the primary source of your income—"

"Dash it all, how can I put them in order without money? This is a fine state of affairs, I must say, when I am forced to discuss such things with a son who owes me both his duty and respect. Had your mother inherited Augustus Benthall's fortune as, by rights, she should have, I'd have full control of that fortune, instead of you, and I could do all that needs doing at Sellafield and more. But as it is . . ."

He went on, but Justin had heard it all many times before and did not bother to listen now. He had kept his temper in the past, not only because he knew it was his duty to show respect to his father but also because he felt a certain guilt at inheriting the fortune that Sellafield had counted on for so many years. Now, however, he found himself running out of patience.

"My dear sir," he said when the earl paused at last for breath, "I cannot undo what has been done, nor in all candor, do I want to. For years you lived on an expectation that proved to be false. Indeed, you must see by now that you had small cause to be so certain of getting the money. Cousin Augustus might just as easily have left it to one or both of my great-aunts."

"Poppycock! The man was a mischief-maker, God knows, but he'd never have been so daft as to leave such a vast fortune to those two dotty old women. I own, I did fear he might leave them the house, but how could anyone have guessed he'd bequeath everything *but* the house to you and leave the house right out of the family, and to a damned Tory, at that? What devil can have possessed him to do such a crack-brained thing? Why, he did not leave your poor mother a sou, and she was his favorite relative. I heard him say so myself, many and many a time."

"He did not forget her, sir. He left his mother's jewelry to her."

"Bosh, trumpery stuff," sneered the earl. "Nothing even worth selling, except for the one diamond set."

"Mama is very fond of those diamonds, sir," Justin said with an edge to his voice. "You must not try to sell them."

Sellafield dismissed with a gesture any interest in the diamonds. "Couldn't raise more than a thousand on them, anyway."

"I collect that you need more than that to settle your account at Tatt's."

"I do, but only fifteen hundred, so don't fly into alt over it. You can spare that amount easily enough."

"Yes, I expect I can. I'll write you a draft on Drummond's Bank, but I feel it only fair to tell you, sir, that I will not serve as your banker indefinitely. I intend to abide by Cousin Augustus's wishes, so do not think you can continue to waste the ready as though you and not I had inherited it. As I said, you would do better to tend to your estates."

"Why should I work to increase your inheritance?"

"Perhaps because at present your fortune, not mine, derives from them."

"If you could see your way clear to putting money into them . . ."

"I'd do it if I could be certain you would not just take it out again; but so long as I cannot control what you do, sir, I'll not waste a penny on them."

"Then will you agree to break the entail so I can sell some of the land?"

"I will not. I have every right to expect you to set them in order."

"Aye, you do, but the expectation is empty, lad. I'll take that fifteen hundred straightaway, if you please."

"Certainly," Justin said, rising without haste. "I'll write the draft."

Borrowing paper and a wafer from one of the several writing desks in the room, he did so. Then, leaving his father, he found Puck upstairs in the dining room, discussing a large breakfast.

"Sit down," Puck commanded. "I ordered enough food for both of us. Call it luncheon, if you must, but fill a plate. Some ale for his lordship," he said to the steward who had moved quickly to draw a second chair to the table.

As Justin sat down, he became aware of a shrewd, appraising look from his friend, but by the time the steward had poured Justin's ale and left them alone, Puck had returned his attention to his plate. Justin helped himself from a platter of rare beef running in juice, and broke a large chunk of bread from the loaf. He did not think the silence would last long, nor did it.

Puck reached for the jam pot and spooned a generous dollop onto half of a crusty bun. Pausing before taking a bite, he gazed at Justin, his eyes half shut. Long, dark lashes hooded their expression, giving him a sleepy look. Gently, he said, "Sellafield in the suds again?" When Justin grimaced, he added, "Don't tell me it's none of my business. I'm a slave to curiosity, as you know; and besides, it's as plain as a pikestaff that he's put you out of sorts, and that's the most likely reason."

"I don't want to talk about it, however," Justin said. "He is still my father."

"He's a sponge," Puck said roundly. "And if I didn't like your brother, Ned, I'd call him the same." He bit into his bun but kept his eyes fixed on Justin.

"I don't want to talk about my family, Puck, not any of them."

There was warning in his tone, but either Puck did not hear it or he chose to ignore it. Talking as he chewed, he said musingly, "Now, Ned don't know any better. Can't blame him for expecting someone to frank his entertainment when someone's always done so. As for the expense of his tuition and his chambers . . ."

"I promised long ago to bear his expenses while he studies law."

"I know you did. Know, too, that your father don't like it. Thinks Ned ought to purchase a pair of colors or become a parson. Can't imagine Ned a soldier or a psalm-sayer, myself, but those *are* more traditional occupations for a second son."

Justin smiled at the thought of his mischief-loving brother preaching sermons.

"That's better," Puck said, smearing jam on the second half of his bun. "I won't ask how much the earl wanted this time. That jolly well *ain't* my business. But I don't mind telling you I've seen the look you get whenever he wants more, and dashed if I don't think you somehow believe you owe him the money."

Justin cut his meat without comment.

"I knew it," Puck said, waving the remains of his bun to

punctuate the words. "You think Augustus Benthall ought to have left his fortune to Sellafield!"

"I never said that."

"Never denied it, either."

"Damn it, Puck, I don't know why I bear with your impertinence."

Puck chuckled, and the resulting expression would have enlightened at once anyone desiring to know how he had come by his nickname. He said, "You bear with me, my lad, because you've known me since the first day we found ourselves abandoned at Eton, and at the mercy of Jack Sproul, deciding which of us he would force to fag for him."

Justin smiled at the memory.

"Aye, you can smile. He didn't knock you tail over topknot."

"He was just trying to see which of us could bear punishment better," Justin reminded him.

"He was a damned bully. I daresay he never expected a new boy to floor him, though. You had a pretty left hook even then, my friend."

"Even so, my introduction to Eton might have been exceedingly painful if Sproul had succeeded in having me flogged for my insolence." The word reminded him of his father, but Puck was chuckling again.

"The beak could have flogged us both. It's a good thing he laughed instead."

"He couldn't help it," Justin said. "You were half my size even then, and both of us were smaller and younger than Sproul. When you insisted that you, rather than I, had floored Jack Sproul, the absurdity of your claim sent the beak into whoops. No one of sense could have blamed him, either."

"I suppose not." Popping the last bit of bun into his mouth, Puck chewed silently for a moment. Then, swallowing, he said, "It must have occurred to you that Augustus Benthall left his fortune to you because he knew your father would reduce it to a pittance in a twelve-month. Sellafield learned from the best,

Justin—from the old king and his profligate brothers. It's habit makes him the way he is, not intent."

Though no one could like hearing facts put so baldly, Justin held his temper. He was used to Puck's plain speaking and, in truth, was surprised that his friend had taken so long to speak out. Still, there were details that Puck did not understand.

"It would be hard for any man to stomach such an insult," Justin said quietly. "To cut him off without a penny like that was cruel when Cousin Augustus must have known he expected to get the money."

"Shouldn't have expected to inherit," Puck said. "Not related to Benthall."

"Don't quibble. He had every right to expect my mother to inherit, which would have given him control of the money. That's generally the way of things, and most folks expected it. He borrowed more than once on the expectation, after all."

"Oh, aye, everyone knew he expected it. My own father, rest his soul, said Sellafield was a fool to think he'd get the lot, though. My father thought Benthall would put portions in trust for your mother, her aunts, your brother, and you. That would have been the sensible thing to do."

"Yes, I've wondered about that," Justin admitted. "Had he left me the house and everything else to Mama and the aunts, I'd not have been surprised."

"You didn't know him very well, though, did you?"

"I met him fewer than five times in my life," Justin said. "How well could I have known him?"

"Well, I didn't know him, either," Puck said, "but people interest me a deal more than they interest you. Probably a form of self-defense when all is said and done. All you need do to depress a bully's inclination to violence is to stand up and narrow your eyes a bit. Not being blessed with your height or muscle, I must pay greater heed to character. Thus, I listen to what people say about themselves and each other, and I observe their actions and mannerisms more than you do."

"And what, my bantam, did all this listening and observation tell you about Cousin Augustus?"

"That he knew perfectly well what your father expected, and it amused him. He also knew a good deal about you."

"Good Lord, how could he? He never even came to London. The aunts have lived in his Upper Brook Street house for donkey's years."

Puck shook his head as he pushed his plate away. "You really must take more interest in what makes people behave as they do. Augustus Benthall may not have set foot off the grounds of Benthall Manor in thirty years, but he corresponded with everyone. A collection of his letters would rival that of the prolific Horace Walpole. He not only knew everyone, he knew what they were up to. And from what I've learned, I'd say the man liked creating situations. He would pass on a titbit from one person to another, guaranteed to stir up strife. It amused him, they say. I daresay it amused him to leave his money to you just because he knew your father expected to inherit it and would loathe having to appeal to you for funds."

Though Justin longed to tell Puck he was wrong, he did not. The description of Augustus Benthall seemed too likely to be true. Instead, he said thoughtfully, "That might explain why he left the house the way he did. He must have known it would irritate us all to learn that a Tory owned it."

"Perhaps," Puck said, "but in truth a Tory don't own it. Women don't take sides in politics, old chap. Can't vote, after all. What point would there be?"

Justin did not argue the point, although he had known women who certainly took interest in politics. He found himself suddenly thinking of the young woman he had nearly knocked down on Clifford's stoop. It was an odd, errant twist of mind at best. He recalled little more than that she had been a small woman swathed in green velvet, with a pair of speaking gray eyes and a mass of dark red curls.

She was unlikely to enter his orbit again. No *lady* would visit a solicitor's office, so the grim dragon at her side most likely meant she was a wealthy tradesman's daughter. That fact alone would preclude future acquaintance. Clearly, the chit was beneath his notice, and he could not think why he was wasting time thinking about her. Recalling that he was due at the royal court by one, he turned the subject to political matters and firmly put the young woman out of his mind.

THREE

Jervaulx London House

"Pull those laces tighter, Jenifry," Miss Dibble commanded two hours later as she supervised Letty's preparations to appear at Buckingham Palace.

"Elvira, I cannot breathe as it is," Letty protested, holding on to a doorpost between the dressing room and her bedchamber so that Jenifry's exertions would not topple her over.

"Then do not waste your breath complaining," Miss Dibble recommended. "You are going to court, after all. From what I hear of the place, the smaller your waist looks, the better you will fare."

Letty laughed, then gasped when Jenifry yanked the strings tighter. "That's enough, Jen! I shall have to stand up in the carriage to breathe if you draw them any tighter. Moreover, since this gown is intended for morning wear, I wore only a demi-corset when Sarah Glass fitted it on me. Do you fear that the queen will think me enceinte, Elvira, like she thought poor Lady Flora Hastings was?"

"What I think," Miss Dibble said severely, "is that you will do better to give no cause for speculation. They will look for anything amiss with you, that lot of precious Whigs, if only to cast disparagement on a proper Tory lady. If you are wise, you will wear nothing so informal as a demi-corset at court."

"I should think they must have learned the dangers of gossip

by now," Letty said thoughtfully as she moved to stand in front
of the nearby cheval glass so that she could see herself full
length. "Poor Lady Flora, to have been the butt of such wicked
speculation, all because she had fallen ill."

"Who is Lady Flora?" Jenifry asked, catching her mistress's
eye in the mirror as she shook out the lilac challis gown Letty
would wear to Buckingham Palace.

With tart disapproval, Miss Dibble said, "Such a question
springs most inappropriately from your lips, my girl."

Abashed, Jenifry begged pardon, but Letty only laughed
again and said, "Don't scold her, Elvira. You must know by now
that I have been telling Jenifry my secrets since we were children. There is no reason, moreover, not to tell her about Lady
Flora, particularly since her ladyship's brother, Hastings, seems
to have sent copies of all their mama's letters to the *Times* for
publication. Anyone who reads the newspapers knows nearly
the whole sordid tale by now."

"The topic still is not suitable for polite conversation, Letitia."

"Very well, then, I promise that I shall not mention it to the
queen," Letty said. When Miss Dibble looked scandalized, she
added with a repentant chuckle, "Truly, ma'am, I wish you
would not excite yourself so easily. I rarely do anything in company to put you to the blush."

"That is true," Miss Dibble admitted, "but you say such
wicked things privately that I am constantly in fear that your
tongue may slip on other occasions."

"I'm well aware of the position I shall occupy at court,"
Letty said, holding up her arms so Jenifry could slip the gown
over her head. When she emerged from the sea of lilac challis,
she said, "Lady Flora is sister to the Marquess of Hastings,
Jen. She served for years as a lady of the bedchamber to the
queen's mama, the Duchess of Kent. Victoria never liked her
very much, though, and upon taking the throne, told Lord Melbourne to beware because Lady Flora was a spy who would
repeat everything she heard to Sir John Conroy and the duch-

ess. The queen's ladies, in consequence, hold Lady Flora in great contempt."

Miss Dibble clicked her tongue in disapproval.

Ignoring her, Letty went on. "At the beginning of this year, matters reached what Papa called a dangerous stage. Lady Flora spent the Christmas holidays at her home in Scotland, and when she returned, she did so in a post chaise that she shared with Sir John Conroy."

Jenifry gasped. "Lor', then, she never!"

"Oh yes, she did. They said afterward that for the previous month she had felt unwell, and indeed, on the very day of her return, she consulted the court doctor, Sir James Clark. The symptoms she complained of included a tendency to biliousness and pain low on her left side; but the worst one, from the court's point of view, was that Sir James reported that her abdomen was considerably enlarged."

"Letitia, really!" Flushing deeply, Miss Dibble clutched a hand to her breast and said in the sternest tone she had yet employed, "This conversation must cease at once. You have no business to be talking of such private things."

"But isn't that just the point?" Letty demanded. "They took one look at her belly, for goodness' sake, and jumped to the worst possible conclusion, when the poor woman was quite ill! The queen and her ladies detected the strange alteration in her figure at once, Jen, and it was not long before they demanded that she be banished to protect their purity."

"Is it true, then, that she was sick all along?" Although Jenifry had dutifully twitched Letty's skirts into place, adjusted her sleeves, and begun to fasten the tiny buttons up the back of the gown, she clearly was paying close heed to the tale.

"Indeed, she was sick," Letty assured her. "However, before they discovered that trifling fact, the queen had accused her of being with child by Conroy. He is a firmly fixed bosom bow of the Duchess of Kent, you see, and Victoria despises him because between them, he and the duchess kept her closely restricted during her adolescence. Some say that Victoria has actually banished him from court."

Miss Dibble said quickly, "Not from court, Letitia, but only from her private rooms. He was accustomed in earlier years to enjoy quite intimate discussions with her, you see, and doubtless expected to become the true power behind the throne. Really, my dear, if you must repeat gossip, you should get the facts right."

"Yes, ma'am," Letty said with a mischievous twinkle. Restraining a base impulse, she forbore to point out that Miss Dibble seemed even better acquainted with the details than she was. "In any case, Jen," she went on, "Sir James Clark next requested that Lady Flora allow him to examine her with her stays off—"

Jenifry gasped again. "Lor'!"

"Needless to say, Lady Flora refused, but that only made things worse. Victoria banished the poor woman from her presence, and it was at that point, I believe, that the Duchess of Kent discovered the whole sordid tale."

"If Lady Flora was her bedchamber lady, she must have been vexed," Jenifry said, hanging on every word now, her duties forgotten. "What did the duchess do?"

"She said that if Lady Flora was not welcome, then she, too, would stay away. She also discharged Sir James, who was her doctor as well as the queen's."

"And then?"

"Well, I think Lady Flora must have been utterly distraught at having caused such a stir, because she agreed then to let both Sir James and a second doctor examine her. What's more, she emerged triumphant from the examination. The doctors issued a certificate declaring that they found no grounds to suspect that she was then or ever had been with child."

"Lor'," Jenifry said softly. "Did the queen apologize to her after that?"

"She did, but the apology came to naught."

"Letitia, it is not your place to criticize the queen," Miss Dibble said sharply.

"I'm not criticizing her, ma'am. In my opinion, the blame falls upon any number of folks. At all events, Jen, the queen expressed contrition and Lady Flora assured her that for the sake of the Duchess of Kent she would contain her wounded feelings instead of voicing them to all and sundry."

"Then it all came right," Jenifry said, gesturing for Letty to sit at the dressing table so she could smooth a few curly auburn wisps that had escaped her coiffure.

"It might well have done so but for a few awkward details," Letty said as she obeyed. "Unfortunately, the queen retained private doubts about Lady Flora's virtue. Worse, the doctors apparently admitted to Lord Melbourne that they, too, still had doubts. To make matters even worse, a number of trouble-makers aligned themselves with Lady Flora. Many were Tories, I'm sorry to say, who wanted to discredit the Whig government."

"Oh, dear," Jenifry said.

"Then, Sir John Conroy, who Papa says is the greatest trou-blemaker in all London, incited Lady Flora to fling fire and flame everywhere she went. And, of course," Letty added, "there was also the duchess. She believed it was all a plot to discredit her by casting aspersions on Sir John and her favorite bedchamber lady."

"What happened next, then?"

"The letters happened next," Letty said. "Lady Flora must have written to everyone in her family, but most importantly to her brother, who, as I told you, is the Marquess of Hastings. He is an excitable individual at the best of times, they say, but his brain then was more than ordinarily enfevered by an attack of influenza. He flew into a frenzy and demanded audiences with both Melbourne and the queen. When that course proved unproductive, he apparently wrote letters to everyone he knew. The *Times* has already published some of them, unfortunately."

"Truly? The newspaper really published their private letters?"

"Very private, some of them."

"Lor'." Jenifry carefully set Letty's straw bonnet in place, then stepped back, cocking her head and narrowing her eyes to examine her handiwork in the dressing-table mirror. When she nodded approval, Letty stood and turned to examine herself from tip to toe in the cheval glass again.

The lilac-colored dress had a plain high corsage trimmed at the neck with a frilly white tulle ruff. Its long sleeves were fashionably tight, with narrow bands of white lace at the wrists. The skirt flared wide, and although the waistline was slightly higher than Letty's natural one, as fashion demanded, the wide, dark lilac belt emphasized her narrow waist nonetheless.

Miss Dibble had insisted that she wear morning dress to meet the queen's mistress of robes, but they would take another, more elaborate gown for her to wear if Victoria desired her to take up her duties at once.

Drawing on a pair of lilac kid gloves, Letty stood still while Jenifry draped an ermine-trimmed lilac pelerine over her shoulders. Then, with a last look in the glass, she grinned impishly at her two companions. "Will I do, do you think?"

Miss Dibble said sternly, "You look quite charmingly, as usual, Letitia, but I pray that you will show the good sense to leave your levity at home."

"I shall be as solemn as a funeral mute, ma'am, I promise you."

Miss Dibble clicked her tongue again, then shot the giggling Jenifry a look.

Sobering at once, Jenifry said anxiously, "I'll warrant your knees must be quaking, Miss Letty. Mine surely would be if I was going to meet the queen."

Letty picked up her lacy reticule but smiled at the girl who had become such a close friend over the years. "You know that I have practically no sensibility, Jen. What's more, you must recall that I have met Her Majesty before, first when she was

still the Princess Victoria, and again last year after her coronation."

"Still, miss, she *is* the queen."

"So she is," Letty agreed, "and that means one must approach
her with all due pomp and circumstance, but she is still quite
young and even shorter than I am, for she is not even five feet
tall. Moreover, I have lived with pomp and circumstance all my
life, thanks to Papa's being with the embassy in Paris, so ceremony does not frighten me. Nor do even the most pompous
heads of state. And few people, you know, pay heed to the ladies
of the court in any event."

She knew, as she said the words, that she was understating
the case, for never before in Britain's history had the royal bedchamber ladies drawn such interest. No doubt the attention was
due to Victoria's youth and to a general perception—in Tory
circles particularly—that the Whig ladies with whom the young
queen had surrounded herself must exert undue influence over
her.

The two most powerful Tories in the land, the Duke of Wellington and Sir Robert Peel, had requested two years previously,
at the onset of her reign, that she appoint a few Tory ladies to
balance the mix. Victoria had refused their request outright,
preferring to remain surrounded by ladies friendly to, and frequently, even related to, Prime Minister Melbourne and some
of the most powerful Whig families. Only as a cushion to increasing public disapproval had she reluctantly agreed to appoint a lady from one of the Tory families, and although she
had chosen an influential family it was one that for many years
had played a small role in politics. Therefore, Letty had no
illusions about the position she was about to assume.

The Marquess of Jervaulx had explained these details to her,
and in his usual frank manner had said, "Victoria thinks you
will cause her no trouble, and my expectation is the same. She
will underestimate you, however, because you will rarely draw
notice—no more, in fact, than a new chair or painting. Naturally,
people will talk about you at first, but only briefly, before they

take pains to ignore you. You will be there only to appease the more outspoken grumblers, but you can help our side by showing Her Majesty that we Tories are not monsters but only ordinary subjects with opinions that frequently differ from those of her favored Whigs."

Letty was still remembering the gist of their several such conversations when she entered her town carriage with her two faithful companions in attendance. She settled herself as comfortably as her tight stays allowed while her footman carefully bestowed the box containing her second dress in the boot. She felt the sway of the carriage as he swung himself up behind, and almost immediately thereafter, heard the coachman give his team the office to start.

As the carriage passed out of the courtyard, she glanced back at the huge house. Jervaulx London House was impressive by anyone's standard, but today Letty felt as if it were her anchor, as if it would keep her steady when she entered the unfamiliar new world of Victoria's court.

She was not nervous. Indeed, she could not remember ever having been a victim of her nerves. Instead, she felt excitement and anticipation, not unlike what she had felt the first time she had come to England without her parents. At nine, she had looked forward to spending a few months in Cornwall with her maternal grandparents and her much older cousin, Charley. Although the visit had resulted instead in tragedy, adventure, and a more intimate acquaintance with smugglers, wreckers, and spies than her fond parents or anyone else could have anticipated, Letty had enjoyed her adventures. She expected to enjoy her service to the queen, too, although she doubted that it would prove nearly as exciting.

The carriage approached the palace from the north, rattling along the gravel drive, passing through the magnificent Marble Arch—erected as a memorial to the victories of Trafalgar and Waterloo—to the entrance front. Drawing up beneath a two-story portico of coupled Corinthian columns, the carriage swayed when Letty's footman jumped down to open the door and put down the step.

Jenifry, last to enter, was the first to emerge. Miss Dibble followed, and then Letty accepted the footman's outstretched hand and, carefully managing her skirt and reticule, stepped down to the pavement. Not one of the colorfully-uniformed guardsmen standing stiffly outside boxes that punctuated the colonnade screening the inner courtyard, so much as looked their way or moved to speak to them.

Letty said to her coachman, "Wait here, Jonathan, until we learn where you are to go and when you should collect us."

"Aye, m'lady. Leastwise, I'll wait till they sends me away."

"Perhaps, in that event, Lucas should stay here with you," Letty said.

Miss Dibble protested, "Lucas must attend you, Letitia, both to lend you consequence and to carry your second gown."

"They will hardly let me keep my footman with me when I am attending Her Majesty, or when I meet with the mistress of robes," Letty pointed out. "However, Lucas had better carry the gown inside, I expect, and I daresay someone will know where to send for Jonathan when we want him. Come along for now, then, Lucas. Since no one is moving to stop us, I presume that we are to use the main entrance. Ah, yes, I see someone coming out to meet us now."

A liveried porter of indeterminate age and magisterial bearing approached them without haste, causing Letty to stifle a sudden urge to chuckle. "He looks as toplofty as Grandpapa's butler, Forbes," she said. "I thought I'd never see Forbes's equal for depressing pretension, but I am very glad we have an appointment here today. I am Lady Letitia Deverill," she said to the man when he was near enough to hear. "I am to see the Duchess of Sutherland. Show him the letter, Elvira."

Miss Dibble did so, and without a word the porter signed to a minion to hold the doors open for them. Inside, Letty and her companions found themselves in a grand hall sixty feet long, forty feet wide, and twenty feet high. At the far end rose an imposing winged, white-marble staircase with a broad center flight and two slightly narrower returning flights.

Noting her gaze, the porter said austerely, "That staircase leads to the state apartments, your ladyship, but if you will be so kind as to follow me, I shall take you to the Duchess of Sutherland."

Letty smiled and thanked him, adding, "My companion will accompany me, of course, but perhaps you will be kind enough to have someone direct my servants to a room where they can await my return."

"Indeed, my lady," he said with an imperious gesture toward another of his minions. "Naturally, we have allotted a chamber to your use. They can wait there."

"Excellent," Letty said.

He spoke briefly to the palace servant, then nodded to Letty and said, "If you and your companion will follow me, my lady."

Although the route by which he took them was not as elaborately decorated or as elegantly appointed as the magnificent grand hall and its impressive staircase, the difference did not dismay Letty. She had much experience with stately homes and knew that often the corridors and rooms beyond the state apartments were austere to the point of bleakness. Apparently Buckingham Palace was no different in this respect from any other great house.

They passed through several long, dimly lighted corridors and up a flight of narrow but carpeted stairs, emerging on a landing with four closed doors. A footman beside the one directly in front of them leapt to open it, and they entered a pleasant, sunny, pink-and-pale green sitting room, presently occupied by two ladies.

Letty recognized Harriet, Duchess of Sutherland, as the elder of the two. The duchess, nearing her thirty-third year, had grown plumper since the last time Letty had seen her, but she still retained a great portion of her justly acclaimed beauty. As a granddaughter of that diamond of the first water, Georgiana, Duchess of Devonshire, Harriet Elizabeth Georgiana Howard had taken London by storm on her entrance into society. Marriage to Earl Gower, the heir to the Sutherland dukedom, had only increased her stature, and now she occupied one of the most powerful positions in the country as mistress of robes to the young queen. When the door opened, the duchess was sitting on a pink velvet claw-footed sofa. She put down the book she had been reading and looked expectantly at the intruders.

Her companion, a younger woman, who sat bolt upright on a scroll-ended bench in a nearby window embrasure, continued knitting placidly. The results of her labor spilled over her lap to the floor in a riot of bright colors. Either she had not heard the door or she had chosen to ignore the interruption.

The porter said, "The Lady Letitia Deverill, by appointment, your grace."

"Thank you, you may go," the duchess said as Letty and Miss Dibble made their curtsies. "Step forward, Letitia, and let me have a look at you." Her voice was pleasant enough, but Letty detected no welcome in her manner.

Complying with what had clearly been an order, Letty remained standing for the next quarter hour while the duchess described her new duties. She learned, primarily, that while she served she would have to be present whenever the queen was up and about unless Her Majesty specifically dismissed her.

"You will help with arrangements for state events, as well as other, less extraordinary ones," the duchess added. "I mention that only because Her Majesty is to give the first state ball of the Season a month from today, on the tenth of May. Your primary duty is to serve her and to help entertain her guests. I understand that you are fluent in both French and German, which will be a great help to you."

"Yes, ma'am," Letty said.

"You will also help entertain the company after dinner whenever the queen invites you to dine with her party. I trust you can play the pianoforte and sing."

"I've had years of lessons," Letty said. "As to whether anyone will want—"

"No false modesty, if you please. There is one more, very important thing."

Letty waited silently.

"Discretion is a quality prized above all others here, Letitia," the duchess said. "One expects any lady in royal service to be a model of circumspection, but we no longer live in the time of Mrs. Burney. Her Majesty strictly forbids anyone to keep a diary while at court, and our ladies must guard even their correspondence. As a result of recent difficulties, the queen becomes quite furious if she thinks anyone has written so much as a word about what goes on here."

"I quite understand, ma'am. I grew up in diplomatic circles, you know."

"Yes, Letitia, but you also represent a group who are politically opposed to the government in power. Her Majesty would be most displeased to learn that you had repeated things you've heard at court to any member of that group."

Choosing her words with care, Letty said, "My parents also would be displeased, ma'am. They both warned me—not that they thought it truly necessary to do so—that in whatever concerns Her Majesty, my lips must remain sealed."

"Excellent," the duchess said, nodding. "If you are prepared to begin at once, then I think you should do so. Tomorrow and every Thursday thereafter, Her Majesty will hold a drawing room. On such occasions, she likes to have all her ladies in attendance, so it would perhaps be as well if you can learn to find your way about the palace before then."

"I was aware that I might have to begin today, ma'am," Letty said calmly. "I brought another dress with me, and my people can fetch more if necessary. I believe, however, that I am not required to move permanently into the palace."

"That is correct," the duchess said. "Maids of honor no longer receive bed and board as part of their compensation, but you will receive board wages and you will have an apartment

to use here. Before you leave the palace you must always as-
certain that Her Majesty does not further require your presence.
You should know, too, that if you are late or fail to appear when
you should, Her Majesty will instantly dismiss you."

"Yes ma'am, I understand."

"Excellent. For today, I assume that you have brought a dress
appropriate for an afternoon at court. You must decide if it will
serve to dine with the royal party later, if Her Majesty invites
you to do so. Since this is your first day, no one will be too
critical, and there is little difference in the required dress since
Her Majesty encourages a feminine display of décolletage at
all times, not just in evening dress."

Well aware of that fact, knowing that Victoria was quite vain
about her lovely shoulders, Letty had chosen her court dresses
accordingly.

When the duchess dismissed her, she and Miss Dibble found
the same footman on the landing outside the sitting room, waiting to show them to Letty's apartment. That chamber, on the
third and uppermost floor of the palace, proved to be a bleak
cubicle, barely large enough for the narrow bed, dressing table,
stool, and wardrobe that comprised its meager furnishings. Lucas, standing stiffly outside the door, contributed much more
importance to the room than Letty felt it deserved.

However, she wasted no time in criticism but changed quickly
to her second gown, an elegant confection of pale green silk,
made very full in the skirt with a pointed waist in the antique
style. The heart-shaped bodice—cut low and well off the shoulders—clung tightly to her figure. Around her neck she wore a
simple pearl necklace. Matching drops graced her ears, and over
her long white glove on her right wrist she wore a single-strand
pearl bracelet.

Having removed her straw bonnet and smoothed her coiffure,
Jenifry pinned a small, beribboned lace cap at the back of her
head, saying, "You'll want to wear a more elaborate cap in the
evening, won't you, Miss Letty?"

"Yes, but Her Majesty will dismiss us at some point to dress for dinner," Letty said. "Will I do for now, Elvira?"

"Very elegant," Miss Dibble said, nodding her approval. "Your hair does want to curl rather too much here in London, but that cannot be helped. Pinch your cheeks a bit, my dear."

Letty shook her head. "I cannot go about pinching them all afternoon. In any event, I doubt that anyone but you will think them too pale."

"You should use a bit of rouge perhaps."

"I don't like rouge, nor do I have time for more primping. I ought to go."

"Your shoes, Miss Letty!"

Letty chuckled, slipping out of the black slippers she had worn with her challis gown and into the green silk ones that Jenifry held ready for her. "Now?"

Solemnly, Jenifry nodded.

Letty turned to Miss Dibble. "Will you wait for me here, Elvira, or do you prefer to return to Jervaulx House?"

"I shall await your return here, of course."

"Well, I don't know why you say of course. In your place, I'm sure I should prefer the warmth and comfort of Jervaulx House, and if you think for a minute that I shan't be able to get home without you, you are much mistaken. I'll be on duty only until dinner unless she invites me to join the party dining with her. Even in that event, I can manage to send word to you when and where to send the carriage to fetch me. Indeed, perhaps I can arrange for a palace carriage to take me home when my duties here are done."

"I will wait, Letitia. Moreover, Lucas, Jonathan, and Jenifry also will wait."

"Very well, ma'am, I won't debate the matter with you. Indeed, I daresay I shall be most grateful to see all your friendly faces by the end of this day."

Letty found the duchess's footman standing silently outside her door with Lucas. She expected the palace footman to take her directly to the queen, rather daunting though that prospect was. Still, it was with mixed emotions that she discovered he was returning her to the Duchess of Sutherland's sitting room.

Rising, the duchess greeted her, then looked her over critically.

Letty stood calmly, awaiting her verdict.

"Quite suitable," the duchess said at last, adding as she held out an object mounted on a white-ribbon bow, "You must wear your badge of office."

The badge proved to be a miniature of the queen surrounded by diamonds. The duchess helped Letty pin it to her bodice, saying, "You have style, Letitia. I believe Her Majesty will be pleased to approve of you."

A half hour later, however, when the duchess presented her to the queen, who sat amidst her ladies in a vast, elegantly appointed drawing room, Victoria frowned. "You have our permission to rise, Lady Letitia. We remember you well, as it happens. Your papa has kept his family in France for many years, has he not?"

"Yes, Your Majesty," Letty replied as she arose from her curtsy. "Having faithfully served the Crown at our Paris embassy, he returns home next month only because my grandfather's death nine months ago makes it both inconvenient and unwise for him to delay any longer in taking up his duties at Jervaulx Abbey."

"That gown is French, is it not," Victoria said abruptly, adding before Letty could reply, "We insist that our ladies wear only English-made clothing. Perhaps no one informed you of that fact."

"One naturally hesitates to contradict Your Majesty, but this gown is entirely English, ma'am. An English dressmaker fashioned it from fine English silk."

"Indeed?" Victoria looked at the gown more narrowly. "It is well made, certainly, but have you not just recently arrived in England?"

"Yes, ma'am. However, you will doubtless recall that last year you asked all the ladies attending your coronation to wear only English-made gowns. Thus, knowing then that I would be in London for the Season this year—even before you so graciously invited me to serve you here at court—my mother and I ordered a number of gowns to be made according to this year's English fashions."

"Indeed. You must have found a most wonderful woman for her to have made them fit you so well, what with you in France and she here in England."

"Sarah Glass is very skilled, to be sure, ma'am, but she did not fit me sight unseen. Once we knew I was to serve at court, my father sent for her, and she very kindly traveled all the way to Paris to attend to my formal fittings."

"I assume that Sutherland has explained your duties," Victoria said, clearly tired of talking about fashion.

"Yes, ma'am," Letty said.

"Excellent. Lady Portman," the queen said, raising her voice and turning her head slightly toward a small group of women talking quietly nearby, "perhaps you and Lady Barham would care to play three-handed whist now for a short while."

Two ladies separated themselves at once from the others and moved to attend to the queen. Footmen swiftly set up a card table, and no one seemed to notice as Letty walked away. For the moment she stood alone, for the Duchess of Sutherland had apparently abandoned her. Seeing another lone young woman look her way, Letty moved toward her, saying as she approached, "Hello, I am Letitia Deverill."

"Are you indeed?"

"Well, I was the last time I looked."

The smile that began to tug at the corners of the other young woman's mouth vanished in an instant when a stern masculine voice spoke from behind Letty.

"Catherine, Lady Tavistock is looking for you."

"I shall go to her at once, Sir John. Thank you."

Letty had thought the drawing room populated entirely by

members of the fair sex, but as she glanced toward the stern voice, she saw at once that she was mistaken. The man who had spoken turned on his heel without so much as a word to her, but she scarcely noted his rudeness.

Directly behind him, looking right at her, was the very handsome man who had nearly knocked her off Mr. Clifford's front stoop that morning.

FOUR

Justin stared in astonishment at the young woman in the pale green dress, hardly able to believe his eyes. However, when he blinked, not only was she still there but she was walking straight toward him.

Such effrontery unmanned him. Young ladies simply did not walk bang up to unknown gentlemen, let alone smile at them in that disarming way.

She had small, even, white teeth; and her rosy lips were promisingly full and softly seductive. The dusting of freckles on her small, tip-tilted nose did nothing to mar the beauty of her skin, which was smooth and creamy all the way down to the fashionably deep décolletage that revealed the round softness of her breasts.

"I have the advantage of you, I'm afraid, my lord."

Her voice startled him out of his brief trance, and an unfamiliar feeling of heat in his cheeks thoroughly disconcerted him. "I-I beg your pardon?"

"You need not do so," she said kindly, making him flush all the more when he realized that she had misunderstood and thought he had apologized for staring. Fortunately, before he could disabuse her of the notion, she added, "I know who you are, you see, and you cannot possibly know me."

"Do you always walk right up to strange men and begin a conversation? For that matter, do you—?"

"Are you a strange man?"

Unaccountably he found himself chuckling. "Perhaps we ought to begin this conversation again. In fairness, though, I should warn you that Lady Tavistock is looking our way. I daresay she will not approve of your forward manners."

"She will not approve of me in any event."

"You say that quite calmly. I should think that since she is chief lady of the bedchamber her disapproval could well end your welcome here."

"I doubt that she will pay me that much heed, sir. As a maid of honor, I am little more than a lowly attendant, and besides, I am only a sop."

"A what?" What mad sort of female was this?

"A sop," she repeated. "It's what my brother Gideon called me. We're Tories, you see—my family, that is—and the queen does not want any Tory women here. She appointed me only to appease the grumblers who deplore the fact that she is attended only by members and toadies of the most powerful Whig families. Now that I come to think of it, though, that must include you."

"I confess to being a Whig," he said cautiously. Then, impulsively, he added, "You are certainly an original, ma'am, if I may say so."

"Well, I wish you wouldn't," she retorted. "It makes me feel like some sort of *objet d'art* that you'd like to stick up on a shelf somewhere."

"You pronounce that phrase like a veritable Frenchman."

"Like a French*woman,* I should hope. The fact is that I spoke French before I spoke English, or at all events, from much the same time."

"Then you had a French nurse as well as a French governess, I expect."

"Yes, but my situation was not quite what you must be thinking."

"What I am thinking is that you are a most unusual young woman, who will likely find herself in the suds before long."

"Do you think so?"

"My dear girl, I found you on a solicitor's doorstep with no one to protect you but another female. I grant you, she looked a proper dragon, but that is *not* an area of town in which I should be pleased to find my sister."

"Have you got a sister?"

"No, but—"

"Then I don't think you should set yourself up as an expert on the subject," she said. "For that matter, Mr. Clifford's office is quite near St. James's—"

"Exactly my point. Many gentlemen's clubs sit in that district, you know."

"Are you suggesting that I might have been molested by a gentleman?"

"No, of course not, but—"

"Now that you put me in mind of it, I very nearly was, was I not?"

"What the devil are you talking about now?"

"You say that you found me, but the truth, sir, is that you nearly knocked me flat. Although that is not *molesting* in the truest sense of the word—"

"It certainly is not!"

"Well, I just said so, didn't I? Still, I do take your point."

He felt dizzy. She made it sound as if she were agreeing with him, but he found it hard to remember what his point had been. He certainly felt none of the satisfaction that such agreement ought to have given him.

Drawing a slow, deep breath, careful to let none of his disconcertion show, he said gently, "I feel obliged to offer you some advice, my girl."

"Then I must warn you, sir, that I do not take kindly to unsolicited advice, particularly not from strange men, and *most* particularly not from one who addresses me as his girl. Moreover, I daresay Lady Tavistock's disapproval of me would pale by comparison with her disapproval of your addressing me in such a rude and heedless fashion. We've not even been properly introduced!"

His temper ignited. "Why, you little spitfire, I meant only kindness. How the devil you have the nerve to take me up like that after you accosted *me*—"

"Accosted you! My dear sir—"

"Hush," he said abruptly, when his attention shifted to a familiar figure approaching them. "Sir John is returning, and little though you deserve—"

"Sir John who?" An arrested look in her eyes stirred his interest even more.

"Sir John Conroy," he said, watching her narrowly. "Look here, do you make it a habit constantly to interrupt other people, because I must tell you—"

"Yes, I do. I've striven for years to overcome the fault, but to no avail, I'm afraid. It is my besetting sin—or one of them," she added with a conscientious air of setting the record straight. "Do you admire Sir John Conroy?"

Justin was grateful for the buzz of conversation in the room, because without it both Conroy and the aide who was his constant companion were close enough to have overheard the question. As it was, he could be nearly certain that her voice had not carried to either man's ears. Offending Conroy was dangerous at the best of times. Just now, his mood seemed grim enough for an offense to prove deadly.

"I would offer to introduce you," Justin said, "if I knew your name."

She had turned, frowning, to look at Conroy, who had paused nearby to exchange a word with someone. When she glanced back at Justin, her frown vanished, and an engaging twinkle lighted her silvery eyes.

"I shall be sorry to end our conversation," she said. "Still, I expect I must tell you my name, for I can scarcely refuse now. I'm afraid I am Letitia Deverill."

"Good Lord." He stared at her, dumbfounded.

"I want to speak to you, Raventhorpe," Conroy said, startling him. Justin had not noticed that he and his shadow were on the move again.

Still dazed, he greeted the other man vaguely.

Conroy shook his hand. Then, shooting a glance at Letitia, he added in a falsely jovial tone, "I see that you have met our little Tory. Are you growing accustomed to life at court, Lady Letitia?"

"Yes, thank you," she said politely.

Justin looked from one to the other. "I was about to introduce her to you, sir. I did not realize the two of you had met."

"We haven't," she said bluntly. "Nor do I know his companion. I believe Sir John interrupted a conversation I was enjoying a while ago, however."

Justin experienced an unaccustomed collision of emotions. Although he felt a tickle of amusement, a surge of anger banished it, and much as he disliked Conroy, he did not think the anger he felt was in any way that gentleman's fault.

Conroy smiled, bestowing upon Lady Letitia the sort of look that made Justin glad he did *not* have a sister.

Keeping his temper on a firm rein, he said, "In that case, let me introduce him properly, ma'am. This is Sir John Conroy, onetime close advisor to the queen, and his aide, Charles Morden."

Conroy's eyebrows snapped together, and his jaw clenched, but these signs did not move Justin. He had no cause to fear Conroy.

"Goodness," Lady Letitia said, looking at the latter with widened eyes. "Do you no longer advise Her Majesty, Sir John?"

Conroy's lips pressed to a thin line, and Justin knew from experience that the man strove to control a temper even more volatile than his.

"The queen has much to learn about her august position," Conroy said grimly. "She inherited the throne at a very early age, as you must know."

"She will celebrate her twentieth birthday next month, sir," Lady Letitia said. "I am nearly that age myself. Do you think a sensible woman of twenty too young to take full responsibility for her duties?"

"What I think is not relevant," Conroy said. "She is the queen. All I meant by my observation is that if she sometimes acts impulsively, we cannot wonder at it. In my experience—and I have known her nearly from the cradle—her intelligence generally outweighs her impulses. Therefore she will soon seek advice again from those she knows she can trust to act in her best interest."

"I should think she would want what is best for the country," Lady Letitia said demurely.

Seeing color leap to Conroy's cheeks, Justin said quickly, "To be sure, that is always Her Majesty's main concern. From what I have seen, she is wise beyond her years. I do not think we need fear she will act rashly."

"Nor do I," Conroy said testily. "So don't think you can make mischief, Raventhorpe. Look here, I want a word with you. Forgive us, my lady."

Letty watched the three men walk away, feeling oddly bereft. For a short time, while she had been chatting with Raventhorpe, she had seen others watching them with open curiosity. Some had even looked as if they might approach, and she had harbored a small hope that he would introduce her so that she could make some friends. It was not to be, however. As Sir John Conroy led him away, she saw the others turn back to their previous conversations.

She tried several times to approach other ladies of the court, but they haughtily kept their distance.

A gentleman approached her shortly before Lady Sutherland dismissed the queen's ladies to change for dinner, but he wanted only to tell her that he had the honor to be her dinner partner. Turning on his heel the moment he had spoken, he neglected even to offer his name. By then she had come to understand that, although she had previously met only a few of the people in the room, everyone there knew exactly who she was and why she was there.

That thought would have depressed a less resilient spirit, but Letty had spirit to spare. Since her duty required only her presence that afternoon, she strolled about the room, looking at pictures and furniture, hoping she succeeded in looking occupied and undistressed by her isolation.

It occurred to her that no one had specifically informed her that she was to make one of the royal dinner party. However, since she apparently had a dinner partner, she felt it safe to assume that she was to do so.

Shortly before the queen withdrew to change for dinner, Letty saw Raventhorpe talking with a tall, blond young woman, whom she recognized as Susan Devon-Poole. She knew little about Miss Devon-Poole other than that she seemed to begin every sentence with "my goodness me," but her apparent hauteur now, even while conversing with him, seemed equal to that of anyone in the room.

Aware of an odd disappointment that he had not returned to continue their conversation, Letty told herself she was being foolish. That he had spoken to her once did not mean he would do so again, much as she had enjoyed exchanging verbal thrusts with him.

When Victoria retired to her dressing room, her ladies and gentlemen followed suit. Letty easily found the stairway leading to her apartment, but to her surprise, Miss Dibble and Jenifry awaited her on the landing outside her door.

Had she not been so glad to see them, she might have wondered what they were doing there. As it was, she greeted them with unqualified relief.

"You cannot imagine how pleasant it is to see friendly faces," she exclaimed. Only when both remained silent did she note their distress. "What's amiss?"

"It's really quite dreadful, miss," Jenifry said grimly.

At the same time, Miss Dibble said, "To think such a thing

could happen right in Buckingham Palace. I do not know how you will dress for dinner."

Hearing distant, muffled noises from the depths of the stairwell, Letty said, "Tell me the worst quickly. Someone is coming."

"Hopefully, it's someone to clear away the mess," Jenifry said.

"What mess?"

Miss Dibble grimaced. "I cannot even speak the words. I am surprised that you cannot smell it, Letitia. To think we were away less than a quarter hour!"

"I do smell something horrid. What is it?"

Jenifry said bluntly, "Slops. Someone emptied at least two basins on the floor whilst we were making ourselves familiar with the corridors and stairways."

"One of the gentlemen's valets very kindly showed us to a common room, rather like a servants' hall," Miss Dibble said. "It is for those of us who look after ladies and gentlemen of the court, but I expect we shouldn't have gone so far."

"Fiddlesticks," Letty said. "How could you suspect that you had reason to guard my room?"

"Well, we will guard it after this," Jenifry said angrily. "It's a good thing we didn't bring more of your clothing, Miss Letty. They threw your lilac gown right down in the mess. It will never come clean again!"

"Clearly, someone wants me gone," Letty said, sighing. "Where is Lucas?"

Miss Dibble said, "I sent him to fetch a slavey to clean up the mess. That must be them now."

The stairway doubled back on itself several times, so it was some time after Letty had first heard the voices that a hurried thump of feet on the carpeted flight below heralded the appearance of three men on the half-landing. The first was Lucas, and he led two menials with buckets, brushes, and pails. Bringing up the rear of the procession was the Duchess of Sutherland's footman.

"Your man told me what happened, my lady," he said quietly. "I informed her grace, who gave orders that you are to remove to another chamber. If your women do not want to go back inside to fetch what you need, one of these men can do so. You need only tell them what you require."

Jenifry said quickly, "I'll fetch your dressing case, Miss Letty."

"No, you won't," Miss Dibble said sharply. "You'll come back reeking of heaven-knows-what. Fortunately, there is very little there," she said to the duchess's footman. "One dressing case with her ladyship's initials on it, and sundry articles of clothing. The latter items you can arrange to have properly cleaned and returned to her ladyship. Do not, under any circumstances, allow your people to take them into her new room without a thorough cleaning."

"Yes, ma'am," the footman said, signing to the menials to enter the room. Then he added quietly, "We will do our best to find whoever did this, my lady. I feel bound to tell you, however, that so far no one admits seeing anyone up here."

"I know you will do what you can," Letty said.

Less than ten minutes later, she sat comfortably at a proper dressing table in a room considerably larger than the first.

Jenifry, looking around, said flatly, "They must have given you the smallest chamber in the palace, that first one. I'll wager you've been having a dreadful time of it downstairs, too, Miss Letty."

"Not dreadful, exactly, but I cannot pretend they welcomed me. Except for one, if they spoke to me at all, they did so in a way that would have cast a more sensitive woman into quite a deep depression."

"Poor Letitia," Miss Dibble said sympathetically.

Letty grinned at her. "I expected you to say that it serves me right for all the worry I have given you."

"I would never say such a thing," Miss Dibble replied. "It is not my place to speak so to you. More than that, however, I do not condone rudeness in others, ever, as you should know, Letitia; and this goes well beyond rudeness."

"It does indeed, ma'am; however, Papa warned me to expect small welcome, so their behavior downstairs did not shock me. Slops cast all over my bedchamber is another, more serious matter, certainly. Still, I do not think it will serve our purpose to make an issue of it. As Jen suggested, we will simply take care never to leave my room unlocked or unattended again."

"In this instance, your lack of sensibility quite unnerves me, Letitia."

"I should think you would be grateful for it, ma'am. Only think how trying it would be if I were to cast myself on your bosom, weeping and wailing and demanding to be taken home at once."

"I do not think we could simply leave, you know," Miss Dibble said judiciously. "One simply does not walk away from a royal appointment."

"Certainly not," Letty said, smiling fondly at her. "Moreover, all is not bleak, Elvira. I did meet someone who occasionally talked like a sensible man. You will never guess who he was, either."

"Not being blessed with second sight, I am sure I cannot," Miss Dibble said. "While you tell us, do let Jenifry arrange your hair more suitably for the evening."

"It was Raventhorpe, but there is nothing more to tell," Letty said, getting to her feet again. "In any event, before I say another word, I am going to take off this dress and loosen this devilish corset."

"Letitia!"

"Well, I'm sorry if you don't like the word 'devilish', but no other word aptly describes this thing, Elvira. Jenifry pulled my laces far too tight. Moreover, I have been standing or walking the whole time I've been away, and these shoes pinch my toes. I want to put my feet up on a stool and relax, if only for a few minutes. What I'd really like is a hot bath with lots of lovely French bath salts, but I daresay I should not take so much time."

"I need only ring for a tub and hot water, Miss Letty," Jenifry said. "That nice footman who brought us here said to let the servants know about anything you require, and after what was done to your room, I expect they'll want to make amends. Of course, later we'll make a list of what we need and bring our own things, but in the meantime—"

"First, we want comfortable chairs," Letty said, turning so that Jenifry could unbutton her gown. "The only one we've got is that pole-backed one by the window, which looks amazingly like a device from the Spanish Inquisition. For now, just fetch me a stool."

Jenifry chuckled, but Miss Dibble clicked her tongue. "That Catholic nonsense need not trouble us here in England, Letitia. I know your papa believes in religious tolerance. I do myself, when all is said and done, but any religion that can put its people through such dreadful ordeals as what they say the Inquisition did don't bear thinking about in a civilized land. You just turn your thoughts to something more suitable, if you please."

"Well, I did not mean to discuss the Catholic question, if that's what you mean," Letty said. "However, considering that it's become a major issue here in England just now, Elvira, I think you had better not say such things where others can hear you. You are bound to offend someone if you do."

"As if I don't have better sense than that. If you are going to take off that gown, for heaven's sake, be careful not to crease it. Hang it up carefully, Jenifry."

"Yes, ma'am," Jenifry replied. "Miss Letty, there's a footstool by the door. I'll draw it right up for you; then I'll go fetch a couple of cushions for that chair."

"I can get the stool," Letty said, kicking off the offending shoes and suiting action to words. Sitting in the chair, which proved to be as uncomfortable as it looked, she put up her feet with a sigh. When Jenifry returned minutes later with two cushions, she accepted them with thanks, adding, "It seems you've gotten to know that footman rather well in the short time we've been here."

To her surprise, Jenifry reddened self-consciously. "He's a knowing one, miss, and quite willing to offer his advice."

"Most men like to do that, in my experience," Letty said dryly, thinking instantly of Raventhorpe. "He is very handsome, too, is he not?"

Jenifry grinned. "He is that, miss, but not as handsome as the one what took us to see the common room. You should have seen *him.*"

Involuntarily both young women glanced at Miss Dibble, but she only shook her head at them, saying, "Ten minutes by my watch, Letitia. Then you simply must put your dress back on. They tell me the queen takes no more time than necessary to prepare for dinner, and you must not keep her waiting."

Letty did not argue. Ten minutes later she took her place on the dressing stool and let Jenifry rearrange her hair with pearls and ribbons from the dressing case woven into the ringlets. Then she got back into her gown and shoes.

Drawing on her gloves, she picked up her lacy reticule and went downstairs, finding herself neither first nor last to return. Although no one spoke to her, she saw the young woman with whom she had conversed earlier and remembered that Sir John had addressed her as Catherine. Taller than Letty, she had hair the color of old guineas. When she saw Letty looking her way, she smiled briefly before turning to an older woman who had plucked at her sleeve.

Shortly thereafter, Letty's dinner partner appeared, introducing himself as Althorn, as if the brief appellation were sufficient to tell her all she needed to know about him. His air of abstraction made normal conversation impossible, and she found herself watching for Raventhorpe. When he did not appear before queen and company went into dinner, Letty felt an unexpected stab of regret.

* * *

Dinner passed minute by crawling minute. Neither her partner nor the man on her left seemed to feel the least obligation to speak to her. After a quarter hour of finding that her conversational gambits fell on apparently deaf ears, she gave up.

Conversation buzzed around her, for the dining table filled the long room, with no fewer than twenty-five chattering diners on each side. Servants scurried to and fro, carrying huge platters, carafes of wine, and buckets of iced champagne. Letty drank water and sipped only occasionally from her wineglass, a trick her father had taught her the first time he allowed her to drink wine with her dinner.

"He who remains in control of his senses throughout a meal is the one who will remember the most of what was said and done there," the marquess had told her. "He also will make fewer errors of judgment in his conversation during the meal or afterward." Letty had long since taken that lesson to heart.

As instructed, she kept her ears open and paid heed to those around her, but she learned nothing that she could imagine was important or even interesting, politically or otherwise. She would not pass on anything to do with the queen, certainly, but what others said about party politics was fair game.

Generally, she found the evening more boring than any other in her memory. If she looked forward to the queen's drawing room the next day, it was only in the hope that it would prove more eventful.

She had attended royal drawing rooms before, of course. Not only had her mother presented her to Victoria shortly after the young queen's accession to the throne, but Letty and both of her parents had attended two coronation drawing rooms the previous year.

The next day's event took place at St. James's Palace, to which the queen traveled in state with her suite, in three royal carriages, escorted by a party of Life Guards. Letty rode in the third carriage with two bedchamber ladies and another maid of honor. The two bedchamber ladies chatted to each other. The maid of honor stared out her window.

At St. James's, a guard of honor from the Life Guards stood on duty in the courtyard, and members of the Queen's Guard protected the color court. Martial music stirred the air, and as Letty knew from experience, bands of both royal regiments would play alternately throughout the afternoon.

Before the drawing room began, Victoria received a deputation from Christ's Hospital in the royal closet. Then members of the royal family arrived with their attendants, and soon after that Victoria entered the throne room to take her place, standing in front of the throne, surrounded by her ladies.

The diplomatic presentations began, and when those with the entrée had come in, and the Countess of Kinnoull moved to present the lady mayoress of London, Letty began to see more familiar faces. Both the Russian ambassador and the Danish minister had dined with her parents in Paris. Each smiled when he saw her, and minutes later, she saw a pair of familiar, twinkling eyes that nearly moved her to leave her post in order to greet their owner. He clearly lacked her scruples, for he came to her at once.

"Herr Hummelauer, how delightful to see you," she said when he took her right hand and bent over it, clicking his heels together as he did.

"Gnädiges Fraülein," he murmured, kissing the air just above her hand, then looking up with his twinkle still firmly in place. "I hope I find you well."

"You do, indeed," she replied in his language.

No one seemed to be paying heed as she continued to chat amiably with the little man in German. He was the Austrian Chargé d'Affaires and a good friend of her father's. When he excused himself, she was sorry to see him go, for the general presentations had begun. Again, time crawled at a snail's pace.

"I heard what happened in your chamber yesterday." Viscount Raventhorpe's now-familiar voice, coming abruptly, and apparently out of nowhere, startled her out of her boredom.

Turning to face him, she found herself fighting a flurry of mixed emotions but managed to say evenly, "How kind of you to concern yourself, sir."

He retorted, "Concern myself? I, I thank heaven, need not concern myself. What the devil was your father thinking, to let a chit like you come here all alone?"

FIVE

Letty drew herself up to her full height to glare at the viscount, and gave her words measured force when she said, "My father considers me perfectly capable of managing my affairs, Raventhorpe. It would please me greatly if you could bring yourself to do likewise."

His reply being more in the nature of a snort than anything else, she could not flatter herself that she had made her point, but she was wise enough not to embellish it. Instead she waited patiently to hear what he would say next.

"My dear girl . . ."

She ground her teeth together.

". . . I am sure you must overrate his opinion of you. He undoubtedly thinks you beautiful, for anyone of sense must see that. I do not doubt that he admires your accomplishments, for they must be legion. However—"

"You *would* have a 'however'," she said sourly.

"Well, any idiot might guess I had a reason for offering you a string of compliments," he retorted. "No, don't interrupt me again," he said when she opened her mouth to do just that. "If you think that your father would admire your visit to Mr. Clifford's office, you are mistaken. Nor would any right-thinking man want his daughter to face the outrageous sight you faced last evening without the benefit of his protection. If I am wrong and he does think you capable of handling that sort of thing, not to mention worse that may come, he is a fool."

"How dare you!" Angrily she turned on her heel, only to stop in her tracks and stiffen when his hand gently touched her arm.

"Don't storm off in high dudgeon," he murmured, "unless you want to provide your enemies with grist for their mills."

Knowing he was right, and oddly calmed by both his tone and his touch, she curbed her temper and looked ruefully at him. "I apologize, sir. You seem to have a knack for sending me into alt, and I confess, I do not understand it, for it is not my custom to indulge in distempered freaks. Moreover, I have two brothers who delight in teasing, and they never can infuriate me. You managed to do it with one sentence. You should not have called my father a fool."

For a moment, he hesitated, saying nothing. Then he smiled.

It was, she decided, a singularly attractive smile. There could be no doubt that Viscount Raventhorpe was a disturbingly attractive gentleman. It was a pity that he was also arrogant and presumptuous. Had he proper manners, she could perhaps come to like him rather well.

Still smiling, he said, "I don't believe I actually called him a fool, you know. If you will recall my exact words, I said only that he *would* be a fool if he did not believe that you stand in need of protection. I do him the honor to believe he would agree with me."

Feeling her temper stir again in that unfamiliar fashion, Letty decided that further acquaintance with his lordship would do untold damage to her disposition if she did not take charge of her emotions. Therefore she suppressed the wish to throttle him and said sweetly instead, "Since you clearly believe my papa to be a sensible man, sir, I shall accept your apology. Oh, dear," she added quickly before he could deny having made one, "I see Lady Tavistock beckoning. I must go to her at once, so if you will excuse me . . ." Without looking back, she hurried through the crowd toward the principal lady of the bedchamber.

Lady Tavistock had turned to speak to another woman before

Letty reached her, so she stood patiently until the second woman moved away again. Then she made her graceful curtsy.

Lady Tavistock said haughtily, "I want to make your acquaintance, Letitia."

"That is kind of you, ma'am."

"Yes, well, I understand that you have no one from your family here at court," she said. "To tell you how you should go on, that is. So I thought perhaps I should drop a word in your ear, to save you grief in future, you see."

"Indeed I don't see, ma'am. Have I erred in some way?"

"You will not want to develop a shabby reputation, Letitia."

"Certainly not, ma'am. I cannot think how I should do so."

"A lady's reputation is everything in court circles. You must bear that in mind at all times. Her Majesty does not easily forgive transgressions."

"I do not know what transgression I have committed."

"This is a drawing room, Letitia. You are a maid of honor. Your attention should be on Her Majesty and the presentations, not idling away in flirtation."

Stifling annoyance for what seemed like the tenth time since her arrival at court, Letty said evenly, "If you refer to Viscount Raventhorpe, ma'am, perhaps you are not aware that we recently became acquainted through a shared inheritance. He was kind enough to ask how I am adjusting to my duties."

"You share an inheritance with Raventhorpe?" Her ladyship's tone was doubtful, which in Letty's opinion could not surprise anyone of sense.

"Perhaps I should not put it quite that way," she admitted. "In truth, each of us inherited property from the same man. That is how we came to be acquainted."

"You are related to Raventhorpe's family, then?" Lady Tavistock's tone softened noticeably, making Letty almost sorry to have to contradict her.

"Not related, no, ma'am. I inherited a house that his lordship had reason to expect he would inherit. It's rather a complicated business, I'm afraid, but he has been most considerate. Perhaps you can understand why I hesitated to snub him."

"I do not desire you to snub him at all," Lady Tavistock said stiffly. "I thought only to drop a hint in your ear. You may go now, and when your duties are done for the day, Her Majesty will not require your presence again until Saturday morning at eight. You must dress for riding then, since she intends to visit the riding school, as is her frequent custom. I assume that you ride competently. I believe the Duke of Wellington has mentioned that you do."

"It was kind of him to say so," Letty said, smiling at the thought of her old friend. Her father had served under the duke at Waterloo, and she had met him several times since then, both while he was prime minister and afterward. Though he, like her father, was a staunch Tory, he was still one of England's greatest heroes and a particular favorite of hers. She was grateful for what clearly had been an attempt on his part to smooth her path at court, and she would tell him so when next they met. His son, the Marquess of Douro, was to marry the following week. If she had not encountered Wellington before then, she would see him at the wedding.

Lady Tavistock dismissed her with a nod, and Letty returned to her post, keeping her eyes dutifully fixed on the flow of presentations, which already had begun to seem unending. The low buzz of conversation ebbed and swirled around her, and for a time she paid little heed to any of it. Then a particular exchange wafted its way to her ears above the general stream.

The speakers, both female, were somewhere close behind her. She did not recognize their voices. The first said, "They meet nearly every day, I'm told."

The second, higher-pitched voice, said, "Mercy me, where?"

"I'm sure I don't know. Finding a place to be private is the great difficulty, is it not? But if his lordship gets wind of this, heaven knows what he will do."

"Well, at least she's given him his heir. That is all one is bound to do, after all, so he ought not to fuss too much about a simple *affaire de coeur,* especially since he's indulged himself in several of them over the years."

"Wicked girl! How can you say such things?"

"Keep your voice down, do. Everyone will hear you."

Letty heard no more, for the queen's chamberlain chose that moment to announce that the first state ball of the Season would honor the state visit of Alexander, hereditary grand duke of Russia. As he spoke, Letty turned, hoping to catch a glimpse of the interesting pair she had overheard, but she could not decide which ones they were. The woman, Catherine, was nearby, but she was talking with the man Letty had seen the previous day in Sir John Conroy's company. Raventhorpe had mentioned his name, but she did not recall what it was.

Since Catherine was the only female at court who had shown any inclination to be friendly, Letty glanced her way several times after that, hoping to find an opportunity to approach her again. It was not to be, however. One moment Catherine was there, talking with the tall, blond man; the next she had vanished.

Letty remained at her post until the drawing room ended. Then the queen and her company returned to Buckingham Palace, and since Letty had received no invitation to dine that evening, she joined Miss Dibble and Jenifry in her new apartment long enough to collect her mantle and gloves. Then the three of them met their carriage and returned to Jervaulx House.

As they alit from the carriage in the flagstone courtyard of that noble residence, Miss Dibble said, "If Her Majesty does not require your presence at court tomorrow, Letitia, we should go to Bond Street and buy some new white gloves."

"Order a dozen if you wish, Elvira," Letty said. "I mean to visit my house tomorrow, and meet my tenants."

"Are you certain that is wise, my dear? Mr. Clifford, who seems to think just as he ought, was of the opinion that your fa—"

"I remember his opinion clearly, Elvira, and if we are not to fall out, I would prefer that you not repeat it to me. The Upper

Brook Street house is mine now, and I have every intention of seeing what it looks like and meeting my tenants. New gloves are an excellent idea, though, and since you know precisely what I require, you can see to their purchase. Jenifry can go with me to view the house."

Miss Dibble looked for a moment as if she might dispute this plan, but she did not, and Letty gave her credit for good sense. The good woman could scarcely imagine that her charge would meet with danger while paying a formal call upon two elderly ladies in the fashionable environs of Upper Brook Street, Mayfair.

After changing to less ceremonial clothing, Letty and Miss Dibble enjoyed a quiet supper. Then Letty retired to her sitting room to write a letter to her parents, informing them of her safe arrival in London. She described her visit to Mr. Clifford, her meeting with the Duchess of Sutherland, and her impressions of the drawing room in detail but mentioned Raventhorpe only briefly, saying that she had met him and that apparently he had expected to inherit the Mayfair house.

Thoughtfully, she nibbled her pen, then added,

> As you know, I have thought it odd from the outset that Mr. Benthall left his house to me. Now it seems stranger than ever. That he enjoyed a distant relationship to Grandmother Jervaulx and an acquaintance with my grandfather seems a trifling reason when he was much more nearly related to Raventhorpe's mother. Odder still, why leave it to me, rather than to one of my brothers? Can either of you think of any other reason for the bequest?

After dutifully inquiring about her brothers, both of whom were at school in England but would communicate with their parents many times before it would occur to them to write to her or pay her a visit, she sanded and sealed her letter and put it aside for the post. Then she rang for Jenifry and prepared for bed.

* * *

Upon rising the next day, she attended first to her morning post. Since friends knew she was in town, she had received several invitations to balls and parties. The London Season was under way, and if she chose, she would not have to spend a single evening at home.

Not knowing yet what her exact duties were, however, she accepted none of them, explaining her reluctance to commit herself, and knowing her friends would understand. The ladies of the bedchamber had specific schedules and knew weeks in advance when they were to serve. But the younger, less experienced maids of honor served whenever others deemed their presence suitable or necessary. Thus, her duties at the queen's court would be Letty's first concern throughout the Season.

When she had finished her correspondence and her breakfast, she returned to her dressing room and rang for Jenifry.

"I want the blue-and-grey-striped foulard dress and a white chemisette," she said when the dresser came. "I'll wear the grey cloak and my cottage bonnet with it. We'll leave as soon as I have dressed."

"We're paying a morning call on your tenants, then," Jenifry said.

"In a manner of speaking," Letty said, grinning. "As you know, in London, 'morning calls' generally are paid in the afternoon. Only one's closest friends and family darken one's doorstep before noon. However, I don't want to share this visit with other callers, so I mean for us to arrive by eleven. Then, hopefully, I can have them to myself for a bit. I mean to make friends with them, so that they will not mind telling me when things go amiss. I am going to be a model landlord, Jen."

"Your papa will approve of that, at any rate."

"He will. He said he has faith in me, and I mean to show him it is not misplaced. I've got until he and Mama arrive at the end of May to get my affairs in perfect order. In my mind, that does *not* mean turning them over to Mr. Clifford."

* * *

Promptly at eleven, Letty's carriage drew to a halt before number 18 Upper Brook Street. Before descending, she gazed at the house with serene satisfaction.

Set behind a forecourt marked with black iron railings at the street frontage, and wider than an average terrace house, its three-bay facade of fine ashlar was enlivened by a columned porch and superb ironwork. The wide arched entrance and balustraded window aprons above, Letty found especially pleasing to the eye.

Giving Lucas her hand, she descended, then paused to let him open the iron gate for her and Jenifry. Red geraniums in clay pots provided splashes of color throughout the flagstone forecourt, and someone had scrubbed the three wide stone steps leading to the porch till they were as white as the flanking marble columns.

Lucas stepped past her to wield the bright brass knocker, and a stout, liveried porter opened the door. In formal tones, Lucas said, "The Lady Letitia Deverill to see Mrs. Linford or Miss Frome."

The porter blinked. Then, visibly collecting himself, he said in even more stiffly pompous tones, "I shall inquire as to whether the mistress is at home, your ladyship, if you will kindly step into the entry hall."

"Thank you," Letty said. "Lucas, you may wait for us in the carriage."

After the promise of the exterior, the entry hall was disappointing. A modest, stone-flagged room, its furnishings comprised only a single straight-backed chair, clearly intended for the porter's use, and two quite ordinary side tables set opposite each other against cream-colored side walls. Unlit candles in plain brass sconces provided the only wall decoration. They also informed Letty that, most likely, modern gas lighting had not yet made its way into the house.

The porter opened one of a pair of tall white doors in the

wall facing the entrance, slipped through, and shut it after him. Two matching single doors faced each other from the side walls.

Letty and Jenifry were alone only a few minutes before the porter returned, opening the double doors wide this time.

Nodding, he said, "If you will be good enough to follow me, your ladyship, Mrs. Linford will receive you in the little drawing room."

Stepping through the doorway in his wake, Letty had all she could do not to stop and gawk. The cool, restrained entrance hall had not prepared her for the splendor of the stair hall.

Lighted from the top, the highly polished oak staircase swooped upward in an open spiral between large-scale, colorful murals depicting Reubenesque women and heroic men in mythical scenes. When she and Jenifry followed the porter up the winding, wide oak treads, she admired the splendid plasterwork and fine doorcases. As they reached the landing, she heard distant notes of a pianoforte and wondered which of the two elderly ladies played with such skill.

The porter opened a door to the right of the landing, and the music grew louder as they passed through an elegantly appointed anteroom, redolent with the scent of roses. Huge bouquets decked nearly every table in the room. The porter opened another set of double doors, and the music washed over them for the few seconds before he announced loudly, "Lady Letitia Deverill, ma'am."

The music stopped as Letty stepped into the room. In the same instant that she noted four females staring at her, rather than the two she had expected, she saw with shock that the pianist was none other than Viscount Raventhorpe.

"Good morning, your ladyship. Won't you and your companion take a seat. Jackson, ask Mary to bring in more refreshments."

Suppressing her shock, Letty looked quickly at the plump, elderly woman who had spoken, and said, "Thank you, ma'am. You must be Mrs. Linford. I hope you will forgive my calling upon you so early in the day."

"I expect you wanted to see your house, my dear," said one of the others. She was a lady nearly as elderly as the first, wearing a huge creation on her head, so extravagantly decorated with ribbons, beads, and rosettes that it took every ounce of Letty's training not to stare at it in astonishment.

Taking a seat on a plumply upholstered, claw-footed chair, she replied with forced calm, "Even more than that, ma'am, did I want to meet my tenants and assure them that I have no intention of disrupting their serenity. Can you be Miss Frome?"

"I am, indeed, though most folks call me Miss Abby. How clever of you to sort us out so quickly. But you cannot know our dear niece Sally, or Liza."

"Sally is Lady Sellafield," Mrs. Linford said reprovingly. "As I have told you many times, Abigail, you ought not to introduce her or yourself so informally."

"Pish-posh," Miss Abigail said with an impish grin that, if unexpected in so elderly a countenance, was nonetheless charming. "I cannot think how you expect me to introduce Liza with any formality," she said, adding in an aside to Letty, "She thinks she is our daughter, don't you know. She is no such thing, of course. Miranda was never blessed with children, and I was never cursed with a husband."

"Indeed, ma'am?" Letty said, hardly knowing what else to say. She looked at the fourth female, a girl of no more than fifteen years, who stared back at her with a vapid expression on her pale, homely face. Beginning to think she had entered a madhouse, Letty glanced at Raventhorpe. That gentleman's countenance was unreadable, but she thought she detected a gleam in his penetrating dark blue eyes.

"Abigail, that will do," Mrs. Linford said on what clearly was a warning note. "Letitia, my dear, do take some time to make yourself known to us. We know that you came to London from Paris, and Justin tells us that the two of you have met already, so we need stand on no further ceremony."

Irrepressibly, Miss Abigail interjected, "But I do think you ought to introduce Liza to her, Miranda. She will see her whenever she chooses to call upon us, which I, for one, hope she means to do quite frequently."

"Liza lives with us, and we look after her," Mrs. Linford said. "That is sufficient for anyone to know. Tell us all about your journey, Letitia."

"It was uneventful, I'm afraid, ma'am. Perhaps you would be so kind as to tell me about the house instead. I am quite curious about it—and about Mr. Augustus Benthall, whom I was never privileged to meet."

Lady Sellafield spoke for the first time. "Is that true, indeed, that you never knew Augustus? How very odd it was of him, then, to have left you his house."

"Yes, ma'am, it was," Letty said frankly. "Moreover, I would not blame you in the least if you despised me as an interloper, for surely you must have expected to inherit it yourself. He was much more nearly related to you than to me."

"Yes, he was," Lady Sellafield agreed. "However, Augustus was eccentric, my dear, so there was no relying on him at all. He did as he pleased, and I promise you, I do not resent it in the least. It *was* his house, after all, and he took care to see that my aunts will not have to leave it, which is the only important thing."

"You are kind to say so, ma'am," Letty said sincerely.

"Augustus was always kind to us," Miss Abigail said with a reminiscent air. "We saw him, you know, in his coffin."

"Abigail!"

"Well, we did, Miranda. You know we did, and he looked ever so odd, Letitia, because they had put his spectacles on his nose, but his eyes were shut, of course, and so it looked as if he had gone to sleep and forgot to take them off."

"That must have seemed strange indeed, ma'am," Letty said faintly. Feeling Raventhorpe's gaze upon her, she turned, looked him straight in the eye, and said, "I did not know that you played the pianoforte, sir."

"No, how could you?"

"Justin!" His mother gaped at him in surprise.

"I beg your pardon, Mama. I am sure that Lady Letitia's skill with the instrument far surpasses my own."

"I only wish it did," Letty said frankly. "I have had lessons, of course—years of them—but I dislike practicing. Thus my skill, as you are kind enough to call it, sir, is limited at best. You, on the other hand, play exceedingly well."

"I like to hear Justin play," Liza said. "Justin always plays for me when he comes to our house. Oh, here's Puss," she added in much the same even tone when a large marmalade cat strolled through an open doorway opposite the one through which Letty had come. "Come, Puss. Come to Liza, dear."

The cat glanced at her but padded straight to Letty, sniffing her skirt, then sitting with front paws neatly together to look up at her with unblinking amber eyes.

"He is deciding if he likes you," Miss Abigail said. "I hope you are not one of those very odd persons who dislikes cats, my dear."

"No, ma'am, I am fond of all animals."

The cat sniffed again, made a spitting noise, then got up, collected its dignity, and left the room with its tail held stiffly erect.

Liza gave a cry of dismay, leapt to her feet, and ran after it.

Miss Abigail said, "Oh, dear, he seems to have taken you in dislike. I cannot imagine why."

"I can," Letty said dryly. "It's possible that he does not approve of monkeys, and I'm afraid I keep one as a pet. No doubt he detected its scent on my clothing."

Mrs. Linford said austerely, "That would certainly explain his distaste."

"But a monkey, Miranda," exclaimed Miss Abigail, clapping her hands in a childlike expression of delight. "Only think how dear! What is his name, Letitia?"

"Jeremiah, ma'am. I have had him since I was eight, and I can assure you, he is just as finicky about choosing his friends as your cat seems to be."

"You must bring him to visit us," Miss Abigail insisted. "I

should very much enjoy making the acquaintance of such an exotic beast."

"The house has seven rooms on each floor," Mrs. Linford said in a tone that ended any further talk about animals. "You will be interested only in the reception rooms, Letitia, which all lie on this floor and open onto the landing. This room adjoins the dining room, which adjoins the library, and so forth. Jackson or Mary, or one of the other maids, can show you through them when you are ready to depart."

"But I want to see the whole house," Letty protested. "And I daresay there must be a stable and coach-house, as well."

"There are three coach-houses in the mews behind the house, and stables that can accommodate ten horses," Mrs. Linford said. "However, it is not convenient to show you over the whole place today. I am sure you must understand. Perhaps if you give us notice of your next visit, we can arrange for our housekeeper to set aside time for a proper tour."

"Yes, of course," Letty said.

An awkward pause followed before Raventhorpe said gently, "I have other engagements this morning, Aunts. I know that Mama wants to enjoy a good long visit with you, however, so perhaps you will let me show Lady Letitia the other reception rooms on my way out, if she does not object."

"That would be kind of you, sir."

"Indeed, it would be just the thing, Justin," Miss Abigail said. "You can tell her all about Mr. Robert Adam and how he came to design this house. I am sure you know as much as we do about that, and far more than Mrs. Hopworthy does."

"I will attempt to tell her whatever she desires to know," Raventhorpe said. "If you are ready to depart, Lady Letitia . . ."

"But she's not had any refreshment yet," Miss Abigail protested.

"I really should go, ma'am," Letty said with a smile.

As she got to her feet, Lady Sellafield said, "Do not forget that we are to dine at Devon-Poole House this evening, Justin, my dear. Susan and Lady Devon-Poole will be disappointed if you forget."

"I won't forget, ma'am. I shall be home in good time."

"Excellent, because your father very likely *will* forget, and Ned is not to be depended upon either, I'm afraid."

"I'll engage to bring them up to scratch," he said. "Shall we go, my lady?"

With Jenifry following silently in their wake, Letty allowed him to guide her into the dining room. When he began to tell her about the architect, Robert Adam, however, she cut in, saying, "I know about the Adams, sir, the father and his equally talented sons. I know also that Robert Adam designed this house. Indeed, I'm told it's one of the three finest examples of his work in London." After a pause, she added, "I have met Miss Devon-Poole. Is it a particular object with you to please her?"

"It is not my intention to disappoint her. I intend to make her my wife."

She had hoped to disconcert him with the impertinent question, but to her astonishment, his casual reply brought a surge of dismay that seemed to tie her tongue in knots. Choosing her next words with more care, she said, "I had not heard of your engagement."

"There isn't one, so there is no reason that you should have heard."

"Does the lady know of your intent?"

He grimaced. "She does not, and I'll thank you not to tell her."

"Oh, Letitia dear," Miss Abigail said from the doorway, "don't forget to bring Jeremiah when next you come, and do come soon. Do say you will."

"Yes, ma'am, I will. I am to ride with Her Majesty at the riding school near the palace tomorrow, and I may have to attend church services with her on Sunday. Perhaps I can manage to come to you Sunday afternoon or on Monday, if one of those days will suit you and your Mrs. Hopworthy."

"Oh, there can be no objection to either one! I'll tell Miranda."

"If you will accept my counsel," Raventhorpe said when Miss Abigail had taken herself off again, "you will not—"

"Raventhorpe, do stop offering me advice. It does nothing more than make me want to run counter to it. What a fine library this is, to be sure."

"You, my girl, had better be careful at the riding school," he said grimly. "You are quite clearly ripe for a fall."

"I am sure you will look out for me," she said with a sigh.

"I won't be there," he retorted. "I leave for Newmarket tomorrow. If my horses run well, I expect to stay there through Wednesday."

Hiding her disappointment, and wondering if Miss Susan Devon-Poole also meant to attend the Newmarket races, Letty turned the subject by asking about the contents of the library. Nonetheless, the unexpected train of thought both startled and dismayed her, for she could not imagine what attracted her so to a man like Raventhorpe. Not only was he arrogant and dogmatic, but he was a Whig, his politics thus guaranteed to run counter to those of her family and friends.

Determined to overcome her odd attraction, she managed by the time they reached the street outside the house to persuade herself that his allure lay in nothing more than that he had been the only person at court to pay her any heed. Doubtless she was grasping for friendship with anyone, out of sheer loneliness and isolation.

During the next few days, she did manage (for the most part) to put him out of her mind. The riding school proved interesting, although it was not a particularly stimulating arena for one who was an expert horsewoman. Letty soon discovered that Queen Victoria did not love riding like she did, that the royal rides were sedate and generally boring. Attending the royal chapel proved no less so. Most people clearly attended only to see and be seen.

By Sunday afternoon she was more than ready for a second visit to Upper Brook Street, but when she sent her card round to inquire if the ladies would be at home, she received a polite reply from Mrs. Linford, informing her that they would be out all afternoon. They would, however, be happy to receive her on Monday at one, if that would suit her.

Letty decided that it suited her perfectly, even if she had to send word to the palace of an incipient illness. As it transpired, however, although the queen required her presence again at the riding school, Victoria intended to spend the rest of the day closeted with her ministers. Thus Letty was free to do as she pleased.

At one o'clock precisely, she and Jenifry stepped down to the pavement in front of the Mayfair house. Shifting the large muff she carried, and petting its small, furry occupant, Letty said, "You need not knock, Lucas. I want you and Jonathan to take the carriage round to the back. There are coach-houses in the mews, I'm told, and I want you to see if they are well tended."

The front door opened as they approached it, and the porter, Jackson, greeted them politely. "The mistress is expecting you, my lady. She is presently entertaining the vicar, but I am to take you straight up, so perhaps you would like to leave your cloaks here in the hall. Ah, Lady Sellafield," he added when that lady appeared in the stair-hall doorway, "I've sent for your carriage, ma'am. It'll be round directly."

While Letty exchanged pleasantries with Lady Sellafield, Jenifry took off her own cloak then moved to help Letty with hers. As she did, the porter reached for Letty's muff, but she said, "I'll keep it, thank you. I think we should go up now." Smiling at Lady Sellafield, she added politely, "if you will excuse us, ma'am."

"Indeed I will, for Aunt Miranda will be glad to see you," Lady Sellafield said. "She finds conversing with Vicar somewhat tedious, I'm afraid, but I could not lend her my support any longer, for I am to take tea with my mama-in-law at two. It is pleasant to see you again, dear. You must come to Sellafield House to visit me."

"Thank you, ma'am."

Lady Sellafield smiled. "I'm giving a dinner party soon. I shall send you a card. Take them up now, Jackson. I'll watch from the window for my carriage."

"Yes, my lady," the porter said, draping their cloaks over the one chair and leading the way into the stair hall.

Letty and Jenifry followed him to the first landing, but when he turned toward the doorway through which he had taken them before, a feline hiss and snarl startled them all. At the sound, Jeremiah came to life inside Letty's muff and with a shriek, slipped free before she realized his intent. The cat, with another snarl of fury, gave chase; and, chattering wildly, the little monkey sprang to the banister and leapt to the next landing, disappearing with the cat in hot pursuit.

"Merciful heavens, he can't go up there," Miss Abigail exclaimed from the anteroom threshold. "Jackson, catch him! Quickly!"

"I'll go," Jenifry said, but Letty caught her arm.

"Stay here, all of you," she ordered, snatching up her skirt with her free hand and hurrying after the monkey. Over her shoulder she cried, "You would just frighten him more. He'll come to me. I'll only be a moment, I promise you."

Miss Abigail cried, "But, my dear, you mustn't!"

Letty paid no heed. She had reached the landing and at the end of the corridor ahead, she caught a glimpse of Jeremiah tearing around a corner with the cat skidding wildly in his wake. She ran after them, rounding the corner in time to see the little monkey hurl itself at a door at the end of the hallway. To her astonishment, the door flew open and he disappeared inside, still chattering at the top of his lungs. Another, definitely human shriek accompanied his.

Reaching the doorway, she stopped, amazed at the sight that

met her eyes. Jeremiah, perched atop a nearby curtain, still chattered angrily, and the marmalade cat clung determinedly, swaying, halfway up the curtain. The couple in the bed was what astonished her, however. Recognizing the wide-eyed, clearly embarrassed, and quite naked Catherine, Letty deduced that the man who had flung the covers over his head before she had entered was not Catherine's husband.

"Oh, dear," Miss Abigail said behind her, "we were afraid you might find out. Miranda will be vexed."

SIX

Letty glanced at Miss Abigail, who wrung her hands in clear distress. In her agitation, the elaborate confection of lace, ribbons, feathers, and beads atop her little head twitched and bobbed in a colorful dance.

"Miranda particularly asked Lady Witherspoon *not* to come today," she said fretfully, "but her ladyship insisted, and now look what's come of it. Miranda will be so dreadfully vexed, and I am sure one cannot blame her."

"Ma'am, really, what on earth . . ." Letty began, only to fall silent when she could not think of an acceptable way to word the question she was burning to ask.

Catherine had dived beneath the covers to join her companion. The bed quaked with their movements, while Jeremiah hurled simian epithets at the marmalade cat, still inching its way slowly but determinedly up the curtain.

Stepping away from the door, and clearly expecting Letty to follow her, Miss Abigail said, "I know that you said I should stay below, dear, but you must see now that I simply could not let you come up here alone."

"Yes, I understand why you felt you could not," Letty agreed, watching her but not stirring from the threshold, "especially if you knew what I would find."

"Well, of course, I knew *that,* although naturally, I could not know precisely where your dear little monkey would run.

I did not know *exactly* what you would find, either, even here, but Miranda says that when the worst possible thing can happen, it does happen. I fear this proves that, as usual, she knows whereof she speaks. Do come away now, dear."

"Surely, ma'am, you and Mrs. Linford do not condone what they are doing in there. I must tell you, I do not believe that man can be Lord Witherspoon."

"No, of course he is not," Miss Abigail said with an air of surprise. "My goodness me, Lord Witherspoon has a perfectly good house of his own in Berkeley Square. Why would he need to come here to go to bed with his own wife?"

"But if you knew what I would find, and if you know that those two are not man and wife . . ."

When Letty paused expectantly, Miss Abigail said with a sigh, "I know what this must look like to you, my dear, but truly—"

"It looks like a brothel," Letty said, glancing again at the bed, which continued to twitch spasmodically.

"Oh, dear, no, *not* a brothel," exclaimed Miss Abigail. "Not at all! We prefer to think of it in the French fashion, as *une maison de tolérance*. You will understand the difference, I expect. After living in France for so many years, you must speak at least a little of their language. Oh, what are you doing now?" These last words came with a shriek of dismay, for Letty had walked right into the bedchamber.

Over her shoulder, she said, "Pray, calm yourself, Miss Abigail. I am merely going to get Jeremiah down before that cat gets close enough to attack him or he attacks the cat." As she spoke, she reached for the marmalade cat, grasped it firmly, and detached it from the curtains, ignoring the low growl it emitted in protest of her intrusion into its affairs. "I do speak French," she added as she set the cat on the floor and turned to coax Jeremiah from his perch. "You mean that this is merely a house of assignation, do you not, a place of rendezvous for lovers?"

"Yes, exactly, so you see, it is nothing in the least bit objectionable to anyone of sense," Miss Abigail said placidly. "Will he bite you?"

"No, ma'am, but perhaps you might just encourage the cat to leave the room. I expect these people would like us to go away, and Jeremiah is unlikely to descend if the cat remains."

"Oh, to be sure. Come along, Clemmy."

Letty glanced at her again. "Clemmy? I thought it was called Puss."

"No, only Liza calls him Puss. His name is St. Clement's," Miss Abigail explained as she picked up the cat and stroked him. "Perhaps you do not know our English nursery rhymes, but because he is orange and yellow—"

"Oh, of course. 'Oranges and lemons, sang the bells of St. Clement's.' I must say, though, he does not behave much like a saint."

"No, and the name became too much for us to say every time, so he soon became just Clemmy. I'll shut him up in my bedchamber for now, dear, and then I shall wait for you on the landing."

"Thank you. I'll be along directly."

Although finding it difficult to ignore the couple in the bed, Letty forced herself to act as if she were alone with the monkey. She coaxed patiently, and was rewarded when he dropped to her shoulder and rubbed his face against her neck.

"Poor Jeremiah," she crooned, stroking him and holding her muff open until he slid down her arm and curled up inside. Then, without another word, she left the room, shutting the door securely behind her.

In the hallway, she found Jenifry, her eyes wide with astonishment. "Miss Letty," the maid said, "was there people in that bed? It looked like—"

"There were," Letty said. "I don't know whether to laugh or to shriek like Jeremiah. I begin to think that I have inherited a most unusual household, Jen, and I am not at all certain what I should do about it."

"I expect you should tell his lordship, miss. That's what you ought to do. Why, it's wicked, what they're doing. Unless, of course," she added with a conscientious air, "those two are husband and wife."

"You know they are not," Letty said, "but I am not sending word of this to Papa. I don't want you talking of it to anyone, either, particularly not to Elvira."

"Lor', I wouldn't," Jenifry said indignantly. "You know I'd never—"

"I do know," Letty said, "and I did not mean to offend you. I just want to be certain you understand that I depend upon your discretion. If you write to your friends in Paris, you must not mention this, lest it somehow get back to Papa."

"It's not like you to keep secrets from his lordship, my lady."

"If I've sunk to being my lady, I know you do not approve, but I am not keeping it from him, exactly. I just want to show him I can manage my own affairs."

"This *affaire* is not yours, however, but someone else's."

Letty chuckled. "It is, indeed. Mercy, what a coil! But come along now. Miss Abigail will have shut up the cat and is doubtless impatiently awaiting our arrival. I wonder what Mrs. Linford will say about this."

"Not much just now," Jenifry said, her eyes twinkling. "Don't you remember, miss? Jackson said she's got the vicar with her."

Stifling a childish urge to giggle, Letty led the way down to the first landing, where they did indeed find Miss Abigail awaiting them. She rubbed her hands on her skirt, and although no trace of dampness showed, Letty wondered if the elderly lady's palms were sweating at the thought of telling her sister that Letty had discovered the house's little secret.

"As you see, I've got him, Miss Abigail," Letty said.

Nodding distractedly, Miss Abigail said, "I wonder if I might ask you not to call me Abigail, my dear. To have both you and Miranda calling me Abigail, which I promise even Papa never did, is quite unnerving. I much prefer Abby."

"Yes, of course, ma'am," Letty said. "I shall be delighted to call you so."

Miss Abby led her to a drawing room larger than the one she had seen before, but the old lady had no sooner stepped inside than she stopped in her tracks, exclaiming, "Vicar! My goodness me, I thought you must have gone by now. That is to say . . . W-won't you have another biscuit? Liza," she added in an overloud voice to the girl, who was straightening items on a side table, "don't you see that Mr. Shilston's plate is empty? A hostess does not neglect a guest's needs, my dear."

"Vicar is just leaving," Mrs. Linford said calmly. "He waited only to meet Letitia. Letitia, my dear, may I present Mr. Shilston, our vicar from St. Michael's Chapel. Vicar, this is Lady Letitia Deverill, who now owns this house."

"That was a very odd thing for your cousin to do, I must say, and 'tis fortunate indeed that your father had left you two dear ladies well fixed for life," the vicar said in reedlike tones as he got to his feet and made a ponderous bow. He was a stout man of medium height, and when Letty held out her hand, his proved chilly when he grasped it. His grip was light, however, and his smile delightful. He said, "I am sure you must have found it odd, too, my lady, for if you even were acquainted with Augustus Benthall, I am sure I never knew of it."

"You are kind to concern yourself, sir," she said, gently removing her hand from his grasp.

"It may be no more than kindness to inquire," Mrs. Linford said, "but I cannot imagine why you should know about our cousin's affairs, Vicar. It would be even odder, in my mind, if you did, for Augustus rarely confided in anyone and his opinion of the church don't bear repeating in polite company."

"Yes, yes, my dear Mrs. Linford, but we must give him the benefit of our superior knowledge of religion, must we not? He was kind enough to establish your tenancy here, and thus I am convinced that he is now with our Lord, which is what I have said over and over to you, in hopes of comforting you for his loss."

"My dear Vicar, Augustus has been gone for over nine months now. Any comfort we might have required—and in truth, I don't believe we required any—would be long overdue had you not been so conscientious in the meantime about expressing it every time we have chanced to meet."

"Ah, yes, but two ladies living all alone! One must attempt one's poor best. I know that you, my dear ma'am, are quite capable of looking after yourself, but—"

"Do you think I am not?" Miss Abby demanded.

"That will do, Abigail," Mrs. Linford said, glancing at Letty. "Letitia has come here to take a tour of the house, Vicar, so I daresay you will not object if I ring for Mrs. Hopworthy now, and arrange for her to do so."

"Bless me, I have already stayed longer than I ought," he said, bowing in her general direction but keeping his eyes on Letty. "You would prefer to show her the house yourself, I daresay, and I am keeping you from that pleasant duty. No need to ring for anyone to show me out, either," he added. "If after all these years I do not know my way to your front door, I do not know anything at all."

Despite this assurance, Mrs. Linford pulled the bell, and Jackson appeared with sufficient speed to inform Letty that he had been awaiting the summons. He glanced from her to Miss Abby, then nodded to the vicar and held open the door.

When it had shut again behind them, Mrs. Linford sighed and said, "I daresay there are vicars in this world who are not tedious bores. It would be a pleasant change of affairs if we could get one of them at St. Michael's, but I daresay I should not speak ill of any servant of God. How do you do today, Letitia?"

"Very well, thank you, ma'am," Letty said. "I hope you know you need not trouble to show me over the house yourself. I shall be quite content with Mrs. Hopworthy, I promise you."

"Yes, I daresay. I'll just ring for—"

"Not yet, Miranda," Miss Abby said urgently. "There is something that we must . . . That is to say, a certain unfortunate event has occurred that—" Breaking off again with a gesture that set the ribbons and beads on her hat fluttering, she tried again. "Not unfortunate, no," she said. "At least, that is not the word I should use. The plain fact is that . . . well . . . Oh, dear Miranda, you will be so vexed!"

"I will certainly be vexed if you do not explain yourself, Abigail," Mrs. Linford said austerely. "Liza," she added, "it is time for your walk in the garden, my dear. Bid Lady Letitia good afternoon and then be on your way."

When Liza had gone, albeit with visible reluctance, Mrs. Linford said, "Now, what on earth were you trying to tell me, Abigail?"

"Letitia knows. She didn't peek, exactly, but . . ."

When she paused again, the resulting silence grew heavy. Mrs. Linford looked from her to Letty and back before she said, "You are unnecessarily cryptic, Abigail. Be plain, if you please, so that one need not guess what you mean to say."

When Miss Abby's mouth opened and shut several times, making her look like a distracted fish, Letty took pity on her.

"I am afraid Jeremiah escaped, ma'am," she said. "I did not bring his chain today, because he can detach it from his collar himself, and I thought my muff would suffice to hold him. It did not, however, and I'm afraid he got upstairs and into one of the bedchambers before I could recapture him."

Mrs. Linford's eyes narrowed. "Jeremiah? Oh, yes, your pet monkey. Abigail was in raptures all morning at the expectation of his coming today. You say he escaped. Where is he now, if I may ask?"

"He is curled up, asleep, in my muff now," Letty said, raising it slightly, "but your cat frightened him, you see, and he got away and dashed up the stairs."

"I am happy to say that the cat is not mine. It belongs to Abigail."

"They interrupted Lady Witherspoon, Miranda!" Miss Abby spoke in a rush, with the air of one confessing to a great crime.

Mrs. Linford looked long at her, then said calmly, "I see. Sit down, Letitia. It becomes plain that we must talk."

"Yes, certainly, ma'am," Letty said, taking a nearby chair.

Miss Abby chose a straight-backed chair by the door, and sat poised as if to take flight at any moment.

Letty said, "I don't know what there is to discuss, ma'am. Surely you know that I cannot be associated with such goings-on. Indeed, I daresay you ought not to be associated with them, either. Lady Witherspoon's assignations here must stop."

Matter-of-factly Mrs. Linford said, "Where would you have her go instead?"

"Yes, where?" Miss Abby echoed. "She must go somewhere. Moreover, we have many other friends who have such difficulties as you cannot imagine, finding appropriate places in which to enjoy themselves. We are doing them a great service, my dear. You would not have us abandon them all, I hope."

"All?" Letty felt her composure slipping. Only too easily could she imagine her father's reaction to this discovery. "H-how many people are involved?"

"Only a dozen or so, I believe," Mrs. Linford said.

"Oh, no, Miranda," Miss Abby said. "I am sure we must have at least a score or more by now. You must have forgotten that both of the ladies Bar—"

"That will do, Abigail," Mrs. Linford interjected sharply. "You must not name names, if you please. Suffice it to say, dear Letitia, that a number of people now depend upon us for the service we provide. I do not think there can be so many as twenty, but we will not argue the point."

"Twenty," Letty repeated. Even to her ears, her voice sounded weak.

"At least twenty," Miss Abby said earnestly. "I am quite certain."

"But how can you?"

"Why, I counted them!"

"I don't mean—"

"I understood you, I believe," Mrs. Linford said. "You desire to know how it is that we are able to accommodate them."

"Yes . . . at least . . ." Letty fell silent, unsure that she had made herself clear but not at all certain how to phrase her questions to the two very odd old ladies.

Mrs. Linford went on, "It is quite simple, really. The women call upon us, as they would, in any event. Then the gentlemen arrive more discreetly through our mews and back garden. We are most fortunately placed here, you see. Since numerous houses share a central mews, one can approach this house from Green Street, Park Street, and South Audley Street, as well as from Upper Brook Street."

"I meant . . ." Letty strove to retain her self-control, then began again. "If you will forgive my saying so, ma'am, neither you nor Miss Abby seems the sort to condone such activities, let alone to encourage them. Still, if so many people are finding accommodation here, you certainly must be encouraging them."

"Well, goodness me, of course we encourage them," Miss Abby said, her eyes wide. "We have our image to support, after all."

"But that's what I mean," Letty said, trying to ignore the feeling that she had blinked and somehow ended up consorting with the inmates in Bedlam. "To protect your image, not to mention your reputations, I should think you would do all in your power to avoid associating with people who so casually break their marriage vows."

Mrs. Linford stiffened. "We allow no married woman here who has not produced a proper heir for her husband, and we allow no unmarried women at all."

"I . . . I see." Taking care to avoid Jenifry's gaze, Letty drew a deep breath and said, "Perhaps you might just explain the whole thing quite slowly to me, Mrs. Linford. Clearly, I do not understand all of what you are trying to say."

"It is quite simple, really," Miss Abby said.

"Hush, Abigail. I will explain, if you please."

"Of course, Miranda. I would most likely make a mull of it, in any case."

After a brief pause, during which Letty forced herself to remain silent, Mrs. Linford said, "It is most unfortunate that we should be reduced to such a course, naturally. And certainly we would be exceedingly distressed if our services were to become widely known. At present, the only people who know are persons with an even stronger motivation than we have to maintain silence. We do realize, however, that one day someone might speak too freely, in which event, we hope that our reputations will protect us and that no one will believe it. If by some mischance everyone did believe it, we would be ruined, of course, but when the whole thing began, we never expected it to come to this."

"At the time, there was nothing else we could do," Miss Abby said.

"How did it begin, then?" Letty asked.

"Oh, it was dreadful," Miss Abby said. "Our dear friend, Lady Fram—"

"Abigail! No names," Mrs. Linford snapped. In a gentler tone, she added, "You really must let me tell the tale, my dear."

"Yes, of course, Miranda. My tongue just keeps rattling, I'm afraid."

"It is true that our situation was frightful, Letitia," Mrs.

Linford said. "We were in sad straits when our brother, Sir Horace Frome, died. Everyone thought we were quite well to pass, however, because Papa had left us so and Horace had made no bones about telling everyone we were rich. After his death, however, we had that image to maintain, and although it was a struggle, we did our best."

"You did, Miranda," Miss Abby said. "You managed things with a truly magical touch. Had you managed everyone's money from the outset, instead of allowing poor dear Horace to do so—though you had no choice, of course—we should all have grown quite as rich as he said we were, I'm sure."

"Thank you, dear, but as you say, I could do nothing about Horace, and my efforts to look after the two of us would have failed had Fate not intervened. We had a dear friend some years ago, Letitia. She married well, but I am afraid that her husband proved unworthy of her. Worse, he was quite brutally abusive. Many was the time she fled to us in tears, bruised and battered from his beatings."

"Oh, yes," Miss Abby murmured. "He was a horrid man."

"My Mr. Linford was no saint," Mrs. Linford said. "I would be the last to say that he was, but he was kind to me. Moreover, he proved quite willing to provide a home for my dear sister after our parents died, which was more than his heir was willing to do when Mr. Linford passed on. Had it not been for Cousin Augustus letting us live here, Abigail and I might have ended in the poorhouse."

"Oh, Miranda, you cannot believe that," Miss Abby exclaimed. "Dearest Sally would never have allowed it. You know she would not."

"Don't be foolish, Abigail. If you can tell me what she could have done when she had been married no more than a week at the time, I should like to hear it."

"Oh." Miss Abby looked daunted. "Why, that is perfectly true. Sally was still in leading strings when Papa passed on, and Horace . . . Horace was her papa, you see, Letitia, and

our brother, of course—Miranda said that, did she not? Poor
Horace never had a feather to fly with except what Papa allowed him. Nor was he at all discriminating in his financial
habits, and to our great misfortune, he controlled our trust for
fifteen years before his death. The only good thing he did for
us was to arrange for Miranda to control our trust afterward,
so no one else ever learned what a fix he left us in when he
died. He was only forty-four then, so most folks thought it a
most untimely demise, but I can tell you, we were utterly—"

"You need say no more on that head, Abigail," Mrs. Linford
said. "Pray, let me get on with explaining the facts to Letitia,
if you please."

"Oh, yes, Miranda. I am exceedingly sorry to keep inter-
rupting."

"I believe I had got to when our friend begged us for assistance."

Letty nodded. "Yes, ma'am, someone with an abusive husband."

"Yes, quite horrid, but as good fortune would have it, she
met someone more suitable and in the end managed to leave
the brute and begin a new life in France."

"I am happy for her, ma'am, but pray, what has this to do
with the scene I interrupted upstairs just now?"

"Everything," Miss Abby said fervently. "Just everything!"

Quelling her this time with a stern look, Mrs. Linford said,
"We felt sorry for her, you see, and as you must realize, her
deliverance did not occur overnight."

"No, it took years," Miss Abby said. Encountering another
look, she ducked her head, pressed her lips together, and folded
her hands in her lap.

"She confided in us," Mrs. Linford said reminiscently. "We
could do nothing to help her against her husband, of course.
He had every power over her by law. But when she came to
us and said she wished she had some peaceful, innocent-look-
ing place where she could meet her friend for just a few min-

utes of happiness once a week or so, Abigail and I instantly invited her to do so under our roof."

"Cousin Augustus's roof by then," Miss Abby added irrepressibly.

"Just so," said her sister. Then she hesitated, shooting Letty a speculative look before she added with a sigh, "The next bit is difficult to explain, because it is not sufficient simply to say that it happened. We saw it coming. We should have had to be fools not to see it."

"They fell in love," Letty said.

"Yes, but they wanted more than mere love, you see. Their behavior had been quite circumspect. We frequently left them alone, but never above this floor, and they always left the door to the room ajar. Then, one day, they confided to us that they desired more privacy. I daresay we might have refused, and perhaps you will say that we should have, but our friend was the one person who knew our true circumstances, and that gave her an unfair advantage. She offered us money."

"Quite a lot of money," Miss Abby said. "A quite staggering amount."

Letty said dryly, "Not her husband's money, one trusts."

"No, no, her friend was . . . is . . . quite wealthy. At first, he said only that he wanted to help pay our servants, and perhaps for the food he and she ate here, but then he began giving us a quite generous sum whenever they came here. He said it was worth every penny, because the most difficult thing about such liaisons is finding a place where a couple can be truly private."

Miss Abby nodded. "And *that* is when Miranda had her quite blindingly brilliant idea. You see, my dear, many members of the beau monde, having married for reasons of property or other convenience, look for true love outside marriage. Their primary problem is to find an appropriate meeting place, and we had all those extra rooms upstairs, just going to waste."

"Yes," Letty said, recalling the exchange she had overheard

at court, and wondering if they had been talking about Catherine. "I do see. I shall have to give this some thought, ma'am. I don't suppose you could simply tell Raventhorpe about your financial problems. He is quite wealthy, I believe——"

"Oh, yes," Miss Abby said. "Justin is quite the wealthiest man in London, but we couldn't tell *him*. Why, that would cut up all our peace. We couldn't entertain the notion for a second, could we, Miranda?"

"It is not to be thought of, my dear," Mrs. Linford agreed. "You see, Letitia, we have become quite accustomed to looking after ourselves, and Justin cannot be trusted simply to give us what we require without also forcing us to accept his advice and counsel. I don't know if you quite understand what I am saying——"

"Oh yes, ma'am," Letty said sincerely. "That I do understand. I had not known him for two minutes before he began giving me the benefit of his counsel. He is, if you will forgive my saying so, quite the most arrogant man I know." And the most stimulating, murmured a little voice in the back of her mind.

Mrs. Linford said with a sympathetic smile, "I don't know if I would go so far as to say *arrogant,* but I do know that his . . . um . . . protective attitude would soon give others to wonder what sort of hold he had over us. We have managed to maintain an image of wealth and independence for more than twenty years——"

"Mercy," Letty breathed. "I have heard all you've told me, ma'am, but I had not realized it had been such a great length of time. Is it truly so many years?"

"Oh, yes indeed," Miss Abby said brightly. "Nearly twenty-two, in fact, because Justin just turned twenty-five, don't you know, so we have lived in this house nearly twenty-six years."

"So you can see, Letitia, why we would be loath to beg help from anyone. Moreover, as you must know if you have read Cousin Augustus's will, if anyone else pays our rent, we should have to forfeit our tenancy here."

"My dear ma'am," Letty said, truly distressed, "I hope you know that I would never allow anyone to throw you into the street."

"You are kind, my dear, but that is not the point. We do not wish to hang on your sleeve or anyone else's. We are quite discreet, I promise you."

"Still, ma'am, it is most improper."

"Dear me, no," Miss Abby said. "The people we help come from the highest ranks of the nobility. Really, they do."

"Yes," Mrs. Linford said. "Moreover, some of our gentlemen occupy the highest places in government circles and the military, so you need not worry that anyone will speak out of turn. They dare not."

"Only think what a scandal they face if discovered," Miss Abby exclaimed.

Letty said, "But that's just it. Think of the scandal!"

"They *need* our services," Miss Abby insisted.

Calmly Mrs. Linford said, "No one has yet spoken out, after all. Until now we have gone on quite comfortably." She sighed. "It is such a pity that you had to discover our little secret."

"Yes, ma'am, I begin to agree," Letty agreed, wondering what on earth she was going to do.

She continued to ponder the question after she had had her tour and returned to Jervaulx House. At first, she thought of her dilemma merely as an absorbing puzzle requiring a delicate touch. That, however, was before Tuesday morning, when she received a letter that lent urgency to finding a satisfactory resolution.

When Jenifry entered the breakfast room a few minutes after Letty had put down the letter, she found her mistress in an uncharacteristically pensive mood.

"Is something wrong, Miss Letty?"

Letty smiled ruefully. "Under ordinary circumstances you

would find me in transports, but you will understand why I have mixed emotions when I tell you that Papa and Mama have put forward their arrival date to the first week of May."

"So soon?"

"Yes," Letty said. "Papa writes that Wellington and Sir Robert Peel believe that the Whig position on Jamaica will soon lead to their downfall. Therefore, he has decided that he and Mama will depart as soon as possible after the farewell celebration the ambassador insists upon holding for them. That gives me little more than a fortnight, Jen, to decide what to do about my house of ill repute."

SEVEN

Newmarket Heath

The fair-haired young gentleman standing near the enclosure, waiting for the Queen's Plate to begin, said enthusiastically to his companion, "I tell you, Jerry, I never crossed a better tit in my life. If her eyes stand, as I daresay they will, she'll turn out as tight a little thing as any in England."

"If you think that, Ned, you're tight yourself," his friend retorted. "That mare of yours is too long in the fore."

"She's not, I tell you. She's as fleet as the wind. Why, I raced with Dicky and Will all the way from Cambridge to Newmarket. Dicky rode his roan, and Will his chestnut mare—and you know both have speed—but I beat them all hollow."

With true sportsman's taste, the one called Ned wore the single-breasted dark green riding coat known as a Newmarket, over buff smallclothes, with cordovan boots and a top hat with a narrow, turned-up brim. His friend wore similar attire, giving both the look of fashionable sporting men. Neither, however, had yet found cause to suppress youthful enthusiasm in favor of the more fashionable air of ennui.

The one called Jerry grinned. "If you expect a victory over Dicky and Will to convince me that you're a knowing one where racers are concerned, you're out, Ned. I've no intention of wagering my blunt on another nag of your choosing."

"That's unfair, Jerry! I own I had bad luck yesterday, but that

was through taking someone else's advice. Those chaps we met
were jolly bucks, too. You thought so yourself. You didn't object
to making their acquaintance, but I don't deny they let us in
damnably. I lost thirty guineas myself, after all. I made up half
of it on Jersey's Glenmara, though, and I mean to double that
sum this afternoon."

"Not with that silly nag you've chosen, you won't."

Their exchange carried easily above the chatter of nearby
onlookers to Viscount Raventhorpe, who had been watching the
pair for some time. He was aware that neither had noticed him
even when he strolled near enough to overhear their conversation. "Which silly nag did you choose, Ned?" he asked.

It did not surprise him to see his brother jump nearly out of
his skin at the sound of his voice.

Ned's face was pale when he whirled to face him. "Justin!
Good God! I did not know you were here. That is, n-no one
t-told me you were coming." He tugged at his light-green cravat,
artfully tied with a full, soft bow. "I-I thought your duties at
court must keep you away. What I mean to say is—"

"I know what you mean to say, Ned. Do stop tugging at your
neckcloth. It's already a sad-looking thing. You'd have done better to choose black or white. Do I know your friend, by the
way? I cannot recall that we have met."

"Oh, this is Jerry Bucknell. I'm sure you have heard me
speak of him. He is from Devonshire, don't you know, and
studies at the Inner Temple with me."

"Have the pair of you been called to the bar before your
time? You certainly must be flush enough if you can afford to
have lost thirty guineas yesterday."

"Well, I know you mean that for another setdown," Ned said
with a look of irritation, "but I am flush, as it happens, because
I've still got most of my quarterage. It's only a bit over a fortnight since Ladyday, after all."

"Yes, but perhaps you have forgotten that your quarter's allowance is supposed to last you three months, not merely three
weeks."

Reddening, Ned shot a sidelong look at his friend, then an angry one at his brother. "How you do take a fellow up, Justin! If you heard that about my thirty guineas, you must also know that I've already won fifteen back. Moreover, if Mr. Craven's entry in the Queen's Plate don't win, I'll be very much surprised."

"Mr. Craven's entry?"

"A mare called I-Wish-You-May-Get-It. What name could be more likely to win for me?"

"I think I'd have more faith in a certainty than a wish. Don't you think Jersey's Caesar in the Handicap Sweepstakes would be a better bet?"

"Pooh, everyone will put money on Caesar. That horse has taken every race it's entered this year, so the odds will be nothing. Indeed, Jersey's horses have won nearly every race they've entered, so even though I managed to win a few guineas this morning on Glenmara, I don't mean to risk more on his nags. He hasn't entered for the Queen's Plate, though. Someone else *has* to win."

"That's a point, certainly," Justin said. "I have only one other question for you, and perhaps for Mr. Bucknell, as well, since you mentioned that he is also a student at the Inner Temple. Were you not keeping commons this week?"

Ned avoided his gaze, saying glibly, "That's nothing to rag a chap about. I've kept seven of the twelve terms already. I can afford to miss a dinner or two."

"You cannot afford to displease your bench master, however," Justin pointed out. "Not when he is the one who will decide in the end whether to call you to the bar or reject you. There can be no appealing his decision, you know."

"I do know," Ned said. "I think it's dashed unfair, too, that he should have the power to act at his pleasure. They say we law students *eat* our way to the bar, and that's true, I suppose, since dining with the barristers and other members is how we learn all they can teach us. There can be no harm in that, though, because clients can take the liberty later of judging how far we have otherwise qualified ourselves. Still, every man who dines with a society should be called to the bar. Otherwise, rejection should be founded solely on his ignorance of the law and be subject to appeal to a higher jurisdiction. As it is, benchers can and do exercise their power on private or political motives, rather than on any basis of law."

"Another good point," Justin said, "but you would be better off making it where it might influence someone with power to change the rules. Since your intent was to divert me from what I have to say to you, however, you shot wide of the mark. You're behaving recklessly, Ned. When you find yourself at low tide later in the term, I hope you will remember—"

"Justin! Thunderation, you here, my boy? I am excessively glad to see you!"

Recognizing his father's voice, Justin turned with a sinking feeling and said, "Good afternoon, sir. Behold me as amazed to see you as you are to see me. I distinctly recall your telling me you intended to forgo the spring meeting."

Sellafield dismissed the comment with an airy gesture. "I may have said something of the sort, I suppose. A man never knows when he will take it into his head to do a thing, after all, which brings me back to the point, my boy. I find myself with my pockets to let for the moment, but for half the share, I'll put you on to an excellent thing. You've only to look at Craven's mare to know . . ."

Detecting familiar signs of his parent's overfondness for drink, Justin gritted his teeth and thought how fortunate it was that his mother, at least, did not constantly apply to him for money. Affecting a politeness he did not feel, he let Sellafield finish before he said quietly, "Sorry, sir. I'm afraid I don't share your faith, or Ned's, in that mare's ability."

"How can you say that? I tell you, that little girl's near as swift as Eclipse was in his day. You've only to look at her. She's got the finest . . ."

Noting that Ned had already taken advantage of the interruption to slip away, Justin hoped the lad would not soon have occasion to beg him for funds. He would be sorry to refuse, but he could not in good conscience encourage him to take the road their father had taken. Again he waited until Sellafield finished speaking before repeating his unwillingness to bet on I-Wish-You-May-Get-It.

"Damme, lad, but you don't know a good thing when you see it," the earl snapped. "It don't matter, though, because even if it should chance that you are right—which it won't—I've got a bet on with Conroy that cannot miss."

"A bet with Conroy? Has he got a horse running?"

"He does, and a loose screw it is, too, wholly untrustworthy."

"Is that why you bet against it? I am surprised he would take your bet if he does not think the nag a good one," Justin added, recalling that for some time Conroy had been pressing him to help in his quest to regain royal favor. He wondered if the man hoped to sweeten him up by allowing Sellafield to win.

Sellafield chuckled. "He didn't even want to bet with me, but I made it impossible for him to refuse. I bet two thousand the tit would neither win nor come in last, that it would place where no one would notice it. He took offense—as who wouldn't? Indeed, I had counted on that very thing to make him put up his money."

"I don't think that was wise, sir. Conroy is no man to challenge."

"Ah, bah; there's no talking to you," the earl snapped, turning on his heel.

Justin sighed but made no attempt to call him back.

Another familiar voice said mockingly, "Having a hard time keeping your team in harness, old man?"

"That's hardly an appropriate or proper metaphor, Puck," Justin said, turning with a slight smile to greet his friend. "If you mean to encourage me to wager a huge sum on I-Wish-You-May-Get-It, you, too, can save your breath."

"I'll be jiggered. Is that what they wanted? What fools. That mare's a zero. General Grosvenor's Daedalus will take the Queen's Plate. Uh-oh," he added in a lower tone, "don't look now, but here come Devon-Poole, Conroy, and that aide of his, Morden. Talk about zeroes! I'll just take myself off again, and you can find me at the Jockey Club later, if you want me, or at the Rutland Arms." He nodded to the approaching trio, then departed without another word.

"Good to see you here, Raventhorpe," Sir Adrian Devon-Poole said heartily, extending a hand in greeting. He was a tall, slender man with an air of distinction reinforced by a full head of silvery grey hair. Without waiting for a response, he added, "Dare I hope that you require companionship this evening, my boy? I've come to Newmarket without my family, and I should be delighted to share a meal."

"That's kind of you, sir, but I have arranged to meet friends," Justin said, briefly shaking the outstretched hand. "Good afternoon, Conroy," he added, nodding at the aide, Morden, without formally addressing him.

"Afternoon," Sir John said, looking intently at Justin. "I trust you've found time to talk with Melbourne since last we met."

Devon-Poole interjected in his hearty way, "John, John, this is no place to conduct business. The weather is mild at last, the heath is well attended, and the lad has come to enjoy the races. Leave your politics in London, man!"

"But—" Conroy began, only to have his chief companion divert him again.

"I've told you, I'll talk to him," Sir Adrian said more brusquely. "Here now, they're up and running. Pay heed. I've got my blunt on I-Wish-You-May-Get-It. I own I could not resist the name."

Unfortunately for Sir Adrian, and for Ned, after several false starts due to the awkwardness of an entry called Sister-to-Plenipo, the list got away in good order with one exception. I-Wish-You-May-Get-It lost ground from the first. Despite the shouted urging of onlookers, including Sir Adrian (and Ned, too, Justin was sure) and its own best efforts, the mare chased Sister-to-Plenipo and the others for only half a mile before giving up altogether. Daedalus, having taken the lead at the outset, kept it to the end, winning cleverly by half a length.

Justin excused himself to the other two men, earning a look of displeasure from Conroy, which he ignored. He did not like him at the best of times. Since Conroy had begun pressing him to take his side at court, Justin liked him even less.

The rest of the afternoon afforded only two races, a proposed handicap not having filed. Neither race interested him, although he noted with resignation that Conroy's horse finished dead last in the second.

He began to wonder why he had honored the Spring Meeting with his presence. His mood improved slightly, however, as he strolled back to the center of town. He met a number of friends, for his route took him along the southern side of the High Street, past the post office, to the dignified entrance of the Jockey Club.

Originally a coffee room, the building was now much grander, having undergone several bouts of improvements and alterations in the years since 1752, when club members had acquired their first lease. A screen with an ornamental gateway enclosed the betting court, and when Justin passed into it, the old clock at the back of the yard showed the time at nearly half past five.

Handing his cloak, hat, and gloves to the porter at the members' entrance, he asked if Sir Halifax Quigley was still on the premises.

"Yes, my lord. He is still at table with Admiral Rame, sir."

Justin's mood improved even more, and he made his way to the dining room with more lightness in his step. The admiral was a man he—like all members of the Jockey Club (and all Newmarket, for that matter)—much admired. Practically every man in England over the age of five knew the admiral's history well.

A younger son of the Earl of Thruxton, the Honorable Robert Rame had attended Harrow School without remarkable achievement. Then, as was the custom of many younger sons, he had taken up a career in the navy. After seeing action in numerous locations around the world, once nearly losing his life while in charge of a prize vessel that sank, he enjoyed a six-year sojourn ashore, discovering a deep love of sporting activities before the call of the sea (and the British navy) demanded his return.

It was then that he had achieved his greatest naval triumph. Commanding a frigate of thirty-six guns called the *Vandal,* through difficulties of which the landbound public had small conception, Rame had brought her back from Newfoundland without a rudder and leaking badly, the menace of a watery grave constantly threatening him and his crew. His judgment and ingenuity had forcibly struck all patriotic Englishmen when, upon the *Vandal's* successful return, they read in their morning papers detailed descriptions of its terrifying adventures. When he retired soon after his return, members of the Jockey Club unanimously chose him to be one of their stewards, the sole arbiters of equine matters at Newmarket.

Seeing Puck and the admiral at a table set beneath a painting of the *Vandal* that the admiral had recently presented to the Jockey Club, Justin made his way toward them. As he drew near he heard the admiral say in the clear tones that came from years of shouting orders on the deck of a windblown frigate, "Handicapping is quite an art, my lad. A public handicapper should be a man of independent circumstances in every sense of the word, and beyond suspicion of accepting illicit compensation for favors received. Ah, good evening, Raventhorpe," he added, catching sight of Justin. "The lad here said we might expect to see you."

"Good evening, sir. Don't get up, I beg you. Hallo, Puck. Did you order enough food for me?"

"Don't I always? Look here, sit down and tell us what you think about this. I told the admiral I thought the most interesting one of his duties must be the setting of handicaps for each horse in a race. He says it's a dashed great responsibility."

Sitting, Justin smiled at the older man. "A difficult and thankless task is what I should call it, sir. I don't envy you finding yourself saddled with it. Not only must you try to satisfy the owners but you have to put up with censure from every capricious scribbler who chooses to display his opinions in the newspapers."

"I was about to point that out," Rame said. He reached for the wine carafe strategically placed in the center of the table, and refilled his glass. His countenance was ruddy and weathered, but his features were even and well formed. Above middle height, he had kept himself fit and trim over his fifty-some years, and was a favorite with the ladies. Even other men thought him damnably handsome.

"A fresh plate," Justin said to the servant who materialized at his side, "and decant a new bottle for us, if you please. This carafe is down to its dregs."

"At once, my lord."

"A good handicapper must attach himself to no stable," the admiral went on. "He should be a spectator of every important race in the United Kingdom, but he should never place a bet. And," he added with a twinkling look at Puck, "he should treat all the remarks made about his handicaps with the utmost indifference."

Justin chuckled at Puck's grimace. His plate arrived within minutes, the food as always was excellent, and the admiral's presence at their table drew others, who stopped briefly to chat before leaving them to return to their conversation. When the admiral drew a watch from his waistcoat pocket and opened it, Justin was surprised to realize they had been talking for nearly two hours. He would not have thought it had been half that time.

"Still early yet," Puck said. "Hope you ain't meaning to retire, Admiral. I wanted to ask you what you think about—"

"Damme, Justin, I've near turned the town upside down looking for you!"

Repressing a wince, Justin turned to greet his seemingly ubiquitous sire. "You have found me, sir. You might say good evening to Admiral Rame."

"Aye, of course, of course. Good to see you, Rame. In fact, you're just the man I need, damned if you're not. Conroy's trying to cheat me, damn his eyes!"

"I presume you mean Sir John Conroy," the admiral said.

"I do, and it's a measure of his wickedness that you deduced that so quickly."

"Not really," the admiral replied. "He is the only Conroy who presently holds a membership in the Jockey Club. That you wish to consult me must derive from my position as a steward—"

"Just so, just so," Sellafield interrupted impatiently.

"Cut line, sir," Justin recommended. "Clearly your displeasure springs from your wager with Sir John. I saw that race."

"Then you know that I ought to have won!"

"I know nothing of the sort," Justin said. "You told me you bet his horse would come in neither first nor last. I saw myself that it finished dead last."

"Aye, it did, damn his eyes; however, just before the race began, I saw him talking to his rider. He ordered him to hold the horse in, that's what he did. Had the gall to admit it to me afterward when I challenged him. If that ain't cheating, I don't know what is, so I want to lay my case before the stewards."

The admiral said calmly, "I don't think that will be necessary, my lord."

Sellafield smiled triumphantly. "As plain as a pikestaff, ain't it? Well, I don't mind telling you that having you decide the case will suit me down to the ground, Rame. Conroy will have to heed any decision you make, for I doubt there exists another man in England more admired than you are for his steady brain, his integrity, and his judgment."

"You flatter me, my lord, but I am very glad to know that you hold my opinion in such high esteem. If I understand you correctly, you made a wager with Conroy that his entry in the afternoon stakes would place neither first nor last. Is that substantially correct?"

"It is."

"The horse subsequently placed last. Is that likewise correct?"

"Yes, but—"

"I understand that Conroy admits to giving his rider certain orders to that effect. However, deplorable as I personally consider his action to be, I cannot see that it affects your wager with him."

"What? What the devil do you think you are saying? You agree that he cheated, but you say he did nothing wrong?"

"Deplorable is what I called it," the admiral corrected gently. "The plain fact, however, is that you must pay Conroy. You laid your bet not upon the place the horse would obtain if its rider remained uninformed of the bet but upon your opinion that the horse lacked speed enough to place first or tractability enough to be brought in last."

"The devil you say! That's rubbish, that is. I won't pay the scoundrel."

"I am sorry to hear that," the admiral said. "You had better hope, in that case, that Conroy does not put the matter before the stewards. If he does, I shall be obliged to reveal the details of this conversation to them all. I advise you to pay up."

Sellafield glared at him but said no more, a fact for which Justin was grateful. It was at times like this that his father showed to worst advantage and made him wish he could reverse their roles as father and son just long enough to bring the earl to his senses. After a brief but pregnant pause, Sellafield said, "I'll think on it," and walked away.

Rame looked ruefully at Justin. "I wish I could have served him better."

"You can hardly throw your ethics out the window to please my father, sir."

Puck said, in his irrepressible way, "It was worth something to see the look on his face when you said your piece, though,

Admiral, after he'd talked of your steady brain, integrity, and all."

The admiral shut his eyes in what was nearly a wince, and Justin said, "Sneck up, Puck. Let's change the subject."

Puck looked from one to the other. Then, with a shrug, he said, "Well, I did want to ask the admiral what he thinks about making Newmarket rules apply to other courses. I've heard talk of doing some such thing, you know, but I'm dashed if I can see how it would work."

This promising topic engaged the three amiably for twenty minutes before another of the admiral's many friends came to remind him that he had promised to play cards at eight. The admiral excused himself, and when he had gone, Puck poured himself and Justin another glass of wine, saying, "Fine chap, the admiral. Glad to see him here."

Justin smiled. "Where else would you see him? He practically lives at Newmarket."

"No, he don't. Got a house in London, don't he?"

"In Richmond, actually," amended Justin. The admiral was a friend of his family, and he had known him since childhood. "You know what I meant, Puck."

"Aye, I do, but if you saw him here before tonight, it's more than I did."

"He is not answerable to you, after all."

Puck raised his eyebrows. "Was that a setdown? By God, I think . . . Now, what the devil is *he* looking at?"

Justin resisted the impulse to turn. "Who?"

"Devon-Poole, that's who. Staring right at us, steely-eyed. Have you offended him somehow?"

"I don't know. He did ask me to dine with him. I told him I was engaged."

"That won't do, you know, if you still have your eye on his daughter. Not," he added when Justin frowned, "that it will make a ha'pworth's difference in the end, of course. Not with all your filthy lucre. Or have you changed your mind?"

Justin grimaced, but his scowl did little to deter his friend.

"No use looking at me like that. *Have* you changed your mind?"

Sighing, Justin said, "She is no doubt still perfectly suited to my purpose, but I had failed to consider that I should also have to put up with Sir Adrian."

"And her mother," Puck reminded him. "Have you seen the woman?"

"Of course I have. Very haughty, but I do not see how that concerns me."

"Lord, what a novice you are at some things," Puck said, shaking his head. "You just listen now, because I see things, my buck. Have you never noticed how very much like their mothers girls become?"

"Do they?"

"Look at my sister. Used to be a sprightly little thing, all smiles and teasing. Got married, and overnight turned into my mama. Not a bad thing, because Mama has style and common sense, and Priss seems somehow to have acquired both, but imagine Lady Devon-Poole's attitudes and affectations draped around your Susan."

"A daunting vision, I'll agree, but I don't agree it's inevitable. I suggest that we pursue this topic no further," he added, giving his friend a direct look.

With a wry twist of his lips, Puck raised his wineglass. "As you wish. In any event, it brings to mind something else that I wanted to ask you. Is there any truth to the rumors I'm hearing about your interest in a certain little Tory?"

Caught off his guard, Justin nonetheless managed to reply evenly, "Certainly not. Where on earth have you heard such stuff?"

"Oh, here and about," Puck said airily. "So you don't like her, then."

"On the contrary," Justin said. "I am sure she is just the sort of young woman most men want to marry; however, her independent ways would not suit me."

"Perhaps you could tame her," Puck suggested with his mischievous grin.

"I doubt that she would respond to the strongest hand on her bridle," Justin said curtly, adding, "I have to return to London tomorrow night, Puck. Douro's wedding is Thursday morning, and I must also attend a state dinner party Thursday night. Have you picked your favorite yet for the Thousand-Guinea Stakes?"

The gambit succeeded in diverting his friend at last, and for the next half hour they discussed the topic most frequently discussed in the Jockey Club. After that, the two men retired to their favorite gaming hell to play hazard.

If Justin found his thoughts drifting less frequently to the tall, stately, and divinely beautiful Miss Devon-Poole than they did to a young woman whose description included none of those qualities, he also found that he was able to thrust away the latter thoughts when they did appear. That they returned was a nuisance, but he believed his mind would prove strong enough to ignore them.

Returning to London Wednesday evening, he dined at Brooks's but soon found himself wondering if he would meet Lady Letitia at the Marquess of Douro's wedding the next day. As usual, he thrust the thought aside, chiding himself for foolishness. Much of Britain's nobility would be present, he knew, both at the ceremony and at the sumptuous *déjeuner* to follow later at the bride's father's home in Belgrave Square. Still, Lady Letitia's parents were out of the country, and the likelihood of an unmarried young woman attending such an august occasion on her own was remote.

So thoroughly did he convince himself that she would not attend, that the next day when he entered St. George's Church, Hanover Square, and hers was the first figure his gaze fell upon, he recognized her with near shock. She walked ahead of him, making her way up the central aisle, and although he could not see her face, he was as certain as he could be of her identity.

Her companion was the dragon he had seen with her on Solicitor Clifford's doorstep.

His mother, whom in his father's absence he had agreed to escort, murmured quietly, "Is something wrong, Justin?"

"Nothing, ma'am. Here is our place, I believe."

"What a crush this is," Lady Sellafield said as they took their seats.

He agreed. Outside, the crowd in Great George Street was so dense that their coachman had found it difficult to make progress, and a strong body of police stood at the church portico to maintain order. Inside, the galleries and aisles filled with spectators desirous to witness the ceremony; and Justin soon realized that nearly anyone who wished to do so, and who looked prosperous enough to persuade the protectors outside to let him or her pass, had been allowed to enter. Perhaps, he thought, that was how the chit had gained entry.

He changed his mind when he found her at the Marquess of Tweeddale's home in Belgrave Square, although it was some time after he arrived before he did so. The house was huge and full of people, so many that it was hard to decide where one ought to go. He and Lady Sellafield made their way at last up the stairs and into a front drawing room, where the wedding cake held pride of place. Surrounded by sugarwork baskets filled with orange flowers tied tastefully with white satin bows, it was the biggest cake Justin had ever seen. Even so, it held his attention for the shortest of moments. Just the other side of the table, he saw Lady Letitia.

Surprised though he was to see her, he noted at once that something was wrong. She stood face-to-face with a young woman he recognized as the erstwhile Catherine Lennox, now wife to Lord Witherspoon, a Whig politician actively involved in the current Jamaican question.

The sight stirred his curiosity, because the tension between Letitia and Catherine was nearly tactile. Doubtless the chit stood ready to cast herself into the suds, and he ought to intervene. However, remembering Puck's warning that others suspected he had some sort of an interest in her, he steeled himself to turn away. Lady Letitia apparently delighted in rejecting good advice. Perhaps she would learn something this time from the consequences of her actions.

EIGHT

Absorbed in her conversation, Letty did not see Raven-thorpe. She had enjoyed the wedding very much. When the bride arrived at the church, accompanied by her bridesmaids, the folks outside had cheered loudly, and when she entered, everyone had turned to catch a glimpse of her. She was as beautiful as a bride ought to be, and Douro, despite a beaky nose just like his famous father's, had looked unusually hand-some as he waited for her at the head of the aisle.

Letty had seen Wellington at the front, as well, and thought he seemed to be in excellent spirits. She knew she had him to thank for her invitation, but she had not expected to enjoy more than the ceremony itself. It had been a special pleasure to receive an invitation to the Tweeddale *déjeuner*.

The marriage ceremony was solemn and dignified. Indeed, such a stillness prevailed that even the bride's most timid, "I will," had carried clearly to all but the deafest ears. But at the end, cheers erupted again when the newlyweds left the church, and when Wellington followed, even louder cheers had greeted his exit.

Afterward, it took Letty and Miss Dibble more time than expected to get to Belgrave Square. Indeed, it had taken so much time that Letty had begun to worry that she might have to leave the moment she arrived, to reach Buckingham Palace in time for the state dinner party the queen was giving that evening.

She was sorry that Victoria had thought it inappropriate to attend the wedding. The young queen frequently displayed her love for gaiety, and would have enjoyed the occasion, Letty knew; but she knew, too, that Victoria had to consider factors other than her own pleasure. The crowds in the streets, as large as they had been to see Wellington's son and the bride, would have doubled at the chance of seeing Her Majesty. The occasion then would have become a royal one, and on a wedding day, the bride and groom deserved to take center stage. In their honor, however, she had canceled her usual Thursday drawing room.

At Tweeddale House, Letty enjoyed a few seconds of conversation with the duke, agreeing with him that it was a pity her parents had been unable to leave Paris in time to attend the wedding. Then others claimed his attention, and she moved on.

Flowers decked every table and niche, and the air was fragrant with their scent. As she exchanged polite remarks with first one person, then another, she lost sight of Miss Dibble, but upstairs, when she saw the splendid wedding cake, she knew she had only to wait nearby and the good lady would eventually appear.

"They say it weighs a hundred pounds," Catherine Witherspoon said as she emerged from the general crush to join Letty in staring at the huge confection.

Letty had not set eyes on Catherine since barging in on her and her lover at the Upper Brook Street house. She felt the other young woman's tension, and knew her own must be as great. For once in her life, she could think of nothing to say.

"Did you know," Catherine said evenly, "that under those favors round the edge of the cake, roses, shamrocks, and thistles lie alternately with the armorial bearings of the Duke of Wellington and the Marquess of Tweeddale?"

"I don't think you want to discuss the cake," Letty said.

"On the contrary, Lady Letitia, I would *much* rather discuss the cake. However, I own that I must first ask if you . . . That is, some days have passed since . . ." Her voice trailed to silence again, and an unbecoming flush tinged her face and throat. She licked her lips.

"I have told no one what I saw," Letty said. "I am sure that is what you want to know, is it not?" When Catherine nodded, she added, "I have never acquired the habit of gossip, Lady Witherspoon. In any event, few people in the circles that concern you encourage me to converse with them."

"We have behaved horridly to you, I know. You have no reason to care what becomes of me, certainly, but I thank you for your discretion."

"You need not," Letty said, beginning to feel as if an unseen force were drawing her inexorably into the other woman's transgression. "My reputation is as much at stake here as yours is, as you must guess. The house is mine, after all."

"Is it? I didn't know."

"Now that you do, I hope you will meet your . . . your friend elsewhere." She would have preferred more bluntness, even to put a snap in her voice, but she kept it low, hoping it would reach only Catherine's ears. With people milling around them like they were, it was entirely possible that someone else might overhear.

Catherine bit her lower lip, avoiding Letty's gaze briefly before she looked right at her again and said, "I wish I could promise we'd stay away, but I cannot. My . . . my friend, as you choose to call him—did you not see him?"

Letty shook her head. She still did not have the faintest idea who the man in bed with Catherine had been. Neither Miranda Linford nor Miss Abby had been willing to enlighten her on that head. Indeed, Miss Abby had said they did not know his name or even what he looked like, because he usually wore a greatcoat, a hat, and a muffler that concealed everything but his eyes.

"Which," Miss Abby had added in her fanciful way, "generally look as dead as Cousin Augustus's eyes did on that last occasion, only he don't wear spectacles, of course, and his eyes are usually open, which Cousin Augustus's were not."

That Lady Witherspoon had vouched for her lover and he had paid their fee had evidently served as sufficient recommendation for the two old ladies. And clearly Catherine Witherspoon did not intend to reveal his name.

"I'm glad you did not see him," she said. "He was furious as it was. If he thought you knew his . . ." Falling silent again, she shook her head.

Seeing Miss Dibble making her way toward them, Letty said quickly, "But why can you not promise to meet somewhere else?"

"I have little influence over him," Catherine said with a frown.

"But if you love each other—"

Catherine's eyes widened with fear. "Oh, hush, someone will hear you! If I could tell you the whole, I would, but please don't say we may not— Oh, mercy," she added, clutching her breast. "M-my husband!"

Following her gaze, Letty saw a large, rather stout middle-aged man moving purposefully toward them in Miss Dibble's wake. Both were still some distance away, working against the general flow of persons wanting to look at the great cake.

Catherine caught her elbow. "I simply must speak more with you."

"This is scarcely the place for such a talk," Letty pointed out, but she let the other woman draw her toward the nearest wall, away from the general surge.

"I know it isn't," Catherine agreed, still watching her husband's approach through lowered lashes. "Please know that I have not purposely snubbed you, Letitia. You cannot imagine how much I've wanted to know you. There are so few young women at court. Other than the maids of honor, I am the only one. The other married ladies are much older than I am, and rather disapproving, you know."

"I do know," Letty said with a smile. "They certainly disapprove of me."

"They cannot afford to do otherwise," Catherine said frankly. "Nor did I think I could, particularly after Sir John warned me off."

"Why did he?"

"I'm not sure, exactly," Catherine said, but her instant flush told Letty she was not being truthful. Apparently aware that she had given herself away, Catherine added ruefully, "You must know that he desires to regain the favor he once enjoyed with Her Majesty. He approached me, and I think certain oth— Oh, help, here's Witherspoon. Do you attend Her Majesty this evening?"

"Yes," Letty said, exchanging a look with Miss Dibble, who had paused nearby, evidently unwilling to interrupt their conversation.

"Good," Catherine said, adding in a louder, more cheerful tone, "There you are, my lord. I had begun to think this crowd must have swallowed you up."

Casting a disapproving look at Letty, Witherspoon brushed past Miss Dibble with a muttered apology, and said ponderously, "It is you who vanished, my dear. You would do better to stay at my side, I believe. One never knows whom one might meet in such a mixed crowd. Moreover, you are due at the palace in two hours, and you will want to change your gown."

"May I present Lady Letitia Deverill, sir?"

Witherspoon nodded, saying brusquely, "Jervaulx's daughter, I believe."

"That's right, my lord," Letty said, making her curtsy.

"Come along, Catherine," he said without further comment to Letty. "You don't want to be late."

"We should leave, too, my dear," Miss Dibble said when the other two walked away. "Who are those people?"

"Lord and Lady Witherspoon," Letty said absently. She was not surprised to see Catherine glance back, nor did she have difficulty interpreting the look the other woman sent her. They still had much to discuss. Collecting her wits, she smiled at Miss Dibble. "I do not know them at all well, Elvira, but she is the woman who very nearly conversed with me that first day at court, when no one else would."

"She is kindhearted, then," Miss Dibble said. "Perhaps she will become a friend. The good Lord knows you could use one in that place."

"It is not so bad. Indeed, I find the queen's court interesting, and at least there have been no more horrid incidents." As she spoke, she experienced a slight chill. Telling herself she was being fanciful, she agreed to Miss Dibble's proposal that they not wait for the bridal couple's departure before taking their own.

Despite all Letty's efforts to reach Buckingham Palace in good time, by the time her carriage had wended its way through the streets of London to the palace gates, she found herself dangerously near to being late. Already guest carriages stood in line to disgorge their noble passengers, which meant the queen's ladies would be taking their positions in the green drawing room. The bedchamber ladies would be helping Her Majesty dress, of course, but her other ladies were to await her entrance in the drawing room.

"I'll use the main entrance, Elvira," Letty said. "That will take less time than going round. Tell Jonathan, please."

Miss Dibble obeyed at once, letting down the window and shouting the order without bothering to point out that it might be better to wait till the carriage stopped at the end of the line. No doubt her reticence was due to relief that Letty had not put her own head out to shout at the coachman; however, it was too much to expect her to keep her counsel indefinitely. "You should not go in alone, my dear."

"I'll take Lucas with me," Letty said. "He can return once he's escorted me upstairs to the state rooms."

She had learned more about the palace in the days since her arrival, and she knew that maids of honor generally entered through a side door, but on an occasion like this, she had every right to use the main entrance and the grand stair.

The carriage stopped, stirring her impatience. "I cannot wait here, Elvira. If I am late, I'll lose my position."

"You cannot simply get out and run the rest of the way, Letitia."

"But there must be a half dozen carriages ahead of us, and they are not moving. Tell Jonathan to pull out of line and drive me up the verge to the arch."

Reluctantly Miss Dibble obeyed, and soon the carriage rolled to a halt beside the first one in line. Lucas jumped down and helped Letty alight.

The Life Guard posted at the Marble Arch stepped forward, clearly meaning to tell her she could not enter yet, but Letty anticipated him. Opening her cloak so that in the dusky light augmented by ceremonial torches flanking the arch, the ribboned badge showed clearly on the bodice of her aqua-colored gown, she smiled and said, "Please let me pass. I shall be ever so late if you do not."

"Certainly, miss," the guard said, stepping back.

Inside the grand hall, reassuringly, she found only palace servants scurrying to finish last-minute chores, their footsteps silent on the elegant red carpet. The haughty porter nodded when she let her cloak fall open again to display her maid of honor's badge. Apparently he saw nothing amiss in her hasty entrance.

Gathering her dignity, she approached the red-carpeted marble staircase with Lucas a step behind her. The white-and-gilded walls flanking the stairs glowed like burnished gold in the candlelight from myriad chandeliers, and the banister gleamed. As Letty reached the first landing, a voice spoke behind her.

"Letitia, wait."

Turning, she saw Catherine in a close-fitting, extremely décolleté evening gown of rose-colored *chiné* silk, hurrying toward her with a handsome young man at her side. Letty wondered if he might be the lover who had thrown the covers over his head, but Catherine's first words sent that notion flying. "This is my cousin, Hector Lennox, Letitia. He is a groom-in-waiting, so he'll gladly escort us. You can dismiss your footman, if you like."

Signing to Lucas that he could go, Letty moved on to the right-hand branch of stairs, saying, "We'd better hurry. We are already later than we ought to be."

Catherine nodded, saying no more in her cousin's presence. He, too, clearly was eager to take up his duties.

The two branches of the stairway came together again at the top, where doors to the guard room stood wide. Passing through this ceremonial entrance to the stately green drawing room, they soon saw by the number of Her Majesty's attendants already present that they were among the last to arrive.

The green drawing room was the central apartment on the west side of the palace's inner quadrangle. To the east, three windows opened onto the loggia over the grand entrance, and to the west corresponding mirror-doors led to the picture gallery. The chairs and sofas bore green silk upholstery, and brocade of the same color covered the walls, giving the whole room a softly muted effect.

Neither Lady Tavistock nor the Duchess of Sutherland was there yet, for their duties would keep them with the queen until she made her entrance. However, Lady Portman stood at the entrance to the drawing room; and Letty knew that her primary purpose in standing just there was to make certain that no one who ought to arrive before the general company did, failed to do so.

"Letitia, perhaps you can help me sort music for the entertainment after dinner," Catherine said when they had greeted Lady Portman and Hector Lennox had left them to tend to his duties. "The royal pages generally make a mull of it, I've found, and the queen may call upon any of us to perform, as you know."

"I hope she doesn't ask me," Letty said with feeling. "It is at times like this that I wish I had been more diligent in practicing my lessons."

Catherine chuckled. "The first time she singled me out, I nearly fainted at her feet, but now I rather enjoy performing. One gets accustomed to it."

"Do you dare being seen talking to me like this?" Letty asked bluntly when Catherine handed her a pile of music sheets to sort.

"Alphabetically by title works best," Catherine said. "People can quickly find what they want." She turned, clearly searching for more music. Letty had begun to wonder if she would ignore her question, when Catherine said, "I don't think it is a matter of daring, so much as of being circumspect."

"Circumspect?"

"Yes. You see, Her Majesty has grown rather distrustful of gossip in light of certain things that have happened recently."

"You mean the fuss over Lady Flora Hastings."

"Exactly. I don't know if you have seen her brother's letters in the papers."

"I should think everyone has seen them. They've been printing them for nearly a week now. Has Hastings decided to send the *Times* every letter any member of his family has written this past year?"

"Apparently," Catherine said. She was still sorting, not looking at Letty, and Letty followed her lead. Anyone watching them would assume that if they conversed they spoke only about details of their task. "In any event," Catherine went on, "you must understand Her Majesty's increasing fear of gossip. As much as any other factor, it keeps people from approaching you in friendship. Many fear that to be seen talking to you might leave them open to suspicion of consorting with the opposition, and the exaggerated Tory outrage over Lady Flora has not helped."

"But the queen is not supposed to take sides politically," Letty protested.

Catherine shrugged. "Perhaps you can tell her that. I do not know anyone else who can, particularly when people dare to criticize her devotion to the prime minister. She quite dotes on Melbourne, you know, although I did hear that today she told him she is thinking of marrying."

"Marrying! Well, she can't marry him, so who can it be?"

"A cousin of hers named Albert, one of the Saxe-Coburg lot. Her uncle, the King of the Belgians, desires the union, and she has great respect for him."

"But if she adores Melbourne . . . Is she so anxious to get married?"

"More eager to be rid of her mama, I think," Catherine said. "She has complained because Melbourne insists that as an unmarried queen she must have a chaperone, and only the Duchess of Kent is of sufficiently high rank."

"I should think the news of a possible marriage will upset any number of people when it gets out," Letty said. "Sir John Conroy, for one. He will never regain favor if Her Majesty has a husband."

"No," Catherine agreed, looking troubled. "Melbourne is not pleased, either, from what I hear. He said he did not think a foreigner would be popular. He persuaded her to put off making a decision until Albert visits in October."

"Did it take him two days to persuade her?" Letty asked, chuckling.

Catherine smiled. "That is hardly all they talked about," she said, "what with Hastings' letters, the intensifying debate over the Jamaican question, and deciding whether to allow the House of Commons to install gas lighting. The men talk of little beyond Jamaica, of course. Certainly, my husband talks of little else."

"He is not coming tonight?"

"No, he had a meeting to attend." She smiled ruefully, adding, "It is just as well that he did not come, since he suggested, quite firmly, that I not encourage you to talk to me." She grimaced. "He said it would do my reputation no good."

After a heavy silence, underscored by the buzz of conversation around them, Letty said, "We've got away from what we meant to talk about, have we not?"

In an undertone, Catherine said, "Why shouldn't I have an affair? Everyone does. My own husband has his *chère amie*. A woman has her pride, after all."

"The affair is your business," Letty said. "In truth, I am more interested in what you were telling me when your husband interrupted us."

"I don't recall what I was saying."

"You said that Sir John Conroy had approached you and certain others."

Casting her a look of sardonic amusement, Catherine said, "He hoped we would try to influence Her Majesty on his behalf, of course. As if I had any such influence. Her Majesty is far more interested in building an image of authority than in cultivating friendships amongst her younger, less important ladies."

"She does keep a certain distance, I've noticed."

"Yes. Moreover, I owe my position to my father's power in Parliament, not to my husband's; and no one—least of all the queen—would think I could influence Papa. He arranged my appointment as a maid of honor soon after she ascended the throne, thinking that the position would help me marry well. Most fathers think that, I believe, and, in my case at least, with good reason."

"Most, perhaps," Letty agreed, grateful that her father was not one of them. He had left to her the decision of whether to accept the appointment, and had taken great care to be sure she understood all it entailed, both privately and politically.

They chatted a little longer, until they had arranged the many sheets of music in good order. Then, other duties parted them, and before the invited guests began to arrive, Letty noted that Raventhorpe was also in attendance. She saw him look her way once, speculatively, while she chatted with one of the guests, but he made no effort to seek her out, and she took care not to look toward him again.

Before the queen's grand entrance, Letty's duties kept her occupied. She circulated among the guests to see that no one was ignored or neglected. She performed the same duties, in fact, that she had frequently performed in her parents' home, and at the Paris embassy. The company included representatives of many factions, and as a result, she found old acquaintances and even some new ones who did not instantly stiffen when she approached them. Little by little she began to relax and enjoy herself.

When the queen arrived, accompanied by her bedchamber ladies, her other ladies quickly gathered round her. Victoria liked to impress her company with the splendor of her entourage, and on this occasion, Letty thought they did her proud. Their gowns were lovely, well made, and colorful. Jewelry flashed on arms, around necks, and in their coiffures. The energy level in the room increased noticeably.

The chamberlain soon announced dinner, and the guests followed Victoria two by two, strictly by rank and precedence, into the picture gallery. There, the long dining table awaited them, splendidly laid with the royal linen, plate, and sterling.

When everyone had taken their places, and footmen had seen to their immediate needs, servants presented the first course for Her Majesty's approval. Receiving it, they began to serve the company.

Somewhat to Letty's consternation, Raventhorpe had taken a chair nearly opposite her. She encountered another narrow-eyed look, and wondered what on earth he could be thinking. His presence stirred unfamiliar sensations throughout her body, and at first it was all she could do not to keep looking at him.

No doubt, she thought with a sigh, he would soon offer his advice again, especially if he should discover his great-aunts' little secret. The thought gave her sufficient strength to avoid looking at him, and she soon forgot his presence in the need to attend to her dinner partner. That gentleman, an elderly, somewhat deaf lord of the realm, clearly expected to impress her with his opinions on subjects ranging from Parliamentary politics to the world at large.

Again her experience at diplomatic tables served her well, and she managed to keep the old gentleman talking without ignoring the man on her right when his partner temporarily deserted him. She paid little heed to her food, accepting and eating what her footman served her. Still, her partner caught her off guard when, after expounding at length on certain activities of the East India Company, he said abruptly, "What do you think, Lady Letitia? Will the directors sanction the introduction of paper money in Bombay? Will they authorize the Company to become shareholders in a joint-stock bank there or in Bengal?"

About to assure him, demurely, that he must know more about such things than she did, Letty unexpectedly caught Raventhorpe's eye. Noting a gleam of condescending amusement, she realized that he had been listening (most improperly, too, since he sat across the table from them and ought to have been attending to the fat countess on his right).

Impulsively, she smiled at her partner and said clearly, "In my opinion, sir, the East India Company cannot legally become copartners or shareholders in any banks established in Bombay or Bengal. To do so would clearly be engaging in commercial business as much as if they were to buy and sell tea or indigo. As you surely know, the act of Parliament authorizing their new charter in 1833 requires them to discontinue and abstain from all commercial business, with but certain exceptions. Therefore, the only question is whether the business falls within any of those exceptions. In my opinion, it does not."

The elderly lord blinked.

"Shall I explain my reasons, sir?"

"Good Gad, no! I mean, I quite agree with you, my dear, but who on earth has been filling your pretty head with such stuff?"

She smiled, taking care not to let her gaze drift across the table. "I'm afraid I read the newspapers, sir. Quite shocking behavior in a female, is it not?"

"Good Gad."

Thus encouraged, she said, "Now, the business of bank notes, I find interesting and rather bewildering. Imagine a place where such paper promises-to-pay have hitherto been quite unknown, despite the fact that commerce has flourished there for ages. But is that an evil or a blessing, do you think?"

"Paper money would make things much easier for everyone in both states, I should think," her companion said warily.

"Ah, but Calcutta, sir, like the United States, Great Britain, and France, is overrun with banking establishments and deluged with paper money. And Calcutta has suffered all the evil money panics that those countries have suffered, whilst Bombay and Bengal have endured none of them. Introducing paper money sounds a most risky business to me, but perhaps you see the benefits more clearly than I do and would be kind enough to explain them."

He was happy to do so, and long before he had tired of the subject and exchanged it for a new one, Letty had recovered

from the brief, uncharacteristic impulse that had driven her to
puff off her knowledge of world affairs.

With the savory before them at last, her partner nodded toward the head of the table, where Victoria was deep in conversation with the prime minister, who sat at her left, and said,
"Quite a fetching young thing, ain't she? But she oughtn't to
cast such sheep's eyes at Melbourne. It don't look at all
proper."

Knowing better than to comment on either the queen's appearance or her conduct, Letty said with a smile, "Her Majesty
is most considerate, sir."

"Aye, she's a sweet lass," he said. "Quite a contrast to what
her murderous uncle Cumberland would have been if he'd got
his claws on our throne as well as Hanover's when the old
king snuffed out. Of course, Cumberland could still inherit the
crown if he outlives Victoria and she don't marry and have
children first, but I daresay we're safe enough for now. Mind
now," he added earnestly, "I don't know but what England
might be better off under a law like the one those Germans
have, which prevents females from inheriting their throne. Still,
they're welcome to keep Cumberland in Hanover, and that's
my opinion on the subject."

Well aware that she had no more business discussing Her
Majesty's uncle, the King of Hanover, than discussing the
queen, and aware, too, that her companion was feeling the
effects of numerous glasses of wine, Letty said, "I find our
laws quite as fascinating as you do, sir. I only wish females
were allowed to study them."

The diversion worked, as she had been sure it would, and
the old gentleman spent the remainder of the time before the
queen's departure from the table explaining kindly why it was
quite impossible to allow women to study law.

When Her Majesty had departed, the rest of the ladies retired
to the green drawing room again to await her return and that

of the gentlemen. The men had an exact quarter hour to enjoy a glass of port, two if they were swift about it.

Lady Portman, again overseeing the behavior of the lesser ladies, asked one of them to take a seat at the pianoforte and to play until the others joined them.

"Something quiet," she said. Then, catching Letty's eye, she moved toward her, but before she spoke, Catherine approached, looking anxious.

"Forgive me, Lady Portman, but may I be excused for a few minutes? My dinner partner stepped on my lace and tore it. I've got pins, of course, and although it's at the back, I think I can mend it quickly." She said the last bit doubtfully.

Lady Portman said, "How very careless, but you must not look untidy. You may have five minutes, Lady Witherspoon, but do not dawdle. Use the ladies' withdrawing room beyond the throne room. Perhaps if Lady Letitia were to assist you, you could manage the task in less time."

"Thank you, ma'am," Catherine said. "Do you mind, Letitia?"

"Not at all," Letty said.

"I hoped she would suggest that," Catherine said with satisfaction as they passed through the empty throne room to the corridor beyond. "I've been talking with the most tedious man, and I simply must get away for a moment to breathe."

"Is your lace really torn?"

"Oh, yes, but it's the merest trifle. I daresay if I tie my petticoat strings tighter it won't show, for it's my petticoat lace that tore. Look here, can I call upon you at Jervaulx House, or will that cause a fuss?"

"Of course, you may; I'd be delighted," Letty said with perfect sincerity. "I am to ride with Her Majesty in the morning at the riding school, but perhaps you can call tomorrow afternoon, or the next day, if we need not be here."

"The Jamaican affair appears to be reaching a boiling point, so I daresay Her Majesty will be conferring long hours with her ministers," Catherine said. "Witherspoon said Melbourne is having difficulty holding his majority together. I am not sure what difference it makes, but one knows that if the prime minister is feeling pinched, Her Majesty will want to do all she can to help."

Aware that their conversation was straying into dangerous territory again, Letty smiled and said, "Do come to call at the first opportunity."

"Well, I will, because you cannot come to my house. Witherspoon would have an apoplectic fit. I don't know when I shall manage, though, because there is always—" Breaking off with a rueful grimace, she fell silent.

"We had better go back before Lady Portman sends someone to find us," Letty said. "Her Majesty will be returning this way soon."

The sound of masculine voices warned her that the gentlemen had returned to the drawing room, and she found herself hoping that her dinner partner had found someone else to whom he could expound his views. As she and Catherine entered, she glanced swiftly around, hoping to spot the elderly gentleman before he saw her, but she found her view suddenly blocked by Raventhorpe's large figure.

"Good evening, Lady Letitia," he said.

Something in his tone warned her to tread lightly, so returning his greeting, she added simply, "You know Lady Witherspoon, I trust." As she said the words, she had a mental vision of him walking in on Catherine the way she had, and a bubble of laughter rose in her throat. Ruthlessly suppressing it in the time it took him to assure her that he knew Catherine, she missed what he said next. "Forgive me, sir, what did you say?"

"You should attend when someone speaks to you," he said sternly. "I merely said I hoped you had not been sharing your political views with Lady Witherspoon."

Unable to resist, she said, "Are you afraid I might convert her to a Tory, sir?"

Sounding shocked, Catherine said, "Pray, don't even suggest such a thing!"

Raventhorpe's eyes gleamed with sudden humor. "Take care, Lady Witherspoon. I have heard her discuss Bombay banking matters with an expert. If you don't take care, she will doubtless try to persuade you that the Tory position on Jamaica is the correct one. Witherspoon would not approve."

With an answering gleam, Catherine said saucily, "You are impudent, my lord. We did speak briefly of Jamaica, but if you mean to scold her for such things, you should know first that I have decided to count her as my friend."

"Have you indeed?"

A little smile played on Catherine's lips. "I believe I have. I can see that you wish to have a private word with her, however, so I will leave you, but beware, sir." With another smile at him, she drifted away.

"She was flirting with you," Letty said in surprise.

"She flirts with every man she meets. Haven't you noticed?"

Much as she would have liked to contradict him, she could not. Catherine did flirt. She said instead, "I would never try to influence her politics, you know."

He said, "I hope not. Do you even know the Tory position on Jamaica?"

"Of course I do, and in my opinion, it is the correct one. The British government has no business sending arbitrary orders to the Jamaican assembly, ignoring the fact that the island has enjoyed self-rule for centuries."

"Indeed, Lady Letitia," the queen said grimly from the nearby doorway, where she stood with several of her bedchamber ladies. "Do you deny the transcendental power of our Parliament over colonial legislation?"

"No, ma'am," Letty said, sinking hastily to a deep curtsy. "Forgive me if I failed to make my point clear. It is not Parliament's power that I question, merely its wisdom in this particular instance."

"Indeed," said the queen haughtily.

Letty distinctly heard Raventhorpe groan.

NINE

Raventhorpe waited for the royal ax to fall. He could scarcely believe his ears when, instead of remaining sensibly silent, Lady Letitia said, "Your Majesty, again I failed to make myself clear. I do apologize."

To his further amazement, Victoria said, "Do you honestly think you *can* make yourself clear on such an important government question?"

Raventhorpe stifled another groan. He would have given much for the power to tell the queen not to be such a fool as to bait the chit. However, not only did protocol strictly forbid him to address Her Majesty before she had spoken to him, but the impertinent chit was already off and running.

"As you are doubtless aware, ma'am," Letitia said earnestly, "no one in Parliament has condemned outright the bill to supersede the Jamaican assembly's powers. It arose, after all, from a simple misunderstanding over an earlier act."

"Did it indeed?" Victoria's tone was icy.

"Yes, ma'am, the bill that puts control of all colonial prisons into the hands of a council of three salaried Whig commissioners. The assembly has freely legislated all regulations in Jamaica since the reign of Charles II, as you know, and there can be no doubt that management of their prisons falls under their general powers. Surely a wise government would make some effort toward conciliation before superseding any, let alone all, of those powers."

" 'Tis fortunate that our government is wiser than you, Lady Letitia," Victoria said with an austerity worthy of a matron at least twenty years her senior.

"Forgive me, ma'am; it was never my intention to displease you," the chit said hastily, giving Raventhorpe hope that she had come to her senses. That hope died, however, when she added, "It does seem unfair that some members of Parliament have insisted upon making this a party issue when—"

"If that is so," Victoria interjected tartly, "it is Tories who are to blame."

"But Sir Robert Peel speaks for the Tory party, ma'am, and his position all along has been that the government should grant the Jamaican assembly time to deliberate. If they do, one of two things must happen. Either they will submit to the wishes of Parliament and pass a prison law of their own, conforming with the one passed here, or else they will remain obstinate. In the first case—"

"In *any* case," Victoria interjected grimly, "it is no concern of yours."

Apparently regaining her wits at last, Letitia made another deep curtsy, saying, "As you wish, ma'am. I did think, when you asked if—"

Unable to stop himself, Raventhorpe snapped, "Lady Letitia, Her Majesty has guests awaiting her, and you have duties to attend."

Turning scarlet, she held her tongue.

Victoria waited a beat, as if to be sure the chit would say no more. Then, with the austere tone she had employed earlier, she said, "If you cannot recall your duties, Lady Letitia, you must ask Lady Tavistock to explain them to you."

"Yes, Your Majesty." Letitia remained in her curtsy until the queen had swept past her into the green drawing room, where conversation still hummed but the music of the pianoforte had given way to the soft thrumming of a harp. Rising at last, she looked around as if hoping to find a supporter, but Catherine

Witherspoon had vanished moments after the queen had spoken. Only Raventhorpe remained.

Fighting to control his anger, he said grimly, "You deserve—"

"Don't say it. I know what I deserve. Looking at her, I somehow quite forgot she is the queen and saw only another person my age who had asked me a question. I was already annoyed with you, and not thinking straight, but—"

"So it is my fault, is it?"

"No, of course not, but how she can support one of the most arbitrary measures ever presented to a British House of Commons, I do not know. They want to suspend the Jamaican assembly for years, saying they need the time to prepare the former slaves to vote properly for new members. Those are the same men who, on all former occasions, represented the freed slaves as already ripe for every enjoyment of civil liberty. If I could have made her understand that—"

"You couldn't do it," he said harshly. "Moreover, you have oversimplified the situation beyond all reason."

"Well, I know that varying opinions exist within the Whig party on this issue, and I'll do you the honor to think yours must be one of the more sensible ones. But the liberal wing of your party, sir, see themselves as the exclusive lovers of freedom. Yet they are now up in arms to suspend a free constitution, and to do so on utterly false pretenses."

"That's enough!" He caught her by one arm and pulled her well away from the entrance to the drawing room. With the queen's return, the noise of conversation had grown louder, and the throne room was empty but for the two of them. Since no one else could hear what he said to her, he decided to give his temper full rein. "You listen to me now, my girl."

"How dare you!" She wrenched her arm from his grip, but although her quickness surprised him, he caught her easily again, grabbing her by both shoulders and giving her a shake.

"Someone has to dare," he snapped, "before you find yourself banished from court and shunned in society. Can you honestly tell me that your father would approve of what you've done here tonight?" When she remained silent, he gave her another shake. "Would he? Look at me, if you can, and say that he would."

After a small silence, she looked at him. His gaze locked with hers, and in that moment something happened that neither would later be able to explain. In the first second or so, he thought it was no more than an unnatural (considering that he felt like murdering her) awareness that her eyes were not truly silver, but blue, with a sunburst of white rays coming from the pupils. But he knew it was much more than that, a different kind of awareness, one that stirred feelings far removed from anger.

"You know I cannot say he would approve," she said quietly. "He would probably feel like doing just what you want to do to me."

"I doubt that," he said dryly.

"Well, he has never beaten me, so I daresay he would not threaten it, but I am not sure that he would not want to. And he can certainly make me quake in my shoes when he gets angry with me."

"Since he knows you well, perhaps he will realize there was provocation."

"Even so, he would say that I ought to have ignored it, and he would be right. At the very least he will be exceedingly disappointed in me."

To his shock, tears welled into her beautiful eyes, and he felt a nearly overwhelming impulse to make them go away again. Before he could think of anything to say, however, she added, "I don't know what came over me. I certainly know better than to set my opinions against Her Majesty's. She began it, of course, by commenting on an observation that was not intended for her ears. Still, she *is* the queen, and I ought simply to have apologized and then kept silent."

Since this analysis exactly matched his own, it was with dismay that he heard himself say, "She did provoke your response, and that was not well done of her. It is not always easy to hold one's tongue merely because it is the proper thing to do."

Her eyes widened with surprise. "Mercy, sir, I never expected to hear you say such a thing."

"I never expected it, either," he retorted.

She managed a watery chuckle as she pulled a lacy handkerchief from her reticule and dabbed her eyes. "You must think me a dreadful watering pot, but I am no such thing, I promise you. I rarely give way to tears. Moreover, I was about to explain to you that, in a way, it was perhaps your fault that this happened."

"Indeed?"

"Mercy, you sounded just like her when you said that!" This time her laughter was more natural. "Don't frown. I meant it before when I said it was my fault. But I think it's because of you that I felt obliged to puff off my reasons to her. The same impulse overcame me at dinner, you see."

"Bombay banks?"

"Yes, I knew you were listening, because you looked at me as if you felt sorry for me, or thought I was helpless before the flood of my partner's discourse. I wanted to show you it was no such thing, and so I succumbed to a horrid temptation to show off what I knew about the East India Company. I think your presence again just now stirred me to debate Jamaica with Her Majesty."

"You don't have to impress me, you know."

"Impress you! I wanted to silence you, to show you that I've got a brain and don't need you or anyone else to give me advice." She grimaced ruefully. "Instead I have probably managed to get myself banished from Her Majesty's court."

Still feeling strongly that she deserved a scolding, but wholly unable to deliver it, he said, "Perhaps it will not be so bad as that. Still, you ought to go back into the drawing room before someone else comes in search of you. I think it would be better—if you will not dismiss my advice this time—if you go ahead of me."

"Yes, it would, because Lady Tavistock would think I had been flirting with you again if we went in together."

"Again?"

Her eyes danced. "Yes, she scolded me for flirting that first day, when I spoke with you. It was the time you accused me of accosting you."

He smiled. "In that event, you can definitely go in by yourself. I shall wait a good long time before following, too."

The wry look she gave him told him that she had recovered her equilibrium, but he could tell, too, that she expected worse to come. The fact that Victoria might dismiss her disturbed him more than he would have thought possible even half an hour earlier. Banishment from court would ruin her, and he knew of only one person with sufficient influence to keep that from happening.

Letty walked away with her head high, but inside she felt an odd and most uncharacteristic mixture of irritation and dejection. Not one to give way to her sensibilities, she felt irritated that Raventhorpe, of all people, had seen her at a weak moment. More than that, though, she was angry with herself for twice giving way to a childish impulse.

No one, in her opinion, was more boring than a person who puffed off his or her political ideas to others who did not want to hear them. Of course, others often encouraged her to express hers, but such encouragement generally came from within her family. She certainly could not say no one had ever taught her to curb her tongue in public, or in diplomatic circles. If Victoria's court did not count in the latter category, she did not know what would.

"Letitia!" Catherine hurried toward her. "I thought you would never come. Lady Tavistock has twice asked what became of you. I told her I thought you were feeling unwell."

"Thank you," Letty said with sincerity.

"Don't thank me yet," Catherine said with an impish grin.

"Her ladyship informed me that maids of honor are not allowed to be ill. Unfortunately, Puck Quigley overheard her, and said that that had been made clear to all and sundry by the Marquess of Hastings' letters about Lady Flora in the *Times*."

Letty groaned. She had met Puck Quigley and liked him. He was as open and friendly as a puppy, and although he had no head for politics, he occasionally turned a phrase in an amusing way. His comment about Lady Flora would not have amused the chief lady of the bedchamber, however. "Where is Lady Tavistock?"

"Yonder with the queen, of course. You know Her Majesty likes to keep her ladies swarming round her. Was she furious with you? I fled, thinking the less she saw of me, the better, but I feel as if I abandoned you. Whatever got into you?"

"The devil," Letty said flatly. She drew a long, steadying breath. "Shall we go to her?"

"Yes, we must, for the entertainments are about to begin. Lady Portman's daughter is to recite a poem about the Battle of Waterloo."

As they made their way to the group around the queen, Letty saw that, as usual, the company would remain standing, even for the entertainment. Sitting in the queen's presence was a rare privilege, and not one that Letty ever expected to enjoy.

Half an hour later she learned she was wrong about that, when Victoria said clearly, "Lady Letitia, we are told that you perform quite tolerably. Doubtless the company would enjoy a ballad or two, if you will honor us at the pianoforte."

Swallowing the fervent protest that leapt to her lips, Letty said in a strangled voice, "Certainly, Your Majesty." Feeling every eye upon her, she made her way to the instrument, fighting a strong urge to turn and flee from the room.

Her brain seemed frozen. She could not recall a single piece that would not blindingly reveal her lack of practice. She had not laid hand to keyboard since her arrival in London, and other than to place the sheets in alphabetical order when she and

Catherine had sorted them earlier, she had paid little heed to the titles.

Clearly, the queen meant to punish her, for Victoria could not have heard anything good about her performance at the pianoforte. There were people present, of course, who had heard her play and sing in Paris, but all of them were diplomats by trade, and none of them would have put her on the spot like this.

By the time she reached the stool, she had herself under sufficient control that she was able to pick up a stack of music and begin to leaf through it, as if she knew what she was doing. That she did not was doubtless the reason she did not sense Raventhorpe's approach before he touched her arm.

Startled, she looked at him wildly.

He smiled and took the music from her hand. "I glanced through these earlier," he said smoothly. "I think the material you want is in this other pile."

She swallowed again, wholly bewildered. "Is . . . Is it, sir?"

"Yes, there are a number of rather amusing French and German folk songs in this lot. I am sure you must know most of them."

He showed her the first one, and when she nodded blankly, he set it on the music rack, saying, "I'll play for you, shall I?"

"If only you could! But the queen said—"

"She said only that the company would enjoy some ballads. These may not be ballads, exactly, but the company will enjoy them. You can sing, can't you?"

"Yes. Yes, certainly I can sing those. They are little more than nursery songs. Anyone could sing them."

"Only someone who speaks French and German fluently could sing them well, however, and the beauty of their simplicity is that most of this company will understand them. The queen certainly will." He took his seat as he spoke, and his hands hovered briefly over the keys. Then he played a few bars of the first piece.

The buzz of conversation, which had continued even through the recitation earlier, suddenly ceased.

Knowing that to avoid the queen's gaze at this juncture would be foolhardy, Letty straightened, folded her hands at her waist, and focusing on the space between Victoria's eyes, began to sing.

The first song told an amusing tale of a mischievous cat, and by the third verse, members of the audience were chuckling, then laughing outright. Letty had a good sense of timing, and as she relaxed and began to enjoy herself, she became more animated, playing up the humor in the songs she sang. She forgot the queen after those first few moments, but midway through the third song, she glanced at her and saw a slight smile. Not a huge triumph, she decided, but certainly not the disaster she had feared.

At the end of the fourth song, she smiled and turned to thank Raventhorpe. Several people called for another, but when she shook her head, Lady Tavistock said clearly, "Thank you, Lady Letitia. We will not impose further on your good nature. Miss Hayworth has generously agreed to play Mr. Beethoven's *Moonlight Sonata* for us now."

Sincerely grateful to Miss Hayworth, Letty turned to express even deeper thanks to Raventhorpe. "I don't know what I'd have done," she said frankly.

"It was my pleasure, Lady Letitia," he said with a formal little nod. Then, as he turned to replace the music, he said grimly for her ears alone, "Do not think I am through with you yet. You still deserve—"

Before he could continue, Miss Hayworth was upon them, saying in a gushing way, "Oh, Lord Raventhorpe, I do not know how I dare to take your place here. Everyone knows how skilled you are on this instrument, whilst I am but the merest novice. I protest, sir, I am quite petrified with terror."

"Don't be absurd, Miss Hayworth," he said. "You play well, and no one paid heed to my performance when Lady Letitia was singing."

Tittering behind one gloved hand, Miss Hayworth turned to Letty and said, "Isn't he the kindest man? Your songs were quite amusing, of course, but everyone knows how well he plays. Even with those funny little songs, one could tell."

"Yes, indeed they could," Letty said, smiling at her. "Shall I perhaps move this branch of candles so the light will fall more clearly on your music?"

"Oh, that won't be necessary. I know this piece by heart, naturally."

"Naturally," Letty said.

Raventhorpe's hand at her elbow tightened as he guided her away from the pianoforte. Then, with a slight bow, he left her and walked away.

Watching him, she was aware yet again of the mixed emotions the man stirred in her. She did feel exceedingly grateful to him, and would have liked to express that gratitude more profoundly. At the same time, she was certain that he had tightened his hand on her elbow as a warning to watch how she spoke. Worse, she could not decide whether he had intended the arrogant nod and bow as he left to tell her or the company at large that he had done no more than assist a competent singer by playing for her.

She had no time to consider her emotions, however, because Lady Tavistock approached as the first few bars of the *Moonlight Sonata* wafted across the room. "The dowager Lady Kirkland is feeling unwell, Letitia. Be so good as to take her to my chamber and ask my woman to look after her until her carriage can be sent for."

"Yes, ma'am." Letty turned to look for Lady Kirkland.

"One moment," Lady Tavistock said sternly. "I have not dismissed you."

"Forgive me, ma'am." Letty assumed an inquiring look, striving to repress unkind thoughts of how much Lady Tavistock enjoyed the power she wielded.

"Her Majesty expects to leave for the riding school at eight o'clock in the morning. Do not be late."

Allowing doubt to tinge her voice, Letty said, "No ma'am, I won't."

"Her Majesty particularly desires your company," Lady Tavistock added, showing that she understood Letty's doubt and did not find it out of place. "She will not require it again after her excursion to the riding school, however, so you will have the rest of the day free to contemplate your duty." Having thus made it clear that Letty was to present herself so early as punishment, she added, "You will find Lady Kirkland sitting quietly in the guard room, near the landing entrance."

"Thank you, ma'am."

Dismissed at last, Letty went in search of Lady Kirkland, whom she knew only as an elderly dowager who seemed friendly with the queen's mother. She found her sitting with Catherine in the guard room.

The other young woman looked up with a smile. "You are surprised to see me here," she said. "I overheard Lady Tavistock say she would fetch you, so I stepped out with Lady Kirkland so she would not find herself bereft of company whilst she waited for you. She is feeling much more the thing now, I believe."

"Perhaps you might ask me," the old woman said tartly.

To save Catherine the embarrassment of responding, Letty smiled and said, "Do you feel well enough to retire to Lady Tavistock's rooms now, ma'am? She said that I might take you there to await your carriage."

"What, go up the stairs and down again, when I could more comfortably wait in the hall? Don't be absurd, gel."

"I merely obey orders, ma'am. I shall do precisely as you command."

"Then send someone to fetch my woman. I daresay Anna Maria never thought of that. She's a considerate child, though a bit of a jumping jack, and I daresay it wouldn't suit her to sit in the hall, so she assumes it don't suit me. But I don't mind. Much easier on an old body, when all is said and done."

Finding it hard to suppress her amusement at the thought of the demanding (and greying) marchioness seeming childlike to anyone, Letty avoided Catherine's gaze. "I will be glad to take you down to the hall, ma'am," she said to the dowager. "Moreover, I will stay with you until your woman joins us. Perhaps Catherine will not mind asking one of the footmen to be sure that someone went to fetch her."

"Of course I don't mind," Catherine said instantly. "I believe Lady Tavistock did send someone, but I can find out very quickly."

"You are a kind child, Letitia," Lady Kirkland said as they descended the stairs slowly to the grand hall. "I don't care what anyone else says."

"Dear me, ma'am, I hope no one has been saying anything too horrid."

"Well, I did hear that you are a Tory," Lady Kirkland said, shooting her a glance that held a wicked twinkle. "However, I have lived long enough to know that one's politics rarely have much to do with one's character."

"Well, if that is all you heard, then—"

"Oh, that wasn't all," the old lady interjected airily.

Letty had begun to suspect that Lady Kirkland felt perfectly well, and merely had been bored and ready to go home. Since protocol demanded that no one leave a royal dinner before the queen had retired, it would not be the first time that someone had employed such a stratagem.

"Dare I ask what else you have heard?" she asked, deciding the old lady would appreciate bluntness more than tact.

"That would be telling," Lady Kirkland said archly. "Still, although I like you, there are others who don't, so you mind your step, gel."

Recalling that the dowager was close to the Duchess of Kent, Letty asked no more questions and, when they were seated in the grand hall, changed the subject to one less likely to stir coals. They had only a few minutes to wait, however, before Catherine appeared with a woman who proved to be the dowager's companion. Her carriage arrived shortly thereafter.

"She recovered nicely from her indisposition," Catherine said with a knowing smile.

Letty nodded but said nothing. She was beginning to feel comfortable with Catherine, and she wanted to know her better, but she was not yet ready to trust her with statements that would not bear repeating to the world at large.

They went upstairs together to find that in their absence the queen had retired. The rest of the party was preparing to do likewise, but there were still duties to attend. It was another hour before Letty was able to slip away to her chamber.

She was very tired, so when she walked in to find Miss Dibble sound asleep in the one comfortable chair, and no sign of Jenifry, her irritation stirred.

Shaking Miss Dibble, she said, "Wake up, do, Elvira. Where is Jenifry?"

Blinking away sleep, Miss Dibble sat bolt upright and said, "Good gracious, what time is it?"

"Nearly two," Letty said, "and I must be back here before eight tomorrow morning. Where's Jen?"

"Isn't she here?"

"Elvira, wake up and look around you. This room is not so large as that."

Rubbing her eyes, Miss Dibble got to her feet. "You must be exhausted, for I've no doubt you have been on your feet since dinner. Sit down, child. Sit down."

"I will, because I want to take these shoes off. But if Jen has disappeared, we must search for her."

"She hasn't . . . Oh, yes, I remember now. She said she was going to take a walk, that she was sure you would not be back till the small hours. And how right she was about that! But, dear me, that was before midnight. Where can she be?"

Seeing clearly that Miss Dibble was going to be of little help until she came fully awake, Letty stood up again, intending to ring for a footman to start a search for Jenifry. Before she had done more than reach for the bell pull, however, the door opened and Jenifry entered.

"Oh, you're back already," the dresser said cheerfully.

"Yes," Letty said, looking at her searchingly. Jenifry looked wide awake, as if it were the beginning of the day rather than the end.

Miss Dibble said sharply, "Where have you been, girl?"

"Never mind that now," Letty said. "Collect my things, Jen. Elvira, send for the carriage. If I've got to be back here before eight, I want to get straight home now. We can talk in the carriage if you like."

However, by the time the carriage had come, Letty could hardly keep her eyes open, and once inside, Miss Dibble began snoring gently almost at once. Soon, the rocking motion of the coach lulled Letty to sleep as well.

When they reached Jervaulx House, Jenifry woke them, but when Miss Dibble insisted that she would accompany Letty to her bedchamber, Letty refused.

"You need your sleep, ma'am, and you are not to drag yourself out of bed at dawn, either. Jenifry can dress me and accompany me to the palace. I'm only riding with the queen. I shall not have to stay afterward."

"Very well," Miss Dibble said, shooting a stern glance at Jenifry. "I hope you will explain to this young woman that her behavior tonight is not acceptable."

"I'll talk to her. Good night, Elvira." Going quickly upstairs, Letty kicked off her shoes and began pulling pins from her hair when she entered her bedchamber. The fire on the hearth had burned nearly to embers, but the room was still warm. "Never mind brushing my hair tonight, Jen. I can just push it into a cap to sleep. I'll wash my face and put on my nightdress, but that's all."

"Yes, miss," Jenifry said, hurrying to pour warm water from the kettle on the hob into the washbasin. Except for the noise of their movements, silence reigned for the next few minutes before Jenifry said quietly, "Are you vexed, miss?"

"Not particularly, but it's a good thing that you came back when you did."

"I-I expect you want to know where I was."

"I doubt that it would surprise me if you told me."

Jenifry stared at her. "Do you know, then?"

Letty chuckled. "I daresay you have been making friends with the Duchess of Sutherland's footman. I remember how you looked at him."

"Him?" Jenifry sniffed disdainfully. "He's all right, he is, but I've got more than one string to my bow, Miss Letty. I have found that a gentleman's man is not so high in the instep as a duchess's footman, and far more genteel."

"And which particular gentleman's man would that be?"

"None in particular, yet," Jenifry replied with her nose in the air. She added with a grin, "But there be two that make my heart beat faster, and that's fact, miss."

"Who are they?"

"I'm not one to kiss and tell," Jenifry said, winking as she handed Letty a towel. "I will say that one of them has a deal of charm and the other can make a girl feel as if she lacks guts in her brain, as often as not."

"Jenifry! Where on earth did you get such a phrase?"

"Me dad used to say it," Jenifry confessed, reddening. "He said it just meant to be knowledgeable, but he did say I wasn't to say it. I didn't know I was going to just now till I did. It's the effect that one has on me, I expect. He's a one. I met him that first day, if you must know. He's the one as showed us the common room."

When she said no more, Letty knew she was hoping for a demand to continue, but Letty felt too tired to coax her. It would serve as a suitable punishment for her lateness, she decided, if for once she treated Jenifry like most people treated their servants instead of like the friend she had become.

TEN

After less than four hours sleep, Letty nonetheless awoke feeling much her usual self. Jenifry, too, seemed cheerful and as if she had got more than enough sleep, for she hummed a little tune as she opened the curtains to let in the early-morning light and fairly danced across the room with Letty's chocolate.

"I'll fetch your riding habit, miss," she said as she plumped the pillows. "This room's much warmer than the dressing room today. The girl lit the fire in there, but it don't seem ever to have caught hold, and the place is like an icebox."

"Very well," Letty said, settling back against her pillows to enjoy the rich chocolate for the few moments left before she would have to get up and dress.

Jenifry returned a few moments later and, still humming, laid the blue-green riding habit on the bed, along with Letty's frilled chemisette. The round, ribboned hat she would wear Jenifry placed carefully on the side table before collecting the tray to set outside the door for one of the maids to take away.

"You're mighty cheerful this morning," Letty said as she got out of bed.

"I expect I am, miss. It is going to be a fine day."

"It can't be the weather that has put you in such good trim, because it looks like another drizzly day," Letty said. "Therefore, it must be the glory of knowing you've got a number of handsome gentlemen dangling on your string."

Jenifry chuckled as she poured water from the hob kettle into

Letty's basin and handed her a towel. "I like London, miss, that's all. I say, did you know the queen is thinking of marrying?"

"I did hear that," Letty admitted, "but I'm surprised the news has reached the servants' hall already. Until there is an official announcement, Jen, I think we had better not talk about it, or I'll find myself accused of gossiping about the court. Are you ever going to tell me your gentlemen's names?"

After a pause, during which Letty continued to scrub her face and hands and Jenifry apparently weighed the pros and cons of complying with her seemingly offhand request, the dresser said, "The best-looking one calls himself Walter, miss. He can be a bit abrupt at times, but he's that handsome, Walter is."

"And the other?" Letty folded the towel.

"Mr. Leyton, but I think it's Walter I fancy most. Mr. Leyton is too full of himself to suit me. I'll just fetch your boots now, miss."

"Whom do these paragons serve?" Letty asked when she returned.

Jenifry blushed. "I don't know who Walter serves, miss. One don't like to ask, and he didn't say, only one gets the notion from his attitude that his master is someone important. Mr. Leyton . . ." She eyed her mistress warily, then said in a rush, "You won't like it, I daresay, but he is my lord Raventhorpe's man."

Letty shrugged. "I cannot see why that should distress me, Jen, especially if he is not the one you fancy most." Striving to sound casual, she added, "What manner of man is he?"

"Mr. Leyton?"

Letty nodded.

Jenifry grimaced. "He's the sort who thinks he knows everything, and he's that toplofty, too, miss. I asked him what his Christian name is, and he said it would not be appropriate for me to use it. Always trying to tell a body what she should do and what she shouldn't, is Leyton. Looks down his nose when he does, too."

"Like master, like man, then," Letty said without thinking.

"They usually are, miss. It's getting on for half past now," she added.

Letty dressed quickly, then hurried into the chilly dressing room to glance at her reflection in the cheval glass. The tight-fitting, pointed bodice with its soft velvet collar revealed her cream-colored, neatly tied cravat and frilly chemisette. The habit boasted short swallowtails, gigot sleeves, and a full pleated skirt, beneath which the lacy edges of her pantaloons would occasionally peep when she mounted, dismounted, or rode at a canter.

"I'll do," she said, adjusting her hat to a more rakish angle. "Fetch my whip and gloves, will you, Jen?"

Jenifry already had them in hand, along with her own cloak. They found Jonathan Coachman waiting below with Lucas and the carriage. Letty's groom was also with them, ready to ride behind the carriage; and he led her favorite mount, a bay gelding she called Denmark.

At that hour tradesmen's carts and wandering pedestrians comprised the only traffic, so they made good time to the palace, and she arrived with twenty minutes to spare. Catherine arrived several minutes later, and they chatted while they waited for the queen and the other ladies who would ride with them.

The more Letty came to know Catherine, the better she liked her. She had assumed after surprising her with her lover that the other woman was not happy in her marriage. Today she learned that Catherine had a small son whom she adored, which clearly made up for a much-older husband who displayed little interest in his marriage. Catherine did not complain or speak ill of him, but Letty had seen him for herself. His age alone, she thought, would preclude their having much in common. Hopefully the lover, whoever he was, provided more harmonious companionship.

They talked together amiably until the queen arrived with her bedchamber ladies, then continued to chat during their ride to the nearby riding school. The school possessed a large ring in a parklike setting, and the proprietor could admit members of the *haut ton* who possessed the entrée while shutting his doors to any commoners who might wish to ride at such an early hour. Thus, he assured the royal party some privacy.

At first, the ladies had the ring to themselves, but they had been riding for less than half an hour when Letty saw several gentlemen arrive, including Raventhorpe and, to her surprise, the prime minister. Victoria greeted the latter enthusiastically, instantly signing to the ladies nearest her to fall back and allow her to ride alone with Melbourne.

Letty and Catherine had been talking together almost without interruption. Not only did Letty learn much about Catherine's precocious young son but she soon found herself telling the other woman about her own childhood in Paris, even describing some of her more daring escapades.

"Surely, you did not go about that huge city untended," Catherine exclaimed at one point. "How did you dare? I would be terrified even now to do such a thing."

"I wasn't entirely untended," Letty said. "I made friends with many of our servants and their children, you see, and because I spoke French, I was able to go about with the other children quite unnoticed. My parents did not approve at first, certainly, but I was intrepid and rather headstrong, I'm afraid. Fortunately, they soon came to realize that I would come to no harm."

Catherine pretended to shudder. "I can just imagine what my father's reaction would have been to *my* playing with servants' children."

Letty chuckled reminiscently. "Mine didn't like it much, either, at first. And, even after he grew more accustomed, whenever my grandfather visited us, I did not dare go in search of adventure, as I called it. Papa is quite an indulgent parent compared to most, but he would not allow us to displease his papa. Nor did one wish to. Grandfather had no sense of humor and his temper was so icy that it utterly froze one stiff."

"How many siblings do you have?"

"Two brothers," Letty replied. "Both are in England now, at school. Gideon is at Oxford, and James at Eton."

"It must be pleasant for all of you to be here together," Catherine said.

"It might be, if we saw anything of each other," Letty said with a grin. "They are both busy at present, but I daresay I shall see them next month when my parents arrive in town."

"Don't they write to you?"

"My parents do, of course, but my brothers do not. I have had precisely one letter from James. Since he has decided the navy might suit him, he blithely chose to assume that I have only to whisper in Her Majesty's ear and she will arrange for him to be put in command of a fine ship just as soon as he is old enough."

Catherine laughed. "What did you tell him?"

"That even if I could get Her Majesty to arrange an interview with the First Lord of the Admiralty, which I most assuredly could not, he would be unlikely to provide a ship for a young Tory naval officer who would rather play cricket than attend to his lessons. Why are you frowning?"

"Because I just noticed that everyone is ignoring us. Her Majesty is riding with Melbourne, of course, staring at him with sheep's eyes, like she always does, so it is not odd that she is paying us no heed. However, when I chance to catch anyone else's eye, that person looks away."

"It's not you," Letty said with a sigh. "They're ignoring me. They have never been friendly, of course, but word must have got round last night that I had stepped beyond the pale at last. Perhaps you should ride with someone else."

"Nonsense," Catherine said. "I choose my friends, *they* don't."

Only a moment later, however, she paled and said, "There is Sir John and . . . and his aide. Whatever do you think he is doing here?"

"I'm surprised they let him in," Letty said, watching Conroy.

He had ridden in ahead of Charles Morden, and for a moment, it looked as if the two would head right toward the queen. Then Raventhorpe turned away from the group he was riding with and made his way toward the pair, effectively cutting off their path to Victoria.

Quietly Catherine said, "I hope they don't make trouble."

"I don't think they will," Letty said reassuringly. "Not now. Sir John cannot want to displease Her Majesty, and to interrupt her when she is enjoying a ride with Melbourne would infuriate her. He must know that."

Apparently Raventhorpe had pointed out either that fact or an equally persuasive one, because Conroy and Morden, after a token turn, left the ring again.

Lady Portman rode up to Letty and Catherine as Sir John was departing. She looked uneasy, and at first Letty assumed it was because the plump woman disliked riding. However, she soon realized her error.

"Catherine," Lady Portman said, avoiding so much as a glance at Letty, "Lady Tavistock would like you to ride with us for a time, if you please."

For a moment it looked as if Catherine would tell her it did not please her at all, but then, with a rueful glance at Letty, she said, "As you wish, ma'am."

Letty understood Lady Portman's discomfort. Clearly her mission had been to separate Catherine from an undesirable influence.

As they rode away, she wondered what she ought to do. The queen did not want her company, nor did the other ladies. If she approached any of them, she could be certain of meeting rebuff. Lost in thought, she did not notice the approach of another horse from behind until Raventhorpe drew alongside.

With a smile he said, "Woolgathering?"

"I was wondering what, if anything, I can do to repair my position here," she said frankly. "I have begun to think it is a lost cause."

"Be patient," he advised her. "Think of something else instead."

"You always have advice to offer," she retorted, more sharply than she had intended. "Do you order *your* thoughts so easily, sir?"

"No, I don't," he said, surprising her. "It might astonish you to know that occasionally I find myself quite overwhelmed. Have you met my father?"

Emerging from her gloom at once, she nearly laughed. She had heard about Sellafield, and guessed that he must be a thorn in his son's side. Changing the subject to one more appropriate for discussion, she said, "How is your mother, sir? I have not seen her in some days now, and I think perhaps I ought to pay her a call. She invited me to do so, and I like her very much."

"Do so by all means," he said, adding with a much warmer smile, "I like her quite a lot myself. In point of fact, I believe she said something recently about giving a dinner party at Sellafield House and inviting you and the aunts." He looked toward the entrance just then, and his expression changed abruptly, giving Letty to fear that Sir John had returned.

Turning, however, she saw only a handsome young man on an elegant black.

With a glance, Raventhorpe said grimly, "My scapegrace brother. He ought to be hard at his studies, but doubtless he needs mon—" Breaking off with a grimace, he said more evenly, "I daresay he has a good reason for coming here."

The younger man looked wary, Letty thought, as he approached them, and his nerves evidently affected his mount, for the black skittered and nearly reared. He held it in skillfully, however, as he drew rein in front of them.

"Good morning," he said cheerfully.

Raventhorpe's reply lacked emotion of any sort. "Good morning. Aren't you rather far afield?"

"Lord, no. I slept at home last night, and Mama told me when I found her in the breakfast parlor that you had already left. Since I particularly wanted to speak with you, I came here first, but if you are otherwise engaged . . ." He paused tactfully, glancing curiously at Letty.

Raventhorpe said, "Lady Letitia, though it goes against the grain with me to do so, may I present my brother, Edward Delahan."

"Certainly, you may," Letty said, as Mr. Delahan touched his hat and made the movement which on horseback passed for a bow. "I am pleased to make your acquaintance, Mr. Delahan."

"Delighted, ma'am. Lady Letitia, did he say?" When Letty nodded, amused, he said, "I say, are you the little Tor— That is," he amended hastily, catching his brother's stern gaze, "I mean to say, you must be—"

"I am Letitia Deverill," Letty said, cutting in with a smile. "I have come to London from Paris, and your brother has been kind enough to give me advice from time to time about how I should go on here."

"I'll wager he has," Mr. Delahan said with feeling. Then, glancing again at Raventhorpe, he colored deeply, adding, "I don't mean to say that. . . . Oh, bother! Justin, you know I never . . . That is, I . . ." His mount stepped nervously sideways, drawing his attention again, and when he had it under control, he looked beseechingly at Raventhorpe.

Letty said, "Shall I ride on, sir, so you may be private with your brother?"

"No," both men said at once.

When she made little effort to stifle a chuckle, Raventhorpe gave her a sour look, but Mr. Delahan looked slightly relieved.

Raventhorpe said, "I warned you, Ned, that I would not prove an easy touch the next time you—"

"I'm not," the other said hastily. "Boot's on the other foot."

"You expect me to ask you for—"

"No, no!" Ned laughed. "I mean that I came to tell you that you have been right all along. I am mending my ways. I learned a lesson at Newmarket when I-Wish-You-May-Get-It failed to finish, and I'm retrenching, Justin, word of a Delahan. And don't say that Father says that whenever he—"

"I won't. I know you mean it, or think you mean it."

"I do, and I'll show you that I do. Only . . ." He reddened, clearly at a loss.

"Only what?" Raventhorpe prompted.

"Well, the fact is that I lost rather more than I thought I had at Newmarket, and I shall need a bit of the ready to tide me over until—"

"No."

"But I've told you that I have come to my senses! I don't know how you can be so . . . so . . ." Glancing guiltily at Letty, Ned fell silent.

"Now, you listen to me," Raventhorpe snapped, making Letty wince. "I warned you how it would be, and your promises at this juncture mean nothing."

He went on in a low but menacing tone, ripping his brother's character to shreds and making Letty wish she were miles away. There seemed to be nothing she could do that would not emphasize her presence. Nor could she doubt, in the mood he was in, that Raventhorpe would order her to be silent if she dared say a word.

Ned's face was as red as a ripe tomato. Moisture glinted in his eyes, and although he stood the dressing-down manfully, a muscle twitched in his jaw, telling Letty that resentment was the strongest emotion he felt. She had seen her brother Gideon look exactly so on more than one occasion; and in her experience, that look led to nothing good. Much as she would have liked to let Mr. Delahan know she sympathized, however, she could not.

"Now, if you know what is good for you," Raventhorpe said, after speaking for what seemed like an age but could not have been but a minute or two, "you will get back to your studying. The best way to retrench, my lad, is to stay in your chambers until you are called to the bar, if that ever happens. Now, go!"

The younger man had looked straight ahead the whole time his brother talked, but now he turned abruptly to Letty and said,

"Your servant, ma'am." Then he wheeled his mount and urged it to a gallop, slowing again only as he left the ring.

Letty looked at Raventhorpe. He was still watching his brother, and she could see that his jaw clenched in much the same way that Mr. Delahan's had. Before she thought, she said, "What a very pretty way to introduce your brother to me, sir. I daresay that not quite half the people here today can have realized you were giving him a devilish scold."

He looked sharply at her, his face reddening in anger. "What I choose to say to my brother is no affair of yours."

"Quite true," she retorted affably. "How much better it would have been had you thought about that before you read him such a sermon with me looking on."

"Forgive me," he said stiffly. "You are quite right. I daresay you'd prefer that I not inflict my presence on you further." With that, he rode away to join a group of ladies, who, Letty suspected, would be only too glad to soothe his anger.

She rode by herself for some minutes before she saw Lady Tavistock riding sedately toward her. Giving Denmark a nudge with her heel, she rode to meet her, wondering if the woman meant to take her to task again for flirting. Little did she know, Letty thought; but in the event, the older woman's words surprised her.

"Her Majesty would be pleased if you would ride with her, my dear."

Since it was quite impossible to suspect the marchioness of levity, Letty said, "Now, ma'am?"

"Yes, of course. Do not keep her waiting, Letitia."

"No, ma'am, certainly not."

Melbourne had gone, and Victoria was indeed waiting with apparent patience on the little brown mare that was her favorite.

"Lady Tavistock said you wished to speak to me, Your Majesty."

"Yes, Lord Melbourne suggested that we speak further, Letitia."

"I must apologize, ma'am, for speaking out of turn last night."

"Your apology is accepted," Victoria said. "Lord Melbourne explained that you are accustomed to a great deal of freedom, for a female. Your father must be a most unusual man."

Uncertain what the queen's purpose was in suddenly befriending her, Letty wondered if Her Majesty wanted something from Jervaulx. Feeling reluctant at first, she became more at ease when she saw that Victoria felt envious of her childhood. Realizing that Melbourne must have exerted his influence on her behalf, Letty considered what his motives might have been. Since she kept half her mind occupied with that exercise while the other half concentrated on the conversation, it was not until she chanced to catch Raventhorpe's eye that it occurred to her that she might have someone else to thank for the queen's change of heart.

Glad though he was to see that his little chat with Melbourne had borne fruit, Raventhorpe was not feeling pleased with himself. He knew that he had behaved badly, and that he owed his brother an apology for ripping up at him like he had with Letitia right there. A horrid thing to have done.

Then to have snapped at her! That, he decided, was so unlike him as to be worthy of some deep thought. She had said nothing more than he had roundly deserved to hear. Was he, he wondered, growing to be such a coxcomb that he no longer considered the feelings of others at all?

His first impulse was to go after Ned at once and apologize to him, but he quickly thought better of it. The damage was done. Moreover, if the lad was to learn anything from it, he would not do so if Raventhorpe went haring after him with his hat in his hand. The arrival just then of the Duchess of Kent with several of her attendants reminded him that he could not simply leave even if he wanted to. He had to remain with the queen, as her lord-in-waiting, and his duties would continue into the afternoon, since she would be holding court.

Lady Letitia was not in attendance during the afternoon, and he found that he missed her. When Catherine Witherspoon seemed to ignore him while she flirted with Conroy and his aide, he wondered if Letitia had confided in her.

By the time he returned to Sellafield House, he had put his brother out of his mind. A note from Puck, reminding him that they were to dine together at Brooks's, gave his thoughts a new direction. He did not forget Letitia—she seemed to lurk in hidden corners of his mind all the time now—but he did succeed in keeping his mind on his dinner and then on his cards, as he and his friends made a night of it.

For the next few days, he attended to his duties at court, managed to avoid Sellafield's renewed demands on his purse, and took his mother and a bosom bow of hers to see the new play at Drury Lane. Her ladyship introduced the only sour note that evening with a wholly innocent observation as they were leaving.

"Thank you, Justin, for a wonderful outing," she said. "Indeed, my dear, I am particularly conscious of your consideration, in view of the fact that you must be anxious to get to Ascot for the races on Thursday."

"I shan't be going to Ascot, Mama. I must remain available for duty at court until Friday, and your dinner party is on Saturday."

"So it is, but . . . Oh, dear, such a pity that you must miss the races!"

"I will survive, ma'am. Have you received replies to all your invitations?"

"Oh, yes, and everyone is coming," she said happily. "Sir Adrian and Lady Devon-Poole, and their Susan, of course. The aunts are quite thrilled to be meeting her at last, for from some cause or other, they never have done so before."

He kept her chatting casually until they had reached the carriage, by which time he had learned that Letitia had accepted her invitation. After that, he lost interest in the dinner party, but he recalled the conversation the next day when he received the following note: *My dearest Justin,* it began. *Pray meet me at your great-aunts' house at two o'clock. It is a matter of some urgency. Yours, Susan.*

He knew of only one person who might thus sign a note to him, but it was nearly inconceivable that Miss Devon-Poole would send him so personal a note. He suspected, instead, that his younger brother was playing some prank in an effort to get even with him for their scene the previous Friday. Tempted though he was to ignore it altogether, he decided he could not, on the remote chance that it might be genuine. He had not clapped eyes on Miss Devon-Poole for several days, and much as he would have liked simply to ask her if she had written to him, he could not. To do so would be nearly as improper as the note itself was.

The possibility that disturbed him most was that she might have learned of his erstwhile interest in her. Puck had seemed to think that she did know, and Puck quite frequently was right about such things. Perhaps, Justin thought, he had underestimated her, and she was attempting to bring him up to scratch.

Thus it was that at two o'clock, he presented himself at the Upper Brook Street house, where Jackson admitted him at once, looking relieved to see him.

"Thank heaven, sir," the porter murmured.

"Is Miss Devon-Poole—" Justin began, only to break off in astonishment when Miss Abby fairly erupted from the stair hall. The magnificent hat she wore quivered with colorful beads and ribbons, all clearly chosen with care to match the varicolored stripes in her silk afternoon frock.

"Justin, thank the Lord! Of course she is here, and what you were thinking I cannot imagine. She walked in when Sir John Conroy was here, too, and how I managed to fob him off before she said why she had come I do not know."

"Conroy! What the devil was he doing here?"

"Goodness knows," she said airily. "Fortunately I was in such a dither as to how to reply to his questions that I could scarcely think. Had it been otherwise, I would very likely have said the worst thing possible when Jackson announced Miss Devon-Poole. Miranda will be so vexed when she learns that Sir John called when she was out, but she will be more vexed with you! To have arranged a tête-à-tête with her here when she's not even married, let alone she hasn't produced an heir for her husband, because, of course, she hasn't got a husband—"

"What the devil are you saying?" he snapped. "You can't be talking about Aunt Miranda!"

Miss Abby blinked in bewilderment. "Miranda's gone to Bond Street, thank heaven. I only wish she'd had the foresight to take Liza with her, because poor Liza was with me, of course, and now she's run away. Really, I'm quite vexed with you myself, Justin dear."

"Run away?" Justin's head was beginning to spin.

"Yes, and that's your fault, too, because you've encouraged her to believe that the main reason you come here is to play the piano for her. The minute Miss Devon-Poole said she was to meet you here, Liza knew what the meeting was for, of course. But how could you, Justin? I didn't even know that you knew our little secret, but if you do, you must also know that consorting here with a young woman of quality like Miss Devon-Poole goes right against our rules."

"What rules?" he demanded.

"Well, I know they are not written down, exactly, but they have always been perfectly clear to our patrons, after all, and—"

"What patrons?"

Turning pale, Miss Abby glanced wildly at Jackson, then grew quite still.

Justin, too, looked at Jackson. When the porter looked solemnly, silently back he turned again to Miss Abby. "Well? Answer me, ma'am. I'm waiting."

"I can see that," she said wretchedly. Then, visibly gathering herself, she said with more firmness, "If you do not know, then why did you invite Miss Devon-Poole to meet you here, if I may ask?"

"I did not invite her. I strongly suspect that Ned sent us each a message to meet here. He is out of charity with me, you see, and this smells like one of his pranks. He must have thought that my apparently inviting Susan to meet me here, when she has never met you, would cause me some embarrassment."

"Embarrassment?" Miss Abby shut her eyes for a moment, then said, "No wonder she looked at me so peculiarly when I said your arranging to meet her here was most irregular, but it is, Justin. I hope you'll tell Ned he must not do it again."

"I mean to say much more than that to him, ma'am, I promise you. But you must tell me at once what is going on here."

"Must I? What of Liza? Something dreadful may happen to her if—"

"Liza will come home when she has done with her sulks," he retorted ruthlessly. "Now, ma'am, I do not want to ask you again. Tell me at once."

"Very well," Miss Abby said with a watery sniff, "but Miranda will be so dreadfully vexed with me, and I am sure I cannot blame her in the least this time."

ELEVEN

Keenly aware of the porter's fascinated gaze, Justin hustled his reluctant relative into the central stair hall and shut the door. When she would have gone upstairs, however, he stopped her with a touch.

"One moment, Aunt Abby. Before we go to Miss Devon-Poole, I want a full explanation of all this, if you please."

"But I don't please," she protested. "Oh, not at all! Moreover, my dear, we mustn't leave her alone a moment longer than necessary. So rude, you know. I am wholly conscious of that, but when our maid, Mary, quite fortunately saw your carriage from the window, she told me, knowing that Miss Devon-Poole had said she was to meet you here, and I knew I must speak to you before—"

"You left Miss Devon-Poole all alone up there?"

"Not *all* alone, for her maid is with her, of course," Miss Abby said indignantly. "She is not likely to wander about, in any case, Justin. She is far too well bred to do that, and anyway, there is no one else here, now that Lady Wi—" She clapped a hand to her mouth, silencing herself.

"Lady who?" Justin demanded, his temper fraying rapidly.

"Miranda said not to name names," Miss Abby said virtuously. "Moreover, we simply must go up to her—to Miss Devon-Poole, that is—because really, it is quite dreadfully rude to leave her kicking her heels whilst we chat, my dear."

"Chat!" Justin struggled with increasing exasperation but

sternly resisted an urge to strangle the old lady. Lowering his voice, he said, "I will endeavor to smooth things over with Miss Devon-Poole, but you and I—and Aunt Miranda, too—are going to have a very long talk, ma'am, before any of us is much older."

"Are we, my dear? How . . . How very pleasant that will be."

She did not sound as if she thought it would be pleasant at all, however, so Justin said nothing more. He simply followed in her wake when she turned away and hurried up the stairs.

At the landing they met the orange cat, apparently strolling in search of Miss Abby, for it hastened its pace when it saw her.

She scooped it up and began to stroke it, murmuring, "Everything will be quite all right, Clemmy. You will see, my dear. Miranda will be vexed, but she will make things right again, I'm sure."

When they passed through the rose-filled anteroom into the smaller drawing room, they found Miss Devon-Poole sitting by a window. Fashionably dressed in a pale pink challis gown, she was gazing thoughtfully out at the gloomy day.

Her companion sat stiffly erect in a straight-back chair against the wall opposite the doorway.

At their entrance, Miss Devon-Poole turned, exclaiming, "My goodness me, my lord, there you are! I thought you were never coming, sir."

"Forgive me," Justin said, striding forward when she arose from her chair. "I am a villain to have kept you waiting."

"But, my goodness me, why did you want to meet here? And why were you not here before me? I expected you to be, you know, to introduce me to your aunts, only, of course, Miss Frome is alone here just now. But she was not expecting me, sir. You ought at least to have warned them I was coming."

He felt tempted to ask why she had come instead of sending him a civil reminder that she was unacquainted with either Mrs. Linford or Miss Frome. He suspected he would not relish the answer, however, so he held his tongue.

Fortunately, before his silence became noticeable, Miss Abby, still stroking the cat, threw herself into the breach. "Warned us of what, my dear Miss Devon-Poole? I am sure we should be delighted any time you deigned to pay us a call. As you say, though, my sister is not here presently, so perhaps another time might have been more convenient. However—"

"Don't try to polish this apple, Aunt Abby," Justin said with a sigh. "Miss Devon-Poole deserves the truth, I believe, distasteful as it is to me to reveal it."

Miss Abby frowned. "I am sure you know best, my dear, but are you quite sure you know the truth? In my experience, it quite frequently turns out to be something else altogether."

"I am as sure as I can be." Smiling ruefully at Miss Devon-Poole, he said, "I believe we can lay the blame for this mix-up at my scapegrace brother's door. I had occasion several days ago to speak sharply to him, and this is not the first time he has repaid me for such a thing by playing some stupid boy's prank."

"Prank, sir?" Miss Devon-Poole arched her eyebrows. "My goodness me, but I have done nothing to make him play pranks on me."

"No, of course you have not, and I sincerely apologize to you for this. I can assure you that it will not happen again."

She simpered. "As to that, my lord, I cannot pretend that I was prodigiously displeased to receive the invitation."

A tiny chill formed in the pit of Justin's stomach. He saw his great-aunt's mouth drop open comically and feared she was accurately reading Miss Devon-Poole's mind. The chit clearly had decided, either because of his brother's stupid prank or from some other, earlier cause, that the wealthiest man in London wanted to marry her.

An unwelcome gremlin at the back of his mind reminded him that he had once—quite long ago—judged her the perfect woman to be his wife. Telling himself it would serve as an excellent lesson to him never to make decisions before he had gathered all the facts, he exerted himself to remain courteous.

"I daresay your carriage is in the mews," he said, moving to ring the bell. "Jackson can send someone to tell your coachman you are ready to depart."

Miss Abby said politely, "Oh, must you go so soon?" Then, when Justin caught her eye, she added hastily, "But of course you must. What a mix-up, to be sure! Justin will read Ned a dreadful scold for this, I promise you."

"My goodness me, Miss Frome, but it is not so bad as that. I had the pleasure of meeting you, at all events, so now when we meet at Lady Sellafield's dinner party, we will not be strangers. I quite count that an advantage, don't you?"

"To be sure, my dear," Miss Abby said, casting another look at Justin.

Fortunately, Jackson arrived just then in response to Justin's ring.

Justin said, "Miss Devon-Poole is leaving, Jackson. Send a lad to order her coach to the door, will you?"

"Yes, my lord. I told them to take it round to the back. Won't be a minute, sir. Oh, and Mrs. Linford came in some five minutes ago," he added. "She was just going to take off her coat and join you here."

Gritting his teeth, Justin said, "Miss Devon-Poole will wait for her, then."

"Yes, indeed," Miss Devon-Poole said. "I want to meet *all* your relatives."

"I thought as much," he murmured.

"What did you say?"

"Nothing."

Again, Miss Abby stepped into the silence. "Would you like to pet Clemmy, Miss Devon-Poole? He is quite friendly, I promise you."

"I am sure he is, ma'am. I can hear him purring." Obediently, she stroked the cat, which ignored her with a haughtiness unmatched by any human.

Mrs. Linford came in a few moments later. "Well, now, isn't this nice," she said with her customary dignity and poise when

Justin presented Miss Devon-Poole. "Do forgive my tardiness, dear. Justin neglected to warn me that you were coming."

"Oh, I know, ma'am," Miss Devon-Poole said cheerfully. "We have already scolded him roundly, but as it happens it was not his fault."

"No?" Mrs. Linford looked expectantly at Justin.

"Ned's notion of a prank, ma'am." He explained briefly.

"I see. How naughty of him. Nonetheless, it has been pleasant to meet you, Miss Devon-Poole. You must call again one day."

"Yes, ma'am, thank you. You are coming with me, are you not, sir?"

"I will see you to your carriage, of course, but then I must return," Justin said. "I have business to discuss with my aunts."

She pouted but did not argue the point.

When he returned, he saw at once that Miss Abby had opened the budget, for Mrs. Linford was looking severe.

Shutting the door to the anteroom, he said, "Now, my dears, I want to know exactly what is going on here."

Mrs. Linford raised her chin. "I do not see how our affairs concern you."

"Since Aunt Abby told me that consorting with an unmarried young woman here goes against your rules, I think it concerns me very much," he said grimly. "She also mentioned patrons. I am not a fool, ma'am. Moreover, I have heard occasional whispers about a house of convenience in Mayfair. Is this that house?"

Faced with such a direct question, Mrs. Linford winced but did not look away. After a long moment, she said, "Dear me, do you think Ned knows? Is that why he sent that young woman here, do you think?"

"I don't know," he replied, "but I promise you, I will find out."

"Please do. I do not like to speak against your brother, but he is something of a prattlebox, I fear. Having managed to protect our reputations these twenty years and more, I'd think it a pity to have it all come out now through his carelessness."

"Have you gone mad?"

Stiffly she said, "I beg your pardon?"

"You have practically admitted that you are running a house of ill repute, ma'am, and now you say that you have been doing so for twenty years?"

He waited for her to deny the accusation, which was an outrageous one, to say the least.

Instead, to his dismay, she said, "I should not call it a house of ill repute, exactly, Justin. Your first definition was more nearly the correct one."

"We generally call it *une maison de tolérance,*" Miss Abby said earnestly. "In the French fashion, you know."

The phrase instantly brought Letitia to mind. He would have to sort this mess out quickly, before she learned that her inheritance could destroy her reputation and force her to resign her position at court. He could not allow that.

"I will have to stop this, you know," he said quietly.

Miss Abby cocked her head. "Miranda, can he do that? He would spoil everything for us!"

Mrs. Linford was regarding Justin with what seemed to him, under the circumstances, to be an unnatural calm. She said, "I do not think you can, you know. We are breaking no laws, you see, and we do not answer to you."

"I am sure you must be breaking at least one or two laws, Aunt Miranda. And even if you are not—"

"Even if we are," she interjected with that same unnerving calm, "you will find the authorities quite uninterested, Justin. Too many of their superiors take advantage of our service, you see, to want us to stop."

"That's quite true," Miss Abby agreed.

"But you simply cannot do things like this!"

"Why not?" Miss Abby asked, but both ladies regarded him with identical quizzical looks.

Sighing, he said, "If you don't understand, I don't know how to explain it to you, but not only am I sure that it must be against some law or other, it's just plain wrong. Persons of your quality simply don't allow illicit activities to go on inside their houses."

"But it is you who don't understand, Justin," Miss Abby said. "Persons of quite the highest quality seek out our service."

"Nonetheless you must stop it at once," he said firmly.

"Quite impossible," Mrs. Linford said.

"Yes, quite," Miss Abby agreed. "We could not think of it, my dear."

"Nonsense, you must!"

Drawing herself up, Mrs. Linford said austerely, "Pray, do not excite yourself so, Justin. We know exactly what we are doing. So long as you can button Master Edward Delahan's lips, we have nothing to fear."

"Nothing to fear? You *have* lost your minds!" The words came out much more sharply than he had intended; so sharply, in fact, that the cat leapt from Miss Abby's arms and dashed under a sofa.

"Oh, now see what you have done," Miss Abby exclaimed. "You have frightened poor Clemmy."

"Never mind that. I tell you, you must stop this nonsense. Why did you ever begin it?"

Matter-of-factly Mrs. Linford said, "Because we needed money, of course."

"Nonsense, your father left you very well to pass."

"Yes, he did," Miss Abby said, "only Horace spent it all."

"Horace?"

"Your grandfather, of course. Our dear brother. He is deceased now, of course, so one must not speak ill of him, but—"

"That will do, Abigail," Mrs. Linford said.

"Oh dear. Yes, of course." Miss Abby primmed her lips tightly together.

Justin looked from one to the other, then drew a long breath to calm his temper. "I think I begin to understand," he said at last.

"Excellent," Mrs. Linford said. "I shall order some tea." She moved toward the bell pull.

"Wait, Aunt Miranda, I have not finished. There is no cause for you to earn your way, you know. I have much more money than is good for me. The obvious solution to this imbroglio is for me to make you an allowance."

"Oh, no, we couldn't," Miss Abby said, clasping and unclasping her slender hands in visible distress. "Tell him, Miranda!"

"Quite right," Mrs. Linford said. "It would not do for us to take money from you, Justin. We value our independence, you see."

"But that would not change. I promise you, I don't mean to be tight-fisted."

"I am sure you would be all that is generous, my dear, but still it would not do for us." She hesitated, then added, "We prefer to go on as we are, you see."

"I cannot allow that."

Miss Abby said with a sigh, "You see, Justin dear, that's just what you would do, forever and ever."

He frowned. "What would I do?"

"You would tell us what to do and what not to do. We are very fond of you, my dear, but we don't want that."

"I wouldn't do any such thing!"

"Excellent," Mrs. Linford said. "Then we shall go on as we are. You could not pay our rent for us, in any case, you know. That would invalidate the tenancy agreement Cousin Augustus included in his will."

"Cousin Augustus is dead," Justin pointed out. "I am sure we can arrange something with Clifford and Lady Letitia so that you can continue to live here. You must know that she would never put you into the street."

"That is just what she said," Miss Abby said. "But that—"

"Before we put the problem to her, however, you must stop letting your so-called patrons come here to pursue their unfortunate activities. Only think how dreadful it would be if she should learn what you've been doing here."

"Oh, but she knows," Miss Abby said brightly, "and she don't mind a bit."

Stunned, Justin looked from one to the other, utterly speechless.

Mrs. Linford gazed steadily back at him.

Miss Abby nodded, setting the decorations on her hat dancing. Then, helpfully she said, "Letitia is quite French in her ways, you know, so she quite understands these things, my dear. I promise you, she did not fly into the boughs."

"Didn't she?" The fit of temper that had threatened him more than once during the past hour nearly took possession now. He held it at bay, saying through clenched teeth, "I shall discuss that with her. Indeed, I must go to see her at once."

Mrs. Linford glanced toward the little Sèvres clock on the mantelpiece. "I do not think you will find her at home just now. She paid us a morning call yesterday, you see, to offer to accompany us to the Royal Horticultural Society fete, which is to take place tomorrow at Chiswick, of course, and—"

"With her dear little monkey," Miss Abby interjected, smiling.

Justin exclaimed, "Monkey?"

"Oh yes, the dearest creature. This time he wore a red velvet collar to which she had attached the dearest silver chain. The naughty boy did not like it in the least, I can tell you, but it certainly made him less likely than last time to—"

"Abigail, you interrupted me."

"Oh, did I, Miranda? I am so dreadfully sorry, but when you mentioned Letty's visit, I recalled that it was entirely due to Jeremiah that—"

"Quite right, my dear, but as I was saying to you, Justin, I do not believe Letitia will be at home now. You will see her at your mama's dinner party tomorrow, of course, but she told us that the queen is holding court today. I collect that Her Majesty did not require your attendance."

"No," he said, frowning. It would not do to seek her out at Buckingham Palace to discuss such a topic, certainly.

"Her Majesty desired Letty to help greet the ambassador extraordinary and plenipotentiary from the king of the French and his countess," Miss Abby said. "Also, the envoy extraordinary and minister plenipotentiary from the king of the Netherlands. Because of her skill with languages, you know, but such an honor, my dear! Indeed, Letty said that Her Majesty has been treating her quite kindly of late."

"Has she?"

"Yes, and she confided to us that she thought she had you to thank for that. Did you speak to Lord Melbourne for her, dear?"

"I did drop a word in his ear," Justin admitted. "I thought perhaps Her Majesty was in danger of forgetting how powerful Jervaulx is, and what powerful men he counts as his friends. He is very tight with Wellington, you know."

"Is he?"

"How pleasant for him," Mrs. Linford said. "And how kind of you, my dear Justin, to have done such a good deed. I fear that some people at court were not treating Letitia as courteously as they ought, so your speaking up for her quite puts me in charity with you again."

"Does it, ma'am? I am gratified, but that does not alter my decision to put a stop to these activities of yours, one way or another."

"Well, in the meantime, I should be very grateful if you would look for Liza. Jackson told me that she ran out of the house, looking quite distressed."

"Liza will come back when she wants to," he said.

Mrs. Linford frowned. "She is not—how shall I say this? Liza does not always understand things. She . . ."

"She is as daft as a loon, Aunt," Justin said when she paused to choose her words again. "Indeed, ma'am, I do not know why you put up with her nonsense. For a servant girl to act as if she is the daughter of the house—"

"She is not a servant girl, either, my dear," Miss Abby said.

"That is the problem, you see. One does not know precisely how to deal with her. Once, when Admiral Rame was here—"

"That's quite enough," Mrs. Linford said swiftly. "We don't name names, Abigail. I do not know why I find it necessary to remind you of that so often."

"Admiral Rame! Good Lord," Justin exclaimed. "Don't tell me he is one of your so-called patrons! I won't believe it."

"I shan't tell you anything of the kind," Mrs. Linford said with lofty scorn.

"No, certainly not," Miss Abby agreed, flushing to the roots of her hair.

Mrs. Linford said, "I ask you again, however, to show some kindness toward Liza. If you have your carriage, you could drive about the streets until you see her."

"I have not got my carriage," Justin snapped. "Moreover, if I go anywhere, it will be to find Lady Letitia. Failing that, I shall pay my idiot brother a call that he will not soon forget. In any event, your Liza, as daft as she is, is still quite capable of finding her way back to this house. If she is not safely in this room again within a couple of hours at the most, I shall own myself very much astonished."

An hour later, returning to Jervaulx House from the palace, Letty unfolded a note presented to her on a silver salver and stared at its contents in dismay.

> *If you want to learn the truth about Little Liza before she disappears from London forever, you will find her at number 12 Boverie Street. Hurry!*
>
> *A friend.*

TWELVE

Letty did not recognize the handwriting on the note, but the scrawl was erratic, as if someone had snatched up the first bit of paper that came to hand and scribbled the message. A sense of urgency emanated from it, stirring her to haste. As she hurried to her dressing room, she realized that if she ordered out a carriage, it could take half an hour before it was at the door. It would be quicker to hail a hackney coach in the Strand. Moreover, a London driver would be more likely than Jonathan Coachman to know the whereabouts of Boverie Street.

Jenifry had gone out on errands of her own, but Letty did not require help to take her green velvet mantle from the wardrobe and fling it on over her afternoon frock. Finding the reticule that matched her mantle, she counted twenty pounds in coins and notes into it from her dressing-table drawer. Then, as she hastened toward the door, another thought struck her that sent her back to the wardrobe.

Reaching for a wooden box on the shelf, she took it down, opened it, and withdrew the small, silver-mounted pistol that her mother had given her before bidding her farewell from Paris. Making certain it was loaded, she plucked two more bullets from the box and stowed the lot in her reticule.

Then without wasting another moment, she hurried downstairs, out through the courtyard, and along the driveway to the Strand. Hailing the first cab she saw, she did not wait for the cabby to jump down and help her, although as she grabbed the door handle and pulled it open, he bestirred himself as if he meant to do so.

Urgently she said, "Boverie Street, do you know it?"

"Aye I do, that," he said, shifting whip and reins to one hand and scratching his scraggly chin whiskers with the other. "Be that whither ye're bound, then, lass?"

"Yes, number twelve. Is it far?"

"Not much, it ain't. Near the Temple, that be, above Hawker's Wharf."

"The Temple? Do you mean the Inns of Court?"

"Aye, the same. Can ye manage that door, then?"

"Yes," she replied, climbing in quickly and shutting the door with a snap. Letting down the window as the coach began to move, she called out, "As quickly as you can, driver. A child's life may be at stake."

"Wouldn't be the first, not there," he shouted back, but she heard the crack of his whip, and their speed increased. "Is that door shut tight?" he bellowed.

"It is," she yelled back. Putting up the window again, and settling back against the shabby squabs, she noted with distaste that the air inside the coach was distressingly noisome. Still, she forced herself to relax. Learning that the address lay near the Law Institutes had slightly reassured her about the neighborhood in which she would find Liza.

She had taken the precaution of bringing the message with her, and now she took it out of her reticule to look at again. The handwriting was unfamiliar, but that, she decided, might as easily be due to the author's haste as to any other cause. It would serve no purpose to ponder that person's identity until she had Liza safe.

That she would find the girl she did not doubt, as long as they were not too late. The coach made good speed up the Strand to Fleet Street and through Temple Bar. Then, just beyond St. Dunstan's West, the ancient church that over a century before had missed by mere yards being consumed by the Great Fire, the coach slowed significantly. They were now within the confines of the ancient City of London, that enclave of business and trade that frequently made its own laws and ignored those of greater London. When the coach made a wide right turn into a narrow, dirty street, Letty realized that she had misjudged the neighborhood.

Leaving the organized bustle of Fleet Street behind, they had entered the warren of crowded, narrow streets and alleyways abounding the Thames wharves. A moment later, the coach drew up with a lurch, and the coachman called out, "Here ye be, lass. That'll be one and six, if ye please."

Taking two shillings from her reticule, Letty got out of the coach unaided and handed them up to the jarvey. "Wait here for me," she said. "I shan't be long."

He tipped his hat and settled back on the box.

Seeing a number of unsavory characters who lounged nearby watching the pedestrians like feral cats watching a parade of tasty mice, Letty hoped he would not change his mind. Still, thanks to her childhood fondness for exploration, she had been in worse neighborhoods. Some areas of Paris that she had visited would doubtless have shocked her parents more than this street would.

The house before which she stood was three stories tall and quite narrow. Its neighbors abutted it without an inch between them, and its unimpressive entrance consisted of a single grey stone step leading to a wooden door. At one time the door might have been white, but presently it was a dingy color somewhere between grey and mud brown, the result of age, the general filth of the area, and chipping paint. Two panes of its fanlight were missing, there was no knocker, and when she pulled the bell, the cord offered no resistance. It hung swaying when she let go of it.

Undaunted by these details, she applied her knuckles, rapping three times loudly, then stepping back to wait. She had to repeat the action twice before it got results; but at last she heard the spat of footsteps on tile or wood inside. A moment later, the door opened.

A burly man with bushy red hair, wearing a suit of drab clothing that was none too clean, stood glaring at her. He said gruffly, "Wot d'ye want?"

"I am looking for a girl called Liza," Letty said. "I believe she is here."

"Wot if she is?"

"I want to speak with her."

The man looked her up and down, smirked, then glanced past her to the street. "Ye've come alone?"

"Except for my driver," Letty replied.

A scornful look flitted over his face that told her he did not think much of her driver. He looked her over again, and she believed that in his mind he was measuring her slight frame against his own much larger one. Again the smirk flitted across his lips, and he shrugged. "Come ye in, then, but step lively."

A shiver shot up her spine as she crossed the threshold, telling her at once that she ought to turn tail and run. Instead, she squared her shoulders, raised her chin, and fixed a firm, unblinking gaze on her host.

"Ye be a lovely little mort," he said, smiling. The smile was not pleasant. Not only did it reveal blackened, broken teeth, but there was little humor in it.

"Take me to Liza now, please," Letty said briskly.

"Oh, aye, I'll take ye." He gestured toward the narrow, rickety-looking stairs, adding, "Up the dancers, then. She's above."

Holding her skirt up out of the dust with one hand, she followed him up, listening for any sound that might indicate the presence of others on the premises. She heard nothing of the sort, but the hairs on the back of her neck seemed to twitch. Taking advantage of the fact that his back was to her, she managed to open her reticule without losing her grip on her skirts, and took out her pistol. Concealing it in the folds of her mantle, she sent a prayer heavenward.

At the landing, he moved toward a closed door, took a keyring from his coat pocket, and plunged one of the keys into the keyhole. A moment later, he removed it and pushed the door open, saying, "She's there. Go right in, then, me lovely."

"I think we will go in together, if you don't mind," Letty said quietly.

"Now that's where ye're wrong," he said, returning the keyring to his pocket without looking at her. "Ye'll be wantin' a nice long visit with the lass, I expect."

"I don't think so," she said, pointing the pistol at him and taking care at the same time that she did not aim it at the open door. "Liza, stay where you are!"

He looked at her then and stiffened. "What the devil? Give me that popgun!"

"No."

When he stepped toward her, she pulled the trigger. He jumped back again, unharmed. "Damnation! It were loaded!"

"Of course it was loaded," Letty said. "Moreover, it still *is* loaded. This pistol holds more than one bullet, and the only reason you are not lying dead on the floor is that I did not choose to kill you. I can hit anything I aim for at nearly any distance that a bullet will travel. I have shot all manner of guns since childhood, because my father and mother believed I should learn most of the same skills that my brothers learned."

"Then ye had damned unnatural parents," he said with feeling.

"You are entitled to your opinion, of course. No, do not move. I am feeling rather more nervous than is customary for me, so my finger may twitch on the trigger, and it's set for very little pressure. Liza, you can come out now!"

"Be that you, my lady?"

"It is," Letty said, noting with satisfaction the stunned reaction of her captive to her title. "Come out at once. Why did you come here?" she added, when Liza emerged warily from the shadowy depths of the room, looking tired and untidy.

The girl's eyes filled with tears. "They said I was to come, that they had a surprise for me, that I would make lots of money, but they were horrid, miss!"

"Did anyone touch you, Liza?"

"Aye, they dragged me out of that carriage, and they shoved me in that horrid room," Liza said indignantly, pointing dramatically.

Letty nodded, satisfied. Turning to the red-haired man, she said, "What did you think you were going to do with her?"

"It ain't what we *were* going to do but what we *are* going to do. We bought the lass fair and square, and there's a wee house where they're expecting her. She can make a good living, if she behaves 'erself, but it's nothing to what ye could make, me lovely. I think we'll take the pair of ye. I don't believe ye'll shoot me, ye see." As he spoke the last sentence, he leapt at her.

Stepping aside to elude his grasp, Letty aimed and pulled the trigger.

With a scream of agony, he collapsed to the floor, clutching his right thigh. Blood oozed through his fingers.

"Hold your hands tightly over the wound," Letty said calmly, shaking the other two bullets out of her reticule. "Then perhaps you will not bleed to death. Liza, the key to that door is in his pocket. Get it, please. Do not let go of your leg," she said to the man, "or I promise you, you *will* die."

Evidently he believed her, for he did not stir when Liza approached him.

Timidly she removed the keyring, then looked quizzically at Letty.

"Keep it for the moment," Letty said. Then, to her captive, she said, "I must ask you to crawl into that room. No, do not argue with me. I have no sympathy for your pain, and I am feeling extremely short-tempered. Indeed, considering that you intended to take us both prisoner, you deserve more than a mere hole in your leg. Go on now. You can move more quickly than that."

As he began to inch his way, she replaced her bullets. When she snapped the gun closed, she had the satisfaction of seeing she had truly frightened him, for he scooted across the threshold more quickly than she had thought he could.

Liza shut the door and locked it, then turned, saying, "Oh, miss, I—"

"We've no time to talk," Letty said. "We must hurry. I've got a hackney waiting below, but the sooner we get away, the better. I have the most awful feeling that this has been too easy."

When they reached the street, the coach was nowhere in sight.

A piercing whistle shrieked from above.

Realizing that their captive had managed to reach the window and open it, and seeing two men pushing through the stream of pedestrians from the Fleet Street end of Boverie, Letty cried, "Run, Liza! That way!"

The girl needed no other bidding, and took off toward the river, holding her skirts almost to her waist. Letty dashed after her, pistol in hand, but she knew she could not use it in the crowded little street, and she would not have wished the hurrying pedestrians elsewhere. She and Liza slipped between them, dashing through open spaces, then slowing when they had to push past someone again. For all the heed anyone paid, they might have been invisible. When a dimly lit opening appeared on their right, Letty pushed Liza toward it. "In there," she cried. "Maybe they won't see us!"

The alley was empty at the moment. It proved to be short, emerging in another narrow street. Turning toward the river again, solely because she thought her pursuers would expect her to run toward Fleet Street, Letty glanced over her shoulder and saw to her annoyance that one of the men was not far behind.

A larger space appeared before her, a cobbled square that seemed to grow wider at the far end. She could see the river now through a greying mist, and she remembered the jarvey saying that Boverie Street was near Hawker's Wharf. Cutting right, she found herself approaching yet another narrow, dark alley.

Plunging into it, she called, "Here, Liza, quickly!"

She was breathing hard now, and behind her the girl gasped, "I'm fair spent, Miss Letty."

"No, you are not. You are merely winded, which is better than dead, so think about that. Oh, Lord save us, there's a gate at the end!"

Praying that they would not find it locked, since it was too tall to climb over and too close to the ground to roll under, she ran toward it, hearing ominous footsteps pounding the cobbles behind them. When she reached the gate and yanked the handle, it held, and for a moment she wanted to shriek with frustration, but her fingers found the latch, and this time she pushed. The gate swung away from her, revealing a broad expanse of lush greensward bordered by gravel walks and brick buildings, all red, except for two that were cheerfully yellow. A number of men strolled along the paths. Others sprawled on the greensward in groups, talking. All of them were of quite a different cut from that of the men chasing her.

Her feet crunching rapidly along the nearest gravel path, she glanced over her shoulder to see her pursuers stop short in the open gateway. They glared at her, and before they turned back, she saw both clearly enough to know she had not seen either before that day. Still uncertain of her safety, she surveyed the nearest group of men and realized that several of them wore academic robes.

"Liza," she said with a chuckle, "I believe we've stumbled into the Temple."

"Be this some sort o' church, then, miss?"

"No, it is the law courts."

Horrified, Liza said, "Will they take us up, then, miss?"

"No, no. In fact, if I can . . . Forgive me for disturbing you," she said to a young man seated on a bench, poring over a large book.

He looked up in surprise. "I say, I'm dreadfully sorry. I did not see you. But what are you doing here? We practically never see females in King's Bench Walk."

"Is that where we are?" Letty felt disappointed. "I was hoping that we were in the Inner Temple."

"You are," he said with a smile, getting to his feet in belated haste. "I say, I ought to present myself. I'm Jarvis Bucknell. My friends call me Jerry."

"You are a law student, then?"

"Yes, that's right, for my sins."

"I am Letitia Deverill, and this is Liza," Letty said, and instantly experienced a vision of Miss Dibble with features arranged in disapproval of such informality. Somehow, though, it did not seem a time to stand on ceremony. "Dare I ask you, sir, if you are acquainted with Mr. Edward Delahan? He is—"

"Ned? I should say I am. In fact, he's a particular friend of mine."

"Oh, how fortunate that you are the one I approached, then!"

"Well, you could have asked anyone," Mr. Bucknell said modestly. "His brother's the wealthiest man in London, you see. Thanks to that fact, I promise you, everyone here knows Ned. He don't count it an advantage, either, I can tell you," he added with a crooked smile.

Aware that she still held her pistol concealed between folds of her mantle, Letty glanced over her shoulder again. The gateway remained reassuringly empty, so she moved to replace the weapon in her reticule. Hearing a gasp from her newfound acquaintance, she looked ruefully at him. "I beg your pardon if my pistol startled you, sir. Some men were chasing us, you see."

"Well, I don't see," Mr. Bucknell said, "but I do know better than to ask impertinent questions of a lady. Otherwise, I should certainly want to know how one like you comes to find herself in an alley near Hawker's Wharf, let alone running away from bad men with a pistol in her hand."

As heartening as she found his company, Letty refused the bait, saying only, "I am glad you do not ask me, sir. It is a long tale to tell, and I would much rather find Mr. Delahan if he is near at hand."

"I daresay he is," Mr. Bucknell said. "We are members of

the same honorable society, you see, and we'll be keeping commons this evening. That means we'll dine in the society hall, so I expect he'll be there if we don't find him at once. Shall I escort you to his chambers?"

Accepting his offer, although she was well aware of the impropriety of visiting an unmarried gentleman in his residence, Letty followed him toward one of the redbrick buildings. Since Mr. Bucknell did not seem to expect further conversation, she spent the next few moments trying to imagine what Mr. Ned Delahan's reaction would be when he saw his visitors.

He opened the door to his chambers himself, and stood gaping at her until Mr. Bucknell said jokingly, "Shut your mouth, Ned. Even on a gloomy day like this one, there are flies about."

Letty said, "Good afternoon, Mr. Delahan. I hope you remember me."

Giving his head a shake, he said, "Yes, of course I do, Lady Letitia, but what on earth has brought you here? And Liza, too. Crikey! I say, there's nothing amiss at home, is there? Mama? My father? Justin?" His face grew pale.

Hastily, she said, "Nothing of the sort, sir, I promise you. You would not receive that sort of news from me."

"No, no, of course not. Forgive me. I say, ought I to invite you inside? My man is not even here presently, so I am quite alone, and I confess, I don't know precisely what I am to do in such a circumstance."

Letty drew a long breath, then released it to say, "I must apologize for coming to you like this. However, although our pursuers lacked the courage to follow us into King's Bench Walk, I fear they may yet be near at hand."

"Pursuers? I say, what the devil—?"

"Well may you ask, sir," she said when he broke off to stare at her. Aware that Mr. Bucknell was also listening with great interest, she said, "You deserve an explanation, but I cannot think it would do your reputation any more good than it would do mine if you admit me to your chambers. Liza and I would be grateful, however, if you would escort us to hail a hackney coach in Fleet Street."

"I certainly will, but I hope you'll tell me what are you doing here."

"Someone enticed Liza to a ramshackle house in Boverie Street—"

"That's the only sort there is in Boverie Street."

"Yes, well, I received a message telling me where to find her. When I arrived, a man tried to lock me in the room where he was keeping her prisoner, but I had anticipated such a move, of course, and was able to thwart his plan."

"Well done," Mr. Bucknell said, regarding her with fascination. "Uh, how did you thwart him?"

"I expect you have already guessed, sir, since you have seen my pistol. I'm afraid I shot him."

"Shot him," Ned exclaimed. "I say, who the devil was he?"

"I don't know."

"Is he dead?"

"I sincerely hope not. I shot him in the upper leg—the merest flesh wound, I should think—for although he was quite noisy about it, his blood did not flow too freely. Moreover, he was able to get to the window and whistle an alarm to his friends in the street, so I believe I am not being overly optimistic."

Clearly shaken, Ned did not speak for a long moment, nor did Mr. Bucknell. However, the latter looked more amused than upset, Letty thought. She waited for Ned to gather his wits, but when he did, he turned not to her but to Liza. "What the devil were you up to, my girl?"

Biting her lower lip, Liza did not look at him. Instead, drawing a pattern on the step with the toe of one foot, she muttered, "They said they'd give me money."

"Crikey, haven't you got a brain? I can guess what they wanted with you."

"You would be right, sir," Letty said. "The man I shot admitted as much to me. He said there is a house where an abbess waited in expectation of her arrival. He implied that the abbess would likewise welcome me."

Ned's eyes narrowed, but he seemed to accept her knowledge of abbesses. "You said you received a message, telling you where to go, did you not?"

"Yes, and I can see that you are thinking the same thing that I quickly came to believe. Someone appears to have baited a trap for me."

"Can you guess who that someone might be?"

"I have a strong suspicion, because there is one person who has steadily opposed my presence at court, but I should not name names without proof."

He nodded. "Well, Jerry and I will see you to a coach, ma'am, although I daresay I ought not to let you go home in a common hackney."

"I came in one," Letty said. "I told the man to wait for me, but although he seemed agreeable, he did not stay."

"No doubt someone paid him off and told him to leave. Your captors wouldn't want him wondering what had become of you."

"I daresay that's true," she said.

"I should take you home myself," he said.

"No, sir, you need not. Mr. Bucknell told me that your society expects you to keep commons tonight, and I know how important it is that you do so. If you will find us a coach with an imposing driver who can be trusted to deliver us safely to Upper Brook Street, you will have done all anyone can expect."

"But see here, I want to know more about this," Ned protested.

"I shall be glad to discuss it with you later," Letty said, shooting a speaking look in Liza's direction. "This is neither the time nor the place, however."

"But when? May I call upon you tomorrow, or must you go to the palace?"

"I'll be at the palace just in the morning, but I have promised to attend the Horticultural Society's fete tomorrow afternoon with Mrs. Linford and Miss Abby."

"But that's excellent! I need a holiday. I shall meet you in Upper Brook Street at noon and serve as your escort. Whilst my great-aunts are exclaiming their appreciation of all the medal-winners, you and I can find an opportunity to talk."

Though the prospect did not thrill her, Letty agreed, thinking it would be churlish to refuse after he had been so kind. Nevertheless, when they had walked to Fleet Street by a much-less-unsavory route, while Mr. Bucknell gave directions to the brutish-looking jarvey they selected, Letty said to Ned, "I hope you won't think it necessary to mention any of this to your brother, sir."

"To Justin? Crikey, I should think not! You can trust me, ma'am. Not a word of this shall cross my lips. In any case," he added naively, "I won't see him before I see you at noon tomorrow." Turning to Mr. Bucknell, he demanded to know if that gentleman had made it clear to the jarvey that he was to protect his passengers with his life. Upon learning that he had, he helped them into the coach.

Having watched the coach rattle away, Ned managed to extricate himself from Jerry Bucknell's company by the simple expedient of telling him that he knew no more about the matter than what they both had heard and that he needed to study several points of law before dinner. He spoke truthfully, but he did not think he would be able to concentrate very well until he learned more about the incident that so amazingly had brought Lady Letitia to his doorstep.

Strolling back to his chambers, he replayed the conversation in his mind, becoming so lost in thought that he did not realize his cluttered front room was no longer unoccupied until a familiar voice said sternly, "I'm told that you've taken to entertaining females in your chambers, sir. Have you taken leave of your senses?"

"Justin! Crikey, what are you doing here?"

"I daresay I am not welcome, but you will have to accommodate me nonetheless. I have come to discuss your sense of humor, you see."

Ned flushed but said nothing, trying to gather his wits.

"You should just be thankful that no more came of the incident than some small embarrassment to Miss Devon-Poole and myself," Justin said. "Otherwise you would find me much angrier now, and would doubtless suffer accordingly. Just how much do you know about that house?"

Bewildered, Ned said, "I know what you know. What else *could* I know?"

"But you don't deny that you sent messages to me and to Miss Devon-Poole, so that we would meet there."

Ned grimaced. "Would it do me any good to deny it?"

"It would diminish my respect for you."

"I didn't know you had any," Ned said resentfully.

"I am extremely displeased with you, as you will soon learn if you do not already know it, but I will believe what you tell me, Ned. You are not a liar."

With an odd sense of gratification, Ned said, "I did play you a trick. I can see now that it was not well done of me, since Miss Devon-Poole has never done me any wrong, but at the time I thought only of getting back at you. I—"

"But why the Upper Brook Street house?"

Ned shrugged, thinking it a small point. "Mama said the aunts had not yet met Miss Devon-Poole, that's all," he said. "I knew it would prove embarrassing to you if you found her there expecting that you had invited her to meet them."

"But what made you think *she* would go there on such a pretext?"

"Meeting your family, of course. You're going to marry her, aren't you?"

"Since I have taken great pains to avoid giving her or anyone else cause—"

"Oh, Justin, don't be daft! Everyone knows."

"No, everyone does not know," Justin snapped. "Some may suspect. God knows, Puck Quigley says they do. But no one knows, Ned, and until today Miss Devon-Poole certainly had no reason to think such a thing. But thanks to you . . ."

At that point the lecture Ned had anticipated engulfed him. He stood it manfully (having expected it to be much worse) until Justin said, "By heaven, I'll see to it that you mend your thoughtless ways and apply yourself more diligently to your studies. You are going to do exactly as I bid you, or—"

"Or nothing," Ned retorted rudely. "I'll apologize to Miss Devon-Poole because I agree that I should, but you are not my father, and I wish you would remember that. The worst you can do is to stop paying my fees here, but I'd survive. I am very grateful to you, Justin—truly, I am—but by heaven, neither that gratitude nor your generosity gives you the right to control my every breath and step."

"That's a damned exaggeration," Justin snapped. "If I try to keep you from stepping over the bounds, it is through no more than concern for your welfare."

"It is no such thing! You want to control everyone around you. Why, I daresay that is why Lady Le—" He broke off, instantly regretting his unruly tongue.

"Don't stop there," Justin said, his voice growing suddenly very quiet. "Finish your sentence, sir. You begin to interest me."

"It was nothing," Ned said.

"Who were the two females who came here? I want the truth, Ned. The chap who described them to me said that one looked like a servant but the other clearly was a lady and she had red hair. I could not believe my first suspicion, but now . . ."

"I won't tell you," Ned muttered.

"You don't need to tell me now," Justin growled. "Your refusal tells me enough. What the devil was she doing here? Surely you did not invite her."

"Well, I didn't, but I don't know why you should be so certain of that, when you have accused me of much worse things. It just so happens—" He broke off. "No, I won't tell you. I promised—"

"Promised, did you? By heaven, you'll tell me if I have to—"

Startled by the fury in his brother's expression, Ned interjected hastily, "It was nothing, really! She came to me for help, that's all."

"All? That explains nothing! Be plain with me if you don't want to feel the full extent of my anger."

Believing him, and angry himself now, Ned said, "It was Liza. Lady Letitia came to find her, and what I began to say before is that I can certainly see why she didn't go to you for help instead, or want me to tell you what she'd done."

"No doubt you can, but that is no explanation." Justin took a step toward him, and Ned capitulated, telling him all he knew.

"I don't understand the whole of it, myself," he added when he had repeated everything Letty had told him. "I don't think she should be traveling about the city in hackney coaches, and she certainly should not have walked into a house like the one she described to me, or shot anyone."

"Shooting that scoundrel was the most sensible thing she did," Justin snarled. "By heaven, when I get my hands on her—"

"She's got less reason to listen to you than I do," Ned pointed out. "You hold no authority whatsoever over her."

"Perhaps not, but she is going to hear what I want to say to her nonetheless. I'd go at once, but I daresay even if she were at home, her servants wouldn't let me in the house this late in the day, let alone tonight. In any event, I daresay she will be going out somewhere or other. I'll find her tomorrow, though, and by heaven—"

"You'll be disappointed then, too, unless you think you can bellow at her right under the queen's nose," Ned said. "She is attending Her Majesty all morning, and then she is going to the Horticultural Society fete at Chiswick with the aunts, and tomorrow night, of course, there is Mama's dinner party. Perhaps you can imagine ripping up at her there, but it would be dashed bad manners."

Instantly Ned wished he had held his tongue, for Justin said grimly, "You needn't worry about that. I don't intend to wait that long."

THIRTEEN

"This is madness," Raventhorpe growled to Puck Quigley the next day as the carriage wended its way slowly—exceptionally slowly—toward the Royal Horticultural Society gardens.

Under an overcast sky, the line of carriages extended unbroken all the way from Hyde Park Corner to Turnham Green. Despite the seeming snail's pace they moved steadily, so that at numerous points along the road it was impossible for a pedestrian to cross from one side to the other in safety.

"You needn't have come," Puck pointed out, letting down the window on his side so that he could look out. "In fact, we can still turn back."

"You'll soon have us covered with dust," Justin said with annoyance.

Puck grinned at him, unabashed. "Is this the same man who led me and my best hunter through a bog last year, chasing an infernal fox?"

"Put up the damned window, Puck."

"Very well, in just a moment," Puck said amiably, his head still outside. "I must say, it says much for the police and the manner in which they carry out their duties that we have seen no accidents and that they have been able to preserve order here. I should not be at all amazed, you know, to see an outburst of fisticuffs in the midst of all this traffic."

"There will be such an outburst inside this carriage if you

do not put up that damned window. I cannot imagine why I brought you."

"I don't know, either," Puck retorted with his usual candor as he put up the window at last. "You have been most uncivil to me ever since you picked me up at my digs. Since you are in this mood, I don't know why you did not select someone like your hapless brother to be your companion today."

"It was a hard decision, I'll grant you, especially since Ned had made plans to attend," Justin said, but he felt himself relax. Ruefully he added, "Sorry I'm such a bear, Puck. I already bit off Ned's head and ordered him to stay in his chambers today and study."

"Then who besides Ned has had the extreme bad fortune to annoy you? You cannot have got yourself this exercised merely over another tiff with him."

Justin was silent.

"Ah-ha, it's a wench! Tell me, my lad, can it be that the Honorable Susan has— No, no! Oh, my dear Puck, where have your wits gone begging?" he asked himself with a laugh. "It's the little Tory, of course. She's been a thorn in your tea since she first arrived in London. What has she done or said now to annoy you?"

"I am sure that what she says or does has nothing to do with me," Justin said stiffly, irritated that Puck had hit the mark so swiftly. There were a number of things on his plate just now that would strain the temper of a saint, but the first that came to mind every time, was Letitia's foolishness in going to Boverie Street. "Nobody tells her what to do, much less what to think," he said, speaking the thought aloud. "She has her own approach to life, and she's utterly indifferent to criticism."

"And that's what stings you to the prick, my lad," Puck declared triumphantly. When Justin frowned, he added hastily, "It's not altogether true that she's indifferent, you know. She is constantly rising to someone's bait. One has only to tell her that the Whig way of doing things is the best way."

"I certainly don't think she makes it her object in life to convert others to her political point of view," Justin said.

"Didn't say that she did," Puck said. "She just loves a good verbal battle, if you ask me. In that respect, she is no different from you, my lad."

"Don't be absurd. That conceited independence of hers will land her in the suds before long. Indeed it has done so already, and she's lucky to have got away with a whole skin—at least, so far," he added on an ominous note.

Ignoring the danger sign, Puck said, "Conceited independence?"

"You heard me. She's got away with it this long because of her father's lofty position. She's been spoiled, by God, and she wants someone to bring her to heel."

"I'd like to see someone try," Puck said, chuckling. "I think even you might fail in that venture, my lad. Whatever did she do to set you off like this?"

"She nearly got herself captured by villains looking for females to sell to an abbess," Justin snapped, adding, "Has this carriage come to a complete standstill?"

Letting down his window again, Puck stuck out his head and said, "I can see the gate some distance up ahead. Do you hear the music? The papers listed at least seven regiments that have sent bands to represent them at this affair. What a racket it must be! Here now, what are you doing?" he exclaimed when Justin leaned across him to open the carriage door, then got up and kicked the step down.

"What the devil does it look like I'm doing? I'm getting out to walk," he said, suiting action to words, then adding, "Keep the carriage, Puck. I'll find you when I can, but first I've got business with Lady Letitia."

"Dash it all, Justin," Puck protested, "if you think I'm paying the fee for this coach of yours, you've got another think coming. My pockets are to let, so I'll have to get out, too, and leave your coachman to fend for himself. Most likely, he'll turn tail and drive off, leaving you to walk home."

"Oh no, he won't," Justin said, shutting the door with a snap.

"Well, then," Puck said through the open window, "he'll pull into someone's field to wait, and you'll end up walking home because you won't be able to find him again."

"Don't be daft; he's got money to pay the entrance fee," Justin said. "If you *want* to get down and walk, be my guest, but I won't wait for you. My impatience to find her ladyship and tell her what I think of her recent activities is getting the better of me." He turned away, but Puck's cheerful voice followed him.

"Don't kill her, Justin. I can rescue you from the law if you only knock her down, but if you murder her there won't be much I can do to save you."

Justin stopped, drew a long breath, then turned back to the carriage. Having made no effort to step down, Puck observed his return with open interest.

Waiting until he stood next to the open window, Justin said quietly, "I doubt that it is necessary to say this, Puck, but I trust you will keep all this to yourself."

"I'm not the one whose tongue has been flapping," Puck said virtuously, "but if Her Majesty should chance to ask me . . . She will be here today, will she not?"

"I don't know, nor do I care." Justin reached up to grip the other man's arm, giving it a squeeze as he said, "You're a good friend, Puck. Not many would put up with my fits of temper like you do."

"You underestimate your appeal, my lad. Think of your riches and all the friends they draw to your side. Oh, don't throttle me," he added with a chuckle. "Go and do your worst to the Lady Letitia. Despite her lack of inches, she is more up to your weight than I am, assuming you can even find her in that crowd."

Shaking his head, Justin turned on his heel and strode to the entrance gates, his pace much swifter than that of the lined-up carriages. He had to pause briefly to buy a ticket of admission, which he showed to the police officer at the gate, but then he plunged into the crowd to begin his search.

Puck's witticisms had softened his mood, but a few minutes of battling the crowd in search of one small redheaded female soon stirred his temper again. He met more than one friend who tried to point out a particularly fine specimen of horticulture to him, or to draw him into conversation. Resisting these efforts, he continued the hunt, growing more irritable by the moment. Thus when he saw her at last, strolling casually ahead of him between his two elderly great-aunts, he felt a surge of fury quite out of keeping with the gaiety of the occasion.

"We shall view the pelargoniums next," Mrs. Linford said to Letty and Miss Abby, consulting her program. That settled, she added with approval, "The recent showers have proven most beneficial to the turf and flower beds of these gardens."

"Oh, yes indeed," Miss Abby agreed. "The lawns look as smooth as velvet and are quite green, which makes the flower beds look amazingly colorful. Why, every hue and tint of nature must be represented here today. Quite relieving to the eyes, is it not, Letty, my dear, after living in a grey-and-white metropolis?"

Letty agreed that it was all very pleasant. The two old ladies had been behaving strangely ever since she had picked them up in her carriage. They kept up a stream of pointless conversation, flitting from topic to topic like bees buzzing from blossom to blossom in search of nectar.

Upon her arrival in Upper Brook Street, when she had asked politely how they were, Mrs. Linford had said, "Perfectly well; shall we go now?"

Miss Abby had colored up to her eyebrows, saying that she thought she always felt well, except when she didn't. When she went on to provide examples to support the odd statement, Mrs. Linford made no effort for once to silence her.

Letty thought perhaps she had embarrassed them a trifle by showing up the previous evening with Liza in tow, so she did not press them further. Nor did she think it prudent to ask after Liza just then.

In the carriage and since their arrival at the gardens, she had been listening to their errant discourse with just half an ear, but they did not seem to mind that she offered no more than a vague comment from time to time.

The scene before them was delightfully animated. Despite a lack of sunshine, the flowers were lovely and the crowd cheerful, stirred to gaiety by the music of military bands placed strategically throughout the gardens. Not only had many members of the beau monde assembled for the afternoon at Chiswick, but also a great number of much more common folk.

Elderly ladies and gentlemen occupied benches and chairs alongside the paths, while younger, more active visitors promenaded to and fro. The gay costumes of the ladies formed a striking but pleasing contrast to the deep-emerald-green grass and the variegated foliage of the trees, adding to the general effect.

Huge marquees and tents dotted the lawns to afford shelter in the event of rain, which continued to threaten but so far had not manifested itself.

Mrs. Linford had declared the exhibits first-rate, and even to Letty's untrained eye, the fruits, flowers, and plants that had won prizes appeared to be of surpassing beauty and rarity. However, the throng of people was so thick and varied in class that she had not been able to recognize more than a few of the men and women of fashion and rank who were present.

She did not realize that she was looking for anyone in particular until she saw Raventhorpe. The instant she clapped eyes on him, her heart leapt, but at nearly the same moment she saw the expression on his face. A chill raced up her spine.

"Just look at this," Mrs. Linford said, briefly reclaiming her attention. "They've given Mr. Cock the large silver medal again.

Mr. Gaines has won only the Knightian, but in my opinion, his pink pelargonium is superior to Mr. Cock's red."

Miss Abby said, "Do you really think so, Miranda? Perhaps Mr. Gaines will fare better with his heartsease."

Their voices faded from Letty's consciousness as she watched Raventhorpe's approach. She had not felt much surprise when Ned failed to appear at noon as promised, having assumed that he had chosen to study instead. Now, though, seeing Raventhorpe's face, she was as certain of what must have happened as if she had witnessed it herself. Ned had, as her brothers would have said, peached on her. Clearly he had told Raventhorpe exactly what had happened at Hawker's Wharf, and now here was Raventhorpe, intending to ring a peal over her.

A sudden impulse to flee astonished her, and she fought it, telling herself that she had nothing to fear from him. Her self did not seem to listen, though, and the closer he came, the stronger the urge grew to run away.

"Good gracious, there's Justin," Miss Abby exclaimed. "He never told us he meant to come here today, did he? I wonder if he's brought Sally with him."

"If he has," Mrs. Linford said dryly, "he seems to have mislaid her. It is just as well, too, since he looks black as thunder again. This is my fault, I'm afraid, Letitia. Something else happened that we ought to have told—"

"Oh, no, ma'am, don't blame yourself," Letty said. "He has no doubt heard about my adventure yesterday, when I went to fetch Liza home."

"Adventure? What adventure? You told us only that you found her, and after I scolded her for running off so foolishly, she ran straight up to her bedchamber."

Letty had told them as little as she thought she could get away with, but that seemed to be the least of her worries now. She did not even have a chance to reply, for Raventhorpe was upon them.

"I want a word with you," he said curtly. "Privately."

"Indeed, sir," she replied with forced calm. "I do not know how you can accomplish that amidst all these people. Perhaps another time—"

"Now," he snapped. "We'll find—"

"Really, Justin, you should guard your tone, sir," Mrs. Linford said. "One does not address a lady so rudely. You astonish me."

"Do I, ma'am? I doubt that. You have known me all my life, after all. You need not suffer my presence long, however, if you will excuse us both."

"I cannot leave your aunts," Letty said, gathering her wits. "I promised to lend them my escort for the afternoon, and in this mixed crowd, I do not think it is safe for them to—"

"No one will molest them," he interjected grimly. "I won't keep you long."

"Just long enough to murder me," she muttered.

"If that is true, it is no more than you deserve," he retorted.

Miss Abby gave a squeal. "You don't mean that, Justin!"

Ignoring her, he glared at Letty. "Are you coming?"

"You haven't said where you want to take me," she pointed out. "I won't leave these grounds without your aunts, and we can scarcely be private here."

Mrs. Linford said austerely, "It is not at all suitable for you to speak to her privately here or anywhere else, Justin."

"Do not speak to me of 'suitable,' Aunt Miranda. We'll go behind that big tent yonder," he said to Letty. "It backs up to the garden wall, and it is sufficiently large to afford us at least a few moments' privacy. That is all I shall require."

Both elderly ladies began to protest again, but Letty, interpreting the expression on his face to mean that he was likely to pick her up and carry her if she did not go peacefully, said, "I'll go with him. He won't strangle me, you know."

He reached for her then, and it was all she could do not to jump back, but although he grasped her upper arm much like a schoolmaster might grasp an unruly student, his grip would leave no bruises.

The crowd might have disappeared in smoke for all the attention he paid it, and when she tried to dig in her heels, his grip tightened painfully.

"Sir, please, I said I'll go with you. Need you drag me like this? You will draw the attention of everyone we pass."

In reply, he reached for her hand and pulled it through the crook of his arm.

Since it forced her to walk closer to him, she was not certain it was an improvement, but at least no one seemed to be paying them much heed.

Moments later, they were alone behind the tent. Looking doubtfully at the quivering wall of canvas next to them, she said, "Do you think anyone is inside?"

"I don't care if they are."

"I don't suppose you do, but I do. The last thing I need is to have it noised about at court that you rang a peal over me at a public fete."

"Is that what you think I'm going to do?"

"Isn't it?"

"Now, see here, my girl—"

"*Your* girl! *You* see here, Raventhorpe. You have no authority over me, so—"

"By God, authority has nothing to do with it," he snapped, grabbing her by the shoulders and giving her a shake. "You are going to listen to me, because what you did yesterday was foolish beyond permission. How you dared—"

"Don't speak to me of daring," she retorted, wrenching away from him. "And keep your hands to yourself, sir."

"Or what? Have you got your pistol handy? Would you shoot me, too?"

"If you know about that, your brother must have told you everything," she said bitterly. "Did he miss keeping commons so that he could rush off to Sellafield House and tell you the whole tale? I thought he would honor my confidence, but clearly I misjudged him."

"You've misjudged many things, Letitia, but not Ned. I was

in his chambers when he returned from seeing you to your coach. I forced him to tell me."

"Poor Ned." She met Raventhorpe's steady gaze, and something tightened inside her. One moment she wanted to hit him; the next, to appease him. Awareness of that contradiction did not still the tremors in her spine, but it lowered their tempo. "I hope you were not too harsh with him, sir," she said quietly. "He was kind to me."

"What the devil were you doing in Boverie Street?" His voice sounded strained, but she knew that he was still angry. Before she could reply, he added, "No, don't try to answer that. I don't want to hear how you managed to persuade yourself to do such a daft thing. Tell me this instead. Why did you go alone?"

"Whom should I have taken with me?" she demanded. "Jenifry was out."

"Anyone. No one. You should not have gone! Why did you not send for me? Did you think I would not care about danger threatening Liza?"

"I thought that by the time I found you—or anyone else, for that matter—and managed to explain, Liza might be dead or gone where we could never find her."

The look in his eyes had changed, softened, and his eyelids drooped as if he would hide his feelings. Still, his tone was stern when he said, "You knew where she was. You had only to tell someone, a policeman, a constable, me, anyone. Instead, you hailed a common hack and hared off to a district where no lady ought to set foot at all, let alone by herself. That you were not murdered or robbed is a miracle. You are a fool, Letitia, and—"

"By heaven, that's enough," she snapped. "I was never in the least danger. May I remind you, sir, not only that I had my pistol but that I was able to rescue Liza easily and get away." Ignoring a twitching conscience that reminded her it had not been so easy as that, she stood her ground, hands on hips now, glaring at him.

He glared back.

Letty licked suddenly-dry lips. She could feel her heart pounding. Indeed, she could almost hear it, and that despite the noise of the bands and the crowds beyond the tent. She was conscious only of her thudding heart and of Justin, as if they were alone in a world wholly separated from the Royal Horticultural Society fete.

The silence between them lengthened until her nerves began to tingle. She could think of nothing to say, and she could not seem to look away from him.

His lips tightened to a thin line. Then he said in that horrid, grim tone, "The truth is, Letitia, that you got away from that place through pure luck. Your pistol might easily have been taken from you. Had that happened, you would have been at that villain's mercy to be raped, murdered, or sold right along with Liza. Your coachman did desert you, so had the Inns of Court not been near at hand—"

"But they *were* near," she said, her voice rising uncontrollably. "To preach of possibilities that never occurred is infamous, my lord."

"That will do!"

"Oh, no, it won't! I'll thank you to remember that I have got a brain, sir. Moreover, I've probably had more experience than you have with neighborhoods like that one. I don't need your advice or counsel now, nor did I need them before I went in search of Liza."

"You haven't got the brains of a goose," he retorted, "and what you *need,* my girl, is to be put over someone's knee and taught to use what little sense you do have. That your father didn't do it long ago gives me a mighty poor opinion of him."

"Does it?" Her temper flashed. "Does it, my lord?"

He glared at her. "It does."

"Well, if you think beating a woman is the way to tame her, you don't have even as much sense as God gave that goose. You're a barbarian, Raventhorpe, like most men! And, like most men—"

"Be quiet, Letitia." He reached for her. "I shouldn't have—"

Inside her, something snapped. Without a thought for consequence, or indeed for anything, her hand flashed back and she slapped him.

Remorse swept over her before his hands clamped hard on her shoulders again. "I'm sorry," she exclaimed. "I've never done such a thing before to anyone! I don't know what came over me. What a horrid thing to do! I won't blame you in the least if you shake me again, but truly—"

"Be quiet," he repeated gruffly.

"But—"

Pulling her hard against himself, he kissed her.

Even as the impulse to fight him stirred, it melted and vanished. His lips were warm and demanding against hers, and her body came alive with new and quite different sensations.

His hands slid from her shoulders, moving around to her back and waist.

She leaned against him, savoring the muscular warmth of his body beneath the soft wool of his coat. No one had ever held her so, enveloped her so, or stirred her senses the way this man did. She forgot her anger, forgot everything but his touch and the heat of his lips against hers.

She kissed him back hungrily, and a few minutes later, when she relaxed a little, allowing his tongue to slip between her lips, she welcomed the new feelings that swept through her, wondering at his daring but glad of it.

"My goodness me, whatever are you doing, the pair of you?"

The squeal of words and the familiar voice startled Letty, and she would have jumped away from him had his arms not tightened around her. He straightened, still holding her, his very touch calming her so that she was able to turn and face Susan Devon-Poole with her dignity at least appearing to be intact.

Coolly Raventhorpe said, "Did you want something, Miss Devon-Poole?"

"My goodness me, sir, you act as if *I* am the one doing something wrong! I saw you walk back here quite a long time ago. When you did not immediately reappear, I thought at first that you must have found some fascinating horticultural specimen, but I see now that it was no such thing. Lady Letitia, are you quite all right? My goodness me, I do not know whom one should blame for such a scene, but I do know that neither my mama nor Lady Tavistock will approve."

Finding herself speechless for once, Letty did not try to respond. Still, she found it possible to feel sorry for Miss Devon-Poole when, with icy displeasure, Raventhorpe said, "Of course her ladyship is all right. You are a great deal too busy, Miss Devon-Poole. If your mama and Lady Tavistock will disapprove of anything in this scene, I daresay it will be your pursuit of us without first acquiring an escort for yourself. A public affair like this is no place for a young woman to walk about by herself. I certainly do not approve of such reckless behavior."

Miss Devon-Poole, flushing scarlet, gasped, then turned without another word and hurried away.

Letty said quietly, "You know that she will very likely tell the first dozen people she meets what she saw."

"Perhaps," he replied, "but perhaps not. She is just as likely to hold her tongue until she can think up a plausible excuse for following us here that won't make her look like a jealous cat."

Hearing a note of amusement in his voice, she looked up.

His eyes were twinkling, and she knew in that moment that she would have to work hard to insulate herself against her feelings, for never before had she known a man with whom she could more easily imagine falling in love, or one who would make her a worse husband. Too much did she value her independent ways, and too greatly did he want to change them.

Even if love could conquer all, nothing was less likely than that he would fall in love with her. He came from one of the great Whig families, for one thing, which made them—politically speaking, at least—like Romeo and Juliet; and she had no wish to commit suicide. For another, if he were hanging out for a wife, he would have found one by now. To be sure, Catherine had told her that everyone believed he had an interest in Miss Devon-Poole, but she had not credited that even before today; and what she had just seen surely proved it was nonsense.

As for kissing her, he had probably just taken the first route he could think of to end a difficult scene. He must have known he had gone too far in ripping up at her like he had; but she had gone over the mark, too, in slapping him.

He had not even tried to discuss the whole business rationally. He simply had wanted to regain control, for that was what drove him, but having let her guard fall once, she knew it might fall again. That would never do. Only heartache and perhaps even a scene similar to the one Miss Devon-Poole had just endured lay ahead if she allowed herself to succumb to the great physical attraction he stirred in her. She must, she decided, strive to overcome it.

He was watching her, and she feared that he could read her thoughts. Looking him straight in the eye, she said, "You may find amusement in my situation, sir, but I do not. It does not matter when Miss Devon-Poole speaks or to whom. She will do my reputation grave damage in any event."

"You just let me— Oh Lord, rain!"

The clouds overhead had burst without the usual polite, warning drizzle. Water sluiced down in sheets, soaking them.

"Your aunts!" Letty cried, pulling her hood up over her head.

Whatever he had been about to say went unsaid in the scramble to find Mrs. Linford and Miss Abby, and make their way through the teeming crowd to Letty's carriage, but Letty had little doubt what he had intended to say. If she would just let him take control of everything, and would follow his advice, he would protect her. It was just as well, she decided, that he had saved his breath.

Raventhorpe refused to get into the carriage with them, insisting that he had brought his own and that, furthermore, he had come with a friend who would drown before leaving without him.

Glad of the respite, Letty soon felt grateful for the heavy

rain, too, because the racket it created made it easy to evade the old ladies' delicately phrased hints that she tell them all that Raventhorpe had said to her. They fell silent at last, but it was difficult to think. She knew she needed time to collect herself and to consider her options, but she also knew that she was unlikely to enjoy that luxury. Less than four hours remained before Lady Sellafield's dinner party.

FOURTEEN

Rain was still pouring down when Letty's carriage drew to a stop in Upper Brook Street to set down the two old ladies. She feared that the long afternoon might have tired them so that they would not enjoy Lady Sellafield's dinner party, but when she suggested as much, they hastened to reassure her.

"Oh, no, my dear," Miss Abby said, clearing a circle on the fogged window with her handkerchief and peering out. "We wouldn't miss Sally's party, not for anything."

"A short nap will suffice to restore our energy," Mrs. Linford agreed. She looked at Letty searchingly. "I did not quite like to press you before now, my dear, but you look a trifle down-pin. Did Raventhorpe say something to upset you?"

Remembering his kiss, Letty felt warmth flood her cheeks, but she managed to answer calmly, "It was as I suspected, ma'am. He wanted to have his say about my going alone yesterday in search of Liza. He does not approve of women who show the least spark of independence, I fear."

"No, he doesn't," Miss Abby agreed without turning.

"He certainly doesn't," Mrs. Linford echoed, with so much feeling that Letty looked at her in surprise.

"Goodness, ma'am, what—?"

"Did he not speak to you about us, then, dear?"

"Miranda, poor Lucas is standing in the rain waiting for us, and there is Jackson now, hurrying out with our umbrella," Miss

Abby exclaimed. "We must go in at once! It won't do for either of them to catch his death of cold on our account."

Letty wanted to ask what Raventhorpe had done to agitate the aunts, but Lucas and Jackson were waiting and she did not have time to go inside if she was to be ready in time for Lady Sellafield's dinner party. So she held her tongue, certain she would find out soon enough, in any event.

As the carriage made its way back to Piccadilly and then along the Strand, she leaned back, enjoying the pounding of the rain on the roof now, and the added clatter of iron wheels swishing through puddles on the cobblestone streets. It was growing colder, but both Jonathan Coachman and Lucas wore protective oilskin coats and broad-brimmed hats, and the horses would find food and dry stalls in the stables at Jervaulx House. So for a few moments she managed to devote her thoughts wholly to Raventhorpe and to pondering the maze that lay ahead of her.

She could not deny that she liked the viscount. He was handsome, and even her grandfather in his worst temper could not have disapproved of his wealth or his rank in society. Indeed the crusty sixth marquess even would have approved of Raventhorpe's determination to dominate everyone within his orbit. The one thing that he would not have approved, however, was Raventhorpe's politics. If she had heard her grandfather refer to one damned Whig, she had heard him refer to fifty, and although the present Marquess of Jervaulx was not as staunchly conservative as his father had been, he was nonetheless a good Tory. He would doubtless have little good to say about his daughter's interest in a gentleman Whig.

The cold had enveloped her by the time she reached home, and Miss Dibble greeted her with alarm. "My dear, you are drenched to the skin! I collect that that dreadful cloudburst caught you still in the gardens."

"It certainly did, Elvira. Indeed I am glad you did not come with us. How are you feeling? Did you enjoy your day of quiet?"

"Yes, indeed. Jenifry and I have been going through your wardrobe to see what you will want to replace, and making lists of new things you should purchase."

"You haven't rested at all, in fact."

Miss Dibble smiled. "I am glad to have had time to do what needed doing, but perhaps your parents would say I ought to have gone with you. Why did you not linger in Upper Brook Street until you were warm and dry again?"

"I won't melt, Elvira. You're the one who said you feared you might be coming down with something, not I. Here, Lucas, take my wet cloak to the kitchen to dry, and stay there yourself until you have had something hot to drink. I want you to escort us to Lady Sellafield's dinner party tonight, but I shan't need you until seven, when we will be ready to leave."

Miss Dibble said, "Lucas, tell them her ladyship requires a hot bath, and tell them also to put it near the hearth in her bedchamber, not in her dressing room. They can build up the fire, too, whilst they are about it."

Letty did not argue with these orders. Her cloak, wet as it had been, had kept her warmer than she was without it. She was beginning to shiver.

Miss Dibble hustled her upstairs to her bedchamber and rang for Jenifry, who arrived as two menservants carried in the high-backed tub and the first bucketsful of hot water. Jervaulx House did not boast any mechanized arrangement to provide hot water above the first floor, but old-fashioned methods still worked very well.

When the men had filled the tub and gone, Jenifry began to stir delicious-smelling French salts into the water. The fire crackled warmly on the hearth, and even in her wet clothing, Letty began to feel more comfortable.

With Miss Dibble's help, she twisted her wet hair into a knot atop her head and quickly stripped off her clothes. As she stepped into the bath, she said, "You go and get dressed, Elvira. Jen can look after me without your help, but I daresay you will want to be present for the final touches to my dress."

"Yes, indeed, for I mean to see that you look your best this evening. That place will be crawling with Whigs, Letitia. I don't want them to notice a single curl out of place. We'd be hearing about that for a sennight afterward."

Seeing Jenifry stiffen indignantly, Letty quelled her with a look and said, "You know that Jen always sees me well turned out, Elvira. I will be grateful for your advice after you have dressed, of course, but there is nothing for you to do here until I have finished bathing."

When the woman had gone, Jenifry said as she handed Letty a bar of French soap, "Sometimes Miss Dibble makes my tongue fairly itch to tell her what I think."

"Well, don't do it," Letty said. "I don't mind when you say what you think to me, but I would have to take her side if you were impertinent to her. Hand me that cloth, will you? And you might as well wash my hair whilst we're about it. It's already wet, after all."

Jenifry silently loosened Letty's hair and poured warm water over it. While she lathered it, Letty relaxed against the back of the tub with her eyes shut.

"May I ask a question, miss?"

Letty opened her eyes. "Of course you may," she said in surprise.

"Well, I did wonder. You went so quiet, and all."

Letty knew that Jenifry's reticence had more to do with the reproof than with the silence since, but she let the comment pass. "What is it, Jen?"

"About the queen, miss. Why is it she don't allow Sir John Conroy to come near her anymore?"

"Mercy, why do you ask that?"

"Well, it does seem cruel to me that she's pushed him to the background now, when he guided her every step before she took the throne. He's got only her best interest at heart, I should think."

"Sir John and the Duchess of Kent also kept the queen isolated from society when she was a princess, Jen. They scarcely ever allowed her to attend even court functions, let alone any others. If the old king had not insisted that she visit him from time to time, she would not have had the least idea of how to go on at court."

"Then she cannot have learned all she needs to know to rule competently," Jenifry pointed out. "Perhaps she ought to listen to them who care most about her."

"Now that she is the queen, she wants to look like a queen," Letty said firmly. "It is quite understandable that Her Majesty does not want Conroy, or her mother, or anyone else, telling her what to do now, Jen."

"I suppose," Jenifry said. "Still, some say we'd do better with a king now, miss, that other countries have good reason for keeping women off their thrones."

"You, of all people, ought to know that a female is equal to anything," Letty said, striving to retain her patience. "Think of Queen Elizabeth, for heaven's sake. She did more for England than any ten kings."

"Well, perhaps, but she was older, Elizabeth was, and some say—"

"Do they say who would rule this country if the law had prevented Her Majesty from taking the throne? It would be the King of Hanover. You certainly know enough about him to know that he would make us a dreadful ruler, Jen. Why they say he once murdered his own valet!"

"Lean forward, please, miss. I'm going to pour the rinse water now."

Thinking she had finally made her point, Letty shut her eyes until Jenifry had finished rinsing the soap out of her hair and had twisted it up again in a towel.

Then Jenifry said, "Still and all, Miss Letty, they say Sir John was once the most powerful man in the country, and that he's right smart, too. They say that Her Majesty should reinstate him, and not take all her advice from Lord Melbourne."

Letty sighed. *"Who* says?"

"It just ain't right the way Her Majesty looks only to Lord

Melbourne," Jenifry said without answering the question. "They say he is much more than—"

"It is no secret that Sir John hoped to become the power behind the throne," Letty said, cutting in before Jenifry could say more about the queen's relationship with Melbourne. Clearly, Jenifry had been talking to others about all this, and it would do neither her nor her mistress any good if it became known around the court that Letitia Deverill's dresser dared to speak ill of the queen and her prime minister.

Hoping to make it plain that she would disapprove of such unseemly prattle, Letty added gently, "I may not always support Melbourne's political positions, but he is a good man, and he manages Her Majesty much more deftly than Conroy did."

"Indeed, miss, she seems ever so taken—"

"Jenifry, if you want to ask me questions, you may. But since you do not understand British politics, I think perhaps you would do better to keep your opinions to yourself until you understand them better."

"Yes, miss. If you're finished now, I'll fetch your towel."

Letty said nothing more until she was sitting in front of the fire wrapped in her warm robe, and Jenifry had begun to brush her hair dry. Then, hoping to ease the tension between them, she said, "How are all those handsome men on your string behaving themselves these days?"

"I never said they were all handsome," Jenifry said.

"You did say that at least one of them is."

"Have a heart, miss. There's only two."

"I thought I'd counted three, at least."

"That's because you tease me about the Duchess of Sutherland's footman, but I never thought much of him, though he was kind enough to us that first day. In truth, he's so high in the instep that any sensible girl wants to stomp on it."

Letty smiled. "And the others aren't? I thought you said Raventhorpe's man was the stuffy one."

"And so he is," Jenifry said with feeling. "Every time I see that man, he's telling me how I should go on, who I should talk to, and who I shouldn't. He had the nerve to come looking for me here today, when it's not even my half-day. He's a sight more puffed up in his own esteem than what that starchy footman is."

"Well, I expect that leaves the third one, then. Walter, isn't that his name?"

"Yes, miss." Her tone was cool, and she said no more.

The only sounds in the room were the crack of a sparking ember and the rhythmic strokes of the brush through Letty's hair until she said, "I apologize if my questions were too particular, Jen."

"It isn't that, miss."

When she did not elaborate, Letty turned to see a troubled look in her eyes. "What is it, then?" she prompted.

"Nothing, miss."

Gently Letty said, "Are you in love with Walter?"

Jenifry flushed. "I . . . I don't know, miss. He's as handsome as a man can stare, and the other women—they think I'm as lucky as he is handsome. When I'm with him, the way the others look at me makes me feel like a queen, because I'm the one he chose out of all the whole lot of them. But then . . ."

When it became clear that she did not intend to finish, Letty said, "Tell me."

Jenifry drew a long breath, then said in a brisker tone, "Like as not, it isn't anything worth telling, miss. He's just a mite forceful in his nature, that's all. When I'm with him, I don't always know whether I'm on my heels or on my head."

Startled, Letty said, "He hasn't . . . That is, he doesn't force you to—"

"No, miss." Jenifry flushed more deeply than ever. "It's just he slapped me once, is all. I daresay I deserved it, though, and he apologized straightaway, Walter did." She smiled ruefully, adding, "He wants what any man wants, of course, but he doesn't press me for favors I'd as lief not grant him yet. Nor ever, for that matter, without we get married first, but—"

"Mercy, has he asked you? Why didn't you tell me?"

"Well, that's just it. He doesn't ask for marriage. Not yet, at all events."

"Then stand firm, Jen. You know how angry Papa gets if he finds that one of the menservants has seduced a maid. Some men even go so far as to let a girl think they want marriage when they only want to bed her, you know."

"I do know that, miss, and I'm a good girl. It isn't even that he gets angry or such. He just has a way of seeming sometimes to swallow me up when he talks."

Letty chuckled, knowing that Jenifry had meant to lighten the mood with her phrasing, but nonetheless she felt troubled. They had known each other since childhood, and never before had Jenifry expressed interest in a man. Had the man in question sounded like one the young dresser's parents would approve, Letty would have left well enough alone (or so she hoped). But this man sounded as if he could be more dangerous than Jenifry might suspect.

Deciding that it might prove necessary to put a spoke in Walter's wheel, she said casually, "Have you ever learned who Walter's master is?"

"Aye, miss. He serves a man called Charles Morden. A very important man, Walter says. Do you know him?"

"I don't know him, exactly, but I know who he is," Letty said. "He is aide to Sir John Conroy, Jen. I begin to suspect where you got your new political notions."

Jenifry bit her lip, then said, "I'd best get your hair dry, miss. It will take some time, and you'll need to be getting your dress on soon or you'll be late to Sellafield House."

Justin, too, was dressing for his mother's dinner party, and he was not looking forward to it. Not only would Susan Devon-Poole be there with Sir Adrian and Lady Devon-Poole, but Sellafield and Ned would be present, both doubtless still harboring ill feelings toward him. Also, his great-aunts would be there, and he feared that one or the other might say something that would lead to their undoing. It was hard for him to imagine how they had avoided doing so long before now.

Examining the articles laid out on his dressing table, he said with a frown, "I want the ruby cravat pin, Leyton, not this trumpery thing you put out."

"Sorry, sir, I'll fetch it as soon as I finish shaving you."

There would be other guests, too, including the prime minister, Lady Letitia and the dragon who generally accompanied her, the Witherspoons, Admiral and Lady Rame, and other friends of his parents.

His thoughts returned to Letitia's dragon. At this point, he could not decide whether he was grateful for her absence from Chiswick or deplored it. What had she been thinking, to let her headstrong charge go dashing about London on her own? He was certain that Jervaulx had not engaged such a woman merely so she could turn a blind eye to Letitia's activities.

Leyton, after putting away his shaving utensils, brought him the ruby pin. "I'll bring your coat now, sir, shall I? You'll want the dark blue one, I expect."

"The black," Justin said, studying the folds of his cravat in the dressing glass as he pinned the ruby in place. Though he generally gave his full attention to his attire until it satisfied him, then forgot it, he could not seem to control his imagination's present annoying tendency to waft him back to Chiswick.

When he and Letitia had dashed back in search of the aunts, they had found them quickly, in much the same place they had left them. All three women had urged him to accept a ride with them, but he insisted that he had to find Puck.

Though Justin had cursed the carelessness that had caused him to leave his friend and the carriage without making a specific plan for finding both after the fete, he had been sure Puck would not leave without him. At least, he would not do so until he had waited long enough to be certain Justin had gone with someone else.

Justin, having recalled that on his arrival he had passed an area near the main gate clearly reserved for ticketed vehicles, hoped he would find his carriage there and that Puck had had the good sense to wait there with it. Therefore, upon learning that Letitia had left her coach in that area, he had accompanied the three ladies there and left them in the care of her capable-looking coachman and footman.

He had quickly located his own carriage and coachman, but it was some time before Puck returned, looking more like a drowned rat than a gentleman of fashion.

"Good Lord," Puck exclaimed. "What a downpour! Tell them to whip up the horses, will you? It's going to take me hours to make myself presentable again for your mama's dinner party."

Justin had complied; however, they had found themselves in a long line of traffic again, slowed even more when a coach ahead of them had bogged down in a rut and men had had to pull it out again. Still, he had no doubt now that Puck would be among the first guests to arrive, and he was thankful that he would be.

Leyton brought his coat, and Justin stood to put it on before he noticed that it was the wrong one. "I said the black, Leyton, not the blue."

"Sorry, sir. I know you did. Don't know where my mind is tonight."

When Justin found himself thinking about Letitia again while Leyton helped him slip on the snug-fitting black coat, he firmly pushed the thought away. He could not imagine what had stirred him to kiss the willful chit. If Miss Devon-Poole had got notions in her head simply from his occasional notice of her, what on earth would Letitia be thinking now that he had kissed her? He was a fool, and no mistake. Nothing could come of such a relationship except heartache for her and damned inconvenience and censure for him. If her father got wind of it . . . But there his imagination boggled, and he made a vow to be more circumspect in future.

He still would have to discuss the Upper Brook Street house with her, of course. He could not let that imbroglio continue a moment longer than he could help. Common knowledge of such goings-on would ruin not only Letitia but also the aunts, and their social ruin would reflect badly on both him and his parents, as well.

Leyton brought him his cloak.

"What the devil! Leyton, have you lost your mind? I am not going out."

The valet looked at the cloak and shook his head. "Sorry, my lord."

"Look here," Justin said curtly, "what the devil's amiss with you? I can't think of another instance when you've behaved like this."

"Forgive me, my lord. It will not happen again."

"Oh, cut line, damn you! I'm not going to turn you off without a character, but I want to know what's going on. Is it a wench?"

The valet said stiffly, "I am sure that my personal affairs—"

"An affair, eh? Who is she?"

"It is *not* an affair," Leyton said indignantly. "See here, Master Justin—"

"I thought it wouldn't be long before you tried that on," Justin said, grinning at him. "It won't serve, though. If you've got into the petticoat line, damned if I *won't* turn you off. I shan't be able to depend on your knowing where *you* are, let alone where my things are."

"I have not taken to petticoat-chasing, sir, and so you should know. If I have some concern about one particular young woman, because she is foolishly allowing her fancies to overcome her better judgment—"

"Good Lord, I can commiserate with you there," Justin said. "Who is she?"

"I would rather not say, sir. Suffice it to say that she is allowing one who is not worthy to lick her shoes to winkle his way into her favor."

"A real dog, is he?"

"His reputation with persons of the female gender is worse than that, sir. I tried to tell her. I even took the liberty of going to— That is, I took advantage of your absence today, and the fact that you had no duties at court, to pay her a call, with the firm intention of describing to her just what sort of a rogue he is."

"Who the devil is this rogue?"

"He serves Charles Morden, my lord."

"Does he indeed? Does he speak English? His master's German, I think."

"He does, sir, albeit with a dreadful Hanoverian accent. Fancies himself quite a buck, too. If I may take a further liberty, sir, he is not unlike his master."

" 'Tel maître, tel valet,'* as the ancient bard said. You might as well tell me now who the wench is, Leyton. I'll find out soon enough, you know."

"I expect you will, at that, sir." Leyton sighed. "She is obsessed with him, I fear. Her name is Jenifry Breton, sir. She is Lady Letitia Deverill's dresser."

"Oh, Lord," Justin said, staring at him.

"Yes, sir," Leyton said, quietly taking the cloak away.

Letty and Miss Dibble were neither the first nor the last to arrive at Sellafield House for her ladyship's dinner party, and when the carriage drew up before the lovely house at half past seven, it was still light enough in Grosvenor Square to see it. The three-story exterior of modest red brick sported white stone belt courses and window surrounds. Two unpretentious stone pillars mounted with gas lamps flanked the white front door, and the elaborate, well-polished brass knocker gleamed brightly with the lamps' reflected light.

The interior of the house revealed a much more opulent classical look. The entrance hall, saloon, and front parlor through which they passed, as well as the magnificent great drawing room where the company had gathered, had all been embellished and gilded with excellent taste, if (in Letty's opinion)

---

*"Like master, like man."

with a rather heavy hand. Painted decoration and murals decked walls and ceilings, each room boasted at least one marble fireplace, and the huge crystal chandeliers in each room now provided modern gas lighting.

Letty had scarcely greeted her hostess and introduced Miss Dibble before Miss Abby descended upon her and pulled her toward a comparatively quiet corner.

"Letty, dear, do come and talk with Miranda and me. We simply must talk with you, for Justin did not tell you, did he, dearest?"

"Tell me what?"

"Oh, I knew it. I just knew it! We thought we would have time to break it to you gently, in just the right, well-chosen words, you know. But then Justin showed up at Chiswick—so unexpected, you know, and so very likely to tell you he knew, because of course we had told him that you did—and then the storm burst over us all. So when Miranda said she didn't think he had, I just knew she was right. You would have said something to us, even with that din on the way home. She said you mightn't, that you might be afraid to upset us. At least that was her first thought, but then when you looked so taken aback at her last question just before we went in—"

"Miss Abby, please," Letty begged, stemming the tide. "I haven't got a notion what you are talking about."

"But that's just what I've been saying, isn't it? Does Miss Dibble know?"

Letty blinked, trying to make order out of the chaos in her thoughts if not in Miss Abby's discourse. "Ma'am, pray begin at the beginning. Does Miss Dibble know what?" Even as she said it, however, she had an uncomfortable idea that she was not going to like the answer. "Wait," she added hastily, turning to her companion. "Elvira, will you excuse us for a few minutes so that I can sort this out with Miss Abby? There is Catherine Witherspoon yonder, beckoning to me. Pray go and speak to her, and I will join you as quickly as I can."

"Perhaps I ought to hear about this," Miss Dibble said evenly.

"It is nothing that concerns you," Letty said in the same tone. "Do go now, and tell Catherine that I shall be with her directly. Now, ma'am," she added when Miss Dibble had walked away, "what's this about Raventhorpe?"

"I do think you had better let Miranda tell you," Miss Abby said wretchedly. "She is talking to Admiral Rame now, and waiting to talk to Sally, who is still receiving guests, but I shall likely make a mull of it if I try to tell you all by myself."

"Is it so complicated, then?"

"No, but Justin knows, you see. And we thought he was going to take you to task because he knows that you know, don't you know, and so when we went to Chiswick and he was there, looking so . . . you know, so out-of-reason cross—"

"Miss Abby, please," Letty said, drawing her farther into the quiet corner. "Perhaps this is not the best time or place for this discussion."

"No, but if he didn't say anything then, maybe he won't, and you need to be warned, Miranda says, because he is determined to take control like he does, don't you know. And most likely he will be telling you what to do, as well as us, and it is *not* his house, after all, but yours. And you understand, my dear, which is so much better for everyone concerned. Justin will just make a mull of things. Worse than me," she added dismally. "He has already upset Liza, poor thing."

"Mercy, she isn't here tonight, is she?"

"No, but she did so want to come, because she knew Admiral Rame would be here, and Sir John Conroy, and she quite dotes on them both, of course. Well, not 'of course,' perhaps, certainly not in Sir John's case—"

"Ma'am, don't go off on another tangent, I beg you," Letty said. Annoyed to hear that Conroy also was a guest, she wondered fleetingly if there might be some way, if Charles Morden was with him, as usual, to let the latter know that his man's attentions to Jenifry were likely to displease the Marquess of Jervaulx.

Miss Abby's agitation quickly recalled the problem at hand.

"My dear Letitia, you are quite right," she said, wringing her hands. "We must stop Justin."

"I collect, ma'am, that Raventhorpe has learned your secret. I am sorry about that, but I can only say that I am surprised that he did not learn it long before now. I do not know what we can do about it, in any event."

"Good gracious, my dear, do you *want* him to tell us all what to do?"

"I'll talk to him if you like," Letty said, wondering what she could possibly say to him that would do any good.

"Oh dear, I wish you would talk to Miranda first," Miss Abby said. "She is over there with Sally now. Perhaps if we just stroll over to them . . ."

When she paused hopefully, Letty said, "Not now, ma'am, when Lady Sellafield has her guests to look after I will try to talk to Raventhorpe, though, I promise you."

Watching Miss Abby make her way toward Mrs. Linford, with the usual collection of decorations bobbing and shimmering on her hat, Letty sighed at the thought of confronting Raventhorpe. For once, though, she thought he might agree with her. That he hadn't thrown the knowledge in her face at Chiswick was surprising, especially since, if she had correctly interpreted Miss Abby's very confused account, he had learned that she knew about the old ladies' little business. Still, he had been so angry about her going alone to rescue Liza, perhaps he just hadn't got to that point when Susan Devon-Poole and the rain had interrupted them.

Before she talked to Raventhorpe, she realized that she had one other person to warn. Catherine Witherspoon had been kind to her, and if Raventhorpe knew about the house, it would no longer be safe for her to meet her lover there.

Moving to greet Catherine, she waited only until Miss Dibble turned away to talk to someone else before saying in an urgent undertone, "I must tell you that Raventhorpe has learned about the house and means to put a stop to the illicit meetings there. You must tell your friend to arrange something else."

Fear leaped to Catherine's eyes, and she turned away, a hand flying to her mouth. When she had recovered some of her composure, she stammered, "I . . . I can't tell him that. He'll be furious to learn that Raventhorpe knows. Letty, what am I to do?"

"Are you afraid of him, Catherine?" When the other woman nodded, she said, "Who is he, that he can terrify you so?"

"I can't tell you. He would kill me."

"Don't be silly," Letty said, reacting as she always did to absurdity. Then she glanced in the direction of Catherine's stricken look, and suddenly she was not so sure that the other woman's fear was absurd, after all. Catherine had been looking toward a group of men that included Sir John Conroy.

FIFTEEN

Seeing Conroy at Sellafield House irked Justin. He had not far to look, however, to learn how the man had got his invitation. Cornering Sellafield, he said, "You invited that fellow Conroy, didn't you?"

"What if I did?" Sellafield demanded, glaring at him. "My house, ain't it? Your mother went and invited that damned little Tory, didn't she? Whatever else Conroy may be, he's a good Whig, ain't he?"

"He looks out for his own interests and no one else's," Raventhorpe said curtly, suppressing with difficulty a strong urge to defend Letitia's presence. "Moreover, you don't like him, so what's he doing here?"

"He wanted a word with Melbourne, that's all, and I was glad to oblige. It's not right that Her Majesty ignores him. He's served her well and don't deserve such Turkish treatment. If he can get Melbourne to speak for him, she may yet relent."

"Melbourne won't do it, and nor will she," Raventhorpe said. "You know that as well as I do."

Sellafield shrugged, not denying it.

Justin narrowed his eyes. "How much of your debt did he offer to forgive?"

Resentfully the earl said, "Only a quarter of it, damn his eyes. Said he was making the offer only once, too, or I'd have held out for more."

"So for five hundred pounds you sold him access to the prime minister. Very pretty behavior, sir."

"Wouldn't have had to do it if you'd paid my debt like you should have. A fine thing when a father has to go begging to his son, especially when the debt's a paltry two thousand and the son's as rich as Midas." His eyes shifted focus to a point behind Justin, and he said, "Ned, you tell him. Ain't there a law says a son must show respect to his father?"

"Not in British common law, there's not, sir; but there's something in the Bible to that effect, I think," Ned said with an oblique glance at Justin. "I am not going to fight your battle with him, in any case, sir. Boot's on the other foot. I've come to offer him an apology if he'll accept it."

"Certainly I will," Justin said.

"What need have you to apologize to him?" the earl demanded.

Ned flushed, and Justin said, "That will remain between us, sir, if you don't mind. Have you come alone, Ned, or did you bring friends?"

The earl turned abruptly away, muttering about having friends of his own to look after. Watching him, Justin grimaced.

"I wish you two weren't always at odds with each other," Ned said quietly.

"Never mind that," Justin said "Are you on your own tonight?"

"No, I brought Jerry with me. He disappeared, though, when we had the misfortune to run into Sir Adrian Devon-Poole and his family."

"Did you apologize to Miss Devon-Poole for embarrassing her?"

"I didn't get a chance to say a word to her. She took one look at me—which nearly froze me to the bone, I might add—and looked away again, all stony-faced. Jerry took to his heels at once, of course, and that's when I realized that you were right, Justin. I can scarcely cry out at you for treating me like a child when I do still act like one sometimes. I'm deuced sorry. Must I speak to her?"

"I think you must offer her an apology but not when she is with her father and mother. If you see an opportunity, take it, but don't make a great thing of it."

Ned nodded. "Very well, then, I'll do it."

"I'll see if I can pave the way for you, shall I?" Justin said. "I owe her an apology of my own."

"You? What did you do?"

"That, my bantam, is my affair. Do you possess no white neckcloths? That pink one is hardly suitable for a formal occasion."

Ned made a face at him, then left to look for his friend.

Justin decided that there was no time like the present to make his apology. In any case, he thought, it would be easier to speak to Miss Devon-Poole before dinner than afterward. With luck, Latimer would announce the meal soon and make it unnecessary for him to converse at any length with her. His first task, however, would be to separate her from her parents.

Finding Puck, he said, "Can you engage Sir Adrian and Lady Devon-Poole in conversation long enough for me to speak privately with their daughter?"

Puck's eyebrows rose ludicrously. "Of course I can. I'm a dab hand at that sort of thing, as you well know, but is it wise for you to be private with the wench?"

"Wise or not, I must," Justin said.

"I thought you had put the notion of marrying her behind you. Certainly you've shown more interest of late in the little Tory than in Miss Devon-Poole."

"That's just the problem," Justin told him. "I did not tell you earlier, because I'm not proud of what happened, but Miss Devon-Poole chanced to interrupt Lady Letitia and me at a most inopportune moment this afternoon. I fear from her reaction that she harbored expectations that I had taken considerable pains to avoid raising."

"Ah-ha," Puck said wisely.

"So, you see, I must speak with her, for Lady Letitia as much as for myself."

"Then I am at your service," Puck said nobly. "In fact, dashed if I won't take a second look at the wench myself."

"Do your worst," Justin recommended. "For the present, you can help me see that she does not make it her object in life to ruin Lady Letitia."

With his friend's deft assistance, he was soon able to speak with Miss Devon-Poole, but her reception was cool.

"I owe you a double apology," he said quietly.

"Do you, sir?"

"You know I do. Not only was my brother responsible for putting you in an awkward situation yesterday, but I spoke sharply this afternoon when you did not deserve it. You were quite right to point out that the fault was mine, not yours."

She looked surprised. "My goodness me, sir, I did not expect you to be so conciliating. You are not a man known for making pretty apologies."

"I generally feel no need to do so," Justin said. "However, I hope I am not a man known for avoiding apologies when I am at fault."

"The confusion at your aunts' house was clearly your brother's fault, not yours, sir." With a smile and a flutter of eyelashes, she added sweetly, "Moreover, I make no doubt that you were enticed into that most distressing scene at Chiswick."

"I'm sorry if you were distressed," Justin said evenly. "However, I feel obliged to confess that if anyone did any enticing, it was I."

She fluttered her lashes again, looking up from under them to say, "Very noble, sir, but it is not necessary to pretend such a thing to me."

"There's nothing noble about it, nor any pretense," Justin said, nettled. "Lady Letitia wouldn't have set foot back there had I not—" He fell silent, unwilling to explain details he believed were no business of Miss Devon-Poole's.

Clearly she misunderstood him, for she said, "There, you

see! You cannot offer me a falsehood, sir. I know—better than most, I daresay—that such a forward little Tory would never interest a good Whig gentleman like yourself."

"One hesitates to contradict a lady, Miss Devon-Poole, but I cannot imagine why you should think yourself better qualified than most to judge the matter." He looked her in the eye, daring her to say that he had somehow given her that right. He was certain that he had done no such thing, that any encouragement she believed he had given her had sprung from her imagination, if not from pure greed.

She met his gaze briefly. Then her eyes shifted and delicate color tinged her cheeks. "I should not have said that, my lord. Pray forgive me."

"There is nothing to forgive," Justin said. "Moreover, I know your reputation for fairness too well to fear that you might speak of what you alone saw today. The scene was not of Lady Letitia's making, so it would be unfair to speak ill of her."

"I do not indulge in common gossip, sir."

"I know you do not." He knew nothing of the sort, but he hoped his warning would do the trick, particularly since he had, he hoped, made plain to her that she, being the sole witness to the scene, would instantly be suspect if word of the kiss did get around. She might not know as much about him as she had suggested she did, but she certainly knew that he was no man to cross. He felt he could take hope from the cordial reception he had received from Sir Adrian and Lady Devon-Poole. Clearly Susan had not told her parents what she had seen.

The butler announced dinner shortly thereafter, and since Justin's seat was at the opposite end of the table from Letitia's, he did not find opportunity to speak with her until the gentlemen had rejoined the ladies in the drawing room. In the meantime, while the other men chatted over their port, he tried to think how best to approach her on the issue of the house. He still had not thought of a way when Conroy waylaid him as the gentlemen were leaving the dining room.

Drawing him aside, Conroy said, "You have so far seen fit to ignore every request for your assistance in my quest, Raventhorpe."

"You have no need of me if you can enlist Melbourne."

"Melbourne does not want to share Her Majesty's favors."

"So you had no luck with him. Try one of her other ministers."

Conroy shrugged. "I shall, of course, but none has Melbourne's knack with her. You, on the other hand, wield influence with Melbourne, or so I have heard."

"I can see no reason to exert myself for you, Conroy," Justin said, wondering how the man had learned of his assistance to Letitia, for he could be referring to no other instance.

Conroy said silkily, "Perhaps you are not aware that your father owes me a considerable sum of money."

"You must look to him to pay it, not to me."

"I see. You do not mind scandal in your family, then."

Meeting his gaze steadily, Justin said, "I think the scandal would be twofold, Conroy. Do you think it would please Her Majesty to know you had paid someone to gain access to her like you did to gain access to Melbourne?"

Conroy grimaced. "So he told you of that, did he? Well, I am in no good odor as things stand now, but I still think I'd weather that storm better than you. You can avoid it easily, however. All I ask is that you do me a simple good turn."

Exasperated, Justin said, "My help would avail you nothing, Conroy. The only hope you have of regaining Her Majesty's favor is if you were to throw yourself in front of a bullet to save her from assassination."

"You are unnecessarily severe, Raventhorpe, but you can still help me."

Justin raised his eyebrows, wondering where the man was heading now.

"They say you have an interest in the little Tory, and you certainly have a family interest in the house she inherited. Suppose I wanted to buy that house."

"Speak to her," Justin said, wary now. "I doubt she wants to sell, however."

"She would have no say in the matter," Conroy said flatly. "One does not deal with females in matters of property. In any event, no one will buy whilst your great-aunts exert their right to life tenancy. As I see it, though, your family interest strongly suggests that you should persuade them to take up residence elsewhere."

"I do not take your meaning, sir," Justin said, barely keeping his temper.

"Do you not? I think you do. In either case, perhaps you should occupy yourself more nearly with their welfare, and with their rather interesting activities."

The threat, though veiled, was clear now. Whether Conroy had an interest in buying the house or not, he knew, or at least suspected, its damning secret.

For all Justin knew, Conroy was one of the aunts' patrons. If so, however—even if it became known that he was—Conroy would suffer less than they did.

He decided that the sooner he talked to Letitia and took control of matters, the better it would be for all of them. There was no longer any point in racking his brain for a diplomatic way to approach her.

As it happened, he had no need to employ a stratagem, because she walked right up to him when he entered the drawing room.

"Whilst we were waiting, some of the ladies expressed an interest in playing cards," she said. "I thought I had better speak with you before they get the tables arranged, lest you find yourself absorbed in a hand of whist before I could do so."

"I abhor whist," he said.

"Do you? I thought you would like most games, sir. Gentlemen generally do. Your brother certainly likes them. He was my dinner partner, you know, and he explained how very like law is to a game of chess. He wants to be a barrister, he said, because he looks forward to pitting his mind against others' in a court of law."

"First he must finish his studies," Justin said, "but I do not doubt that he will succeed where he chooses. I wanted to speak to you, too, Lady Letitia."

"Yes, I thought you would. Your great-aunts told me that you had learned their secret. I hope I can enlist your aid in helping me sort that out."

"You can leave it all to me," he said. "I've decided that the less you have to do with them or with the house just now, the better it will be."

"You've decided."

"Yes, and for heaven's sake, don't fly into the boughs, because I am only trying to preserve your good name. If word of what they've been doing gets out, it will reflect on all of us, of course; but as you must know, you, as a single, apparently unprotected young female, will suffer the most of all."

"I shan't be unprotected much longer, sir," she said, giving him a direct look that told him his characterization had annoyed her even more. "My parents will arrive in London quite soon now. I look to see them by Wednesday or Thursday."

"Excellent," he said. "Look, I know you do not like taking advice, but if you want my help, you simply must cooperate. Just let me handle everything, and stay away from the house until I can get matters settled satisfactorily. Your parents' arrival will prove helpful. You can simply say that any time you have away from the court you want to spend with them, if my great-aunts invite you to call."

"You are taking a great deal on yourself, Raventhorpe. It is, I remind you, still my house, and they are still my tenants."

Someone who had begun to play the pianoforte struck a sour note just then, making him wince. He saw Letitia's eyebrows rise, and realized that she had mistaken it for reaction to her words. He said, "I mean no offense to you, but my mother's aunts will need financial support that you can scarcely offer to provide for them. I can, however. Furthermore, it is my duty to look after them, not yours."

"You can offer financial support, sir, but they will refuse it—if they have not done so already," she added, clearly reading his expression as easily as he had read hers. "You cannot simply stomp out independence in females, Raventhorpe, much as you would like to, nor can you ignore everything that they think is important."

"I suppose next you will tell me that you know what they do think is important," he said with an edge in his voice.

"Yes, for they have told me. They want to protect their social image, which makes them no different from anyone else, really. You protect yours, after all. The queen protects hers. I suppose even I protect mine."

"Their social image? They are two old ladies with excellent family connections who live in a very pleasant house in an excellent location. How would that change if I help them? The fact is that it wouldn't."

"But it would! Miss Abby explained that very point to me quite clearly, and I sympathize with them. You would not simply give them financial support and leave it at that, sir. You would stick your oar into their affairs whenever you thought it right to do so, and that would be much too often to suit them."

"They need someone to stick an oar in," he said sharply. "Just look at them. They've been carrying on in a mad way, one that would bring censure down on them if it ever became public knowledge, and they have been doing it for years!"

"Which just goes to show that they know what they are doing," Letitia said.

"Keep your voice down."

"I am trying to, but you would anger a stone, Raventhorpe. You do not always know best, whether you can admit that or not. That no one speaks openly of what goes on in that house just proves what your aunts say. It is more to the benefit of those who know the secret to keep it quiet than to speak of it."

"That is true for the most part, but the stakes have grown, I think. There may be more danger of exposure now."

She looked at him narrowly. "I wish you will not talk in riddles, sir. Speak plainly. What is it that you fear?"

"Are you aware that Conroy wants to buy the house?"

"Mr. Clifford told me that he had made an offer. Someone else had, too; however, he withdrew it when he learned of your aunts' life tenancy. I supposed that Sir John had also withdrawn his offer. Certainly he has never approached me."

"He wouldn't approach you in any case. Though it may agitate your sensibilities to hear it, he is—"

"I have no sensibilities."

"One hesitates to contradict you, but—"

"No you don't. You delight in contradicting me."

"I wish you would learn not to interrupt," he said. "Conroy will not approach you, because although he knows you inherited the house, he assumes, as anyone would, that he must discuss any possibility of its sale with your father."

"Oh." She grimaced. "I suppose you are right, sir, horrid though it is. Mr. Clifford still has difficulty accepting that Papa has granted me full control."

"So do I," he said frankly. "It is my belief that your father assumed he could trust you not to empty his bank accounts, and that with Clifford to guide you, you would run into no difficulty the two of you could not handle. But if you can tell me, honestly, that your father expected you to meet with any situation like the one you did meet in Upper Brook Street . . ." He waited a beat. "Well?"

She grimaced. "A point to you, sir. He could not possibly have known about that when he scarcely even knew who Augustus Benthall was."

"He didn't know him?"

"No. My grandmother was a distant connection of Mr. Benthall's, but Papa thinks my grandfather never even liked him. Grandfather died shortly before Mr. Benthall did, so we could not ask him. I wrote my parents some time ago, asking them to try again to think what could account for Mr. Benthall's having left the house to me, but if they've thought of anything, they have not mentioned it to me."

"Very puzzling."

"Yes, but it is just as puzzling why Sir John would want to buy the house."

"I can think of several reasons," Justin said. "For one, it is an excellent property in an excellent location."

"But there are other houses like that. Perhaps they are not quite so fine—"

"Few of them sit on freehold property," Justin pointed out. "That means—"

"Mr. Clifford explained that to me." She looked at him with the quizzical look he had come to expect whenever her mind leapt from one thought to another that some people might think unrelated to the first. "Those aren't his reasons, are they? You think he has some other purpose in mind."

"I do. Conroy's only purpose right now is to winkle his way back into the queen's favor. He thinks I can influence Melbourne."

"You have been known to wield such influence, have you not?" she said with another direct look.

"Yes, in a good cause, and if I so choose," he replied with a smile.

"But you don't so choose this time."

"Not for Conroy. His notion of the best way to alter my course is to exert pressure from all directions. He has already worked on my father, who lost at least one bet to him that he cannot afford to pay. For my own reasons, I chose not to pay it, and Conroy has threatened to make trouble over it if I don't talk to Melbourne."

"But that's extortion! And now he wants my house? That makes no sense, sir. Even if it did, you cannot compel me to sell."

"No, and he must know that. Nor would he expect me to influence your father, which is why I believe his original aim has not altered. I think he mentioned the house only to make known his strongest threat, and for no other reason."

She opened her mouth, then shut it, and he saw the quizzical look leap to her eyes again. "You think he might reveal the secret," she said, frowning. "He could do so, of course, for I'm nearly certain he is a patron there."

"Indeed?"

"Yes, he was at the house only yesterday. Miss Abby told me so when she said that Liza had run away." Another thought struck her. "Someone enticed Liza to Boverie Street, you know. Could Conroy have done that?"

"Frankly, it doesn't seem the sort of thing he would do. Nor do I think he would risk his own reputation merely to embarrass us, but he might be capable of much more than I know. In any case, you must stay away from the house until I can get things sorted out. I'll have to keep my mother away, too."

"It will be hard to stop her, sir. She may say her visits and morning calls are none of your business. You can scarcely command her to neglect her own aunts."

"I would not command her to do any such thing," he said. "I know she has every right, even a duty, to visit them. I will simply ask her to stay away from Upper Brook Street for a sennight as a favor to me. She knows how much I care about her well-being, and theirs. She will not question my reasons."

"How very obliging of her," Letitia said.

"I hope you will oblige me as well," he said sternly. "You said you wanted to help. You can help best by staying away, and by not arguing about it."

"Very well, sir, I won't argue with you."

"Good girl. I'll speak to my mother now, if you will excuse me. She is apparently setting up her card tables in another room, and means to leave this one to those who want to play the pianoforte or sing. Perhaps you would honor us—"

"Don't try my patience too far, Raventhorpe. Go find your mother. Perhaps you will find her more compliant than her aunts will be."

"Or you?"

"I have said I will not argue with you. Don't ask for more than that."

"I know better," he said, smiling. "I shall be satisfied with that."

Letty watched him walk away, wondering how satisfied he would feel when he realized she had promised only not to argue with him. She had not promised to stay away from the house, nor would she make such a promise to anyone. The house was hers. Therefore its problems and those of its tenants were also hers.

She could hardly tell her father she had managed her affairs well if she had to let someone else solve every problem. She disliked even that small deception, though, and as she went to find Miss Dibble, her conscience pricked her. She was glad she would not be flinging her defiance in Raventhorpe's face straightaway.

Having no inclination to play cards, she passed much of the next forty-five minutes listening with half an ear while the amusing Puck Quigley and Miss Susan Devon-Poole performed a series of duets at the piano, the lady playing (and very competently, too) while the gentleman turned pages for her. Their voices blended well, and the audience rewarded them with heavy applause when they finished.

Conversation had continued through the performance, of course. Miss Dibble coughed twice and sneezed once, for she was indeed coming down with a cold, but she seemed content to comment about one guest after another while Letty responded with polite noises. Others spoke to them, as well, making it clear that members of Whig society had begun to accept Letty's presence in their midst. She knew that she had Raventhorpe and Melbourne to thank for that, and was careful to avoid political discussions, even when she found the temptation to enter one nearly irresistible.

For a few minutes after Puck and Miss Devon-Poole had finished singing, the noise of general conversation increased. At one point, she heard Sir John Conroy remark that the Jamaican situation seemed to be reaching a crisis.

"I hope the government isn't making a mull of things," he said.

Ned Delahan said at once, "In my opinion, Parliament ought to give the Jamaican assembly time to act. I have been reading the arguments presented in the *Times*, you know, and I think some of them have made excellent legal points."

Lord Witherspoon, standing nearby with Catherine, said amiably, "I daresay you can safely leave the management of Jamaica to the British Parliament, lad."

"But the law is clear," Ned said. "The Jamaican assembly has every legal right to ignore a law Parliament thrusts upon it. We didn't do that to them even in such a great cause as emancipation. Not only did the assembly support our wish to free the slaves, but it passed its own emancipation act. Clearly, we should give them time to do the same with the prisons act. Once we have explained its purpose—"

"We are not obliged to do that, however," Melbourne said, "and certain factions in Parliament are dead set against allowing any such discussion."

Much as she wanted to cheer Ned's efforts and support them with arguments of her own, Letty kept her mouth shut. She found herself looking around for Raventhorpe, to see if he appreciated her restraint. He was nowhere at hand, however, and although Miss Dibble might have commended her, had she been aware of the exchange, she was talking with the woman on her other side.

The debate continued until several ladies cried out for a cease-fire. Then, those who wanted to continue arguing withdrew to a distant corner to do so.

Letty burned to hear their conversation, and to take part in it. She had begun to consider the possibility of inching her way close enough to the corner to overhear, at least, when Lady Sellafield's approach claimed her attention.

"Will you walk a little with me, my dear? I'd like to talk with you."

"Certainly, ma'am," Letty said, rising at once. "Will you excuse us, Elvira?"

Miss Dibble rose to greet Lady Sellafield and tell her how pleasant the evening had been, then returned to her conversation.

"Come to the terrace, my dear," Lady Sellafield said. "The rain has stopped, and I am persuaded that the air must be quite fresh and invigorating now."

The air was also cold, Letty discovered when she followed the countess through a set of French doors to a flagstone terrace overlooking the back garden. Torches lighted both the terrace and the paths through the garden, bearing witness to the fact that the rain had stopped, but the sky overhead looked black, and the torches flickered in a stiff breeze that rustled branches and shrubbery in the garden. Letty wrapped her arms around herself, shivering.

"Oh dear," Lady Sellafield said, "it is much colder out here than I thought it would be, but this is the only place where I could be sure we'd be quite alone."

"Must we be quite alone, ma'am?"

"Oh, yes, for it would not do to let anyone overhear. Still, I will be as quick as I can. Justin has said I should stay away from Upper Brook Street, that it's not a good idea for me to be seen there now. I bristled up, just as I would have, had I not known exactly what he was talking about—but Aunt Abby and Aunt Miranda had warned me, of course, that he had discovered their little secret."

"Did they?" Letty said, wondering if perhaps she and Raventhorpe had been the only people in London who had not known that little secret.

"Oh, yes, of course they did," Lady Sellafield said, "just as they told me when your amusing little monkey discovered it.

So, of course, then I got to thinking about exactly what Justin had said to me, and I wondered if perhaps you might have let something slip, dear. Could he possibly know about me, do you think?"

Letty forgot her goose bumps and shivers. She stared at Lady Sellafield. "About you, ma'am? But what could I have let slip about you?"

"Why, about me and Teddy, of course."

Just then the French doors opened, and Admiral Rame put his head out. In a voice that carried easily despite the increasing noise of the wind in the trees, he said, "Sally, you idiotic wench, it's as cold as the deck of a ship out there. Come in at once, before you catch your death of cold."

"We'll be right along, my dear," Lady Sellafield called. "Shut the door, will you, before a draft blows out one of the gaslights."

Letty gasped at the endearment, but before she could speak, the admiral said, "Very well, Sally, but don't dawdle."

Letty stared at the admiral until he had shut the door. Then she said, "I understand now what you feared I might have let slip, ma'am. Of course, it is none of my business, but—"

"Since you clearly did not know, you could not have said anything to Justin, could you? I hope you will not do so now, for he would guess at once who it is."

"No, of course I won't, ma'am. I will keep your confidence."

"Then that is all right. We had better go in before we both are blown away."

Thinking the cheerful countess seemed singularly unalarmed at having given away her secret, Letty followed her back into the house. Her thoughts were racing, for Raventhorpe was more right than he knew. The stakes had grown enormously.

Not only was her reputation at stake, and that of the two old ladies, but now his mother and Admiral Rame stood at risk. If he put a foot wrong, he would cast them to the wolves, and he did not even know the peril existed. Nor could Letty tell him, now that she had promised to keep the information to herself. Nonetheless, one thing was clear. To leave the entire burden of keeping them all safe to Raventhorpe would be most unfair. How fortunate that she had made him no promises.

SIXTEEN

For the next few days, Letty's duties at court kept her busy. On Sunday morning, she attended the Chapel Royal, St. James's, with the queen and the Duchess of Kent. That afternoon, the queen took an airing in Hyde Park, and on Monday the royal party attended the water-color exhibit in East Pall Mall. On both days, the Earl of Uxbridge served as lord-in-waiting, so Raventhorpe was not present. Letty did not know whether to be glad or sorry for his absence.

Much as she tried to pretend she did not miss him, she did, but although she was curious to know what he was doing about the Upper Brook Street house, she was not sure she wanted to find out. She hoped he would do nothing to upset the old ladies, and nothing at all about the house without discussing it with her first.

Late Monday morning, not long after the royal party emerged from the water-color exhibit, she heard, to her horror, that someone had assassinated the Duke of Wellington. Rumors spread quickly through London, producing painful reactions throughout the business community as well as the beau monde. Members of the court buzzed with the news, and staunch Whigs expressed as much dismay as Letty felt. The hero of Waterloo was still much beloved by his countrymen.

It was Raventhorpe who brought word to court that the rumors were false, and he approached Letty soon after he arrived. "I know you care deeply about him," he said, "so I came to find you as soon as I'd arranged for the news to reach the queen. Wellington himself announced that he has never been in better health."

"Thank heaven," Letty exclaimed. "Thank you, sir. I am most grateful to you for telling me."

His smile warmed her even more than the news he had brought, but he did not linger. The court was buzzing again, this time with good news.

"Who could have started such a horrid rumor?" Letty asked Catherine as they went up to their palace apartments to change for dinner. Both were to dine with the queen, along with her other ladies, for she had also invited Melbourne, her lord privy seal, and the secretaries of state for the Home, Foreign, and Colonial offices.

Catherine shook her head. "Witherspoon said that no one seems able to identify the source. Nor can anyone imagine a motive for such a wicked business."

Letty was trying to think how to phrase tactfully what she was thinking when Catherine looked at her, surprised by her silence. Letty said, "I was just wondering. Would anyone tell Witherspoon who started the rumors, if they did know?"

"Oh yes, I think they would," Catherine said. "The secretaries of the various departments and most members of Parliament think very highly of him, because he has a reputation—uncommon amongst his peers—for studying issues before casting his vote. They frequently discuss the threat of assassination in those circles, you know. Apparently Wellington has received many such threats over his long career."

"I know he has," Letty said. "Someone tried to kill him once in Cornwall, when I was a child."

"I've heard tales about that attempt," Catherine said. "Still, it's odd that such a rumor would fly about now, when he is older and not so active politically. One does hear occasional threats against Her Majesty, of course."

"Yes," Letty said with a disgusted grimace, "and not just because she is queen but simply because she is a woman. Although she has governed capably for two years now, many men still think she has no business to be ruling the country."

"True. I've even heard—" Catherine broke off, then added hastily, "About Witherspoon . . . I-I know why you wondered if anyone would speak to him of such things. He just does not look like a knowing one, does he?"

"No, he doesn't," Letty agreed, wondering what it was that Catherine had so nearly said. "I ought to know better than to judge a man by his looks, though," she added. "Perhaps I see him as I do because you think so little of him."

"But I don't!" Catherine looked astonished. "Just because he is not the ideal husband for me does not mean that I hold him in contempt, Letty. In many ways, he is much more honorable than—" She broke off again, turning red this time.

"Much more honorable than whom? I do wish you would finish your sentences, Catherine."

"Never mind. I should not speak of him in the same breath as . . . as anyone else," Catherine finished lamely.

With a quick look around to be certain no one else was within earshot, Letty said, "Well, it is plain now whom you mean. Have you spoken with him yet, Catherine? Have you warned him to stay away from Upper Brook Street?"

"Oh, don't even speak of him here," Catherine implored, looking around frantically, as if she expected listening ears to pop out of the wainscoting. "I have not met him privately since you warned me that Raventhorpe knows about the house. Fortunately we've been too busy here, and have had practically no time for personal business. Then, too, even when he might have expected me to find time to myself, he was obliged to . . . Well, he has duties, too, you see."

"I don't see," Letty said frankly. "Who is he, Catherine?"

However, Catherine would not say, and when Letty pressed her, the other young woman said with alarm, "I can't, Letty! Pray do not ask me! He has threatened to kill me if I speak his name to anyone, and I believe him."

"I do wish you would not be so melodramatic," Letty said.

"I have my own suspicions as to who it is, you know. I have seen how you look at a certain man."

Blushing again furiously, Catherine said, "Nevertheless, you have heard no name fall from my lips, Letitia Deverill, nor will you. Moreover, pressing me further will afford you naught." Obviously wanting to change the subject, she said, "Did Tavistock tell you that Her Majesty will drive in the park tomorrow morning and that she expects us to attend the opera at Drury Lane tomorrow evening?"

"Yes," Letty said, accepting momentary defeat. "Also that she will hold a privy council at one o'clock, and an audience with Melbourne and the Marquess of Landsdowne afterward. Thus we are to remain in attendance at the court nearly all day, which is particularly awkward for me. My parents may arrive in London at any time now, and I have things I must attend to before they do."

"Well, with the usual drawing room on Thursday, I doubt we'll have much time to ourselves before Friday," Catherine said, "and I, for one, am grateful."

Letty was not grateful, however. She found herself in a continual fret to know what Raventhorpe was up to. Therefore, at a little past four the following day, when she saw Puck Quigley strolling aimlessly about while Victoria was meeting with her privy council, she seized the opportunity to speak with him.

"We do not often see you here, sir," she said.

"I try to avoid the court as a rule," he said with a smile. "My cousin Landsdowne dragged me along with him today, though. Said it would do me good to be seen here. Don't know how it can, though. Dashed boring place, the court is nowadays. Lacks some of the dash and splendor of years past."

"Goodness, sir, you sound like a graybeard," she said, laughing.

"I do, don't I? Bored, I expect. One grew up hearing about one scandal after another at court, and one expected to see and be part of such things oneself. Ought to have gone to Newmarket with Raventhorpe. Much more entertainment there."

"Oh, has his lordship gone out of town?" Though she tried to sound casual, she was certain he must detect the relief in her voice.

"Left late yesterday to attend the second Spring Meeting," Puck said. "Be back tomorrow night, I daresay. What with the drawing room and all, royal duty will recall him if nothing else does," he added with a mischievous grin.

"Yes, I expect it will," she said, paying no heed to the grin.

Her thoughts were racing. Mrs. Linford and Miss Abby must be wondering by now if she had deserted them, she decided; and, if Raventhorpe had issued any orders or ultimatums before departing for Newmarket, they would be distraught. At the very least she ought to reassure them that she would not allow him to do anything horrid. However, for her to see them before he returned to London meant getting away from Buckingham Palace as soon as possible.

Accordingly, she pinched her cheeks till they hurt, then sought out Lady Tavistock. "Pray, ma'am," she said, "I'd like permission to retire for an hour or two if I may."

Lady Tavistock looked at her with concern. "You look feverish, Letitia. Are you ill?"

Unwilling to lie, Letty said, "I do not think I am ill, ma'am, although my companion did remain at home today because she has caught a feverish cold." That much, at least, was true, although she had not expected to feel grateful for Elvira's sniffles and sneezes. "I do feel that I should take precautions, don't you? One does not wish to prove contagious to Her Majesty or to others at court."

"I rarely excuse anyone who is on duty, as you know, Letitia."

"Yes, ma'am." Letty lowered her lashes, hoping to hide her frustration.

As if she were thinking aloud, Lady Tavistock went on to say, "Her Majesty has been setting quite a pace these past few days, because she does not like to give up her simple pleasures even when larger issues like this unfortunate Jamaican crisis take up so much of her time."

"Yes, ma'am," Letty said.

"Perhaps you are merely tired, my dear. Not everyone can keep up with Her Majesty at such times as this."

Gritting her teeth, Letty said submissively, "I daresay some cannot, ma'am."

"I dare not excuse you from the theater party or from dinner here at the palace afterward, I'm afraid, unless you truly are sick. Her Majesty likes to make a display of her attendants on such occasions, as you know, and I have already told Lady Witherspoon that she need not attend. Her husband is entertaining a number of the ministers at dinner tonight. Naturally she must act as his hostess."

"Yes, ma'am. I see that I shall simply have to bear up," Letty said.

Lady Tavistock smiled. "We do not want you growing ill, my dear. I suggest that you spend the next few hours resting in your chamber. I doubt that Her Majesty will require your presence before she departs for Drury Lane at a half past six."

"Thank you, ma'am."

Letty departed at once, before Lady Tavistock could change her mind, or command her to stay in her apartment. Her first impulse was to send a footman immediately for her carriage, but fearing that word of such an order might somehow reach the chief lady of the bedchamber, she went instead to find Jenifry.

"Find Jonathan and tell him to bring the carriage round," she said when she entered her chamber. "I want to call in Upper Brook Street, and I have little more than two hours before I must return. I've just learned that Raventhorpe has gone out of town, and I want to reassure myself that all is well at my house."

"I've already sent for Jonathan, Miss Letty," Jenifry said. "You see, you told me that you would wear the pale green silk to Drury Lane, since it was here."

"Yes, that's fine. I shall return in plenty of time to dress," Letty said.

"Well, it isn't fine, miss. That's why I've just sent for Jonathan."

Letty blinked. "What has Jonathan to do with my dress?"

"If you will recall, Miss Letty, you got a bit of mustard on the bodice of that gown the last time you wore it."

"Yes, but surely someone has cleaned it by now."

"Someone ought to have done," Jenifry said sourly. "However, although the maid who took it away to clean it brought it back fifteen minutes ago, it won't do. She promised to do no more than sponge the stain with boiled fig-leaf water, which is what I'd use myself, and which generally makes such stains instantly disappear. However, the cure in this instance proved worse than the ill. Look at it." She held up the dress to reveal a large spot in the middle of the bodice front.

"Mercy, is this more mischief then?"

"As to that, I cannot say, miss. My guess is that she was just careless, but I did tell her to throw out what's left of the fig-leaf water."

"Have I nothing else here that I can wear?"

"Only the aqua terry gown, Miss Letty, and you wore that one last night. We've been going at such a pace that, thinking you'd be on duty at least another hour or so, I decided I'd go to Jervaulx House and collect a few more gowns."

"It was a good notion," Letty said, "but I'm glad you hadn't gone yet."

"I could still take a hackney, miss. Then you could take your carriage."

"Yes, but what if Papa and Mama have arrived? They would be so disappointed to hear that I'd taken time to go to Upper Brook Street without seeking first to learn if they were at home. I'll have to go with you, that's all."

The carriage was waiting at the side door when they emerged from the palace, and the trip to Jervaulx House took no longer than twenty minutes. Letty greeted the news that her parents had not yet arrived with mixed feelings. Much as she looked forward to seeing them, she wanted to be able to report with a clear conscience that her affairs were in good order.

While Jenifry collected what was necessary, Letty looked in on Miss Dibble, finding that good lady in bed, with a maidservant in close attendance. "I shall be as right as a trivet in no time, my dear," she said when Letty inquired, "I have everything I need, but I must say, I wish you could take that dratted monkey back to the palace with you. He has escaped from your bedchamber three times today, and led the servants a merry chase each time. He misses you, I fear."

"Well, I cannot take him to the palace," Letty said, laughing. "However, I see no reason that I cannot take him with me to Upper Brook Street. I'll take his chain and collar along, and Jonathan and Lucas can bring him back here after they deliver us to Buckingham Palace."

"Oh, if only you could do that. I declare, I don't get a wink of sleep worrying about him getting out of the house and running free through the city."

"Miss Abby and Liza will be delighted to see him," Letty assured her. "And there can be no difficulty returning him afterward, because I shall be going to the theater with Her Majesty and then returning to the palace for dinner. Jonathan need not return for me before ten at the earliest, and Lucas can look after Jeremiah."

"Then that is settled. What will you wear tonight?"

Letty stayed chatting with her until Jenifry came to say that she had Letty's clothing for the evening all sorted and packed. Then, pausing only long enough to collect a joyful Jeremiah, the two young women set out for Upper Brook Street.

Their reception there put Letty in mind of Jeremiah's raptures, for Miss Abby came rushing into the entrance hall while Jackson was taking their cloaks.

"I saw your carriage from the drawing-room window," she exclaimed. "Oh, how we have missed you, my dear! Do come up at once. Miranda will be so pleased to see you."

"I have my clothing for this evening in the carriage, ma'am," Letty told her. "Since it may begin to rain again at any moment, I wonder if Jenifry and Lucas can take it upstairs and hang up my dress, at least. That is, if they won't be disturbing you, or . . ." She paused tactfully.

Miss Abby nodded emphatically. "Yes, of course. They can disturb no one, for there is no one here to disturb. Nor will there be ever again if Justin has his way. Oh, my dear, we have so been longing to talk to you about all this! And here is dear Jeremiah," she added when the little monkey's head popped from Letty's large muff. "Liza has been asking us every day why Jeremiah does not come to visit her. And today she asked particularly, because *no one* has come to see us."

Fully aware of Jackson's interest, although he was busily bestowing their wraps, Letty sent Jenifry and Lucas to take her clothing upstairs, and encouraged Miss Abby's small talk until they were alone in the stair hall on their way up to the drawing room. Then, when Miss Abby paused for breath, she said quietly, "I collect, ma'am, that Raventhorpe has prevailed upon you to curtail your services."

"Curtail? Oh, my dear, he has said we must stop them altogether, and indeed, I do not know what we shall do. It is just as we feared it would be, you know, for he has already begun to tell us that he thinks we would enjoy a little holiday at Ramsgate or Brighton. As if anyone could enjoy the seashore at this time of year, particularly after all the rain we have suffered! It would be just more damp air. I tell you, I could not abide it, Letty. Even Liza, who generally loves the sea, refuses to go. I am afraid she wants to stay here for the most foolish of reasons, however."

"Goodness, ma'am," Letty said, settling Jeremiah on her shoulder but keeping a firm grip on his silver chain. "What reason can that be?"

"She has decided that she wants to marry Justin," Miss Abby said.

"What? Mercy, does he know?" Letty stifled her laughter,

trying to imagine his reaction if he were to learn that Liza held a tenderness for him.

"No, and I am not going to tell him. Poor Liza, she is very fond of Justin, but she is fond of most men, I think. She treats them all the same from what I can see."

When they entered the drawing room, they found Liza and Mrs. Linford sitting by the fire, the former stitching a sampler, and Mrs. Linford reading. Both looked up at their entrance, and Liza cast her work aside at the sight of Jeremiah. "Oh, the dear!" she exclaimed in delight. "May I take him, Miss Letty?"

Having not seen Liza since rescuing her from Boverie Street, Letty was a little surprised by the casual greeting, but she said, "Of course you may."

With no more than a nudge of encouragement, Jeremiah leapt from her shoulder to Liza's arms. Finding that she still held his silver chain, and realizing that the monkey had cleverly detached it from his collar again, she reattached it with a laugh, and warned Liza to keep a close eye on him.

"I hope you do not mind that I brought him with me, ma'am," Letty added with a smile at Mrs. Linford. "Poor Elvira has contracted a feverish cold, and Jeremiah's antics have driven her almost to distraction."

"He is nearly as welcome here as you are, my dear." Her next statement belied this generous sentiment, however. "Do take him away to the kitchen or somewhere, Liza. Perhaps Cook can find him a tidbit left over from luncheon."

"He likes any sort of fruit," Letty said. "Or nuts, if the cook has any."

"I'll find some," Liza promised, hoisting Jeremiah to her shoulder and directing the rest of her conversation to the monkey.

When they had gone, Letty said, "Miss Abby tells me that Raventhorpe has suggested you might enjoy a holiday by the sea, ma'am."

"Indeed, he has, but the sea does not agree with my constitution at this time of year," Mrs. Linford said.

"I should think it would not agree with anyone," Letty said. "What was he thinking to suggest such a thing?"

"He is determined to direct the course of our lives, Letitia," Mrs. Linford replied with feeling, "and I will not stand for it. We have notified everyone we can think of to stay away until this little tempest blows over, but I will not allow Justin or anyone else to order my life for me. I do understand his point that your reputation will suffer if by some mischance a scandal erupts. But I think he exaggerates the danger, don't you? After all, we have weathered many little upsets like this over the years, and none has amounted to more than a storm in a cream bowl."

Letty nodded, understanding how the two old ladies felt. At the same time, however, she realized that she did appreciate Raventhorpe's taking a hand. That he had persuaded them to curtail their activities could only prove a blessing.

"Soon we shan't be able to pay you our rent," Miss Abby said sadly.

"Surely it hasn't come to that, ma'am," Letty protested. "The rent is quite small. Mr. Clifford told me it can never be more than forty pounds a year."

"To your Mr. Clifford that may be small, my dear, but it is not so to us," Mrs. Linford said. "Much of what our friends pay for our services goes to the servants, you know, and to pay for our food and theirs, as well as the rent."

"But surely you don't believe I will cast you out, ma'am. I promise you, rent or no rent, you are welcome to live in this house forever and a day."

"We have our pride," Mrs. Linford said stiffly. "I thought we had made that clear to you, Letitia. We have never had to depend upon the charity of others, and we do not wish to begin at this late date."

"People would *know*," Miss Abby said in anguished tones. "They would all think we had somehow come to ruin through not seeing to things properly, and that is so grossly unfair, when dear Miranda has managed so very well all these years. How could we ever hold up our heads again?"

Tempted though she was to point out that people were likely to think more highly of a pair of suddenly impoverished gentlewomen than they would think of those gentlewomen running a house of assignation, Letty held her tongue. As she strove to think of something constructive to say, sudden distant shrieks put her forcibly in mind of the day Jeremiah had interrupted Catherine and her lover.

Leaping to her feet, she looked accusingly at Miss Abby. "I thought you said there was no one—"

"But there isn't!" Miss Abby, too, had jumped up. "That's not just Jeremiah shrieking. I can hear Liza's voice, too. Oh, mercy, what can it be?"

"The servants will soon tell us," Mrs. Linford said placidly.

"I don't think we should wait," Letty said, hearing another feminine scream. "That came from neither Jeremiah nor Liza."

Hurrying to the landing with Miss Abby at her heels, she realized the noise was coming from below. Catching up her skirts, she ran downstairs, where it became clear that the noise originated somewhere beyond the green baize door in the wall below the sweeping curve of the stairs.

The door was slightly ajar. Letty hurried to it and flung it wide.

More stairs spiraled downward. As she hurried down toward a corridor at the bottom, the pandemonium increased in volume.

"Oh, don't hurt the poor thing!" Recognizing the shrieking voice as that of the maidservant, Mary, and seeing Liza in the midst of a group of people gathered in a doorway along the corridor, Letty ran toward them.

Liza, who was holding Jeremiah's silver chain but not the monkey, caught sight of her and screamed, "Miss Letty, hurry! He's going to stab Jeremiah!"

Others saw her then, and a hush fell over them, allowing her to hear Mary say clearly above the monkey's angry chattering,

"Put down that dagger, sir. He meant no harm. Oh, please, put it down!"

"Verdammter Affe! Ich werde ihn ermorden."

Pushing her way through the group huddled round the door, Letty said sharply, "You will murder no one!" Pulling up short at the sight of Charles Morden with a bedsheet wrapped around him, waving a wicked-looking dagger, she exclaimed, "Good mercy, sir, what are you doing here? What *is* all this?"

At the sound of Letty's voice, Jeremiah darted out from under the bed, holding a white cravat aloft like a banner as he ran toward her. Leaping to her arms and then to her shoulder, he hurled rude epithets at the man still waving the dagger.

Mary crouched near the bed, struggling to cover herself with a quilt.

Realizing that the maid was naked, Letty snapped, "What's going on here?"

"It's that Mary," Liza said. "He don't like her, and that's true, Miss Letty."

"Don't be foolish, Liza. Jeremiah does not dislike Mary."

"Not him," Liza said indignantly. "Him!" She pointed to Morden, who had been trying to adjust the hastily wrapped bedsheet.

Morden glared at Letty. "You seem to like pushing in where you are not wanted," he said in a guttural growl. "First at court, and now here. Women should not push themselves forward so. Go away now. No one wants you here."

"Perhaps you are not aware that this is my house, Mr. Morden. If anyone is going to get out, it is you. How dare you seduce a maidservant beneath this roof!"

To her shock, he smiled, and the smile was not pleasant. "I know this is your roof, girl," he said. "However, you evidently do not know what goes on beneath it. Perhaps you should ask Mary if I seduced her, *nicht wahr?"*

Involuntarily, Letty glanced at Mary, and saw the maid look away with tears rolling down her cheeks. Turning back to Morden, Letty said, "You may be sure that I will talk to Mary, but no one who threatens my pet with a dagger is welcome in this house. Now, get your clothes on and get out before I send someone for a constable. Here is your cravat," she added, detaching that article from Jeremiah's clutches and handing it to Morden.

"Better you think twice, I think, before you are calling for a constable," Morden said. "I have powerful friends. They can do you much harm."

Knowing he spoke no less than the truth, Letty nonetheless was determined to conceal her fears. Meeting his gaze, she said, "Do your worst, for I, too, have powerful friends. And considering the way things are going in Parliament just now, you may soon find that mine are significantly more powerful than yours are."

"That is quite true," Miss Abby said, startling Letty, who had forgotten that the old lady had followed her. Miss Abby went on, "Jamaica will very likely bring down the present government, you know. Everyone says so. Not that one would expect you to understand about that, of course, being a foreigner like you are. Come away out of there at once, Mary. You should be quite ashamed of yourself."

"What's all this, then?"

The group in the doorway parted instantly at the sound of the strident voice, and the imposing bulk of Mrs. Hopworthy loomed on the threshold. Arms akimbo, she exclaimed, "Miss Abigail! Lady Letitia! Mercy, mercy, what goes on here?"

"Well may you ask, Mrs. Hopworthy," Letty said, catching hold of Jeremiah before he could leap from her shoulder, and affecting a calm she did not feel. "Mr. Morden was just leaving," she said. "You may take that sheet with you, Mr. Morden. I am sure the bootboy can show you somewhere you can dress."

His face scarlet now, and muttering furiously under his breath, Morden brushed past the outraged housekeeper.

Sure that he was cursing her, and wondering how much he knew, Letty shooed the others back to their work and told Mary to get dressed. "We are going to retire to the housekeeper's

room, Mary. Come to us there as soon as you have dressed. I
want to talk to you."

"Yes, my lady." Mary's voice was hoarse, her eyes downcast,
and her cheeks still streaked with tears.

Turning to leave, Letty said, "Mrs. Hopworthy, perhaps you
will just make sure that Mr. Morden has left the house before
you join us."

"Yes, my lady, I certainly will."

As the housekeeper bustled off on her mission, Letty said,
"Miss Abby, I do not want to distress Mrs. Linford unnecessarily, but I failed to consider that perhaps you would prefer to
conduct our talk with Mary upstairs."

"Oh, no," Miss Abby exclaimed. "Not until we find out what
she was doing with that dreadful man. Miranda will be so vexed,
she will very likely say we must turn her off without a character
without even hearing what she has to say, and I don't think I
could bear that. Mary has been with us since she was the merest
child."

"He don't like her. He likes me best. Here, Miss Letty, here's
his chain."

Astonished, Letty turned to find Liza behind her, holding out
Jeremiah's silver chain. In the course of watching Mrs. Hopworthy dismiss the other servants, she had forgotten all about
the girl. Now she did not know what to do with her. If she sent
her upstairs to Mrs. Linford, Liza would give her, at best, a
garbled account of the incident. Nevertheless, it was unthink-
able to allow her to witness the forthcoming scene with Mary.

Taking the chain, she said quietly, "Liza, I think perhaps you
ought to—"

"Mary did a bad thing! He don't like her. He likes me best.
He told me so!"

"Liza, please . . ." Then she realized what Liza had said.
"What do you mean, he told you? When did Mr. Morden tell
you anything?"

Glaring at her, Liza burst into tears, whirled about, and ran
up the stairs.

"Oh, dear, now you've upset her," Miss Abby said. "The poor thing don't know what she means half the time, I'm afraid."

"I think she knows very well this time," Letty said thoughtfully as she reattached the monkey's chain to his collar.

SEVENTEEN

"Oh, what if Miranda comes downstairs to see what caused all the row?" Miss Abby wailed when they stepped into the housekeeper's sitting room.

"Since the row has stopped and we have not yet seen her, I think we are safe for the moment," Letty said calmly, stroking the monkey, still on her shoulder.

"He's gone, my lady," Mrs. Hopworthy said when she joined them. "Would you like some tea? I can have one of the girls bring some in at once."

"No, thank you, Mrs. Hopworthy. Do sit down."

"Perhaps I should go and hurry that Mary along," the housekeeper said.

"I'm here, ma'am," Mary said in a small voice from the doorway.

"Come in and shut the door," Letty said.

"Please, my lady, am I to be turned off without a character?" Tears still trickled down the maid's damp cheeks.

"It's what ought to happen to you," the housekeeper said with a sniff before Letty could speak. "Carryings-on with menfolk is what I won't tolerate, girl."

"We was only trying to help," Mary said with a sob.

"We!"

"How were you helping, Mary?" Letty asked quickly before the housekeeper could further unburden herself of her outrage. "I don't understand."

"Our ladies have been so worried, ma'am, about how they could get enough to pay the rent if his lordship was to make them stop letting people come here like they do. We thought we should help them, don't you see? Me and some of the others thought . . . Well, we knew that some of the men what comes here likes us, and when they offered us money for . . . well, for what they wanted, it didn't seem like such a dreadful thing. Mr. Morden, he's that handsome, ma'am." Mary shot a sidelong glance at Miss Abby's scandalized expression and fell silent.

Frowning, Letty said, "I did not realize that Mr. Morden was one of your patrons, Miss Abby."

"Nor did I, my dear. Indeed, I don't believe he is."

They looked at Mary.

Flushing deeply, she said, "I don't think so either, ma'am, but he did come here once with Sir John Conroy, and he flirted with me. So when he came round asking would I like to make some extra money . . . Oh, my lady, please don't turn me off. I send half my wages to my mother to help feed my little sisters."

Letty said sternly, "I will see if I can persuade Mrs. Linford to let you stay, Mary, but you must never again allow someone like Mr. Morden to have his way with you. How many of the other maids have done anything like that?"

Mary bit her lower lip, looking from one to the other. Then, with a sigh, she said, "Most of 'em lately, my lady. Mostly, they just gives a good time to the coachmen what comes with our ladies' friends. I'm the only one that's done it with anyone grander. We all get paid, though," she added with an earnest nod. "We'd not have done it without we got the money, Miss Abby. We slipped it into the housekeeper's jar, the one what she uses to pay the tradesmen."

A moan escaped Miss Abby's lips.

"You may go now, Mary," Letty said. "Tell the others they must stop, too. I think perhaps you had all better forfeit your half-days until we get this sorted out."

"Yes, ma'am." Mary shot a frightened look at Mrs. Hopworthy, but when the housekeeper only pressed her lips tightly together, the maid fled.

"I don't like this, my lady," Mrs. Hopworthy said when the door was safely shut again. "It is not my habit to keep immoral girls in service here."

Stifling a sudden impulse to point out that morality had not, until this moment, seemed important to anyone in the house, Letty said only, "I am sure it is not your practice, Mrs. Hopworthy. Presently, however, we have more problems to worry about, and I am convinced that Mary and the others thought they were helping." She could not resist adding, "One can scarcely blame them if they did not quite understand that what they were doing is wrong."

Again the housekeeper pressed her lips to a thin line. Letty noted that she was careful not to look at Miss Abby.

Poor Miss Abby was scarlet. "What have we done? Oh, Letty dearest, what have we done?"

"We can talk about that upstairs," Letty said. "I believe Mrs. Hopworthy wants to make certain the other maidservants are not neglecting their duties."

"I do," Mrs. Hopworthy said grimly.

"Please send someone to ask Jenifry Breton to come to me in the drawing room," Letty said gently. "I want her to take charge of Jeremiah."

"I could take him to her for you, my lady," Mrs. Hopworthy said, slanting a wary look at the monkey.

"Thank you for offering, but I will feel much better if I can hand him over to her myself," Letty said. "Now that he seems to delight in escaping from people and making such a nuisance of himself—"

"Oh, pray don't say that he may not visit us again," Miss Abby said. "That would be so unfair. This was not his fault. Indeed I . . ." Glancing at the housekeeper and then at Letty, she wrung her hands together. Then, with a sob, she said, "I expect we should go now and tell Miranda what has happened."

"Yes," Letty said. "I think we must."

"I'll fetch Miss Breton myself, my lady," the housekeeper said.

"Thank you." Letty ushered Miss Abby out of the room and up the stairs.

The old lady went reluctantly, and remained uncharacteristically silent.

"Don't fret so, Miss Abby," Letty said when they reached the landing outside the rose-scented anteroom. "Mrs. Linford can't *eat* any of us, you know."

"She will be considerably vexed," Miss Abby said with a sigh, "but in truth I was not thinking of Miranda."

"You weren't?"

"No, I was remembering the day you said it sounded like we were running a brothel here. I told you then that it was no such thing, but oh, my dear, I'm afraid it was! Oh, what will Miranda say?"

When they entered the drawing room, Mrs. Linford looked up from her book and said calmly, "I trust everything has settled down now. I cannot conceive of what can have stirred all that row." She glanced expectantly from Miss Abby to Letty, then added complacently, "I daresay it was that monkey. I must say, my dear, I do not welcome him in my drawing room."

"No, ma'am," Letty said. "Jenifry is coming to fetch him. Indeed, I think I hear her coming now." When Jenifry hurried into the room a few moments later, Letty said, "Take Jeremiah upstairs with you, Jen. He has slipped his chain twice already today, so take care that he does not do so again."

"Yes, my lady," Jenifry said, taking Jeremiah and holding him against her shoulder like one might hold a baby. "I should perhaps point out that it is nearly four o'clock, Miss Letty," she added.

"Mercy, is it? Where has the time gone? I'll have to change here, Jen. Put out my clothes, and send word to Jonathan that he must have the carriage waiting at the door in half an hour. I cannot be late, but I need ten more minutes before I dress."

"You'll never dress in twenty minutes, my dear," Miss Abby said. "Perhaps you had better go at once."

"We must talk first," Letty said firmly.

Miss Abby's face fell, and she shot an anguished look at her sister. "I expect we must, but I do wish we needn't, you know."

"Sit down, Miss Abby," Letty said gently, taking a seat near Mrs. Linford.

Jenifry turned to leave.

"Wait, Jen," Letty said. "I want to ask you a question." When Jenifry turned back, she said, "Did you ever have occasion to speak of the affairs of this house to your friend Walter?"

Blushing furiously, Jenifry looked at Mrs. Linford and Miss Abby before she said earnestly, "I wouldn't, my lady. You know that I'd never gossip about your affairs or those of people close to you."

"I do know, Jen. I just needed to hear you say it. Thank you."

Without a backward glance, Jenifry hurried from the room.

"Now, Miss Abby," Letty said, "shall I tell it, or would you prefer to tell Mrs. Linford yourself what we learned below-stairs?"

Mrs. Linford said, "You tell me, Letitia, if you please. Abigail never could tell a tale in less than ten minutes, and you do not want to be late to the palace."

"No, I don't," Letty agreed. "Very well, then." As quickly as she could, and for once without any interruptions from Miss Abby, she explained the situation.

Mrs. Linford listened without speaking. As far as Letty could tell, the only indication that the old woman understood the magnitude of what she was hearing was that she grew slightly paler. When Letty finished, Mrs. Linford was silent for a long moment before she said, "I see. How very dreadful. Do you know how long the maids have been engaging in these unfortunate activities?"

"Mary did not say, ma'am, but I don't think it can have been long. Mrs. Hopworthy surely would have discovered it by now if they had a long habit of entertaining men in their bedchambers, particularly since Mary said they have been slipping the money they've made into the housekeeping jar."

"Yes, I expect she would, then. My dear, we must *not* tell Justin about this."

Letty had been thinking the same thing, but hearing her thought spoken aloud somehow put it in a new perspective. "The reputations of people very close to him could be at risk, ma'am. Your niece, for one. We do not know how much Mr. Morden knows of what has been going on here, but that he was able to seduce a maid is enough if he chooses to broadcast it to the world."

Anxiously Miss Abby said, "Surely he will not speak. Like all of us, he has his own reputation to think about, does he not?"

"Don't be foolish, Abigail," Mrs. Linford said. "Men of his stamp are not like the gentlemen we count as our friends. Mr. Morden has no reputation of any consequence, and thus nothing to lose by saying whatever he pleases."

"His master does, however," Letty pointed out. "It is not the same as if Morden were a manservant, of course, but he does serve at Sir John Conroy's pleasure, I believe, and I doubt that Sir John will want the news made public."

Miss Abby said more cheerfully, "I'm sure you are right, my dear."

"Well, he does have his own reputation to consider, and that of at least one other for whom he clearly holds tender feelings," Letty said tactfully, seeing no reason to name names at this point.

"I don't like him," Mrs. Linford said frankly. "Always poking and prying about. The only thing that man *really* cares about is his position at court."

"You are right, ma'am, and for that very reason, we must take particular care now. He may think his knowledge more useful against others than it is damaging to himself, and with what Mr. Morden now has to tell him, I think we would be wise to prepare ourselves for the worst. To that end, I believe we must tell Raventhorpe everything. He is not at home presently—"

"Newmarket," Miss Abby said, nodding.

"Just so, ma'am, but he will be in London tomorrow for the drawing room. I will endeavor to speak to him then or afterward. I must go now," she added, rising, "but please, don't worry, either of you. Somehow we will see this through."

"You are very kind, my dear," Mrs. Linford said, also rising to her feet.

"Nonsense, ma'am. It is no more than my duty to put things in order here. Oh, and that reminds me! I know you have warned Lady Sellafield to stay away, but did you think to warn Admiral Rame, as well?"

"Admiral Rame? Why on earth should we? He is our very good friend."

"Well, I thought . . ." Letty hesitated. "I know you have been very discreet, ma'am, but surely, the man Lady Sellafield meets here has as much right as she does to know that it is no longer safe. I did think briefly that it might be Sir John Conroy, but that was before I saw her at her dinner party with the admiral."

"Oh, not Sir John," Miss Abby exclaimed with a shudder. "But not Admiral Rame, either, my dear. He has a new young wife whom he quite adores."

"I didn't know," Letty admitted. "But if it is not the admiral . . . Really, ma'am, I ought to know who it is, lest I inadvertently say something I'll regret."

"There is no harm in your knowing now, I expect," Mrs. Linford said placidly. "It is Teddy, of course."

"Teddy? I do remember her mentioning that name. But Teddy who, ma'am?"

"Why, Teddy Witherspoon, of course."

Letty stared at her, stupefied. "Witherspoon?"

"Yes, my dear. They have known each other since they were children, and I believe she would have married him had her father not insisted that Sellafield was a far greater catch. Indeed, it is my belief that she named dearest Ned after Teddy."

Letty gasped. "Ned is not Witherspoon's . . . That is— Oh, mercy!"

"No, my dear," Mrs. Linford said. "Simple arithmetic will tell you that Ned cannot be Teddy's son. Ned is twenty now, after all, and although her relationship with Teddy began years ago, before he married Lady Witherspoon—"

"We think he married her because she looks much like Sally did at the same age, don't you know," Miss Abby said.

"Don't interrupt, Abigail. As I was about to say, my dear, although they began meeting before, once he married Lady Witherspoon, we utterly forbade Sally to meet with him again until after his wife had presented him with an heir. We could not allow any interference with the succession to his title, of course."

"Of course you couldn't," Letty said, feeling weak in the knees though she was sitting down.

Miss Abby's eyes twinkled. "Have we not been clever to keep Teddy from finding out about Catherine? It was a near thing more than once, too, I can tell you, because Catherine's young man likes to make plans on the instant, but we did not feel we could deny her when we had been letting Teddy meet Sally here for years."

Before Letty could think of anything to say to that, the door from the anteroom opened, and Jenifry entered to say, "Miss Letty, it's gone well over the ten minutes. If you don't—"

"Mercy, I must fly," Letty said. "I'll tell Raventhorpe to do nothing further without telling me. In the meantime, though, pray do nothing yourselves to make matters worse, and be sure your servants understand that they must admit no one."

Although she dressed as quickly as she could, and Jonathan and Lucas had the carriage at the door when she ran down again, they reached Buckingham Palace with only minutes to spare. Leaving Jeremiah in Lucas's care, she rushed in at the side entrance with Jenifry, hoping to avoid a meeting with Lady

Tavistock or anyone else who would demand to know where she had been. Unfortunately, she met her ladyship on the first landing.

"Why, there you are, Letitia," that haughty dame said with a frown. "I decided to look in on you myself, to see if you were feeling more the thing."

"I—"

"You need not tell me," Lady Tavistock said. "I can see that you have changed your gown, and assume that you returned to Jervaulx House to do so. It is unfortunate that you did not simply send your woman to collect some things. Under the circumstances, that would have been much wiser, I should think."

"Yes, your ladyship," Letty said meekly.

"We must go directly to the front hall. Her Majesty's party will have assembled by now, but with luck we can be there before she arrives."

"Thank you, ma'am," Letty said. Signing dismissal to Jenifry, she hurried in Lady Tavistock's wake, suppressing the guilt she felt at having deceived the woman. The last thing she needed now was to have to explain everything.

The royal party reached the theater shortly before seven o'clock, and *The Maid of Palaiseau,* based on one of Mr. Rossini's operas, began shortly afterward. Madame Albertazzi, who was making her first appearance for the season as the persecuted but finally triumphant maid, was a favorite with the audience. Her entrance onto the stage was the signal for an enthusiastic and prolonged welcome, in which those gracing the dress circle and the private boxes took a decided part.

As Letty looked around the theater during the clamorous applause, she noted that while patrons occupied nearly every space available in pit, gallery, and box, the boxes straight across from theirs remained empty. Remembering similar empty boxes in European theaters she had visited on royal occasions, she wondered if perhaps they remained so to pre-vent a would-be assassin from taking up a position directly opposite the queen.

The thought sent a shiver up her spine. She was standing behind Victoria and a little to her right, because even in the theater, members of the queen's party did not sit in her presence. If an assassin's aim was off by the slightest amount, Letty re-alized that she herself made an excellent target.

As the play progressed, she forgot her imaginings, caught up in the splendor of the production. Madame Albertazzi was charming, and unlike many of her contemporaries, she did not overdramatize her part but played it naturally, making one feel that the character she portrayed was real. The audience remained unusually silent, as caught up in the story as Letty was. Thus, when the first act ended amidst a thunder of applause, it took a moment more before she realized that the box directly oppo-site theirs was no longer empty. The gentleman seated there raised a hand to her in greeting. The lady beside him smiled widely.

Even then, so much did she feel as if she had wakened from a dream that she did not instantly recognize them. When she did, however, she exclaimed, "Mercy, it's Mama and Papa!" Turning without another thought to Lady Tavistock, she said, "Oh, ma'am, pray excuse me for a few minutes? My parents have arrived, and I should very much like to welcome them."

Lady Tavistock said austerely, "When one is attending Her Majesty, Letitia, one does not ask to be excused. Moreover—"

To Letty's astonishment, Victoria said, "Let her go, Anna Maria. She has not seen them in over a month. Do not dawdle, Letitia."

"No, Your Majesty. Thank you, Your Majesty."

Victoria said nothing more, but Lady Tavistock said evenly, "Go then, Letitia, but I find it rather extraordinary that you did not meet your parents at Jervaulx House since you barely man-aged to return before we left the palace."

Bobbing a curtsy, Letty made no effort to reply to that, and backed to the entrance of the royal box with more speed than grace. Fearing at any moment to hear either Lady Tavistock or Victoria call her back, she did not breathe naturally until she was outside in the corridor with the door to the royal box shut behind her. Picking up her skirts then, she fairly ran past the stair landing to the other side of the house, slowing there only because she was uncertain which door she wanted.

As she hesitated, a door opened and a petite dark-haired woman stepped into the corridor. When her gaze fell upon Letty, her dark blue eyes twinkled merrily.

Letty hurled herself into her mother's arms. "Mama!"

"Darling. Oh, how glad I am to see you!" Daintry Tarrant Deverill, Marchioness of Jervaulx and Countess of Abreston, hugged her daughter tightly for a long moment, then held her away to look at her.

The two were much the same size, and in the glow of lamp-light in the corridor, they looked closer in age than one might expect. The marchioness, at forty-three, retained both her slim figure and the roses-and-cream complexion of her youth. If a few gray threads had invaded her ebony curls, they remained invisible without stronger light. Her smile was merry, revealing still white, even teeth.

She turned back toward the box she had come from and said, "Gideon, come and say hello to your daughter."

At once Gideon Deverill, seventh Marquess of Jervaulx, stepped forward. "Thought I'd give you two a moment alone first," he said, holding his arms wide to welcome Letty.

As she stepped into them, Letty sighed with pleasure and the sense of safety she always enjoyed when he hugged her. "Papa, I'm so glad you're here. I've missed you both even more than I'd expected."

"We've missed you, too, ducky."

Over six feet tall and still as broad-shouldered and powerful-looking as ever, the marquess, at fifty-three, looked like a man in his forties. His hair had greyed more than his wife's had, but his tanned complexion and upright posture made the grey seem premature. Believing him to be one of the handsomest men she knew, Letty could think of only one other whose good looks could compare with his.

"I can't stay," she said. "Lady Tavistock didn't want me to leave, but Her Majesty said I might."

Daintry said, "You look tired, darling."

"Do I?" Letty felt heat in her cheeks, and she was glad for the dim light. Even so, and much as she wanted to linger, she knew that she could not. Her parents would soon see that she had things on her mind that she was not mentioning to them. They were astute at such things, as she had frequently discovered in the past.

Even as these thoughts sped through her mind, Gideon said teasingly, "We've not heard of any explosions at court, so you must be behaving yourself. Have you learned anything more about why Benthall left you his house?"

"No," she said, glad that he had asked a specific question that she could answer with absolute truth. "I had hoped that you could tell me."

"I can't yet," he said. "The duke collected a list for me of people with whom Benthall corresponded, and I mean to ask them if they can cast any light on the puzzle. He seems to have indulged in quite a voluminous correspondence."

"It was kind of Wellington to take an interest," Letty said, having no doubt to which duke her father referred. "Did you hear about the rumors of his death?"

"Yes, we stopped at Apsley House when we first arrived in town," Gideon said. "There is nothing more evident than that the Melbourne government is worn to the stump and must fall any day now, the duke says. The Jamaican crisis is bringing everything to a head. The Whigs depend upon a coalition of their liberal and moderate wings to hold everything together, you see, and it is rapidly unraveling."

"You can't talk politics now, you two," Daintry said with a laugh. "Letty has to get back to her duties. Will you come home after the theater, darling?"

"No, I am to make part of the royal dinner party tonight, so I will be late. Do you and Papa attend the drawing room tomorrow?"

"Yes, your papa has the entrée, of course, and the duke procured our carriage ticket for us yesterday. We are to meet a number of our friends in the Ambassadors' Court, but you need not wait till then to see us, you know. I'll wait up for you tonight, my love. Come to my sitting room as soon as you come in."

"I will," Letty promised.

As she hurried back to the royal box, she heard the bell ring to warn strollers that the next act was about to begin. The chance of being late did not concern her as much, however, as how she was going to avoid revealing to her parents everything that had happened and everything she had learned since she had come to London.

She was not in the habit of deceiving them, but in childhood she had often neglected to tell them about her more interesting adventures until sometime after they had occurred. Her reasoning at the time had been that she did not want to worry them, and she felt much the same way now. However, over time, both Daintry and Gideon had learned to recognize certain signs, not all of which she understood, but that somehow allowed them to sense when she was keeping details to herself. This time, she vowed to herself, she would tell them everything, just as soon as she had got things sorted out. She would never hear the end of it, though, if she had to ask her father to put things right for her before then.

Gideon had retired before Letty got home, and although Daintry had waited up as promised, she was full of news from Paris, and from Eton where they had stopped to visit James.

"He is perfectly well, of course. He always is," Daintry said. "I nearly expired though, through holding back laughter when he told us he had asked you to persuade the queen to reserve a ship for him."

"What do you hear from young Gideon?"

"Nothing of late. I think he persuaded himself he need not

write because we had left Paris and had not yet arrived in London, but your papa says we can go to Oxford to see him next week. Can you get leave to go with us?"

"I'll try," Letty told her.

"You must get some sleep now, darling, or you will look a hag tomorrow."

Feeling nearly exhausted, Letty slept almost as soon as her head touched the pillow. And although she had intended to arise early so that she could breakfast with her parents, Jenifry did not waken her until nearly nine o'clock.

"Her ladyship said I mustn't disturb you till the last possible minute," the dresser said when Letty exclaimed at the time. "She is bathing now, but she said she knows you must leave before she and your papa do, so you are to visit her in her dressing room when you are ready to depart."

Dressing quickly, Letty snatched up her gloves and mantle, told Jenifry to let Lucas know she was ready to leave, and went in search of the marchioness. Finding her still in her frilly dressing gown, seated before her looking glass, Letty said as she bent to kiss one rosy cheek, "You should wear that to the palace, ma'am. As beautiful as you are, you would turn every head in the room."

Daintry chuckled. "You are kind to say so, darling, but my head-turning days are over. I mean to bask in the glory of my lovely daughter. Don't tell me you haven't collected a string of beaux here, for I shan't believe you."

Letty knew she was blushing, but she said calmly, "I shan't tell you any such thing, ma'am. Nor would I be so brazen as to boast of a string. For one thing, until recently, most people at court ignored me, and although I received numerous invitations from our friends, I rarely had time to attend Tory parties or balls."

"Not everyone at court ignored you, surely."

"Not everyone," Letty said, blushing again when a vision of Raventhorpe leapt to her mind's eye.

"Ah-ha, just as I thought," Daintry exclaimed. "Who is he?"

"No one. At all events, I cannot stay to talk or I'll be late."

"Very well, but we are going to have a long talk before we are much older, my dear. I want to hear about everything that has happened to you in London."

With this daunting promise echoing in her ears, Letty hurried to her carriage, where Jenifry, Lucas, and Jonathan awaited her. Twenty minutes later they arrived at Buckingham Palace, and half an hour after that the queen's party, in three carriages, traveled to St. James's Palace for Her Majesty's drawing room.

Letty had seen Raventhorpe astride a magnificent black gelding while everyone gathered to depart for St. James's, but for the next two hours she found no opportunity for private speech with him. Upon their arrival at St. James's, the queen took her place, standing before the throne and facing the wide entryway, the landing, and the grand stair up which the company would stream. The queen's ladies gathered behind her, as always, and Lady Tavistock's gaze seemed to rivet itself on Letty. It remained so until the presentations ended.

The only remarkable incident occurred when a deputation of twelve Quakers courteously but adamantly refused to remove their hats. Their doctrine, they explained patiently to the chamberlain, required that they should never voluntarily uncover their heads in the presence of either sovereign or lesser mortal.

Since the room contained a multitude of foreign dignitaries, as well as young women making their first curtsies to their queen, it seemed that a crisis might erupt, until a quick-thinking official solved the problem. As the Quakers mounted the grand staircase in pairs, two Yeomen of the Guard, one standing to the left and the other to the right, lifted off each man's hat as he passed so that the letter of their rule remained inviolate.

Each man solemnly kissed the queen's outstretched hand, evidently finding that bit of homage inoffensive to his principles. Indeed, Letty heard the leader of the group comment afterward that he found the act no hardship. "I assure thee," he added, "it was a fair, soft, delicate little hand."

At last the final presentation was over, and members of the company remaining in the chamber began to converse in normal tones while they awaited their turn to descend to the carriage hall. The queen engaged Lord Melbourne in conversation, and even Lady Tavistock allowed herself to respond cheerfully when someone approached her to chat.

Letty, having noted that her parents were among the remaining company, hesitated only a moment before making her way toward Raventhorpe, who stood alone for the moment near a window embrasure.

He smiled at her approach. "I like that gown," he said the moment she was within earshot. "You wear lavender better than nearly any other woman of my acquaintance."

"Thank you," she said, surprised at how warming she found the simple compliment and wishing she need not spoil the moment by telling him about the recent events in Upper Brook Street. "Have you a moment to speak privately, sir?"

His eyes twinkled. "Perhaps it would be better to speak later, when Lady Tavistock is not so near at hand."

"Where would you suggest we meet?" Letty asked with a grimace. "I could ask you to call at Jervaulx House now, but my parents are in town, so we cannot be private there, and you have forbidden me to visit Upper Brook Street."

His mouth quirked. "Are you suddenly so obedient, then?"

"No," she retorted frankly. "That is precisely why I must speak with you. I went there yesterday, and—"

"The devil you did!" The twinkle vanished, and his expression grew forbidding. "Just once, I wish you would show some sense, my girl."

"I wish you would not call me that," she snapped. "Moreover, we have no time for recriminations. I must tell you—"

"You have got to stay away from there until I can be certain—"

"You did not even stay in town long enough to see if your

aunts obeyed your orders, sir. You went to Newmarket to the races!"

"I had committed to do so with friends, but what if I did? I could hardly stand over my great-aunts with a whip, you know. I believed them when they gave me their word. Are you telling me now that they broke it?"

"No." She bit her lower lip, suddenly loath to tell him what had happened. She was facing him, her back to the general company, and when she looked at him again, she saw that he was gazing beyond her, his eyebrows knitted in a frown. "I wish you will stop glowering, Raventhorpe. People will wonder what we are saying. It's bad enough already without that."

"Your father is looking at me," he said.

She was glad to note that his expression relaxed. "You can scarcely wonder at it if he is," she said.

Raventhorpe smiled at her then. "No," he said, "but no one warned me that the man cuts such an imposing figure as he does."

Her heart warmed at seeing the smile, but she knew it would be short-lived. "There is no use putting this off," she said a little sadly, "but you are going to be dreadfully angry, I think. I took Jeremiah with me when I visited them, you see."

"I can scarcely be more angry at that than at your putting your reputation in jeopardy again," he said gently.

"No, but that is not all." She sighed, then added in a rush, "The maidservants have been helping your great-aunts by entertaining customers of their own, you see, and what's worse than that is that your own mother is one of . . ."

The black look that descended on his face silenced her. For a moment he said nothing, but faced with that look she felt her knees begin to quake. Then, in measured words and an implacable tone that she had never before heard from him, he said, "Do continue. My mother is one of what?"

EIGHTEEN

The noise of the drawing room seemed to fade, leaving Letty alone with Raventhorpe and his anger. She wanted to look away. Even more, she wanted to run. Never had her courage come so close to deserting her.

"Well?" Still that horrid, implacable tone.

"I should think you would be concerned about the maidservants' activities," she said. Then, before he could reply, she added hastily, "Did you hear what I said, sir? They have been granting sexual favors to all sorts of men."

He said nothing.

"They thought they were helping your great-aunts make ends meet. Jeremiah surprised Mary in bed with Charles Morden, of all people, and she said all the maids have been doing it. She said that mostly they entertain servants who accompany your great-aunts' patrons. She is the only one who has been with someone grander, she said. As if Morden were grand."

Still he remained silent.

Exasperated, Letty said, "Have you nothing to say, sir?"

"I am waiting for you to answer my question."

Feeling a sudden lump in her throat, and wishing she had never approached him, Letty swallowed hard. Then slowly, painfully, she said, "I don't want to tell you. Surely you've guessed that by now."

"But you will."

"Yes," she said with a sigh. "I cannot be party to keeping it from you any longer. The danger has increased past the point where anyone could justify silence. She . . . she is one of those who have made use of your great-aunts' services."

"Do you dare insinuate that my mother is having an affair with someone?" His outrage was unmistakable, his tone a menacing growl.

"I'm not insinuating anything. I'm *telling* you. It's true, sir."

"I hope I do not intrude."

Letty nearly jumped out of her skin at the sound of her father's voice, and Raventhorpe's head snapped up, showing that he, too, had remained unaware of the marquess's approach.

"Perhaps you should present this gentleman to me, my dear." Jervaulx's tone was calm, his words innocent, but Letty knew better than to think he did not know he had interrupted them at a tense moment. She wondered how much he had heard.

All sign of Raventhorpe's fury had vanished. His countenance showed no expression at all, but she knew that his anger still lay just below the surface, that the slightest spark would set it afire.

He did not know her father, and suddenly, fear that he might stir the marquess to forget his diplomatic training became more important than anything else. She did not want to cause strife between them. Without a thought for the consequences, she said, "Papa, this is Viscount Raventhorpe, but I have something that I simply must explain to him, and it cannot wait. Lady Tavistock will summon me at any moment. Please, sir, I will present him to you properly at another time."

Meeting Jervaulx's stern gaze, she knew that she had displeased him, but she did not look away. After a long moment's silence, still looking right into her eyes, he said evenly, "As you will, my dear. I am sure your explanation will be a good one." With a nod to Raventhorpe, he left them.

Letty turned back to the viscount and saw, disconcertingly, that he looked amused. "Do you dare to laugh at me, sir?"

"You never cease to surprise me," he said. "Was he speaking

of the explanation you have yet to give me, or one that he expects you to give him later?"

"The latter, I'm afraid." Knowing that his amusement was transitory, that most likely she would anger him again, she felt briefly overwhelmed. That Jervaulx was unhappy with her as well, only added to her woes. His anger was not as formidable as Raventhorpe's, for he had never made her knees feel as if they had turned to wax. Still, at the least, he would demand to know what she had been thinking, to keep what she had learned about the Upper Brook Street house from him and from Mr. Clifford both. At the moment, she had no good answer to that.

"I would have my explanation at once, if you please," Raventhorpe said.

Drawing a deep breath and hoping she could say what she had to say before anyone else interrupted them, she said, "Mrs. Linford said not to tell you. Matters have reached such a pass, however, that I was afraid you would find out through some other means. For all I know, Morden is aware even now that—"

"How long have you known this?" The anger was returning.

Swallowing again, she said, "For some time, sir, but—"

"How dare you keep something like that from me!"

"I did so because your mother asked me to. Indeed, sir, I should not be telling you now, because she should be the one to tell you, but I feared—"

"You did not trust me. You continue to insist upon managing affairs that are beyond the ability of any female to manage. Had you told me what was going on when you first discovered it, I might—"

"I didn't tell you because your great-aunts begged me not to tell you. They feared that you would do precisely what you have done, which is to take over and begin issuing orders. Don't you understand that they have been independent for years, making their own decisions without interference from anyone—"

"And just see where it has got them!"

"You sound just like your stupid Whig friends in Parliament," she said. "All of you think you know how to run people's lives from a distance better than they can manage them on their own."

"Do we, indeed?" His tone was grim.

"Yes! You issue ultimatums and expect others simply to bow down in abject obedience. Well, sir, people don't behave so! Whether they are Jamaicans or mere British females, people value independence and will do what they must to hang on to it once they've got it."

"Well, in this case, I'm afraid that I—"

"I remind you that the house is mine," she snapped. "It is also your great-aunts' home and your mother's sanctuary. What goes on there is no concern of yours, and I will thank you to keep your notions and orders to yourself henceforth."

"Very well, you little termagant, have it as you will. When Conroy and his friends threaten you with social ruin, perhaps even with criminal prosecution, you can look elsewhere for help. No doubt your father will be happy to deal with such eventualities when they occur. I own I should like to be a fly on the wall when you explain it all to him. Perhaps this time he will give you your just deserts."

She opened her mouth to tell him that she could manage her affairs by herself, thank you, but the words would not come. Her throat ached, and her eyes burned with unshed tears. Determined not to give him the satisfaction of seeing her cry, she glared at him in silence until he brushed past her and strode away.

For a long moment, feeling terribly alone, she stared at the wall in front of her, unwilling to turn, certain that at least a dozen pairs of eyes were watching, waiting to see what she would do. Then the normal noises of numerous persons engaged in social conversation swelled around her, reminding her that most people paid heed only to their private concerns, that to assume they watched her was simple conceit. Drawing a breath to steady herself, she turned.

As if drawn by a magnet, her gaze fell instantly upon her father. He was looking at her with narrowed eyes, and he seemed about to walk toward her when her mother touched his arm and began to speak to him. Experience informed Letty that she had won a respite. She would not have to face Jervaulx until later.

Catherine approached, looking as if she, too, suffered from fraying nerves. "Letty, Her Majesty is ready to depart."

Glad of an opportunity to put aside her own troubles, Letty said, "Are you feeling quite the thing, Catherine? You look as if you are ill."

"I can't talk now," Catherine said, flushing, "but I've learned something quite horrid, Letty."

"Tell me," Letty urged. "Perhaps I can help."

"No one can help. I've brought it on myself, and I must deal with it myself." Abruptly Catherine turned and walked away.

Wondering if she had discovered Witherspoon's infidelity, Letty felt tempted to follow and urge her to say more. However, recalled to her duty by a glance from Lady Tavistock, she hurried to join the others instead.

At Buckingham Palace, the chief lady of the bedchamber told Letty that the queen had invited her to join the royal dinner party again that evening, so once more it was late when she returned to Jervaulx House. Finding a message from her mother on the hall table with her candle, she told Jenifry to wait for her in her bedchamber and went to the marchioness's sitting room.

Daintry was sitting at her writing desk. When Letty entered, she put down her pen and sprinkled silver sand over what she had written, saying, "You're very late again, my love, but at least I have nearly finished a long and chatty letter to James. He will be astonished at how much I have written, for I am persuaded that when we visited him he must have thought we told him everything that had happened in our lives since he last left us in Paris." With a smile, she added, "Your duties at court seem to keep you very busy."

"Yes, ma'am, and there will be no rest tomorrow, either. Her Majesty is holding court to welcome the hereditary grand duke of Russia. She has planned numerous activities for him through the weekend, too."

"Yes, I know," Daintry said. "Your father decided that we should pay our respects to the grand duke, and then go right on to Oxford. He is certain that the present government cannot last much longer, and Wellington and Sir Robert have asked him to stand ready to help form a new one at a moment's notice. Nothing can happen before Monday, of course, but he has decided that if he is to indulge my wish to visit Gideon, we must go at once."

"I wish I could go with you," Letty said, "but . . ." She spread her hands.

"I know, darling." Daintry regarded her silently for a long moment, and Letty's lips and mouth suddenly felt parched. It was all she could do not to fidget. Then her mother said gently, "Your father wanted to speak to you earlier, you know, but I prevailed upon him to wait."

"I . . . I know," Letty said. "I know he is displeased with me. Both of you must wonder . . ."

When she paused, uncertain how to put her chaotic thoughts into words, Daintry said, "He was a little shocked by the way you spoke to him. But he can be patient when he believes it wise to be, and I persuaded him that he must trust you to deal with that very handsome young man in your own way. Nevertheless, darling, you were disrespectful, and you must apologize to him before you leave for the palace in the morning."

"Yes, ma'am, I will," Letty said, thankful to have got off so lightly.

Bidding her mother good night, she went to her room and prepared for bed, certain that she would fall asleep at once. Instead, her thoughts continued to dwell for some time on the events at the Upper Brook Street house, and the scene with Raventhorpe at the palace.

She slept at last, though, and when she awoke, Jenifry was

opening the curtains. Sunlight streamed through the windows. A tray with Letty's morning chocolate sat on the table near the door, steam rising from the little pot's spout.

"Good morning, miss; 'tis a fine bright day today," Jenifry said.

"Is his lordship up and about?"

"He's in the breakfast parlor," Jenifry said.

"Then I will dress. I don't want my chocolate, Jen."

Twenty minutes later, she entered the sunny breakfast parlor to find the marquess alone, reading one of the morning newspapers. He set it down and rose to greet her with a hug and a kiss.

"I like that dress," he said.

"Thank you, sir. I came to apologize for speaking to you as I did yesterday."

"You're lucky I was in a mellow humor, ducky. Your mother says that I am not to ask you any questions about that scene I interrupted, but I must tell you, I did not like seeing that young man frown at you like he did. Had you given him cause?"

"Yes, sir." Letty said no more, but she watched him warily. Experience warned her that her father was not one to let matters rest so easily.

To her surprise, he smiled again, saying only, "You had better get some breakfast, you know. I expect you have to get to the palace soon."

"Are you going out, sir?" she asked as she turned with relief to examine the dishes set out on the sideboard.

"I have a meeting with Wellington and Peel this morning. I suppose your mother has told you that we mean to visit young Gideon at Oxford. We'll leave tonight and return late Sunday."

His casual attitude tempted her to tell him everything. Only the knowledge that he would instantly take the management of the Upper Brook Street house into his own hands stopped her. She had not yet proved her ability to deal with her affairs, and while she might need his help in the end, she was not ready to give up.

Helping herself to some toast, and an orange from the Jervaulx Abbey succession houses, she sat down and turned the subject to politics. Since he wanted to hear what others were saying about the Jamaican crisis, that topic occupied them satisfactorily until they had to go.

As they left the breakfast parlor together, he said, "If the Whigs suspend the Jamaican constitution on Monday, as they seem determined to do, Melbourne's government is bound to fall. In that event, Her Majesty's state ball on Friday will serve as a splendid celebration of the Tories' return to power."

Letty grimaced. "You may greet that notion with delight, sir, but I can assure you Her Majesty will not. The royal household has been on the fidget now for weeks. I cannot imagine what it will be like if Melbourne's government falls."

"Don't fret about it, ducky. There will be changes in the royal household, as well. It won't do, you know, for the queen to continue surrounding herself with Whigs once their party is out of power. Her constitutional duty demands that she present at least the appearance of impartiality."

"She hasn't done so yet," Letty pointed out.

He smiled. "She will."

Letty left soon afterward for the palace, and throughout the weekend, the activities in honor of Russia's hereditary grand duke kept her busy. She saw Raventhorpe frequently, but if he noticed her he gave no sign of it. She might as well have been invisible.

Knowing she had only herself to blame for his attitude depressed her, but she could think of no way to change it, so she turned her mind to solving the problems in Upper Brook Street. Her duties kept her far too busy to do anything more than think about them, but the glimmerings of an idea began to form.

* * *

Her parents returned to London late Sunday night, and on Monday, as Jervaulx had predicted, Parliament suspended the Jamaican constitution. On Tuesday, also as predicted, the prime minister offered his resignation.

Letty was with Victoria when the news reached Buckingham Palace, and to her dismay, the queen dissolved into tears. "All, *all* my happiness gone," Victoria exclaimed. "Dearest, kind Lord Melbourne no more to be my minister!"

Lady Tavistock instantly ordered the other ladies from the room, but word quickly spread through the palace that the queen remained inconsolable.

Melbourne visited her at noon, and she sent for her ladies afterward, apparently determined to put a good face on things. "Lord Melbourne insists I must send for Wellington," she said. "He does not believe the duke will agree to form a government, but I hope he does, for if he won't, I must send for Sir Robert Peel."

The ladies closest to her exclaimed sympathetically. Letty said nothing, nor did anyone ask for her opinion.

"Melbourne says I must strive to conquer my dislike of Sir Robert," Victoria added sadly. "It is very hard to have people forced upon you whom you dislike."

Wellington visited her the following morning, but as expected, the elderly duke declined her offer to take over as prime minister. That afternoon Sir Robert Peel, in full court dress, presented himself at the palace, ready to receive his sovereign's commands to form a new government.

Letty felt no more surprise than anyone else when the interview did not go well. She had met Peel, and had heard much about him. Her father thought him more intelligent than Melbourne and a far more skilled politician, but Sir Robert possessed few social graces and was apt to conceal shyness beneath a reserved, off-putting manner. In any event, as everyone knew, the Tory leader could not hope to compete with his charming predecessor for the queen's favor.

Victoria emerged from their twenty-minute meeting with her

eyes still tear-swollen and her demeanor resentful, but she announced to her ladies that she had remained collected, though she thought Sir Robert had seemed embarrassed and put out. Having said that, the queen added that Peel would return next day to report on his progress in forming a government, and then gave way again to her tears.

In the meantime, Letty spent nearly all her time at the palace, and saw little of her parents. Jervaulx spent less time than she did at home, and her mother was busy as well.

Thursday began with more royal tears and recriminations, but during the morning, a letter from Melbourne cheered Victoria, and led some of her anxious household to think the worst of the storm had passed. An exchange of notes followed, the queen evidently seeking and receiving advice from Melbourne about how she should deal with Sir Robert. Her spirits began to rise.

Peel arrived as promised early in the afternoon, and this time Victoria did not dismiss her ladies. It was, Letty thought, more like a state occasion of the sort that frequently prompted the young queen to display the splendor of her entourage than a normal meeting between sovereign and prime minister.

The audience began smoothly enough. Peel informed her of several of his appointments, including that of Wellington as his secretary for foreign affairs, and she deigned to accept them all. Several more points of business ensued before Sir Robert said quite audibly enough for all to hear, "Now, ma'am, about the ladies."

Victoria said instantly, "We have no intention of giving up any of our ladies, sir. Indeed, we never imagined that you would ask such a thing of us."

"Do you mean to keep them all, ma'am, even your mistress of robes and the ladies of the bedchamber?"

"All," Victoria said flatly.

"But they are Whigs, ma'am, wives of the opposition party. Certainly, *some* change is necessary to show your confidence in the new administration."

"We never talk politics with our ladies, sir," the queen snapped. "Such a notion is absurd. We know that when governments change, a king must change members of his household who are members of Parliament, but unless you mean to give seats in that august body to our ladies, we have nothing more to discuss."

Although Sir Robert continued to try to make his point, he failed, for Victoria remained unimpressed. When he left, his mood was somber.

He returned later with Wellington to try again, but although Victoria heard them out, they made no progress. The following morning, determined to prevent further demands that she remove at least certain ladies of her bedchamber, she sent Peel a flat refusal. She would not dismiss a single one of her dear friends.

Later in the day, Sir Robert, believing that he faced an impossible task, resigned without forming a government.

Victoria joyfully recalled Melbourne; and the state ball, which many in the palace had feared they would have to cancel or hold without the queen's presence, suddenly loomed as a jubilant celebration, albeit not for the party that had hoped to be celebrating.

The queen retired with her bedchamber ladies to dress for the evening, and before following her, Lady Tavistock took Letty aside. "I daresay you intend to return home to dress for the ball, Letitia."

"Yes, ma'am, with your permission."

"Certainly, for Her Majesty will not require your presence at her little dinner for the hereditary grand duke and her ministers, so perhaps you will want to spend the time with your parents instead, and drive to the ball with them afterward."

"Thank you, ma'am, I'd like that." Though she thought it an odd suggestion, she had little time to think about it, and summoned her carriage at once. She had been home less than an hour, however, when a footman rapped at her dressing-room door and handed Jenifry a message for her.

Unfolding the note, Letty stared at it in dismay. The queen had dismissed her. Worse than that, Victoria had banished her from court.

NINETEEN

Jenifry said anxiously, "What is it, Miss Letty?"

"They've dismissed me," Letty told her grimly, "banished me from court."

"Lor', miss, why would they do such a thing?"

"In truth, I had half feared dismissal, because the queen was so out-of-reason cross with Sir Robert for demanding that she change her Whig ladies for Tories, but I never thought she would ban me from court altogether. This note says word has reached Her Majesty's ears that I am involved in certain meretricious activities of which she must forcibly disapprove."

"What's that, then, 'meretricious'?"

"Well, in this instance, I believe it means I've attracted attention in a vulgar way," Letty explained. "Indeed I hope that is all it means. I have a dim recollection that it can also refer to matters relating to prostitutes or prostitution."

"Lor' now, what could Her Majesty know of such things, as young as she is?"

"She is nearly as old as I am," Letty reminded her.

"Aye, so she is, but nonetheless, miss . . ." Jenifry tactfully fell silent.

"If you are on the brink of pointing out that we have enjoyed quite different upbringings, you are quite right," Letty said with a rueful sigh. "I'm afraid Sir John Conroy or his minions have been busy again, but I wonder how much, exactly, he can have told her."

"I swear, Miss Letty, I never—"

"I know you said nothing to Walter," Letty said. "It would not matter, in any case, since between them, he and his precious Morden must know all there is to know about that house. I just never thought he'd dare tell Her Majesty. If he told her the whole truth, he took an awful risk that she would learn about his relationship with Lady Witherspoon."

"He won't want that, miss."

"No, he most certainly won't."

Jenifry glanced at the clock. "It's nearly seven, which is when his lordship said he wanted to leave for the palace," she said quietly. "You had better go and tell him and your mama at once that you cannot go with them."

Letty grimaced. "How on earth am I going to explain this to them without telling them the whole? What a scrape I've got myself into this time, Jen."

"Just tell them you've been dismissed," Jenifry suggested. "You need say no more than that tonight, surely."

"Papa would demand to see the note I received. How would I explain that?"

"Still, miss, maybe his lordship can fix it. If he explains to Her Majesty that you have done nothing wrong—"

"She won't want to listen to any Tory, Jen, least of all tonight," Letty said.

"Still—"

"No, I don't want him to fix things for me," Letty said firmly. "I have thought of a way to deal with Miss Abby and Mrs. Linford, and I won't have people saying I cannot manage my own affairs before I've even put it to them. I forbid you to say a word about this to Papa or to anyone else."

"What will you do?"

"Stop asking questions! If Elvira weren't still sick, you wouldn't plague me like this."

Instantly regretting her outburst, Letty opened her mouth to apologize, but the door opened and a maidservant hurried in, speaking as she came. "Lady Letitia, there's another message come, and the man did say to bring it straight up, no matter that the butler said you was just on the point of leaving the house. And his lordship said to tell you to make haste, m'lady, lest you will be late to the palace."

"Thank you," Letty said, taking the message. "Tell his lordship I shall be down in a twinkling."

"Yes, m'lady," the maid said, turning with quick steps back toward the door.

As the door shut again, Jenifry said urgently, "Miss Letty, you must—"

"One minute, Jen," Letty said. "Good gracious, this note is from Miss Abby. What the devil has happened now?" Reading swiftly, she frowned. "She writes only that I must come at once, that it's a matter of life and death."

"Lor' now, what can she mean by that?"

"Heaven knows, but I'd better go," Letty said. "No doubt she has exaggerated the case, but if she has not . . ." She fell silent, but her thoughts were racing. "At least this gives me a plausible excuse for not driving to the palace with Papa and Mama, but you will have to tell them, Jen. I can't face them yet. They would ask too many questions, and I simply cannot lie to them."

"You want *me* to lie?"

"No, certainly not. Just tell them that I have received a note asking me to stop in at the house. That much is quite true, after all. Say that I am certain the case is not as urgent as Miss Abby writes, that doubtless she wants only to see me in my finery; and say that I will join them as soon as I can. Perhaps you can also beg them to make my excuses if Lady Tavistock complains of my absence. She will not do so, of course, so that will be all right."

"It don't sound all right to me, Miss Letty. His lordship will be turning me off without a character when he learns the truth about all this."

"Don't be daft, Jen." Letty wished she could be as certain as she was trying to sound. Nevertheless, she added firmly,

"Now, do as I bid you. I'll go out to the stables myself and order a second carriage. You can join me there as soon as you've talked to them, because I want you to go with me."

"Well, that's a good thing, that is, because I'm either going or I'm telling his lordship the whole truth, miss. This don't sound right to me, not right at all."

"Go on, Jen, and don't spout empty threats at me. You've never yet cried rope on me. I don't suppose you will begin tonight."

"Maybe I ought to have done long since, Miss Letty, for I'm thinking it's a pity Miss Dibble is still laid down upon her bed. You've gone and got yourself into deep water this time, and no mistake. His lordship's right about that, and I don't mean your papa when I say that, neither."

"We will not discuss Raventhorpe," Letty said grimly. "I don't even want to think about that man tonight. Now hurry, Jen. If Miss Abby does believe it's a matter of life or death, she won't thank us for dawdling."

Letty did not for one moment believe that Miss Abby's description would prove remotely akin to the true state of affairs at the Upper Brook Street house. Still, she hurried the stable-boys, affecting an urgency even greater than she felt.

When it occurred to her that the urgency she did feel likely rose from fear that her father might want to discuss her decision to visit Upper Brook Street, she put the unsettling thought out of her head. However, the sense of profound relief she felt when she saw Jenifry hurrying toward her alone, stirred an equal sense of guilt.

"What did they say?" she demanded as the dresser climbed in beside her and the coach began to move.

"Your mama wanted to know what you could be thinking, but your papa said there was no time to argue with you if you were not all to be late. He told me to remind you that most of the guests, not to mention the queen's ladies, are supposed to be present at a state ball before Her Majesty makes her entrance. I don't mind telling you, miss, he had that look on his face when he said it, too."

Letty did not have to ask what look Jenifry meant. She had seen it often enough to know. The marquess was a mild-tempered parent by most standards, but when one did manage to rouse him to anger, the result was unpleasant for all concerned. She did not look forward to their next meeting, but she could not dwell on its likely consequences now.

"It is not like you, miss, to put off unpleasantness," Jenifry said quietly.

Letty did not speak for a long moment, well aware that she was behaving like a coward. Then, with a sigh, she said, "They are going to be so disappointed in me, Jen. Heaven knows I am disappointed in myself! Still, before I can tell them everything that's happened, I must learn the worst of it. Lady Tavistock's note mentioned no specific crime, only that my activities were meretricious. Until I know what, exactly, has come to light, I simply cannot involve Papa. Not now."

"He would not agree with you, miss."

"I know, but I must deal with this myself. Now hush, and let me think. Surely, Lady Tavistock will tell me what she has heard, at least, if I can just ask her. And the sooner I can do so, the better, or everyone will hear about this. As soon as we can get away from Miss Abby, I'll go to the palace. I won't go to the ball, of course, but perhaps I can arrange for a brief private meeting with Lady Tavistock."

"What if they won't let you in?"

"I've got my badge of office, and I doubt that anyone will have ordered the guards at the front gates to keep me out, so I'll not worry about that until it happens. First we'll attend to Miss Abby's life-and-death matter, though. Not that I believe it is any such thing, mind you."

Everything looked normal enough when the coach drew up before the house, but Letty's complacence disappeared in an instant when the door flew open, and Miss Abby pushed past Jackson to greet her with tears pouring down her face.

"Thank God, you're here at last," the old lady exclaimed, adding in a rush of words, "I thought our man must have missed you! He's killed Lady Witherspoon, all because she would not let him misuse poor Liza in the most shocking way. Oh, my dear, my dear, what devilry have we brought upon ourselves?"

Hastily pulling Jenifry and the old lady inside and telling Jackson to shut the door, Letty said, "Hush, ma'am, they'll hear you in the street. Did you say that Catherine is dead? What is she doing here? She is supposed to be at the palace."

"I know, I know, but she said he made her come here, that it was a test of his power over her, and now he's gone and murdered her in our house, and we don't even know who he is! At least, she must be dead by now, because—"

"Good gracious, could she still be alive? Why did you send for me, then, and not for a doctor?"

"But we did send for the doctor," Miss Abby said, brushing a hand across her cheek. "We did that at once, but we did not know what else to do, or how to keep him from telling the world she died here! We cannot think that would be a good thing, you know, not until we can invent a good reason for her being here at all."

"We can talk about inventing reasons later," Letty said. "Where is she?"

"In the yellow bedchamber, the one where you found them the first time."

Without waiting to hear more, Letty ran upstairs.

Inside the bedchamber, she found Mrs. Linford and a thin little man standing quietly beside the bed. Catherine lay still against the pillows, her eyes shut, her face as white as the lacy pillowcase.

"Is she . . . ?" Letty could not speak the words.

Mrs. Linford shook her head. "Not yet, my dear, though we

fear she will expire at any moment. We must fortify our spirits as best we can."

"The poor, poor dear," Miss Abby said, entering behind Letty with Jenifry right behind her, peering over her shoulder.

"We ought to send for Witherspoon," Letty said impulsively.

"No."

To her surprise, the single, harshly muttered word came from the figure on the bed. It drew the doctor, equally astonished, to bend over her at once.

Catherine's eyelids fluttered, then opened slightly. Her lips parted again. "Letty, don't." The words were barely audible, but the effort visibly exhausted her. When she tried to speak again, Letty moved closer but was not sure she heard correctly. She thought Catherine murmured, "He mustn't know."

Speaking to the others, Letty said, "What else has she told you?"

"That's the first time she has spoken," Mrs. Linford said. "She has been unconscious till now. He must have knocked her down, you see, for we found her crumpled on the floor. The doctor says her head must have struck a hearthstone or the chimneypiece when she fell."

Her words seemed to upset Catherine, for she stirred, grimacing with pain, and tried again to speak. Letty moved right to the bedside, kneeling down so that she would not miss a word this time.

Catherine's breathing sounded labored. She said, "Letty, he hit me so hard."

Trying to think how to learn the most while demanding the least effort on Catherine's part, Letty said, "Miss Abby told me you were trying to protect Liza. That was very brave of you."

"No . . . That wasn't all. I—I don't . . . Letty, you must stop him! He's going to k-kill . . ."

Though Letty strained her ears to hear, no more words passed from Catherine's lips. Her eyes had shut again, and her breathing grew so shallow that Letty could no longer detect even the slightest stirring of the coverlet.

With a surge of terror, she turned to the doctor. "Help her! She mustn't die. We must hear what she wants to say!"

"I can do nothing more," the doctor said quietly. "She may last another hour; she may not. Frankly I'm amazed that she found strength to speak."

Turning to Mrs. Linford, Letty said urgently, "Where is Liza?"

Miss Abby exclaimed, "Liza! What do you want with her at a time like this?"

"Really, Letitia," Mrs. Linford said, "the child has been through enough tonight. Moreover, I do not think that this is an appropriate—"

"Ma'am, forgive me, but did you hear what Catherine said? He is going to kill someone. We must find out who it is and stop him."

"But Liza will not know. How could she?"

"Was she not present when he struck Catherine down?"

"She was, Miranda," Miss Abby said. "You know she was."

"Yes, that's true, she was. Very well, my dear, you are quite right." With that, Mrs. Linford moved to pull the bell.

"Wait," Letty said. "You go, Jen. Find her and bring her here at once."

While they waited, Letty tried again to urge Catherine to speak, but she did not, and it seemed an age before Jenifry returned with Liza.

Before Mrs. Linford could so much as begin to interrogate the girl, Letty said, "Leave her to me, please, ma'am. Liza, did you hear what Lady Witherspoon and the man said before he hurt her?"

"Aye." Liza looked guiltily at Mrs. Linford. "I didn't know it were wrong, what he wanted. The others does it, and they gets money. I wanted money, too, and he likes me best."

Miss Abby gasped, looking wretched, but Mrs. Linford said sternly, "Never mind that now. Answer her ladyship's question at once."

"Yes, please, Liza. What did they say?"

"He said she was to do what he told her, and she said she wouldn't. She said he was to leave me be, and that she wanted him to leave her be, too. She said she didn't believe he cared about her, anyway, only about her position at court."

"About her position? That's what she said?"

"Aye, and he said 'twas true enough, that he seduced her— Be that the right word, m'lady? Seduced?"

"Yes," Letty said grimly. "That's the right word."

"Well, I did wonder, 'cause he said he would tell everyone she did it to him if she said a word about him out . . . out of school, I think he said."

"He threatened to say *she* had seduced *him?*"

"Aye." Liza glanced nervously again at Mrs. Linford, but that lady kept her lips pressed tightly together. "He did say that, miss. Said he would tell her husband as much if she tried to make trouble for him with the queen or anyone, or if she had failed in the task he had set her tonight."

"Task? What task?"

"I dunno," Liza said. "What they said then made no sense. She said she wouldn't give you nothing to give Her Majesty, that for all she knew it might harm her or you. He laughed then, all evil-like, and she got wild. She said she believed it *were* worse than that, that they wasn't really going to pretend to save Her Majesty like he promised, but to assassinate her for real. What's 'assassinate,' Miss Letty?"

"But that's mad," Letty said, ignoring the rider as she fought a chill that threatened to paralyze her. "I don't believe for one moment that Sir John Conroy intends to murder the queen. She is the key to all the power he craves."

Mrs. Linford said, "Sir John?"

At the same time, with surprise in her voice, Miss Abby said, "He wore a mask, as usual, when he arrived, but I don't think it can possibly have been . . ."

"Wasn't Sir John," Liza said, her voice a dim echo of theirs.

"But if not Sir John," Letty exclaimed, "then who was he, for heaven's sake?" Even as she said the words, however, she remembered something Liza had said but moments before. "You said he likes you best! Liza, was it—"

"Mr. Morden do like me best," Liza said, nodding earnestly.

Mrs. Linford said, "Merciful heavens."

Letty felt dazed. "The time I interrupted them I didn't see him because he kept his head under the covers the whole time I was in the room, but a number of things made me think Sir John was the one."

"Oh, my dear," Miss Abby said, "I quite see how you came to make the error, for Sir John *was* here that horrid day when Liza ran away. And it's perfectly true that he has been a patron of ours from time to time. As we told you, many gentlemen in high places have made use of our service. But he never saw Catherine here, nor she him, for we are most discreet, you know. Moreover, that particular liaison of his has come to an end, so I do hope you will not ask us who—"

"No, no," Letty said hastily. "Her identity is of no consequence, but good God, what are we to do? I must go to the palace at once, and— Oh, dear, but if they don't let me in after all, what would I do? What a horrid coil this is!"

"But you must go if our dear little queen's life is in danger," Miss Abby said. "Mr. Morden ran out of here like one possessed. I thought he feared that we would send instantly for the police, but of course we can do no such thing until we decide exactly what we should tell them."

"Hush, Abigail," Mrs. Linford said when Letty looked pointedly from Liza to the doctor, who had turned his full attention to his patient. Nodding, Mrs. Linford said, "Liza, my dear, if you have no more to tell us, you should go to bed now."

"Yes ma'am," Liza said, her shoulders slumping. "I'm sorry I was wicked."

"I should not have said you were wicked," Mrs. Linford said, her face flushing. "You did not know any better, and that is quite my own fault. Go to bed now, child. We will talk more of this in the morning, but you have nothing to fear."

"I'll take her," Jenifry said, slipping an arm around Liza's shoulders.

Letty glanced at the bed, wondering if Catherine had slipped away without even a farewell, but the doctor still hovered over her. Sending a silent prayer heavenward, she fought a nearly overwhelming and most uncharacteristic urge to burst into tears.

Mrs. Linford said, "There is no time to lose, Letitia. You must go at once to the palace, for you can reach Her Majesty more quickly than anyone else here. Only you have the entrée."

Drawing a breath to steady herself, Letty said, "I'm afraid I no longer have it, ma'am. I received word only this evening that Her Majesty has dismissed me. The queen never really wanted me there, you know, and now that she has practically fought and won a war with Sir Robert Peel over her Whig ladies, she apparently has decided to get rid of me."

"Mercy on us," Miss Abby said, clutching a hand to her breast.

"Then you must send for your father," Mrs. Linford said flatly. "I do not like to do that, as you must guess, but we simply cannot delay when Her Majesty's life hangs in the balance."

"But what will people think of us?" Miss Abby wailed. "Everyone is bound to learn *why* Lady Witherspoon was here, Miranda."

"Forgive me, ma'am," Letty said, "but we have reached a point where necessity must take precedence over what people may think about any of us. An image, after all, is only that, Miss Abby. It is time for all of us to face reality."

"Then you must send for your father, I expect," Miss Abby said with a sigh of resignation.

"No, ma'am, I won't do that," Letty said. "I don't deny that he could help, but in fact, he has already left for the palace, and even if I knew exactly how to get a message to him, it would take much longer than if I can get to the queen myself. Raventhorpe can help me do that if I can reach him before he leaves Sellafield House, and much as it goes against the grain with me to beg his help, I can hardly ignore my own advice at a time like this."

"Oh dear, Justin will be so angry," Miss Abby said fretfully.

When Mrs. Linford winced, clearly agreeing, Letty nearly had second thoughts, but she stiffened her resolve. It occurred to her then that she might not find Raventhorpe at Sellafield House, that he might already have gone on to the palace. If that proved to be the case, she decided, she would just have to gain entrance by herself, one way or another.

Leaving the two old ladies and the doctor with strict orders to do nothing until they had heard from her, Letty shouted for Jenifry and hurried to her carriage, knowing well that her chances of finding Raventhorpe still at home were slim. If she missed him, she decided, she would just have to act on her own.

TWENTY

Raventhorpe stood impatiently before the cheval glass in his dressing room, while Leyton twitched the tails of his evening coat into place and brushed away bits of lint that somehow had managed to mar the perfection of the dark blue material.

"My lord, if you will not stand still, I cannot be answerable for the result."

"Tardiness is not a trait Her Majesty will forgive, damn it. I should have been gone twenty minutes ago."

Calmly Leyton said, "Although you have frequently credited me with accomplishing miracles, sir, I cannot turn back the hands of time."

"I know that," Justin retorted. "If I'm short-tempered, blame the damned weather. What the devil do *you* want?" He addressed the last few words to his brother, who entered the room without ceremony, still in his shirtsleeves.

"I wanted to know if I've got this blasted cravat tied properly," Ned said, looking him in the eye. "You're always saying that I should effect a more fashionable style, but if you are going to roar at me, I'll go away again."

Justin sighed. "Don't go. I'm in a black mood, that's all. No cause to take out my temper on you. You've tied that very well."

"I say, that's decent of you, thank you," Ned said, peering around him to catch a glimpse of himself in the glass. "Just for that, I shall warn you that Father is looking for you. I told him you might have already left for the palace, but if you don't leave at once, he is likely to track you down. I daresay he wants to borrow money again," he added, smoothing a fold of his cravat with a fingertip.

"Thank you," Justin said dryly. "Are you ready to go now?"

"No, I'm not, as you can see perfectly well, since I have not even got my coat on. Moreover, I don't mean to go for a while. I ain't a lord-in-waiting, I'll remind you, and I don't want to spend the whole night dancing attendance on Mama or Susan Devon-Poole, although I believe I might try my luck with her since you don't want her."

"You won't succeed," Justin said. "She is looking for bigger game, my lad. She'll most likely refuse Puck Quigley, and he's got more to offer than you have."

"The devil you say! We'll just see about—"

"*Here* you are," Sellafield declared from the doorway. "You might have told me he was still here, Ned. Justin, I want a word with you before you go."

"I'm off," Ned said instantly, shooting a sympathetic glance at his brother as he slipped past Sellafield.

Resigned to the inevitable, Justin signed to Leyton to leave. When that worthy had disappeared into Justin's bedchamber and shut the door, he said curtly, "If you have come to ask for more money, sir, I can only tell you that I meant what I said the last time."

"Thunderation, lad, you can't mean to leave me in debt to an ass like Conroy. I won't have it. No right-thinking son would leave his father in such a fix."

"No right-thinking father would put himself in such a fix," Justin said unsympathetically, picking up his hat and gloves from the table where Leyton had put them.

"Now, see here, Justin," the earl snapped. "I am still your father, and I owe me respect. I won't have you talking to me that way, by God. We'll see bailiffs here in Sellafield House if you don't straightaway set things right with Conroy."

"Just how much do you owe him, for heaven's sake?"

"Five thousand pounds now, I think it is."

Justin stared. "How the devil—? No, don't try to answer that. I don't want to know. Very well, sir, I will pay your debt to Conroy, but—"

"I knew you would," Sellafield said on a note of profound relief. "No son of mine could leave his father in such a pickle. Why, I'd have to blow my brains out, that's what I'd have to do."

Controlling his temper with difficulty, Justin said, "I will pay the debt, sir, but only on the condition that, in return, you relinquish authority over all Sellafield properties to me."

"What? The devil you say! I won't do it."

"I am sorry to hear that. I shall endeavor to visit you occasionally in prison."

"Now, see here, Justin, they ain't going to throw me into debtor's prison. I'm still a peer of this realm, damned if I'm not."

"Then you have nothing to fear."

"I suppose you think your mother has nothing to fear. Bailiffs in the house, me on the penniless bench, finished and aground. How do you think *she* will feel?"

"Perhaps she will convince you to sign authority over to me," Justin said, moving to his desk and opening a drawer. "I had the papers drawn up two days ago. You need only sign them, and I will give you a draft on my bank."

"That's extortion."

"I prefer to think of it as sanity. I'd have done it long since if I hadn't felt guilty about inheriting the money and worried about what people would think." More gently he added, "I will promise to seek your advice when I need it, sir, but the land will fare better in my hands than it does in yours. You know it will."

Sellafield glared at him.

"You will have to decide quickly," Justin said. "I should be at the palace right now, and Mama must be waiting for you to escort her to the ball."

"Well, she ain't," Sellafield growled. "She dined out this evening and means to go with a party of her own."

Fearing he already knew the answer, Justin said, "With whom did she dine?"

"Now, how the devil would I know that?"

"She ought to have told you," Justin said. "Most wives tell their husbands where they intend to dine, and with whom."

"That just shows you don't know much about wives, lad. In my experience, they don't do any such thing."

"Mine will," Justin said grimly.

"If you ever get one. Oh, don't look daggers at me. I'll sign your damned papers. Don't see that I've got much choice, do I? Give them to me."

Justin spread the papers on the desktop and moved so that Sellafield could sit to sign them. His impatience stirred again when the earl chose to read each one first, but he suppressed it, hoping he was doing the right thing.

A rap at the door heralded the entrance of a footman who looked particularly wooden-faced. "Begging your pardon, my lords," he said, "but I've got a message for Lord Raventhorpe."

"What is it?" For once Justin did not trouble to hide his impatience from a servant. To his surprise, the man hesitated, glancing at Sellafield. When Justin held out a peremptory hand, he gave him a folded slip of white paper.

Frowning, Justin unfolded it. The frown deepened and fear knotted his stomach when he read, *I must see you at once. It is a matter of life and death! Letitia Deverill.*

Glancing at his father, he said, "You must excuse me, sir. I have pressing business, I'm afraid. Keep one set of those papers, and leave the others there."

"What about that bank draft?" Sellafield demanded.

"I'll get it to you before breakfast, but I hope you believe me when I say that if you——" He broke off, turning back to tell the footman to await him in the corridor. When the man had gone, and had shut the door, Justin said, "I warn you, sir, if you don't draw the bustle, much as I shall dislike it, I will let your creditors know that henceforth they must apply to me to settle your debts."

"You wouldn't do such a damned unfeeling thing!"

"Oh, yes, I will. Now, will you give me your word that you'll make a real effort to curtail your extravagance?"

Bitterly Sellafield said, "Would you trust my word?"

"I believe it is as good as my own, sir. Do I have it?" Trying not to think about the note he held, he forced himself to wait for an answer.

"Very well, damn you, you have it."

"Thank you." With that, he snatched up his cloak from the chair where Leyton had left it and hurried from the room to find the footman awaiting him. Making sure the door had latched firmly, Justin said urgently, "Where is she?"

"In the little parlor off the stair hall, my lord. With her ladyship gone out for the evening, I did not know what else to do with her."

"Of course not. I, on the other hand, know exactly what to do with her. I shall drop her in the Thames."

The footman's mouth twitched.

Justin grimaced. "Think that's amusing, do you?"

"N-no, sir." He could not meet Justin's gaze.

With a sigh, Justin said, "Look here, I've got a strong notion that I'm going to want Leyton. He's either still in my bed-chamber or he's gone to his room. See if you can find him for me without drawing my father's notice. I don't want his lordship to see Lady Letitia before I can get her out of the house."

"Yes, my lord."

"Tell Leyton to wait for me in the front hall." Turning away, he strode to the stairs and hurried down them, trying to ignore the knot of fear that had twisted his stomach since reading Letty's note. He had not lied in telling the footman what he would like to do to her. He only hoped that she had exaggerated her need.

"Oh, thank heaven you are still here," she exclaimed, starting toward him when he flung open the door.

One look at her told him she had not exaggerated, for her usual confident demeanor had given way to visible distress. Thus, instead of demanding to know what the devil she meant by coming to his house in such an improper way, he crossed the little room in two long strides and caught her by the shoulders.

Peering anxiously into her eyes, he said, "What is it, Letty? What has upset you so?"

Having expected him to shake her or, at the very least, to lecture her before giving her a chance to speak, Letty felt a surge of relief. "They're going to assassinate the queen," she said.

"What?"

"It's true, sir. I did not know what to do, because Papa and Mama have left for the palace already, and I've been dismissed from my post—banished from court, in fact. I've still got my badge of office, but I don't know if it will still get me into the palace, and even if I could get in, I doubt that they would allow me to approach Her Majesty. I was so afraid you'd have gone already!"

"Well, I haven't. My carriage should be waiting at the door."

"Very likely it's there," she said, "but any number of carriages are standing in the square just now. Not only did I not pause to inspect them but your porter answered the door the moment I pulled the bell. I know I ought not to have come here alone, but my companion is still sick, and Jenifry stayed with Liza. That is another whole story, I'm afraid. Oh, Justin, Catherine Witherspoon is dead, or at least she's dying! It's all quite horrid."

"You can tell me everything in the carriage," he said. "We must make haste, though. As it is, we may be too late." Nodding to Leyton, who was waiting in the hall as ordered, to accompany them, Justin urged Letty toward the door.

"How could we be too late?" she demanded. "They won't dare kill Victoria at a state ball with a crowd of people and the hereditary grand duke of Russia looking on. Indeed, for the moment, at least, she must be safe, although I suppose we cannot be certain of that."

Putting a hand under her elbow as they hurried down the steps to the carriage, he said, "It would be easier to get close to her at a ball than almost any other time, I'd think, but what makes you think anyone means to assassinate her?"

"Apparently, Charles Morden gave Catherine something to give to her. Liza said Catherine meant to give it to me, actually, but I cannot think that is right. She must have thought it was a gift from Sir John Conroy—yet another attempt by the horrid man to wriggle back into the queen's good graces. But for some reason, Catherine refused to give it to her. At least, Liza said they fought because Catherine had refused to do as he demanded." Letty fell silent as he helped her into the carriage, trying to remember just what else Liza had said.

Shouting to the coachman to get them to the palace as quickly as he could, Justin climbed in beside her. As they waited for Leyton to follow suit, he said, "Perhaps you had better begin at the beginning. I might understand better if I knew how you know that Catherine is dead, or dying, what the devil Liza has to do with it, and who exactly wants to assassinate the queen."

Explaining quickly how word of her banishment from court had come just before Miss Abby summoned her to Upper Brook Street, she described all that she had heard and seen there. "Catherine said that it was a test of Morden's power over her that he could force her to meet him at the house tonight. Even so, I'm certain that Liza said she had refused to give their gift to me or to the queen."

"I presume he has been meeting Catherine there straight along, then."

"Yes, only I thought she was meeting Sir John."

Justin grimaced. "Just how did Morden force her to meet him tonight?"

"Liza said he threatened to tell Witherspoon that Catherine had seduced him, rather than the other way round," Letty said indignantly.

"Did Catherine know what the gift was? Is that why she refused?"

Letty hesitated. "I think she must have guessed in the end. Liza said . . . Let me think. She said . . . Yes, she said that Catherine no longer believed him, that just before he struck her, Catherine said she did not believe they meant to save her, after all—meaning Victoria, of course—but really to assassinate her. So . . ." Again, she fell silent while she tried to order her scattered thoughts.

"Good Lord, this may be my fault," Justin said, staring at her.

"How could that be?"

"I told Conroy that the only way he would find his way back into the queen's favor was if he had the good fortune to save her from assassination. I was joking . . . No, not joking—I was being sarcastic, trying to show him how futile his quest was. Could he possibly have believed that was a way to impress her?"

"I don't know, sir, but it isn't Conroy who tried to force Catherine to deliver the gift. It was Morden. I'll warrant they told her it was some sort of a harmless device that looked threatening enough to frighten Victoria."

Justin said, "But if Catherine knew they intended to save

her, the notion must at least have come from him, and thus from me. It was a stupid thing for me to say, but the more I think about it, the more likely it is that Conroy might have seen it as a way to prove himself to her. He could be a party to the plot, at all events."

"Justin, Sir John *can't* want Her Majesty dead! How could he benefit?"

"A good point, but nonetheless he must have suggested the sham assassination attempt. Perhaps now Morden means to lay all blame at his door."

"And perhaps we are simply leaping to conclusions," Letty said firmly. "Perhaps they have no intention of killing anyone. After all, if Catherine did not give the thing to Her Majesty . . ." A new thought struck her. "But why would Morden have become so murderous, then?"

"You said Liza told you he struck Catherine when she refused to deliver his gift. Perhaps he simply flew into a rage, and did not mean to kill her at all."

"Even so, if he does mean to kill Victoria, and he suspects that Catherine lived long enough to warn her, won't he feel a certain urgency to carry out his task?" The fear Letty had harbored from the instant that Catherine had mentioned the plot surged again. It had subsided with the opportunity to tell Justin about it, and her belief that the queen was safe for the moment, but now it threatened to overwhelm her again.

"Why do you say 'task'?" Justin asked abruptly. "Do you suspect that he is working for someone else besides Conroy?"

"I do," she said instantly, as her thoughts suddenly grew clear. "Moreover, I think I know who. Morden speaks German when he's angry. I've heard him, and Jenifry once told me that his valet, who's been courting her, comes from Hanover."

Leyton, who had been sitting stiffly erect in the forward seat, made a sound that drew a glance of disapproval from his master.

Ignoring them, Letty went on. "Before Jen began cooling

toward Walter, she once tried to tell me how lucky Victoria is that England allows a woman to rule, and other things that seemed odd for her to say. At first, I thought she had been reading the papers or talking politics belowstairs, but I soon realized that she was parroting someone else. When I taxed her with my suspicion, she admitted that Walter said such things, and she insisted that he sounded sensible. I pointed out certain errors in his arguments, and not long after that, she began having difficulty with him. He even struck her once, I believe."

Leyton growled audibly.

Justin said, "A man like his master, then, but I doubt that you believe that devilish valet aspires to assassinate Victoria and has persuaded Morden to do it."

"What I think," Letty said with a glance at Leyton, "is that although Charles Morden serves Sir John Conroy, he also serves the King of Hanover. And if you doubt motive from that quarter, sir, you are not as astute as I think you are."

"Dear old Cumberland," he said musingly. "It's certainly true that he stands to inherit Britain's throne if anything happens to Victoria before she marries and has a child. If he's heard that she is thinking of marrying her cousin Albert, he must be wild, and many believe that he's killed at least once before."

Letty looked out the carriage window. Traffic clogged the streets. "Please, tell them to hurry, or we'll never make it in time. It's just occurred to me that if Morden does intend to see this thing through, more people than Her Majesty may die. Justin, my parents are there, and doubtless yours as well!"

"The coachman is driving as quickly as he can," he told her. "We've nearly reached Piccadilly, so we'll be there soon. In the meantime, we had better devise a plan for when we arrive."

"Can we not just tell the guards that someone is trying to

assassinate the queen? They might not have heeded me alone, but surely they will listen to you."

"They will listen, but what then? Recall that it is still possible there is no plot. Even if one exists, do you truly expect the queen's guards to storm her ball?"

She chewed her lower lip. "I suppose they might hesitate to do anything so dramatic. The queen would be furious if they spoiled everything and then could find no bomb."

"I don't suppose Morden would show them where he'd put it, either."

"But we must do something," Letty protested. "At the least we must learn what gifts Her Majesty has received tonight, but only think of the time we will waste if we try to ask everyone who might have given her one! It's the first state ball of the Season, after all. I should think a number of people will give her things."

"The best approach would be to arrange for Her Majesty to put off opening any wrapped packages until someone can examine them," Justin said.

"You will have to tell her, then."

"I can't walk bang up to her and begin speaking," Justin pointed out. "Not only does protocol forbid it, but half a dozen people would stop me before I could gain her ear. She is more accessible to her ladies than to her gentlemen, however. If I get you inside, do you think you can manage to speak to her?"

"Yes, I must," Letty said confidently, steadying herself as the coach picked up speed. "Until the bedchamber crisis poisoned her mind against all Tories again, she had grown quite friendly to me. The note I received did suggest that she has heard rumors about the house, though. If she has, she may order me clapped in irons rather than listen to anything I say."

"It's more likely that Conroy has made suggestions to someone close to her. In my opinion, at this point, he would have to be extremely careful about what he said. After all, he'd still have to explain *how* he knew about that house."

Letty said, "Lady Tavistock wrote the note, so he must have spoken to her. Perhaps he only insinuated the worst. The queen is certainly angry enough to accept the merest excuse to dismiss her sole Tory maid of honor."

"Tavistock may not have said anything at all to Victoria yet," Justin said.

"Do you think she would dare dismiss me on her own?"

"Oh, certainly, if she thought she had cause. As you noted yourself, Victoria has no reason to love you. She would readily forgive her chief lady of the bedchamber for such a small offense."

"Well, if Her Majesty doesn't know I've been dismissed, I can easily speak to her. Protocol or not, she knows I frequently act impulsively. Moreover, even if she did order my dismissal herself, I doubt they will have told all the others. They would never expect me to ignore a direct order from the queen, after all."

"Then it's worth a try. Whilst you approach her, I can look for Melbourne, Wellington, or your father. Any one of them will grasp the danger quickly, and two of them can walk right up to Victoria and march her out of the room, if necessary."

Realizing that he referred to Melbourne and the duke, Letty said, "Do you think Papa wouldn't do that if he thought it necessary, sir?"

Instead of answering her directly, Justin said quietly, "Your parents seem to have played little or no role in tonight's incident so far. Am I to believe that they simply went straight on to the ball after learning of your dismissal?"

The silence that fell then took her mind right off what lay ahead.

Justin said quietly, "You didn't tell them, did you?"

"I . . . I couldn't. They would have been so . . ."

"Disappointed?"

She nodded, not looking at him.

The silence in the coach grew heavier, and for a moment

she feared he would demand to know more, or tell her what a fool she had been. Then she realized he would say none of those things with Leyton present. He said nothing more, in fact, until the carriage drew to a halt before the well-lit entrance to Buckingham Palace.

Gaining entrance proved even easier than he had predicted. If the guards had orders to stop Letty, they gave no sign of it. With Leyton following, she and Justin moved with the throng of other arrivals into the entrance hall and up the grand staircase, through the vestibule, and into the green drawing room.

As the flow of people moved from the drawing room into the picture gallery, Leyton suddenly plunged ahead of them toward a man near the door into the saloon, startling Letty. To her amazement, the valet did not so much as pause before his fist shot out, and the man by the door crumpled to the ground. Glancing up at Justin's taut face just as he grabbed her arm and urged her forward at a faster pace, she saw that his eyes had narrowed, and she feared for Leyton's future employment.

As they neared him, she saw the valet look around with great dignity and heard him say in his haughtiest tone, "You there, footman! Remove this debris at once. Can you not see that Her Majesty's guests are likely to stumble over it?"

The footman he had addressed glanced at Raventhorpe, but receiving no contradictory order from that quarter, he stepped forward at once, waving to a fellow servant to assist him. As the pair dragged the unfortunate victim away, Raventhorpe said quietly to Leyton, "The egregious Walter, I collect."

"Just so, sir. I apologize for acting so impulsively, but when I saw him, my fist just took on a life of its own."

"Understandable under the circumstances, but don't you think we might have learned something from him before you silenced him?"

Looking suddenly like a guilty schoolboy, Leyton said, "I do apologize, sir. I did not think of that."

"I daresay we've learned what we want to know, nonetheless, merely by his presence here. One generally does not bring one's man along to a ball unless he has a specific use for him. Go along and tell those lads not to lose him, Leyton. They should tie him up if necessary."

"I'll see to that myself, my lord, and gladly." Leyton walked away with a distinct lightness in his step.

"The dancing has started," Letty said, hearing music from the ballroom, which lay just beyond the saloon. "As much as Her Majesty enjoys the exercise, I daresay that is where we shall find her."

"I agree. You look for her whilst I find Melbourne or Wellington. If you see your father before you find the queen, however, tell him why we are here."

Letty nearly told him that she couldn't, that Jervaulx would demand explanations she had no time to give him, but meeting his steady gaze, she simply nodded. It was more likely that her father would act first and demand explanations later. What would happen then was best not thought about just yet.

Justin left her, and she made her way into the ballroom, trying to look as if she belonged there. She could not let Lady Tavistock or Lady Sutherland see her, however, because either one might order her out of the room. Not only would such an event prove humiliating, but it might well prove fatal to the queen. Thus it was a shock to see Lady Tavistock before she saw Victoria.

Having to elude the chief lady of the bedchamber made searching for the queen more difficult, so Letty surveyed the dancers from behind one of the pink columns that formed a colonnade along the garden front of the room. Windows overlooking the garden, but heavily curtained now, formed the wall behind her.

A moment later she saw the queen dancing with Melbourne. Moving toward them, she knew she would have to wait till they stopped. Until then, trying to keep one eye on the couple, she did her best to scan the room, looking for Morden or

Conroy. The ballroom teemed with guests, however, and it was difficult to see over their heads. An instant later, the diminutive queen disappeared into the crowd.

Not far from where Letty stood, midway along the garden front of the room, she could see festoons of yellow satin drapery edged with silver fringe swooping from the ceiling. The sight told her that she must be near the dais where chairs of state stood for the use of Her Majesty and members of the royal family when they were not dancing.

When the music stopped, and the general conversation grew louder, she made her way quickly along the colonnade, slipping past other guests who wandered there, until she could see the dais right ahead of her. Backed with white satin embroidered with yellow roses, it stood half inside and half outside the colonnade. The only people presently occupying chairs there were the Duchess of Kent and Lady Sutherland.

Letty hesitated, but just then Melbourne and Victoria moved into sight, approaching from the far side. As they did, she saw Sir John Conroy moving toward them, an ingratiating smile on his face, a brightly wrapped package in his hand.

She could not hear what he said when he reached them, because people were laughing nearby, and the orchestra had begun to play again. She saw Conroy bow low, extending the package.

Graciously Victoria took it, and without another thought, Letty sprang forward, pushing people aside, oblivious of their outrage, her thoughts fully occupied with the tableau ahead.

She saw Melbourne glance her way, saw his eyebrows go up in astonishment, saw Victoria begin to turn toward her, then Conroy. His eyes narrowed, and he glanced away as if looking for an avenue of escape, but Letty had eyes only for the package in Victoria's hands. Reaching out as she ran, she snatched it from the royal grasp and dashed to the nearest window. No one moved. Dimly aware of voices crying out in shock, she ignored them and without hesitation shoved the curtains aside.

She grasped the latch. When it stuck, she cried out in frustration, but then it gave and the window swung outward.

Letty hurled the package into the night.

Stepping quickly back away from the window, she became aware at last of the silence behind her. It lengthened until she turned. In the first second or two it seemed as if she faced a tableau, for the entire assembly stood stock-still. The first movement she noted was that of a red-coated guard coming toward her. Then, as the room came to life, she saw other guards and heard men shouting near the far door.

Victoria had not moved. She stood beside Melbourne, looking at Letty, but other than a slight raising of her eyebrows, her composure seemed undisturbed.

At that moment, an explosion shattered the night's calm outside, and inside the ballroom, chaos erupted.

TWENTY-ONE

To Letty's surprise, Conroy had not moved. He stood staring at her, visibly shocked. Then, evidently growing aware of the number of guards moving toward him, he turned to Victoria, spreading his hands in supplication.

"Your majesty, I didn't know! Please, ma'am, you must believe me. I had no idea what was in that package!"

Victoria did not acknowledge his plea. Imperiously, she nodded to the nearest guard, who stepped forward and grasped Conroy firmly by an arm.

"You will have to come with me, sir," he said.

"One moment there." It was Wellington. The elderly duke stepped forward from a group of the excited onlookers. His voice was calm but carried easily over an increasing buzz of murmured exclamations. "Forgive me for intruding, your majesty," he went on, "but I believe Conroy speaks the truth. We have unmasked the real culprit, you see."

Victoria continued to ignore Conroy, but her eyebrows rose again. Letty thought she could even distinguish a note of amusement when the queen said, "You, your grace? You captured the villain?"

"Not I, ma'am. One of your lords-in-waiting had the honor to capture him. We believe the villain serves an unfriendly power."

"Which one?" the queen demanded.

"If it please your majesty," Wellington said smoothly, "upon reflection, I believe you will agree that this is not the time or place to reveal that information."

Victoria glanced around the room at the sea of interested faces. A few looked frightened, Letty noted, but most looked eager, expectant, even excited. Signing to the guardsman to release Conroy, the queen said, "Perhaps, your grace, you might reveal at least which lord-in-waiting it was who captured him."

Wellington said, "Raventhorpe, your majesty. Floored him with as nice a right jab as I've been privileged to see."

The queen nodded. "Excellent. Will you tell us, as well, the name of the villain he has captured?"

"Charles Morden."

Several people gasped, and the buzz of excitement increased. Then silence fell again. Everyone wanted to hear what the queen would say next.

She looked at Conroy. "Morden is your aide, is he not, sir?"

"He is, ma'am," Conroy said wretchedly. "I cannot believe—"

Victoria snapped, "Be silent, sir."

The only sound that followed for several seconds was the slight squeak of someone's shoe against the floor.

The little queen seemed to increase in size. "If he is your man, he is your responsibility. We find it difficult to believe that you were not party to this."

Before Sir John could speak, Wellington said firmly, "It would be better, your majesty, to continue this discussion elsewhere. May I respectfully suggest that you give your orchestra the office to begin playing again."

Victoria looked at the duke for a long moment, as if she would tell him that his respectful suggestion came rather late in his discourse.

Letty could sympathize. The last thing Her Majesty wanted on this night of nights was to take orders from a Tory leader. She glanced at Melbourne, who had remained silent throughout, clearly shaken by what had happened.

Victoria, too, turned to Melbourne. "My lord, we shall withdraw with his grace to learn what he can tell us about this disgraceful event. Pray have someone direct the orchestra to begin playing again."

Melbourne signed to a hovering footman.

Conroy, with tears in his eyes, said, "Your majesty, I beg of you—"

"We will acquit you of wanting to assassinate your queen," Victoria said in an icy tone. "Her death would do you no good that anyone can imagine. We do not, however, wish to hear your voice again."

"With your permission, your majesty, I will look after Conroy," the Marquess of Jervaulx said, stepping forward. "Forgive me for intervening, ma'am, but I do wish to speak with him. I agree that he was most likely an unwitting tool of the villain who sought to exterminate you. However, since my daughter risked her life to prevent that event, I believe I have good cause to learn what lay behind it."

Victoria looked for a moment as if she would refuse, but when Admiral Rame stepped up beside Jervaulx, she said, "We shall expect to hear in good time all that you can learn from him, my lord." Accepting Melbourne's proffered arm, she walked away with him. Wellington followed them.

Jervaulx said, "Thank you for supporting me, Rame. I daresay she dislikes turning even Conroy here over to a Tory to question."

"Just so, my lord," the admiral said with a smile. "I think we all want to get to the bottom of this, however."

"I certainly do," Raventhorpe said, joining them.

Letty's gaze met that of her father, and seeing sternness there, she glanced at Justin, wondering how much he had already told the marquess. As if he could read her mind, Justin gave a slight shake of his head.

"I hope you won't object to a few moments' private speech with us, Conroy," Jervaulx said.

With a wry grimace, Sir John said, "I thought you looked as if you hoped I *would* object. Very well, don't glare at me. I'll go anywhere you like, so long as someone can produce a bottle of whisky."

Justin waved a footman over and gave the order. "Bring it to the yellow parlor off the corridor behind the picture gallery," he said.

As the footman started to turn away, Jervaulx said to him, "When his grace of Wellington returns, tell him where he can find us."

"Yes, my lord." The footman hurried off.

"I want to hear what Conroy has to say, sir," Justin said.

The marquess nodded. "As you like. I daresay Her Majesty prefers the Whigs to be well represented."

"That has nothing to do with it," Justin said shortly.

"I'm coming, too," Letty said.

Conroy looked surprised. "I say, it has nothing to do with you!"

"Does it not?" She glared at him. "Need I remind you that, were it not for me, you would have killed—"

"That will do, Letitia," Jervaulx said.

The tone was one that could always silence her, and the look in his eyes told her that she would do better to take her leave while she could, but curiosity overwhelmed any thought of her own best interest. "May I go with you, sir?"

"Let her come, sir," Justin said. "She has earned the right."

The two men looked steadily at each other for a long moment before Jervaulx said, "Very well. Lead the way to your yellow parlor, young man. Conroy, you go with him. You still with us, Admiral?" he added with a smile.

"I am indeed, my lord," Rame said.

They reached the parlor just a moment or two before the footman arrived with a tray bearing a decanter of whisky and several glasses.

Conroy stepped forward at once. "Good lad," he said.

When the footman glanced at Letty, clearly surprised to see her with the men, she shook her head. "I don't want anything, thank you."

Waiting only until he had served their drinks and everyone had taken seats, Justin dismissed the footman and said, "Now, Conroy, open the budget. Tell us all you know about this business."

"I tell you, I don't know anything," Conroy said. He swallowed half his whisky, then added, "Morden has served as my aide, that's all. I cannot imagine how you—any of you—imagined that I could be party to this. I have served Her Majesty faithfully for years. I certainly have nothing to gain from her death."

"Fortunately for you, even in the aftermath of that terrifying explosion, she realized that," Jervaulx said. "Nonetheless, you did give her the parcel."

Letty glanced at Justin. He smiled slightly, but said nothing.

"Other people gave her parcels tonight," Conroy said. "Many sent gifts earlier, as well. I've heard people talking about flowers they sent, and I've seen some huge bouquets. That explosive device could have been in any of them."

"But it was not in any one of them," the admiral said. "It was in your parcel."

Grimacing, Conroy turned to Jervaulx. "Ask your precious daughter how she knew it was there, when I swear by all that's dear to me that *I* didn't know."

Jervaulx looked at Letty. Indignant at the implication, she opened her mouth to tell them, but Raventhorpe spoke first.

He said, "Trying to shift the blame for this will not help you, Conroy. You have been manipulating people in all sorts of ways for some time now. Why don't you just admit that your little plan went awry?"

"How dare you! Even Jervaulx admits that I had no cause—"

"Spare us your protests," Raventhorpe snapped. "You seized every opportunity to apply pressure where it would do you good. My father, two innocent old ladies . . . Worst of all, in my opinion, when the Tories succeeded in introducing one of their own to the queen's court, did you not see her, too, as your enemy, and do everything in your power to get rid of her?"

"What the devil are you talking about?" Involuntarily, however, Conroy looked at Letty.

"Just so," Justin said. "First there was the incident of the slops thrown on the floor of the chamber first allotted to her."

"Slops," the admiral exclaimed. "Good God, man."

Jervaulx said nothing, but the look he gave his daughter boded no good.

"I-I heard about that," Conroy said. "Shocking affair."

"Soon after that," Justin went on evenly, "a certain chap began making a dead set at her dresser, pressing her to keep him informed, I daresay, of whatever she could tell him about her mistress."

Dismayed, Letty said, "Jenifry wouldn't!"

"No, that's quite true; she refused to tell him a thing," Conroy said. When a pregnant silence fell, he looked from one to the other, and color suffused his face.

"You would do better, I think, to be more forthcoming," Justin said. "There is also the matter of the house Augustus Benthall so mysteriously left to her, and your supposed efforts to purchase it."

"There is no law I know about against trying to buy an excellent property."

"Ah, but you knew the secret of that house, and you threatened to use it to ruin her. I daresay that had you not had your own reputation to protect, you would have arranged her dismissal from court long before tonight."

"I don't understand," Admiral Rame said. "You can't buy that house."

With a grimace, Conroy said, "Has Lady Letitia been dismissed? One would not know it. Oh, sit down, Raventhorpe. Murdering me will afford you nothing."

"On the contrary, it would afford me the utmost satisfaction," Justin said grimly. Exchanging a look with Jervaulx, he remained where he was, however.

Conroy said, "I don't deny that I told Morden we had to limit Tory influence with the queen. That's no more than Melbourne told her, for heaven's sake. But I did nothing more. It was his man who committed the slops offense. Morden's man, not Melbourne's, of course. I was shocked, I tell you, quite shocked indeed."

"I don't doubt that you were," Raventhorpe said. "Were you also shocked when Morden's plot to abduct Lady Letitia and young Liza went awry?"

Admiral Rame exclaimed, *"Liza!* Good God!"

"I know nothing about that," Conroy said firmly.

Jervaulx had been listening with evident fascination. Now he said in a silky voice, "If you are wise, Conroy, you will stick to that line buckle and thong."

Conroy looked at him, and for a moment Letty saw fear in his eyes. Then Jervaulx glanced at her, and she felt a tremor of the same emotion. That there would be a reckoning between them, she could not doubt.

Admiral Rame said, "I don't understand any of this. Am I to believe that Conroy here, whom I have always believed to have the queen's best interest at heart, was party to a plot to assassinate her? Do you also say he has conspired to abduct innocent little Liza and to drum Lady Letitia out of Her Majesty's court?"

Stiffly Conroy said, "I thought we had agreed that I have nothing to gain from Her Majesty's death."

Justin said, "Not from her death, perhaps, but what if you had been the one to save her tonight, Conroy? What then?"

"That's not what happened, though, is it?" Nonetheless, the deep flush on Sir John's face, and the way he gulped the rest of his whisky told everyone there that Raventhorpe had struck a nerve.

"By heaven," Raventhorpe said, "did you honestly think such a plot could prosper?"

"No!" Conroy turned on him, his face filled with fury. "I would never have placed Her Majesty in danger. I love her like my own daughter. Oh, don't sneer. I don't deny that I repeated your words to Morden. Nor will I conceal that he suggested such a plan might work to my benefit, but I refused to hear of it."

"I would like to believe that," Jervaulx said.

"Of course you may believe it," Conroy exclaimed. "Only think what a stir the newspapers will make of tonight's event! Some lunatic, angry with the government or with something—anything—that she might chance to say, might now decide to try where others failed. We must take every care of her!"

Admiral Rame said, "We will, sir. You can depend upon that."

Conroy sighed. "Just the thought of planting such a seed in a madman's mind was more than I dared risk. I told Morden so at the time. Please, believe me."

Unable to remain silent for another minute, Letty said, "Charles Morden comes from Hanover, does he not, Sir John?"

"Why, yes," Conroy said. "Though how you guessed that, I do not know. His English is excellent, though I suppose he does have a bit of an accent yet."

"One presumes that he supplied you with references," Justin said.

"Certainly he did. The queen's own uncle vouched for him." When the others exchanged glances, he said in dismay, "Surely, you don't suspect the King of Hanover of plotting against—Good God, of course. He would inherit the throne!"

Sardonically, Justin said, "You have used men as pawns for years, Conroy. How does it feel to learn that you've become the pawn of someone else?"

What Sir John might have responded to that, they did not discover, for Wellington entered at just that moment, and Letty said, "What news, sir?"

"Her Majesty is suffering from great distress, as you might imagine," the duke said. Then, with a slight smile, he added, "I believe we may all live to be grateful that Melbourne is still in power. Only consider the consequences if it were Peel in there now, trying to soothe her. No doubt the Tories would figure as the would-be assassins. As it is, Melbourne quite understands the necessity of keeping this as quiet as possible. He promises to put about some story or other to stifle the scandal. The only promise I made in return was to see that you cease to be a nuisance to Her Majesty, Conroy. I suggest that you leave the palace at once."

Conroy set down his glass, looking as if he meant to obey instantly.

Jervaulx said, "One moment, Conroy."

Conroy looked at him. A muscle in his cheek twitched, but he kept silent.

"I think you would do well to consider leaving England," the marquess said, as if he were merely thinking aloud. "If you do not, it is possible that tonight's events may soon come back to haunt you. Certain other details we've heard tonight about your recent career, if made public, would ruin you, I believe. In fact, I think I can promise that they would. Do you understand me?"

Conroy looked from Jervaulx's expressionless face to Justin's grim one. "I do, damn you all. I'll give it some thought." With that, he left the room.

"What was that all about?" Wellington demanded.

"I'll tell you later," Jervaulx said. With a meaningful glance at his daughter, he added, "Just as soon as I have a clearer understanding of it all myself."

"Why did you want Sir John to leave England?" Letty asked.

Jervaulx looked from Rame to Justin. "Just a little Tory plot, I'm afraid."

The admiral's eyebrows shot upward, but Justin chuckled. "I collect that you refer to the problem of the bedchamber ladies, sir."

"You are quick," Jervaulx said. "It did occur to me that Peel will continue to demand that the queen make significant changes, and Melbourne's government is too weak to object. If we can offer Her Majesty Conroy's departure in return for her dismissal of Tavistock and Sutherland, I think we can prevail without an upheaval."

"Excellent notion," the duke said approvingly.

Rame nodded. "It will certainly make government of any

sort easier. As things stand now, no one has enough of a majority to get anything done. That will continue to be the case until something occurs to draw the Whig factions together or the Tories win an election. With some give and take on both sides, however, perhaps we can all muddle through."

"I'm glad you approve, Admiral. Shall we go now? I want to have a little chat with my beloved daughter."

Letty sighed but arose obediently.

Justin said, "With your permission, sir, can that little chat wait? I doubt that anyone will object to our leaving the palace now, and we have a rather urgent reason to go to Upper Brook Street. We left things there in rather a chaotic state."

"Surely you can deal with that, young man," Jervaulx said. "As I understand it, Letitia's tenants are your relatives."

"But it's my house, Papa," Letty said. "I must go."

"As to that," the admiral said, "perhaps I can—"

"No, she's quite right," Jervaulx said. "Moreover, we can have that chat in the carriage on the way."

"I'm coming with you," Justin said.

Jervaulx's eyebrows shot upward. "The devil you are."

Justin said, "It's the best way, sir, believe me. I've got my carriage here, but we should go at once, and my mother will want to be there, as well as Lady Jervaulx, I'm sure. My man is here at the palace, and he can collect the pair of them." With a grimace, he added, "He will need to fetch Witherspoon, as well."

Wellington said, "Why the devil—"

Jervaulx looked stunned. "Raventhorpe, I have deduced that you feel some sort of need to protect my daughter—"

"On the contrary, sir, I have frequently wanted to beat her."

"Then you know her even better than I thought. Nonetheless that does not excuse this mad desire of yours to assemble a party in Upper Brook Street."

"Papa, it is not—"

"Let me do the explaining, Letty," Justin said gently.

She looked at him, saw warmth and understanding in his

eyes, and knew that this time he was not issuing an ultimatum. She waited a beat to be sure, but he held her gaze, and his expression did not change. "Perhaps you'd better," she said.

Jervaulx's eyes narrowed. He waited patiently for Justin to explain.

Glancing at the admiral, who seemed rooted where he stood, Justin sighed and said, "I am trusting you to keep this quiet, sir. My lord, Lady Witherspoon is at the house. Charles Morden may have murdered her."

"Murdered her!" Jervaulx, Wellington, and Rame said as one.

"We don't know yet if she will survive, but in any event, we must protect the reputations of your daughter and my great-aunts, not to mention Lady Catherine's. We must hurry, so I'll explain on the way, but if you will just write a note to the marchioness, I'll write to my mother and Witherspoon. Then Leyton can—"

"There is no need for you to trouble your man with those tasks," Admiral Rame said in a tone that reminded them all he, too, was a man accustomed to command. "I'll undertake to collect Lady Jervaulx, Lady Sellafield, and Witherspoon and deliver them to Upper Brook Street. I'll need a moment more to arrange for someone to see my wife home, but then I am quite at your disposal."

"Really, sir," Justin protested. "I cannot impose on your good—"

"It is no imposition, I assure you. I have a stake in this, too, after all." With that, he strode off, leaving them to stare at each other in bewilderment.

"I haven't the faintest notion what he's talking about," Letty said. "Do you?"

"None," Justin said.

Wellington said, "Sound man, Rame is. Wouldn't expect him to push himself in where he has no real interest. Won't, myself. I will leave you to deal with this, Gideon. You may call upon me at Apsley House tomorrow."

"I'll do that, sir," Jervaulx said, "but I begin to think that I am a mere onlooker in this myself. Come along, you two," he added as the duke strode from the room. "The sooner we get this business sorted out, the better it will be for all of us. I still have a few things to say to you, Letty."

Bracing herself, Letty looked at Justin.

"Don't expect any help from me," he said. "You know what I think."

"Well, at least you didn't try to leave me behind tonight," she retorted.

He smiled, taking her hand and drawing it into the crook of his arm. "I was hoping you'd noticed that," he said. "I daresay you cannot convict me of trying to control everything that happened here tonight, either, my girl."

TWENTY-TWO

Letty entered the carriage first, but to her surprise, Justin followed, and when she would have sat in her usual place, he caught her arm and pulled her toward the forward seat, leaving the rear seat for the marquess alone. If Jervaulx disapproved of his daughter sitting beside the viscount instead of beside him, he said nothing.

By the time they reached the house in Upper Brook Street, Letty and Justin had put the marquess in possession of most of the facts. Letty knew her father was unhappy with her, but he did not seem as disappointed in her as she had feared he would be. He said little, in fact, other than to ask one or two pertinent questions.

At one point, he said, "It seems rather ingenuous of your tenants to pretend that they were unaware of their servants' activities, don't you think?"

"No, sir," she replied. "You won't think so, either, when you meet them. It never entered their heads that the maids or Liza, certainly, would take their generous attitude toward their so-called patrons as tacit approval of the activities in which those patrons engaged."

"Moreover, sir," Justin put in, "since the maids only recently began to accept clients, I would not be amazed to learn that Morden put them up to it."

"To what purpose?" Letty demanded.

"Hoping to put you in fear of criminal charges being laid

against you, thus giving him the whip hand," Justin said. "I daresay, even though he ought to have seen what a stubborn chit you are, he hoped to force you to do his bidding."

Letty knew he called her a stubborn chit only because he was trying to keep her mind off what lay ahead. She made a face at him.

"That makes sense," Jervaulx said. "He wanted a scapegoat, did he?"

"Yes, sir," Justin said, "and he seems to have used the queen's preference for Whigs as a means of concealing his true purpose throughout. It is possible, you know, that at one point or other he had planned to get your daughter to give the parcel to Victoria. If they could have blamed the Tories for Victoria's death, it really would have put the cat amongst the pigeons."

They drew up before the Upper Brook Street house a few minutes later, and Jackson opened the door as they were hurrying through the front courtyard. "Good news, my lady," he said to Letty. "Lady Witherspoon has regained her senses twice more, and the doctor says she may very well live, after all."

"Oh, thank God," Letty exclaimed. "I'll go straight up to her."

"There is no need for that, my dear," Miss Abby said from the doorway into the stair hall. "She is sleeping quite naturally now, and the doctor says we must let her get her rest. I don't believe I know this gentleman," she added gently.

Begging her pardon, Letty introduced Jervaulx.

Miss Abby's eyes widened. "H-how do you do, my lord? Has dearest Letty told you . . . ? Yes, I can see that she has told you everything." Her countenance crumpled. "I daresay all our happiness has come to an end. Miranda will be so dreadfully vexed."

"Don't be cast down, Miss Abby," Letty said. "I have an idea that may answer the purpose for everyone. Let us go straight up to Mrs. Linford before I tell you about it, though."

Miss Abby looked unconvinced, but collecting herself, she

said, "Then you had better order refreshments for everyone, Jackson."

They found Mrs. Linford with Liza in the drawing room. Liza looked much her usual self, Letty thought, although at the sight of them, she had colored up to the roots of her hair.

Mrs. Linford murmured something to her, and she got to her feet and bobbed an awkward curtsy. "Is Justin going to play the pianoforte?" she asked.

"Not tonight," he said. "Isn't it time you were in bed?"

"I told her she could stay up," Mrs. Linford said. "The events of this evening have distressed her, as one can well imagine they might."

"Still, Aunt Miranda, I do think—"

She cut him off, saying, "Where have your manners gone begging, Justin? This gentleman looks vaguely familiar, and I imagine I know who he must be, but nonetheless . . ." She paused expectantly.

"This is Jervaulx, ma'am, Letty's papa."

Jervaulx nodded.

Mrs. Linford said, "I expect Abigail has given you our good news. We had a little mishap here earlier this evening, my lord."

"He knows all about it," Justin told her. "He knows everything."

"Everything? Oh, dear."

"Yes, precisely," he said. "The game is up, ma'am."

Looking dismayed, Mrs. Linford seemed to slump a little in her chair.

Letty said sharply, "Don't talk to her like that, sir. Everything will be fine, ma'am, I promise you. I have an idea that I think you will approve."

"Oh, my dear, if only—" She broke off when sounds of new arrivals wafted to their ears from the stair hall. "Who can that be, at this hour?"

Glancing at Justin and at Jervaulx, neither of whom offered to reply, Letty said, "I believe it must be my mother, ma'am, and Lady Sellafield, with Lord Witherspoon and Admiral Rame."

"Merciful heavens," Mrs. Linford said, turning pale.

"Papa!" exclaimed Liza. She jumped to her feet and ran toward the door, startling the marmalade cat, which had curled up on a pillow near the doorway. The cat darted through the doorway ahead of her, and a masculine oath sounded afterward, followed by a gurgle of laughter that Letty recognized as her mother's.

"Well, that was not one's usual ball, I must say," Daintry said as she entered the room. She looked at her husband. "First an explosion, then an arrest, and then you and Wellington disappeared with my daughter. Then, out of the blue, this very kind gentleman arrives to tell me that my husband desires him to deliver me and two strangers to him like a parcel. You have some explaining to do, sir."

Behind her, Admiral Rame entered with Liza clinging to his arm. "I tried to explain what I could, Jervaulx, but I hesitated to say very much, you know, not knowing exactly what you wished me to make known to Witherspoon."

Letty scarcely heard what he said. She was staring at the admiral and Liza. "Did I hear her call you 'Papa,' sir?"

"Yes," he said, putting his arm around the girl. "I guess you had not yet learned all of the secrets of your house, Lady Letitia. Liza is the result of a liaison I had with my housekeeper when I was a carefree bachelor, long before I married my darling wife. When her mother died suddenly, I was still in a position where I thought it necessary to keep her existence a secret. The dear ladies here were kind enough to take her in and treat her as befitted my daughter, which led at times to some confusion on her part, I fear. I have long meant to tell my wife about her, however, and I believe the time has come, don't you?"

Witherspoon brushed past him. "What's the meaning of all this? Who the devil are you, sir," he said to Jervaulx, "and where is my wife? The admiral said I would find her here, but I do not understand how that can be the case."

Lady Sellafield, who Letty suspected had come upstairs with Witherspoon, hesitated in the doorway, looking uncertainly at her son. He smiled reassuringly at her, then turned to Letty.

"No more secrets," he said.

"No," she said. "I think you had better handle this part. Then I'll tell everyone what I think we should do next."

He nodded, then turned back to his mother, saying baldly, "Ma'am, I think you should know that Catherine Witherspoon was nearly murdered here tonight."

Lady Sellafield gasped and clutched a hand to her breast.

Witherspoon exclaimed, "What are you saying? Catherine? Impossible! She was in bed when I left the house. She has been feeling poorly for two days!"

"She told you that only so she could get out tonight to meet her lover," Raventhorpe said. "If I seem brutal, sir, perhaps you will agree that you deserve no less. I mean to tell you exactly what transpired here, so that you can help us put the best face on it for public consumption. I do not care to have my family dragged through scandal, and I daresay you don't want that, either."

"Good heavens," Witherspoon said, clearly very much shocked. "Did you say Catherine has taken a lover?"

"She has been meeting him here, just as you have been meeting my mother," Raventhorpe said.

Witherspoon looked at Rame, then at Jervaulx. "I say, Raventhorpe, I can understand your resentment, but need we air this all before such an audience?"

Letty nearly spoke, but catching Justin's eye, she subsided.

He said, "This house belongs to Lady Letitia, sir, and therefore, whether she likes it or not, her father and mother have a right to know what has gone on here. As for the admiral, I daresay there is little about this house that he does not know."

"Who the devil was she daring to meet here?"

"Charles Morden. Yes, I daresay that shocks you, and you can discuss it with her if she recovers. I remind you that she was gravely injured tonight."

"Dear me, I should go to her," Witherspoon said belatedly.

"You need not hurry. Miss Abby says she is sleeping now, and a doctor is with her. I might add that Catherine risked her life tonight to protect young Liza there when the brute who seduced her attempted to force himself upon the child."

"I'm not a child," Liza said indignantly, "and what's more, he likes me—"

Her words ended when the admiral unceremoniously put his hand over her mouth. "That will do, my dear," he murmured. "You must not speak now unless someone speaks to you first."

She nodded, resting her head lovingly against his hand.

"I don't understand this at all," Witherspoon complained.

"I daresay you don't," Justin said. "All you need to understand just now, however, is the need to make all tidy. You have much to answer for, sir."

"Now, see here," Witherspoon began.

"That attitude will avail you nothing," Justin said. "I understand your feelings for my mother, and hers for you. I know you've been good friends for years, and I have a sneaking suspicion that one reason she is the only one in my family who never asks me for money is that you provide for her when my father does not."

"If I have done so, it is none of your damned business."

"Perhaps not," Justin said. "I am well aware that members of our circle have long turned a blind eye to such relationships as yours. I think, however, that you will find less sympathy for them in the coming years. We no longer have profligate kings running our country, sir, and our virginal young queen takes a dim view of such practices, as you must know by now. In any event, this affair must stop."

"I agree, Teddy," Lady Sellafield said, speaking for the first time. "You have a duty to Catherine. I have long felt that, as you know if poor Justin does not. Had I not been so desperately lonely, and you so wonderfully understanding . . ."

"I know, my dear," he said with a tenderness Letty would not have expected to hear in his voice. "Very well, I will attend to my duty. Poor Catherine. You need not worry that I shall scold her, Lady Letitia. I am in no course to do that."

"Nor she to hear it, sir," Letty said. "But perhaps, before you go to her, we might just decide what tale we will tell of this night."

Justin said, "I've got that worked out, I think. The best thing would be to keep as near the truth as possible, so that whatever that villain Morden says will sound like he's just trying to put a good face on his own actions."

"You need not worry about Morden, sir," Leyton said from the doorway.

Everyone turned instantly to stare at him.

Justin said, "What the devil do you mean? If Morden says anything at all, it will stir up a hornets' nest. That alone . . ." His voice trailed to silence when Leyton shook his head. "What is it?"

"The poor devil appears to have shot himself whilst in custody, sir."

"Where did he get a gun? I'd swear he had none on him."

"They say that Sir John Conroy visited him briefly just before he did the dreadful deed. God rest his soul," Leyton added piously.

"Well, that does make things easier. Thank you, Leyton. Perhaps you will just go now and tell Lady Letitia's woman that she will be ready to leave in half an hour or so. We will ring when we want you," he added, smiling at his man.

"Thank you, my lord. I'll be glad to tell her." Leyton left quickly.

Justin said thoughtfully, "Morden's death, however convenient we may think it, does not alter what I said before. The nearer we can stay to the truth, the easier it will be for all of us. Therefore, I suggest we say simply that Lady Witherspoon fell and struck her head whilst visiting my great-aunts. We need not say when or how, and if people ask questions, we can say that it happened today. She can decide how much more to reveal to her intimates. No one will ask the rest of us for details."

"That's all very well," Witherspoon said, "but I don't know that we ought to say she was here when it happened. I can take her home and simply put it about that she fell down the stairs, or some such thing."

"You must do as you think best, of course," Justin said, "but your servants will know that is not true. On the other side of that coin, we all know that the servants here are a discreet lot."

"But that's just it," Witherspoon protested. "Too many people know what goes on here. I'm sorry, ladies," he added, looking wretched. "I know I should be the last to complain. Nonetheless, won't people guess why Catherine was here?"

"We do have friends who visit without taking advantage of our private chambers," Miss Abby said indignantly.

"And no one will be taking such advantage of them in future," Justin said firmly. "I have decided to provide my aunts with—"

"Just a moment, sir," Letty interjected. "You are encroaching upon my business now, not yours. I will decide what is best to do with my tenants."

"I think we should decide," Miss Abby said miserably.

"You shall do so," Letty said. Looking directly at Justin, she added, "You may choose between Justin's plan and mine."

His eyes began to twinkle.

Her dignity still very much intact, Mrs. Linford said, "What do you suggest?"

Witherspoon, who had been looking from one speaker to another, said in a querulous voice, "You don't need me for this discussion. I am going to see my wife. You and I can talk later, Sally. I hope your son don't think it necessary to spill the beans to Sellafield. That *will* cause a scandal!"

"He won't, Teddy," Lady Sellafield said, patting him on the shoulder. "You run along up to Catherine now. Go on, Letty dear. Pay no heed to us."

"Very well, ma'am, thank you," Letty said. Turning to the old ladies, she said, "It has occurred to me that although Mr. Benthall's very odd will stipulated that you would forfeit your tenancy if anyone else paid your rent, and also that I cannot increase that rent, it said nothing about a lower one. I submit that if I lower your rent to one pound a year, you will be able to make ends meet quite nicely."

Miss Abby said worriedly, "That is kind of you, my dear, but I don't think we could, you know. The upkeep on this house is very expensive."

"Then I will make you an allowance," she said.

"Out of the question," Mrs. Linford said. "Even if your papa would allow it, and even though we know you would not constantly want to order our lives for us, it would be worse to be beholden to you, who are not related to us, than to our grandnephew. I don't know why Augustus put us in this dreadful fix," she added irritably. "It was most thoughtless of him not to have left us some money."

"He wasn't thinking of you, Miranda," the admiral said.

Everyone looked at him.

"Do you know what he *was* thinking, sir?" Letty demanded. "Because, I promise you, sir, none of us has the least notion."

"Augustus was one of my chief correspondents whilst I was at sea," the admiral said. "Whenever we put into port, I would find letters awaiting me, telling me all the gossip of the beau monde. I had intended to speak to you," he added, turning to Jervaulx. "It seemed to me that you were the proper person. I did not realize that your daughter had taken the reins into her own hands."

"She has a habit of doing that," Jervaulx said evenly.

Daintry said hastily, "What do you know of her inheritance, sir?"

The admiral smiled at her. "I don't know for a fact, my lady, but I can guess. Augustus and the sixth marquess were well acquainted, you know."

"We know he was kin to my grandmother," Jervaulx said cautiously.

"They disliked each other cordially," the admiral said, "but he loathed Jervaulx with a passion. Said he had no sense of humor."

Daintry smiled at her husband. "I can recall your saying much the same thing, sir," she said.

He smiled at her.

"Augustus knew everything that went on in London," the admiral said. "He certainly knew that Mrs. Linford and Miss Abby lacked sufficient funds to live here in the style they preferred without his support, and he knew almost to the day when they began their little enterprise here."

"He did?" Both Mrs. Linford and Miss Abby spoke at once.

"Oh, yes, of course. He thought it was clever of them to take advantage of the great many members of the beau monde who so casually discounted their marriage vows. It was he who suggested that I place Liza here, saying you would be glad of the money. I did not tell you that, of course. It would have been most impolite. I merely expressed my gratitude when you agreed to take her off my hands."

"But what has this to do with his bequest to my daughter?" Jervaulx asked.

"I suspect that Augustus thought it would be amusing to cast the whole business into your father's lap. Recall that he deplored the sixth marquess's lack of humor. He expressed a desire more than once to liven him up, so I think it amused him to think of Jervaulx's discovering that his granddaughter had inherited what amounted to a house of ill repute. Forgive me, ladies, if I am speaking too bluntly."

"Good God," Jervaulx said with feeling. "But there is one small flaw in your reasoning. My father died before Benthall did."

"Only by a week or so," the admiral reminded him. "Augustus learned of Jervaulx's death after he himself became ill. He wrote me that he had thought of changing his will, but decided it was proof of his belief in the hereafter that he did not. He believed Jervaulx would know exactly what he had done and why, and would be utterly unable to do anything about it."

"I wish you had told me of this," Jervaulx said grimly.

"I meant to do so, but I did not want to try to put my suspicions in a letter that would have seemed most inappropriate to someone who did not know me. Moreover, you and your daughter were fixed in Paris, the ladies had been managing well for years, and there was no reason to think that would change before you reached England. By the time I realized that your daughter was here and had become so nearly acquainted with them, I had no means to reach you."

"I can see that my daughter and I still have much to discuss," Jervaulx said, giving Letty another look.

The admiral said, "You will want to do that privately, however, so I'll take my leave now. Don't trouble yourself to ring for someone to show me out, Miranda. I'll take my sleepy daughter up to her bedchamber and then be on my way."

When he and Liza had gone, Letty braced herself for the storm.

"This is perhaps not the best time for a declaration," Justin said casually.

After a pause during which one might have heard a pin drop, Jervaulx said, "Are you daring to choose just this moment to ask for my daughter's hand, sir?"

"If she will have me," Justin said.

"Why should I want you?" Letty asked, hoping he could not detect the tremors of exhilaration shooting through her body.

He said blandly, "It occurs to me that an engagement between one of the great Whig families and one of the great Tory families will provide enough grist for the rumor mills that it may take the light off of everything else. Also, I thought perhaps you and I might eventually move into this house. My great-aunts can remain here until we return from our wedding trip, at which time they might perhaps enjoy a holiday in a little house I own in Richmond until we have arranged things so that they can live comfortably here with us if they choose. I am not trying to order everyone's lives, mind you, but that did seem like a plan that might prosper."

"Horrid creature."

Daintry chuckled. "I hope you have more reason for marrying my daughter than simply to smother the flames of rumor, young man."

"Does the fact that I find myself tail over top in love with her count, ma'am? Because I am persuaded that exasperating as she can be, not to mention stubborn and outspoken, I shall not enjoy life nearly so much without her as I will with her."

"It counts with me," Daintry said. "I'm not sure that Letty believes in love."

"I do now," Letty said, looking into Justin's eyes.

He stepped forward and took both her hands in his. "Do you think you can put up with me, sweetheart?"

"Gladly, sir."

Daintry said, "I think perhaps we should leave, Gideon. Justin can see Letty safely home."

"We'll walk out with you," Mrs. Linford said, getting up. "Come, Abigail."

"But, Miranda, do you think we shall like Richmond?"

"I believe we'll enjoy the change, Abigail, and if Letitia is to join our family, we need not worry about Justin telling us what to do. She is equal to anything."

Letty found herself alone with Justin and felt annoyed to see that the twinkle in his eyes had deepened. "Do you doubt that I am equal to anything, sir?"

"Not a bit. It's what I love best about you."

The door opened, and Miss Abby put her head in to say, "Justin, it has occurred to me that people may think you married dearest Letitia just to get the house. You won't like that, I daresay, so perhaps—"

"With fond respect, Aunt Abby, go away," he said.

She shut the door again, and Letty said, "I hope they do think you married me for the house. It's better than thinking I married you for your money."

"Whatever they think, my love, it will keep them talking, and with luck it will keep them from speculating on the interesting things that went on in this house. Now, are you going to kiss me or not?"

She did.

EPILOGUE

July 1839

Lady Raventhorpe's first order of business that warm summer morning was to waken her lord and give him the news she had been hugging to herself for nearly two days. It was his own fault, of course, that she had been unable to tell him earlier, because although he had joined her in her bed upon his return to Raventhorpe from London late the previous night, he had failed to waken her.

He looked very peaceful, lying there asleep with one hand tucked behind his head and a little half-smile playing upon his lips. As she wondered what he was dreaming, a mischievous impulse stirred; and, moving slowly, ever so gently, she slid a hand beneath the covers to clear her way, then inched down beneath them until she could touch her lips to his warm, bare thigh.

He did not move, nor did the pattern of his breathing change straightaway, but as she pressed a line of kisses up and over his thigh, moving ever closer to the juncture of his legs, she felt him tense. Soon it became obvious that whether he still slept or not, his body was aware of her attention. She felt a surge of power, the same feeling she had enjoyed often in the weeks since their marriage. Knowing that she could stir him so gave her immense satisfaction.

He moved, and in nearly the same instant the quilt covering

her rose, and she felt the caress of the light breeze from the open window.

He said with amusement in his voice, "So you missed me, did you?"

"You were gone three whole days, Justin."

"I was indeed, and I fretted about my beautiful wife the entire time. Don't stop what you are doing, sweetheart. You've hardly got started."

"Did Her Majesty notice that you had left your wife at home?"

"She did, and she sent her kind wishes for a speedy recovery when I told her you had been taken ill. She did not even object when I declared that I intended to return at the earliest possible moment. I collect, by the way, that you have recovered from your unfortunate indisposition."

"Yes, of course," she said, hoping that she spoke truly. From what she had heard, most women in her condition became sick only in the mornings. She felt wonderful when she awoke, but for the past fortnight, she had felt anything but well in the afternoon. Still, if this day followed the pattern of its predecessors, she would enjoy a fine morning with Justin first. She grinned at him. "Shall I go on with what I was doing, or would you like to hear about the surprise I've got for you first?"

"Surprise? You terrify me, Letty. Neither of my parents has been near Raventhorpe, so it can have nothing to do with them. Ned has behaved like a saint these past two months, the aunts are safely in Richmond for the summer, and everything here has been running smoothly. Or so I thought." He frowned. "You cannot have come up with another threat to the queen here at home, so my imagination fails to conjure up anything you might have found to surprise me with now. Is it Jeremiah? Has that damned monkey of yours got into mischief again?"

"I don't think I will tell you what it is," she said, raising her chin. "Jeremiah has been an angel, and I think that for maligning him you deserve that I shall not continue seeing to your pleasure, sir. What do you say to that?"

In response, he grasped her nearest arm and pulled her up until she was looking into his eyes. She noted a distinct hint of laughter there when he said, "You have frequently said that you admire plain speaking, have you not?"

"I have," she agreed, "and I tell you plainly, sir, that I will not allow you to tease me this morning."

"Will you not? What if I were to tickle you instead?"

"I should very likely cast up my accounts, as my brothers would say."

He frowned. "So you are not entirely well yet. Why did you tell me that you were, then?"

More to turn the subject than to satisfy curiosity, she said, "Did you find it as hot in London as we heard that it was?"

"Worse. I was glad to get away. When we rode in the park yesterday, the air was as hot as an oven. It was even worse at the opera last night."

"Still, you must have news," Letty said. "Has Melbourne got his new government in order? Have there been any more ructions from the queen?"

"Melbourne met with as much trouble as your father predicted, but things look well enough for him now. As to the queen, she is planning her cousin Albert's visit in October, and she grows quite pink whenever anyone speaks his name."

"If the wind truly sits in that quarter, her Uncle Leopold will have won a few more points over Cumberland. Albert is part of his family, after all."

"I don't much care who she marries, myself." He was looking at her, his eyes narrowed, as if he would peer into her mind.

She said, "It is rude to stare like that, sir. I had a governess once who told me my eyes would fall out if I did that sort of thing."

"I was wondering why you changed the subject a moment ago."

"I don't recall," she said mendaciously, "but thinking of Victoria brings to mind the meeting I had with Papa's solicitor when I first got to London in April. When I declared my intention to look after the Upper Brook Street house myself, he said it was unheard-of for a young woman to take interest in matters of finance or property, and he believed Victoria needed a strong man to guide her. I wonder what he thinks of her now."

"He certainly didn't think much of your retaining the rights to your property when we drew up the marriage contracts," Justin said with a reminiscent chuckle.

"I daresay he thought you as mad as he thinks Papa. He said he would not be surprised to learn, years from now, that I had left all my property to my daughters and ignored the claims of my poor sons. I daresay I shall, too, you know."

"You may do as you please with what's yours, my love. I will struggle to take care of our sons by myself." A new, more gentle note had entered his voice.

Letty grimaced ruefully. "You've guessed, Justin! That's not fair. I wanted to surprise you."

"Then you should have told me straightaway."

"Justin, I—"

She broke off when the door opened, and Jenifry entered.

The maid stopped short when she saw Justin. "Oh, dear, I beg your pardon, my lord. I thought you were in your— That is to say, sir, I didn't stop to think anything, because that dratted monkey's got into the kitchen again. Cook says monkeys in kitchens is something she won't abide, and the little beast has got into the racks over her ovens and won't come down to me, so I came to tell the mis—"

"Go away, Jenifry," Justin said.

"Just a moment, Jen," Letty said. "Perhaps if you ask Cook to find Jeremiah some nuts or fruit, the pair of you can coax him down."

"I tried that, but—"

"You go and try again," Justin recommended, "and don't come back until her ladyship rings for you."

With a glance at Letty and another at Justin, Jenifry said, "I'll get Leyton to help us. We'll get him."

Justin said dryly, "I trust, my love, that she will not encourage Leyton to become as dictatorial as Morden's chap was."

"As if Jenifry encouraged that man, or that Leyton would ever—" Noting the deepening twinkle in her husband's eyes, Letty broke off. "You! I don't know what you deserve for teasing me so."

"I deserve that you should finish what you began, sweetheart, but first I want to hear your news."

"You know it. You already guessed."

"I want to hear it from your own sweet lips, however. Are you quite sure?"

"Yes, quite. Dr. Morrisey came out yesterday from Cambridge, and he confirmed what Jenifry and I had already guessed. I wanted to be certain before I told you that we are going to have a daughter."

"Good lord," Justin exclaimed. "Can Morrisey tell as much as that? I had no . . . You wretch," he added in quite a different tone, giving her a shake. "You dare to talk of what I deserve and then serve me such a trick!"

"Would it distress you so to have a daughter, my lord?"

"It would not, and you know it would not, so you need not poker up like that, little wife, or call me 'my lord' in such a haughty tone."

She chuckled, snuggling down beside him. "Still, sir, you ought to have seen the look on your face."

In response, he took her chin firmly in one hand and turned her face so that he could kiss her. As his warm lips touched hers, her body ignited, and soon they had both forgotten everything but each other. When or exactly how her nightdress ended up on the floor in an untidy heap, Letty could not have said, for her thoughts were all on Justin.

Dear Reader:

For those of you who wondered, Queen Victoria came to the throne in June of 1837 but was not crowned until June 29, 1838.

The Bedchamber Crisis, as the business over Victoria's ladies came to be known, happened pretty much the way it is related in *Dangerous Lady,* and resulted in Lord Melbourne's serving two more years as prime minister before the Tories took over. Because his majority was practically nonexistent, his authority was small, and little of note occurred in Parliament during those years. Victoria did eventually appoint a balanced number of Tory ladies, but only after the intervention of Prince Albert. She later blamed her behavior in the incident on her youth and inexperience, and agreed that a ruler should make every effort to appear nonpartisan.

Both Victoria and the Duchess of Kent made honest intentions to reconcile their differences. Progress was slow, however, and it was many years before they did so. In October 1839 Prince Albert of Saxe-Coburg-Gotha arrived in England. Victoria fell in love with him, and four months later she married him. It was he who did the most to bring the duchess back into favor.

Lady Flora Hastings died in July 1839 of the illness that had overtaken her.

For those of you wondering why Letty is a maid of honor rather than a lady-in-waiting, it is because the latter term is late nineteenth century (1862). A maid of honor was an unmarried lady, usually of noble birth, whose duty was to attend the queen. That term dates from 1586. The term *lord-in-waiting* the author took from the London *Times* of April 1839.

The rumor about Wellington's assassination occurred on April 29, 1839, as described.

The Duke of Grosvenor still owns most of the land in Mayfair. The land is leased to the householders, and freehold properties are much more valuable than those that are not. It will not surprise anyone to learn that a very large part of the Grosvenor fortune derives from these leases.

The heroic achievements of Admiral Robert Rame are, in fact, those of Admiral Henry John Rous, of the Royal Navy. The author has drawn the admiral's comments on handicapping from *Law and Practice of Horse Racing* (1850) by the Honorable Captain Rous, R.N., as cited in *Newmarket: Its Sport and Personalities* by Frank Siltzer (Charles Scribner, 1923). Admiral Rous was for many years the much respected senior steward of the Jockey Club. All other actions and comments of Admiral Rame derive solely from the author's fertile imagination.

For those of you who are interested in learning more about the early Victorian period, the author recommends *The Letters of Queen Victoria, A Selection from Her Majesty's Correspondence Between the Years 1837 and 1861; Melbourne* by Lord David Cecil; and *The Young Victoria* by Alison Plowden. More information on ladies-in-waiting (and maids of honor) can be found in *Ladies in Waiting* by Dulcie Ashdown, and *Ladies in Waiting, From the Tudors to the Present Day* by Anne Somerset.

If you enjoyed *Dangerous Lady*, I hope you will watch for *Highland Spirits* in November.

Sincerely,

Amanda Scott

ROMANCE FROM JO BEVERLY

ROMANCE FROM JANELLE TAYLOR

ROMANCE FROM FERN MICHAELS